the LAIRD

GRACE BURROWES

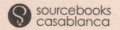

sourcebooks
casablanca

Published by Sourcebooks Casablanca, an imprint of Sourcebooks, Inc.
P.O. Box 4410, Naperville, Illinois 60567-4410
(630) 961-3900
Fax: (630) 961-2168
www.sourcebooks.com

Printed and bound in Canada.
MBP 10 9 8 7 6 5 4 3 2 1

To those who have not yet begun to heal

Author's Note

This book took me down a somewhat different path from its many predecessors.

Michael and Brenna (and their community and family) arrive to a happily ever after, but they must first wade through issues from Brenna's childhood that are among the toughest a child can endure. Brenna triumphs over the intimate betrayals in her past, and she and Michael emerge strong and heart-whole by the end of the book. Their path, though, traverses more sadness and struggle than I usually write.

Conflict this painful and complicated isn't everybody's idea of good material for a love story, and yet, I also think *The Laird* is one of my most heartfelt romances. If you journey with Michael and Brenna to the book's happy conclusion, let me know what you think of their tale.

I love to hear from readers, and can be reached through my website at graceburrowes.com.

One

"Elspeth, I believe a Viking has come calling."

At Brenna's puzzled observation, her maid set aside the embroidery hoop serving as a pretext for enjoying the Scottish summer sun, rose off the stone bench, and joined Brenna at the parapets.

"If Vikings are to ruin your afternoon tea, better if they arrive one at a time," Elspeth said, peering down at the castle's main gate. "Though that's a big one, even for a Viking."

The gate hadn't been manned for at least two centuries, and yet, some instinct had Brenna wishing she'd given the command to lower the portcullis before the lone rider had crossed into the cobbled keep.

"Lovely horse," Elspeth remarked.

The beast was an enormous, elegant bay, though its coat was matted with sweat and dust. From her vantage point high on Castle Brodie's walls, all Brenna could tell about the rider was that he was big, broad-shouldered, and blond. "Our visitor is alone, likely far from home, hungry and tired. If we're to offer him hospitality, I'd best inform the kitchen."

Highland hospitality had grown tattered and threadbare in some locations, but not at Castle Brodie, and it would not, as long as Brenna had the running of the place.

"He looks familiar," Elspeth said as the rider swung off his beast.

"The horse?"

No, Elspeth hadn't meant the horse, because now that the rider was walking his mount toward the groom approaching from the stables, Brenna had the same sense of nagging familiarity. She knew that loose-limbed stride, knew that exact manner of stroking a horse's neck, knew—

Foreboding prickled up Brenna's arms, an instant before recognition landed in a cold heap in her belly.

"Michael has come home." Nine years of waiting and worrying while the Corsican had wreaked havoc on the Continent, of not knowing what to wish for.

Her damned husband hadn't even had the courtesy to warn her of his return.

Elspeth peered over the stone crenellations, her expression dubious. "If that's the laird, you'd best go welcome him, though I don't see much in the way of baggage. Perhaps, if you're lucky, he'll soon be off larking about on some new battlefield."

"For shame, Elspeth Fraser."

A woman ought not to talk that way about her laird, and a wife ought not to think that way about her husband. Brenna wound down through the castle and took herself out into the courtyard, both rage and gratitude speeding her along.

She'd had endless Highland winters to rehearse the speech Michael deserved, years to practice the dignified reserve she'd exhibit before him should he ever recall he had a home. Alas for her, the cobbles were wet from a recent scrubbing, so her dignified reserve more or less skidded to a halt before her husband.

Strong hands steadied her as she gazed up, and up some more, into green eyes both familiar and unknown.

"You've come home." Not at all what she'd meant to say.

"That I have. If you would be so good, madam, as to allow the lady of the—*Brenna*?"

His hands fell away, and Brenna stepped back, wrapping her tartan shawl around her more closely.

"Welcome to Castle Brodie Michael." Because somebody ought to say the words, she added, "Welcome home."

"You used to be chubby." He leveled this accusation as if put out that somebody had made off with that chubby girl.

"You used to be skinny." Now he was all-over muscle. He'd gone away a tall, gangly fellow, and come back not simply a man, but a warrior. "Perhaps you're hungry?"

She did not know what to do with a husband, much less *this* husband, who bore so little resemblance to the young man she'd married, but Brenna knew well what to do with a hungry man.

"I am…" His gaze traveled the courtyard the way a skilled gunner might swivel his sights on a moving target, making a circuit of the granite walls rising some thirty feet on three sides of the bailey. His expression suggested he was making sure the castle, at least, had remained where he'd left it. "I am famished."

"Come along then." Brenna turned and started for the entrance to the main hall, but Michael remained in the middle of the courtyard, still peering about. Potted geraniums were in riot, pink roses climbed trellises under the first-floor windows, and window boxes held all manner of blooms.

"You've planted flowers."

Another near accusation, for nine years ago, the only flowers in the keep were stray shrubs of heather springing up in sheltered corners.

Brenna returned to her husband's side, trying to see the courtyard from his perspective. "One must occupy oneself somehow while waiting for a husband to come home—or be killed."

He needed to know that for nine years, despite anger, bewilderment, and even the occasional period of striving for indifference toward him and his fate, Brenna had gone to bed every night praying that death did not end his travels.

"One must, indeed, occupy oneself." He offered her his arm, which underscored how long they'd been separated and how far he'd wandered.

The men of the castle and its tenancies knew to keep their hands to themselves where Brenna MacLogan Brodie was concerned. They did not hold her chair for her, did not assist her in and out of coaches, or on and off of her horse.

And yet, Michael stood there, a muscular arm winged at her, while the scent of slippery cobbles, blooming roses, and a whiff of vetiver filled the air.

"Brenna Maureen, every arrow slit and window of that castle is occupied by a servant or relation watching our reunion. I would like to walk into my home arm in arm with my wife. Will you permit me that courtesy?"

He'd been among the English, the *military* English, which might explain this fussing over appearances, but he hadn't lost his Scottish common sense.

Michael had *asked* her to accommodate him. Brenna wrapped one hand around his thick forearm and allowed him to escort her to the castle.

తుం

He could bed his wife. The relief Michael Brodie felt at that sentiment eclipsed the relief of hearing again the languages of his childhood, Gaelic and Scots, both increasingly common as he'd traveled farther north.

To know he could feel desire for his wedded wife surpassed his relief at seeing the castle in good repair, and even eclipsed his relief that the woman didn't indulge in strong hysterics at the sight of him.

For the wife he'd left behind had been more child than woman, the antithesis of this red-haired Celtic goddess wrapped in the clan's hunting tartan and so much wounded dignity.

They reached the steps leading up to the great wooden door at the castle entrance. "I wrote to you."

Brenna did not turn her head. "Perhaps your letters went astray."

Such gracious indifference. He was capable of bedding his wife—any young man with red blood in his veins would desire the woman at Michael's side—but clearly, ability did not guarantee he'd have the opportunity.

"I meant, I wrote from Edinburgh to let you know I was coming home."

"Edinburgh is lovely in summer."

All of Scotland was lovely in summer, and to a man who'd scorched his back raw under the Andalusian sun, lovely in deepest winter too. "I was in France, Brenna. The King's post did not frequent Toulouse."

Outside the door, she paused and studied the scrolled iron plate around the ancient lock.

"We heard you'd deserted, then we heard you'd died. Some of the fellows from your regiment paid calls here, and intimated army gossip is not to be trusted. Then some officer came trotting up the lane a month after the victory, expecting to pay a call on you."

Standing outside that impenetrable, ancient door, Michael accepted that his decision to serve King and Country had left wounded at home as well as on the Continent.

And yet, apologizing now would only make things worse.

"Had you seen the retreat to Corunna, Brenna, had you seen even one battle—" Because the women saw it all, right along with their husbands and children. Trailing immediately behind the soldiers came a smaller, far more vulnerable army of dependents, suffering and dying in company with their menfolk.

"I *begged* you to take me with you." She wrenched the door open, but stepped back, that Michael might precede her into the castle.

She had pleaded and cried for half their wedding night, sounding not so much like a distressed bride as an inconsolable child, and because he'd been only five years her senior, he'd stolen away in the morning while she'd slept, tears still streaking her pale cheeks.

He searched for honest words that would not wound her further.

"I prayed for your well-being every night. The idea that you were here, safe and sound, comforted me."

She plucked a thorny pink rose from a trellis beside the door and passed the bloom to him.

"Who or what was supposed to comfort me, Michael Brodie? When I was told you'd gone over to the enemy? When I was told you were dead? When I imagined you captured by the French, or worse?"

They stood on the castle steps, their every word available to any in the great hall or lurking at nearby windows. Rather than fret over the possibility that his wife had been unfaithful to him—her questions were offered in rhetorical tones—Michael stepped closer.

"Your husband has come home, and it will be his pleasure to make your comfort his greatest concern."

He even tried a smile, letting her see that *man and wife* might have some patching up to do, but *man and woman* could deal together well and very soon.

She looked baffled—or peevish. He could not read his own wife accurately enough to distinguish between the two.

"Have you baggage, Husband?"

Yes, he did. He gestured for her to go ahead of him into the hall. "Last I heard, the coach was following, but I haven't much in the way of worldly goods."

"I'll have your things put in the blue bedroom."

When she would have gone swishing off into the

bowels of the castle, Michael grabbed her wrist and kept her at his side. She remained facing half-away from him, an ambiguous pose, not resisting, and not exactly drinking in the sight of her long-lost husband, either.

"What's different?" He studied the great hall he'd stopped seeing in any detail by his third birthday. "Something is different. This place used to be…dark. Like a great ice cave."

And full of mice and cobwebs.

She twisted her hand free of his.

"Nothing much is different. I had the men enlarge the windows, whitewash the walls, polish the floors. The room wanted light, we had a bit of coin at the time, and the fellows needed something to do."

"You put a balcony over the fireplace." She'd also had the place scrubbed from the black-and-white marble floor to the blackened crossbeams, freeing it of literally centuries of dirt.

"The ceilings are so high we lose all the warmth. When we keep the fires going, the reading balcony is warmer than the hall below it."

She'd taken a medieval hall and domesticated it without ruining its essential nature, made it comfortable. Or comforting? Bouquets of pink roses graced four of the deep windowsills, and every chair and sofa sported a Brodie plaid folded over the back. Not the darker, more complicated hunting plaid Brenna wore, but the cheerful red, black, and yellow used every day.

"I like it very much, Brenna. The hall is welcoming." Even if the lady was not.

She studied the great beams twenty feet overhead—or perhaps entreated the heavens for aid—while Michael caught a hint of a smile at his compliment.

That he'd made his wife smile must be considered progress, however miniscule.

Then her smile died. "Angus, good day."

Michael followed her line of sight to a sturdy kilted fellow standing in the doorway of the shadowed corridor that led to the kitchens. Even in the obscure light, Michael recognized an uncle who had been part older brother and part father, the sight of whom now was every part dear.

"Never say the village gossip was for once true! Our Michael has come home at last." Angus hustled across the great hall, his kilt flapping against his knees. "Welcome, lad! Welcome at long last, and God be thanked you're hale and in one grand piece, aren't you now?"

A hug complete with resounding thumps on the back followed, and in his uncle's greeting, Michael found the enthusiasm he'd hoped for from his wife.

From anybody.

"Surely the occasion calls for a wee dram," Angus said. His hair was now completely white, though he was less than twenty years Michael's senior. He wasn't as tall as Michael, but his build was muscular, and he looked in great good health.

"The man needs to eat before you're getting him drunk," Brenna interjected. She stood a few feet off, directly under crossed claymores that gleamed with the same shine as the rest of the hall.

"We can take a tray in the library, woman," Angus replied. "When a man hasn't seen his nephew for nigh ten years, the moment calls for whisky and none of your fussy little crumpets, aye?"

Brenna twitched the tail of her plaid over her shoulder, a gesture about as casual as a French dragoon swinging into the saddle.

"I will feed my husband a proper meal at a proper table, Angus Brodie, and your wee dram will wait its turn."

Angus widened his stance, fists going to his hips, suggesting not all battlefields were found on the Continent.

"Uncle, Brenna has the right of it. I haven't eaten since this morning. One glass of good spirits, and I'd be disgracing my heritage. Food first, and then we'll find some sipping whisky."

Brenna moved off to stick her finger in a white crockery bowl of roses, while Angus treated Michael to a look of good-humored disgruntlement.

"She runs a fine kitchen, does our Brenna. Do it justice, and find me in the office when you've eaten your fill. I'm that glad you're back, lad."

He strode off, the tassels on his sporran bouncing against his thick thighs, while Brenna shook droplets of water off the end of her finger.

"Does my uncle often cross swords with you?"

She wiped her finger on her plaid. "He does not, not now. He leaves the castle to me. I'm sure your arrival is the only thing that tempted him past the door. What are you hungry for?"

He was hungry for her smiles. A soldier home from war had a right to be hungry for his wife's smiles.

"Anything will do, though I've a longing for a decent scone. The English can't get them right, you know, and they skimp with the butter and must dab everything with their infernal jams, when what's wanted is some heather honey."

Compared to the little curve of her lips he'd seen earlier, this smile was riveting. Brenna had grown into a lovely woman, but when she aimed that smile at Michael, he had the first inkling she might be a *lovable* woman too. Her smile held warmth and welcome, maybe even a touch of approval.

"A batch of scones has just come out of the oven, Michael Brodie. If we hurry, you can get your share before the cousins come raiding."

He followed her into the depths of the house, watching her skirts twitch, and entertaining naughty, husbandly thoughts.

Until he recalled that the blue bedroom where Brenna was sending his baggage was a guest chamber, across a cold, drafty hallway and several doors down from the laird's apartments.

❧

He was Michael, and he was not, this Viking come calling. His table manners were still fastidious—some might say elegant—without being pernickety, his eyes were the same shade of green, and he still bore a light scent of vetiver... And yet he was not the man she'd married.

Brenna buttered him another scone—his third—and set it on his plate. "I have tried without success to hate you, you know."

He paused, a bite of roast grouse speared on his fork. "To what do you attribute your failure?"

Good of him, not to scold her for raising the topic when he'd been home less than an hour. "I used to like you." She had not meant to sound so wistful.

His smile was the same as her many memories of it, tipping up at the right side of his mouth first, and revealing a dimple in his right cheek. "One hopes you married a fellow you liked."

She would have married nearly anybody who'd offered. "You used to tease me, but you were never mean about it."

He'd also kept his hands to himself—hands that didn't sport dirty fingernails, no matter how hungry he'd been when he came to the table.

He offered her the scone she'd just buttered. "You've been watching me eat for nigh half an hour, my lady, and the food is ambrosial. Please have at least a nibble."

Brenna accepted the scone, tore off a bite with her fingers, and set the rest back on his plate. Before she took a bite, she tried to steer the discussion in the direction it needed to go. "I wondered if you regretted our marriage."

"Never."

She popped the bite of sweet into her mouth, mostly to give herself time to digest his answer, for it had been as swift and certain as a bolt from a crossbow. "Then why did you leave me a maid, Michael?"

"So I would not instead leave you a mother." He spoke gently and held out another bite of scone to her, his fingers glistening with butter and honey.

His green eyes used to be full of laughter and confidence, and now they held shadows. He wasn't lying, but neither was he being entirely honest. Brenna took the food from his hand, realizing she was hungry too, and dinner still some hours away.

"We eat late this time of year. The days are so long, and the nights so short."

He went back to cleaning his plate, suggesting he was prudent as well as hungry. "Do I have time for a bath before the meal?"

"You do." Brenna dispatched her bite of scone, licked her fingers, and caught her husband watching. "I'll order you a bath."

She scooted her chair back, and Michael was on his feet with a speed that astonished.

"You needn't observe the parlor courtesies with me, Michael. I've been doing without somebody to hold my chair for years." She moved away, she did not scurry.

"When you remind me of that, you don't mean it as a scold, but I hear it was such. Will you assist at my bath? One anticipates a wife might perform that service for her husband."

He was reminding *her* that their separation had not been entirely easy for him either, drat the man.

"I'm not scolding. I'm..." She was hungry and tired, and not a little resentful of her husband now that he had returned—though she'd also resented his absence. Part of her wanted to assist at that bath, to touch him and make sure he was real. Another part of her nearly hated him.

Nearly.

"I did not wake up this morning anticipating that my husband might come home today. I got out of the habit of wishing for that, and now here you are, and what's to be done with you?"

What's to be done with us?

In some fashion understood only by soldiers who'd seen years of death, did he nearly hate her and all who'd spent those same years at peace?

He slid her chair back to its place at the table. "We will talk about what's to be done, but first I'll wash the dust of the road from my carcass, have a wee tot with Angus, and then a ramble around the castle. My thanks for the food. It's the best I've had since leaving home."

He seemed sincere, but that was the problem with men—they could so easily seem sincere. Or maybe, and this was an old conundrum, the problem was Brenna's discernment.

She took herself off to the kitchens, both to relay the laird's compliments and to arrange his bath. Under the circumstances, Angus might have assisted at his nephew's bath, but Brenna couldn't stomach such a notion.

Angus hadn't even used the front door to come into the castle, but had let himself in through the kitchens, as if he still lived here or was perhaps anticipating living here again.

Which he might do, over Brenna's dead body.

Brenna was Michael's wife, and Michael had asked her to assist him at his bath. She was prepared to meet that challenge until she found the tub, not in the blue bedroom, but in the laird's very bedchamber.

The presumption of it, that he'd countermand her orders, added more than a dollop of rage to her near-hatred.

"You've changed things in here too," Michael said as the maids dumped the last of the water into the tub, all the while stealing glances at the prodigal laird. "My wife likes our home light and cheery. This is fortunate, because I do too."

Did he expect a light and cheery marriage? *With her?*

"Give me your boots, sir. Hugh's eldest does a wonderful job with them. Have you a shaving kit that I can fetch from among your things?"

He settled into the rocking chair where Brenna preferred to do her embroidery at the end of the day. The chair was old and quite heavy—like much about the castle—and yet it creaked under Michael's weight.

"I shaved this morning. Do I still have a kilt somewhere on the premises? I have a dress kilt among my things. I assume I'll wear that tomorrow when we review the staff."

A dusty boot came off, revealing a stocking-clad, muscular calf and a big right foot.

Brenna pretended to test the temperature of the water, which was wonderfully hot. "You haven't developed a taste for southern attire?"

"I've had a bellyful of southern everything. I've missed home, missed it terribly." The second boot came off, and he held them out to her.

He hadn't missed *her* terribly, and while that ought to be a relief, it also rankled. Exceedingly.

Brenna took his boots and found wee Lachlan waiting for them outside the door, which denied her the excuse of taking the boots all the way down to the kitchen.

"Thank you, Lachlan, and mind you do a good job.

Fetch me one of your da's work kilts and a clean shirt from the laundry, and leave them in the sitting room before you start on the boots."

The boy scampered off, his grin revealing two missing front teeth. Behind her, Brenna heard her husband rising from the rocking chair.

"You will be happy to know you're a baroness," he said, unbuttoning his waistcoat. "Or you will be shortly. I was hoping to escape with a mere knighthood, or a baronetcy, but the Regent gets sentimental about his soldiers."

"I'm a *baroness*?" If he'd told her she was with child, she could not have been more surprised. "You're to be given a title?"

He draped the waistcoat over the shoulders of the rocker, where it looked both odd and cozily appropriate. "When you heard I'd gone over to the enemy, I was in fact on the King's business, or so my superior officer would have it. Would you help me with this knot?"

Brenna crossed the room and stood before him as he raised his chin. "Conducting the King's business in Toulouse could not have been very safe, Michael Brodie." She loosened the knot, which he had indeed yanked into something entirely unfashionable.

Staring at the breadth of his shoulders, Brenna was abruptly reminded that in addition to being her errant husband—and now a peer of the realm!—Michael Brodie was the smiling, teasing, decent man who'd married her when he might have repudiated the bargain their fathers had struck years ago.

How many times had he cheated death in the past nine years?

A queer feeling assaulted her knees as she studied

his throat. "I would not have liked to find myself your widow."

Whatever emotions she was battling—anger, resentment, bewilderment, relief—any of them was a better bargain than sorrow.

His arms as they came around her were tentative, but surprisingly welcome. "One is cheered to hear this."

"You sound English," she said, pulling back but smiling to be able to insult him. "You dress English."

"And yet, the English could barely understand me, at first." He passed her his wrinkled cravat, which she hung over his waistcoat. "You are not pleased about being a baroness."

The voluminous linen shirt he unbuttoned probably cost enough to feed a crofter and his family for months, and yet, Michael expected her to be pleased about this title business.

"A title is another surprise, and I do not like surprises. Have you ambitions to join the Scottish delegation?"

"No, I do not. Those poor bastards must mince about London for much of the year, pretending they have some influence with a group of lords who've never dug a potato or imbibed decent whisky in their fat, pampered lives. No more French for me, no more English, and I'm not entirely keen on the Irish or the Germans at present, either."

The shirt came off over his head, which necessitated that Brenna test the water again. It had not cooled in the least. "Your mother was Irish, sir, and the daughter of an Irish earl. A true lady."

And his sisters had been sent to Ireland not long after he'd left the castle.

"As Wellington is Irish," he said, tossing her his shirt, "though His Grace disdains mention of it. It was the duchess's friendship with Mama that brought me to Wellington's notice."

Brenna folded the shirt, an extravagance of pale fabric, meticulous seams, and tiny stitches, a shirt she might have made for him had he remained at home. A shirt he might have died wearing.

This peculiar, domestic conversation juxtaposed with increasing displays of Michael's bare skin had anxiety cresting up toward panic in Brenna's belly.

"Are you used to ladies assisting you at your bath?" Because she was surely not used to this casual disrobing he accomplished all too quickly. Maybe a soldier learned this lack of modesty, along with how to march and shoot. Michael's chest and shoulders rippled with muscle, his arms were roped with it, and his belly… She draped the shirt ever so carefully over the chair back.

Michael paused, his hands on his falls. "I am not used to having anybody's assistance with a bath. For months, the only places I could bathe were ponds and streams, and to do so was to risk the loss of my clothing, if not my liberty or my life." He undid a couple of buttons on each side of his breeches and shot her a puzzled look. "Are you shy, Brenna Maureen?"

He'd gone a bit Scottish on her. *Are ye shy*?

While she'd gone a bit red in the cheeks. "I've seen many a naked man, more than I've ever wished to."

She shouldn't have said that, and not because it piqued her husband's interest.

"Oh, have you now?" He prowled across the room. "So if I drop these breeches you won't be torn between the urge to shamelessly stare at the long-lost family jewels and the inclination to run from the castle in a maidenly fright?"

In the next room, somebody opened the door, then a moment later, closed it.

"That will be Lachlan with your clean clothes."

Brenna might have ducked past her husband, but he stood there, naked to the waist, his tone not quite teasing, and his mouth not quite smiling. "Brenna Maureen?"

She'd always liked the way he said her name, musically, like an endearment. Now was an inconvenient moment to recall such a thing.

And yet, as angry as she was with Michael, she did not want to hurt him avoidably, not even for the sake of her pride.

"I see my cousins and the fellows from the village bathing in the loch all the time. They know good and well when Elspeth and I are on the parapets or in the solar, and those men have no modesty. Elspeth finds them vastly entertaining. She fancies Lachlan's papa, though I doubt he's aware of her feelings."

Michael peered down at her. "What does Lachlan's mother think of a devotion to cleanliness that requires strutting and pawing in the altogether before decent women?"

"Annie's been gone five years, Michael." Brenna moved off to the wardrobe, where she stored her soaps and flannels. She rummaged longer than necessary, trying to locate her emotional balance and failing.

"Would you mind fetching my clean clothes?" Michael asked. "You'll have to make me a list of who's left us, who's been born or wed. I ought to know these things before I start on my tenant calls."

He sounded neither resigned nor resentful, but perhaps resolute. Brenna left the room, starting that list in her head, for many families had departed for the New World, and in nine years, any family seat would see its share of deaths—also a few births. When she returned to the bedroom, Michael was ensconced in the tub and busily lathering his chest.

Which was a kindness on his part, truly it was.

Two

If Brenna had strayed during the years of Michael's absence, she hadn't wandered very far or very often. Judging from her excessive modesty, she'd done her frolicking in the dark of night under several blankets and without a single candle lit.

Which in one sense was a pity—virgins and their near equivalent were rumored to be a howling lot of work—and in another was a sweet, sweet relief.

"I think I'll shave after all," Michael said when he'd rendered himself cleaner than he'd been in days. "Perhaps you'd retrieve my kit for me?"

His wife left the room as if a squad of dragoons were galloping down on her, which allowed Michael time to climb out of the tub, towel off, and pin on the plain, dark work kilt. The only assistance he'd asked of his wife was to rinse his hair when he'd made use of her soaps, and even this had provoked blushes from her.

And silence. Brenna had been a quiet girl; she was a silent woman.

"Thank you," Michael said, taking his kit from her

and moving to the window. Castle Brodie was in truth an Elizabethan manor with a stone keep anchoring its central wing, but in deference to Highland winters, the walls were thick throughout.

Michael unrolled grooming scissors, a razor, comb, whetstone, and shaving brush, the last of which he swished in the tub and lathered up using Brenna's soap.

"You scent the soap with heather and what else?" he asked, because small talk seemed the safest undertaking with a wife who had reason enough to hate him.

"Lavender, a bit of rosemary, a drop of vetiver. I use what's on hand, and what's in season. The rose oil I save to make gifts."

Michael wet the razor and lifted his chin. "What time should we muster the castle staff tomorrow? They're impatient to inspect me, I'm sure."

In the mirror, he saw that his wife had stopped tidying up in the vicinity of the tub—or stopped pretending to tidy up. He'd been careful not to splash a single drop on her floors. She instead watched him as he scraped whiskers off his throat.

"We'll get that out of the way early. There's work to do, and the weather should be fair."

Early by Highland summer standards was not a sanguine thought for a man who'd traveled hundreds of miles on horseback. "Early it is. Is auld Maudie still keeping house for us?"

"She is."

"And does Dabnich mind the tenants and farms?"

Brenna's expression gave away nothing, which piqued Michael's curiosity.

"Angus has taken on those responsibilities. Dabnich's boys moved to Boston, and he and the missus followed."

Michael considered this while tending to his upper lip. "Would you mind if I grew a beard?" He hated beards. They itched and made eating a fussier undertaking. He was becoming none too keen on conversation with his wife either.

"You must do as you please."

"Have you time to trim my hair then?"

Because he was determined that she not spend their entire marriage across a room from him, and even as a very young lady, Brenna had not easily abided untidiness.

"I like your hair."

He nicked himself on the jaw. "You *like* my hair?"

She opened the wardrobe to put away her scents and soaps. "Aye. There's more red in it now. Two red-haired people usually have red-haired children."

Because she might turn and see his face in the mirror, Michael did not smile, but she'd recalled the color of his hair when he'd departed years ago, and she contemplated procreation with him.

More progress, but like the damned French, she gave up ground only grudgingly.

"May I have that shirt?"

She had folded the clean shirt at least twice, but tossed it to him now. "That one might be a bit small on you. Hugh isn't as broad through the shoulders."

Michael's baroness was not offering a compliment.

Hugh hadn't access to the London tailors, said to be the best in the world. The shirt was clean and well made nonetheless. Michael left the top two buttons open to accommodate the more snug fit.

"I'm sure I have a clean cravat somewhere in my bag." This time, rather than provide his lady with yet another excuse to depart from his presence, he crossed the corridor himself and retrieved his entire traveling bag.

As he stood before the mirror and wrapped his neckcloth around his throat, Michael caught sight of Brenna in the mirror, arms crossed, plaid shawl wrapped tight. "Why the frown, Wife?"

He wished she'd object to his moving his effects into what was clearly her bedroom. Wished she'd join battle, because an altercation of any sort required that two parties *engage* each other.

"Will you sashay about the castle barefoot?"

"Half the women in Edinburgh are barefoot as we speak, shoes being too precious to waste on summer wear."

When he expected she'd inform him he was not a fishmonger's wife plying her wares on the lowland docks, Brenna instead tossed his shaving water into the tub, wiped off his razor, threw his towel onto the stack of damp flannels on the floor, and started rolling up his kit.

"You would have made an excellent officer's wife."

She passed him his kit, the ties fastened in a tidy bow. "Some might say I *am* an officer's wife."

She would have made an excellent *officer*. Rather than lay himself open to another telling toss of her uxorial dagger, Michael focused on brushing his too-long hair back from his face.

"Angus will be expecting you," Brenna reminded

him. "Mind he doesn't get you too drunk. The staff began inspecting you the moment you rode into the bailey. You were right about that."

He set the shaving kit aside, determined to gain some concession from her. "If that's so, I'll sleep here tonight, Brenna Brodie. We are man and wife, and a baron needs an heir."

She wrinkled her nose, which made her look young and not as formidable. "Any particular baron?"

Brenna sidestepped as nimbly as if swords had been crossed beneath her verbal feet.

"We are the Baron and Baroness Strathdee." He liked the sound of it, even if their title did not impress his lady wife.

"We've good fishing in the River Dee. I'll see you at dinner."

She left the field, off to clean, tidy, polish, or otherwise organize some corner of the house, and yet, Michael did not have the sense he'd inspired his wife into a retreat. A baron might need an heir, but a man married to Brenna Brodie needed his wife's cooperation if any heirs were to be forthcoming.

On that daunting thought, Michael headed barefoot for the lower floors, and a wee dram—or two.

⁂

"I hate Scotland. The mountains are gray and mean, the roads are bumpy, and everybody talks funny."

Maeve's nursemaid might have been deaf for all the impact this litany had on her, so Maeve resorted to heavier artillery.

"I have to use the necessary."

Prebish stopped gawking out the window and aimed a smile at her charge that did not fool Maeve for a moment.

"You used the necessary at the last posting inn, and if you're about to tell me you're famished to flinders and dying of thirst yet again, you know the basket is under the seat."

"There's nothing but scones in the basket, and they're stale by now. The tea in the flask has gone all cold and nasty too." Like Maeve's life had gone cold and nasty.

"Best appreciate good food while you have it, child. Times are hard, and not every little girl is as fortunate as you."

Prebish was a Papist, which Maeve took to mean she prayed frequently, was on a first-name basis with a lot of saints, and didn't mind so much when people died. When Maeve had been a truly little girl, she had heard many a good story perched on Prebish's ample lap. On the basis of that long association—and a certain tight feeling in her tummy—Maeve posed a question that had been plaguing her since they'd left Ireland.

"If I'm so fortunate, why did Bridget send me far, far away?"

Such a scary distance too. The Scottish roads were nothing compared to the pitching of the Irish Sea and the odd languages people spoke in Belfast and Glasgow. In the port towns, Prebish had held Maeve's hand, and Maeve hadn't protested.

"Your sister is expecting a child of her own, young Maeve, and your older brother is now a Scottish baron. He's the head of your family, and the proper fellow to look after you now that all that nonsense is over with on the Continent."

Nonsense was what Prebish called everything from a disagreement among the maids to war to Maeve's very reasonable arguments against having her hair braided every single day.

"Tell me again what my brother looks like."

Prebish's smile shifted and became wistful—or sad?

"He's a grand fellow, your brother Michael. As tall as Hamish Heckendorn, with green eyes and blond hair. He liked to laugh when I knew him, and your sisters adored him."

"Does he still like to laugh?" Because what did it matter if a man was taller than the blacksmith in Darrow if that man was grumpy and sour all the time?

"He's been long away to war, Maeve. That can take the laughter out of a man, but there's nothing like a child to bring it back."

Who was to bring back Maeve's laughter?

The mountains never changed here. They took all day to get around, and the roads only got worse the farther the carriage traveled from the coast. In Aberdeen, Prebish had declared they needed a day to rest, but they'd also picked up baggage, the weight of which made the ride even rougher.

"Will my brother like me?"

Prebish was not ignoring this question. Maeve could see her old face was creased in thought. "He will love you, and you will love him, because that's what family does."

Maeve reached under the seat for the basket of

scones—which were not stale—and took a bite, hoping to settle her stomach. Prebish had told the truth—families loved each other, even families who sent their dearest little girl off to strange, cold, bumpy lands—but Prebish had also not answered the question Maeve had asked.

Would Michael, a brother she'd never met, *like* her?

∽

Brenna had parted from her newly scrubbed husband at the first opportunity, needing activity to keep her from flying at him in a flat panic.

Heirs were not a fit topic for the dinner table, though, so a lovely meal had been served an hour earlier than usual.

Of which, Brenna had tasted not one bite.

"Angus said you set a good table, and he spoke the truth." Michael offered her a smile and put a slice of cheese on the end of a small bone-handled knife. Brenna took the cheese, knowing she hadn't eaten enough dinner to sustain a hare in summer.

She ignored the compliment and the smile, for Angus offering compliments was the local equivalent of Greeks bearing gifts.

"Thank you." She nibbled the cheese rather than speculate on what else Angus had said over a glass or three of whisky.

"Does Angus usually dine here?"

"He dwells in the dower house, and is well looked after there. This is our own cheese, you know. I like it particularly well."

From Michael's expression, Brenna's dodge hadn't worked.

He cut himself a thick slice of cheese in a single, clean stroke.

"Why is my uncle residing in the dower house when we have an entire castle available to shelter our family?"

"The castle is drafty, dusty, and without many modern conveniences, according to Angus." While the dower house, built at the insistence of Michael's mother, was an architectural gem full of comfort and innovations. "Your father gave him the tenancy of the dower house with your mother's permission."

This was not far from the truth, if the late laird's semi-drunken ramblings could be trusted. Brenna had been too grateful for Angus's absence to question the explanation.

"I suppose it's the least we can do for Angus, as much of the running of the place as he's taken on. Will your cousins join us for meals?"

As Brenna finished her cheese and washed it down with the last of her wine, it occurred to her that Michael was much concerned with reconnecting with his people. He wanted to review his staff first thing in the day, had asked for a list of the departed before he'd taken his bath, and now wanted to know the comings and goings of Brenna's cousins and their families.

"Come," she said, rising. "I will answer your questions as we walk."

Because she'd moved dinner up, and because they were in the Highlands, the sun was not yet set. In high summer, the gloaming lasted for hours—hours when work might be done, or a husband might be reasoned with.

"Where are you taking me, Brenna?" He was amused, not in fear of a kidnapping.

"You asked me to list for you all of those who've left your holdings in your absence. We'll start that list down by the kirk."

The castle chapel had been demolished in some long-past wave of reformatory zeal and the stones reused for other structures, so Brenna led her spouse through the postern gate and down the wooded hill toward the village.

"Even the trees are taller," Michael said. "Do we still have as much venison as we want?"

"We do, and thank God for it. Venison and potatoes, salmon when they're running, grouse, mutton, oats most years, and we trade wool for much else. I'm jealous of my kitchen gardens, and the conservatory provides a few delicacies. I suppose Angus would have discussed the crops with you."

That was as close as Brenna could come to asking about the hour Michael had spent behind a closed door with his uncle. Angus would share his version of Brenna's history with Michael, and he'd do it at the time and place most likely to benefit Angus and burden Brenna—or destroy her.

Michael took her hand. Just slid his fingers through hers, and kept right on walking, while Brenna lost track of every thought in her head.

"Angus complained, of course," Michael said. "Cheerfully, because we Scots always complain cheerfully, but he let it be known I am much indebted to him for cobbling together ten more years of solvency on land that begrudges even the hardiest sheep a living."

"Five years," Brenna said. "Your da didn't fall from his horse until five years ago, and he managed his land properly until the end." Though he hadn't managed much else well.

"May we rest a moment?" Michael didn't drop her hand, but instead came to a stop at a small clearing. Heather sprang up amid the bracken, and evening sunlight slanted through deep forest shadows. The scents were fresh, green, and soothing.

Michael had endured hardship after hardship with the military. He was not asking to rest because his feet were tired.

"It will be dark soon," Brenna observed.

Still, Michael did not drop her hand. "A soldier learns to treasure beauty where he finds it. Tell me about the day my father died."

Five years ago, Brenna hadn't known where to write to her husband, or if he was even still alive.

"Shall we sit, Husband?"

Ages ago, somebody had graced the clearing with a plain plank bench, and that bench had endured too. Brenna untangled her hand from Michael's and took a seat, but the infernal man simply came down beside her and recaptured her hand.

"Were you here when he died?"

"I was with him. He asked that I remember him to you and tell you he was proud of you."

Michael hunched forward, one forearm braced on his thigh. He stayed that way for a long moment before he spoke.

"If we are blessed with children, we will tell them we are proud of them, but we will also tell them we love them, and when they are gone from us, we will tell them we miss them and pray for their safety every night."

"Aye."

She hurt for him, despite all intention to the contrary, because he wasn't the cheerful, braw fellow who'd gone off to war years ago. He was both more and less than that young man, and the changes had been wrought through privation, violence, and misery.

"Was it awful, in France?"

He lifted her hand to his lips and kissed her knuckles.

"Yes, it was awful, for many reasons. In some regards, the wars were hardest on the French people. They gave untold thousands of their best and boldest young men to the Corsican's bloodlust, and eventually, few were left at home to tend the crops or raise the children. One couldn't help but admire the French, just as they grudgingly admired the bravery and tenacity of their foes."

"All this gallantry only made for more widows and orphans." And wounded, starving soldiers.

"Just so."

Brenna searched for anything she could give him that might be of comfort. "Your father was always a bit tipsy toward the end, but no more so than any other aging laird. The gout plagued him, and drink was his consolation. He was on his favorite horse, and they simply took a bad step before a jump."

More quiet passed, such as the woods at dusk were quiet. Squirrels chattered and leaped about, and birds fluttered in the canopy above.

"Even on the battlefield, it can happen like that,"

Michael said softly. "We lost many a soldier to disease and exposure, rather than to bullets. Too many."

She could not tell if his use of "we" referred to the French or the British. Probably both.

"Your father also told me to give his love to your mother and sisters. I wrote to your mother to let her know this." He'd been proud of his son, but his wife and daughters had had his love—too late, of course, but they had.

Another absent kiss to her knuckles. "Thank you."

His expression was so bleak, Brenna's heart ached. "I ride his gelding, you know. Boru is a fine mount, though Angus wanted to shoot him."

"We'll ride out tomorrow, then, you and I."

"If the weather's fine." Except first they had a night to get through. "Shall we be on our way? Soon it will be too dark to read the headstones."

"You were taking me down to the cemetery?"

"Aye." And still, he kept her hand in his. He'd been like this as a young man too, affectionate, full of casual touches and easy smiles. She had loved him for that, loved him desperately. "Michael, I realize we will share a bed tonight, but if you expect…"

He sat beside her, her hand in his, his expression unreadable in the forest shadows. "If I expect—?"

She rose and walked across the clearing, twigs snapping under her boots. Maybe this was a discussion best held outside the castle walls, or at least begun there.

"I cannot join with a stranger."

"I would be alarmed if you could, but I'm not a stranger. I'm your husband."

He'd followed her across the clearing, and she

hadn't heard a sound. The heat coming off of him, the scent of vetiver, and his voice told Brenna her husband stood immediately behind her.

"Why didn't you come home, Michael? The armistice was more than two years ago, and you didn't serve for the Hundred Days. You've been on British soil for more than two years, and I've received exactly one note from you in all that time."

"You're angry," he said, his hands settling on her shoulders. "I can under—"

Brenna wrenched out from under his grasp and faced him.

"I am *not* angry, and you can*not* understand, any more than I can understand why you'd remain behind enemy lines in France, year after year, bound by some duty you haven't taken the time to explain to your own wife."

"One doesn't generally advertise one's location behind enemy lines, Brenna."

"One doesn't generally spend years behind those lines, then wait two more years to come home, Michael." The light was waning, and this topic wasn't the point of their errand beyond the castle walls.

"I had yet to discharge my duties to my satisfaction or to my superior's satisfaction."

Bother his superior.

"Every soldier gets leave, Michael Brodie, and yet, I had no leave from being your wife. I thought about haring off to London, you know. Presenting myself on your doorstep to see if you recognized me."

He remained silent, did not even try to apologize or explain.

"Your parents separated for all practical purposes," she said, because any reaction from him was better than his continued silence. "Many couples do."

"We'll not separate." He sounded exactly like his father, and exactly like his uncle, too.

"You failed to consummate our union when you had the chance, went marching off to war for longer than was necessary, could not be bothered to write to your own wife twice a year, and now you come wandering home in expectation of...what? An heir on the way by Christmas? *Are you daft?*"

"We'll not separate, Brenna Brodie. Angus tells me our finances are precarious, many of the tenants have left for the New World, the English pass one tax after another, and the people remaining need their laird and lady. Mother should never have gone back to Ireland."

"You are so certain of that," Brenna said, "and you know nothing of it, because you were not here, were you?" The bitterness in her tone must have registered, because Michael's expression was shocked.

"Michael," she said gently, "we *have been separated* for nearly a decade. I no more want to be your cast-off wife than you want to follow in your parents' footsteps, but creating a family is not another order from headquarters to be dispatched with all haste."

"I fail to comprehend—" He went silent, and in that silence, Brenna could see him building up a wall of masculine pride and Scottish male stubbornness. If he had his way, he'd bed her by morning, preferably more than once, and mark it off his list of obligations to be seen to.

Her soul—and her dinner—rebelled at the very thought.

"I don't know your favorite dessert," she said. "I don't know which of the dances you prefer, or if you still know them. Do you fancy heather ale, or does your taste run to English drink? Will you spend days out on the moors, shooting as your father did, or have your mother's head for figures?"

"What has that to do with begetting an heir?" he shot back, moving closer. "A soldier becomes accustomed to both the hardships and the limited comforts available in times of war. I can well assure you, madam, a man and woman need not know each other's particulars to enjoy—"

Brenna put her hand over his mouth. "If you're about to compare your wife to a camp follower, Michael Brodie, I suggest you rethink your words."

He spoke around her fingers. "You find this amusing?"

She dropped her hand. The first time she'd touched him voluntarily, it had been to shut him up, and yes, she found humor in that—also hope.

"I think it's sad that your only comfort has been whores. I, however, am not one of them."

Brenna was damned sure of that.

"I never meant to imply you were, but Scottish baronies are not awarded every day."

"Spare me," she said, heading back up the path toward the castle. "You care naught for titles and pomp, particularly not the kind handed out by an English sovereign. I have been loyal to you *and* faithful to you for the duration of this farce of a marriage, Michael Brodie, and if you're honest, you will admit many other women would not have honored their vows to the extent that I have."

She left him in the deepening shadows, having resolved nothing, except her own position on the matter of his almighty *heirs*.

And that Michael did not agree with it.

❧

"I've bungled things already."

The sound of Devil's steady chewing said the master's clumsy handling of his wife was of no moment to the horse, but then, Devil was a gelding, and the summer grass was lush.

"She's not the Brenna I left behind," Michael added. "Not the Brenna I used to pray for each night, bivouacking beside my horse on the alarm grounds, waiting for death to snatch us from sleep."

Then, as now, the steady chomp, chomp, chomp of a nearby mount was reassurance that all was well, and no raiding parties were stealing through the countryside intent on wreaking havoc on Wellington's army.

"I don't miss France, God knows. Don't miss London either."

Devil shifted a few feet away, having a nose for clover like no other horse Michael had known. Michael shifted too, trying to find a smooth patch of pasture from which to watch the stars come out.

"I do miss something." Missing something had become a habit, a bad habit. Rather like the whisky in his flask could become a bad habit. "I should not have tarried so long in London, but St. Clair needed me."

Michael's wife had implied she had needed him too, though Michael was at a loss to say how. Brenna appeared as self-sufficient as a woman could be, with a ready ability to state her wishes, needs, and wants.

Also her dislikes, among which, her marriage—or her husband—apparently numbered.

Equine lips wiggled over Michael's hair. He scratched the horse's ear, as the beast had trained him to do.

"I failed to do adequate reconnaissance, horse. Wellington never went into battle without conferring with his intelligence officers if he could help it, and St. Clair seemed to know things the very birds of the air were in ignorance of."

Michael did not miss his former commanding officer either, much. The damned man was wallowing in wedded bliss, for one thing.

"Angus said Brenna can be difficult." This daunting thought required another pull on the flask. "I surmise my uncle and my wife are not in charity with each other, but then, Uncle was against the marriage."

His father had told him that, which at the time had only increased Michael's determination to see the wedding take place.

"I used to be protective of our Brenna. She was such a quiet, wee thing." And pretty—she was still pretty, but no longer wee, and her quiet had become the brooding of a discontented female.

Lights winked out in the castle windows, while overhead, the night sky filled with stars.

"Uncle says Brenna will need a firm hand, and that she's standoffish and given to strange fancies." Though Angus had shared this reluctantly, Michael had wanted to plant the older man a facer for speaking ill of a woman who had put up with much.

He tipped the flask up rather than think of all Brenna had endured without her husband at her side.

"Bloody hot in Spain. We slept in our clothes, though." Did Brenna sleep fully clothed, even in summer? Was she prepared for a sneak attack in the dead of night?

"I'm a bit half-seas over, you understand." Another light went out, this one in the laird's chamber. "'Tisn't helping."

Michael lay in the cool, fragrant grass and tried to recall exactly when the discussion between him and his wife had gone astray. Dinner had been delicious, abundant, and pleasant enough. Then in the clearing, Brenna had announced that he wasn't welcome to exercise a husband's privileges in her bed, and matters had gone abruptly to Hades.

"What did I expect?" he asked, scratching behind the horse's chin. "Brenna had the right of it. I did not mean to compare her to a whore, but I compared coupling with her to what passes between a prostitute and her customers. A woman is entitled to expect a great deal more from her husband, or why marry the bugger?"

Something in the conversation had cheered him, nonetheless. Something about…

"She has not strayed, horse. My Brenna Maureen has not strayed even once."

Though Angus had said she was overly partial to her widowed cousin, and cousins often married.

"Do you think she'd believe me, if I told her I hadn't strayed either?"

The horse moved off in search of more clover,

while Michael got to his feet, took a few moments to get his bearings, and then headed in to spend the night beside his wife.

To whom he had been faithful, and of whom he was still—to his surprise, pleasure, and relief—protective.

❧

Sometime after Brenna had fallen exhausted into her bed, she felt the mattress dip and shift. A pleasant whiff of vetiver, whisky—and meadow grass?—came to her as her husband arranged himself two feet to her left.

The next sound was harder to decipher, but she managed—the soles of two big male feet rubbing together, the bedtime equivalent of shaking the dust of the day from one's feet, a small safeguard in the direction of keeping the sheets clean if conducted with those feet hanging over the side of the bed.

Michael punched his pillows next, several stout blows that would have knocked wayward notions from grown men.

"Are you trying to wake me up, Husband?"

The punching stopped, and she felt him flop down onto the mattress—and heard the put-upon male sigh with which he tucked himself in.

"You did not lock the door, Brenna. My things are in this room."

So was his wife.

"Neither one of us wants talk." The bed was huge, and they weren't touching, but Brenna could feel her husband thinking.

"I did not want you to conclude I was sneaking up on you."

"You're hard to miss when encountered in a bed, Michael. Go to sleep. Morning comes quickly." And yet, she was pleased the pillows had taken a few warning shots on her behalf.

"You want time."

"I want a good night's sleep." Though she should have anticipated that, like any man, Michael would want to beat a topic to death once broached. He could not ponder a discussion and undertake it in manageable portions; he must have done with it, regardless of the hour.

"I want time too, Brenna Maureen."

Brenna rolled to her side, wishing she'd left a candle burning, despite the extravagance. "Time for what?"

"I was a good soldier, once I saw what was expected of me. It's part of the reason I went to France. I was to look after my men, the same as a laird looks after his people. In France, it was much the same, though I was in a garrison with soldiers of a different nationality. We looked after one another, most of the time, and when a man lapsed in that duty, he suffered consequences."

What was he saying, and why must he say it to her in pitch darkness?

"If I were planning to run off, Michael Brodie, I would have scarpered long since. Many and many a family has left the Highlands, including entire branches of clan MacLogan. I could easily have gone with them." Though her own clansmen had hardly recalled where they'd stashed her, once she'd come to live at Castle Brodie.

A considering pause ensued, and then Brenna felt a single, callused finger trace down the side of her jaw.

"You might have left, but you stayed. I'm glad you stayed."

The quality of the darkness changed, sheltering fragile dignity rather than frustrated curiosity. Because Michael had made a concession, Brenna offered him one of her own.

"You need not have come home at all. I know this. You're a baron, or a lord of Parliament, or some such. You could have set up housekeeping in London, and you could easily have set me aside."

He still could.

"Such a thought never occurred to me. This is my home, you are my wife, but I'm asking you to give us time, to not dismiss our marriage out of hand because we're getting a late start on being husband and wife."

Asking.

All day long, Brenna answered questions: What to serve for dinner, when to schedule a wedding or christening, what to put in a basket for a family suffering illness, and how to manage old Davey MacCray when he was once again three days gone with drink.

Those questions were easy, and this one was too.

I'm also glad I stayed, Michael. I've learned to be patient. Maybe you can learn to be patient with me, as well."

The mattress shifted again, bobbing Brenna about as if she were a small craft on a stormy loch. She felt Michael come near, felt the shocking warmth of his bare chest against her arm, and then his lips brushing against her forehead.

Before she could flinch or bat him away, he subsided.

"Good night, then, Wife. Though I'm warning you, a man learns a deal of patience in the army."

He rolled over, giving her his back. She'd seen his bare back earlier in the day, when he bathed, and she knew the skin over his shoulder blades would be smooth, the muscles along his spine lean and graceful.

Brenna rolled over too, so they were back to back, and any stray temptation to touch him less likely to overtake her good sense. "Good night, Husband."

Why had he kissed her, and why hadn't she panicked? "Michael?"

"Hmm?"

"I feel safer with you here."

He said nothing, did not ask if she meant safer with him back home, safer with him in the castle, or safer with him in the same bed.

He also did not ask what or who she felt safer *from*.

Three

ARMY LIFE, WHETHER IN A FRENCH GARRISON OR among British troops in Spain and Portugal, was intimate. Michael had seen a woman giving birth in the snow along the road to Corunna, and rejoiced with his entire unit when he'd learned mother, child—and father—had safely made it aboard the evacuation ships.

He'd also seen a couple lying in the snow, arms about each other, both dead of the exhaustion and exposure that had claimed many on that hellish retreat.

Combat held worse intimacies yet, as when a French officer whom one chanced upon foraging with his men along a riverbank—and shared a bit of gossip and commiseration with—showed up the next day at the business end of a bayonet charge.

The garrison in France had been no different, with domestic squabbles, short rations, and news of the occasional victory or defeat equally shared by all. Thus, it should not have bothered Michael to spend the night in the same bed with his wife, to hear her sighs and murmurs, and feel her stirring in the dark.

"You sleep like a recruit after his first forced

march," Michael said, untangling himself from the sheets. "Though you don't snore, and you smell a good deal better."

Like roses, and like home.

"This time of year, nights are short, days are long." Brenna sat on the bed with her back to him, wrapping herself into a wool dressing gown. She wouldn't even cross the room without donning as much armor as the situation might afford her.

"Why do you wear the hunting plaid?" The darker hues flattered her vivid coloring more than the red everyday plaid would, but it was still an odd choice.

"This pattern doesn't show the dirt as easily, and the colors suit me better." Still, she sat with her back to him, as if the knot of her sash required all of her attention.

"Brenna, I'm decently covered."

She peeked over her shoulder. "So you are."

And yet, she blushed to find him wearing pajama trousers, though they were held up by a properly knotted drawstring rather than a morning salute from his cock.

"Do you break your fast here, or go down to the kitchen?" He could not imagine her putting the staff to the effort of serving her a solitary breakfast in a dining parlor.

"I take a tray, something light, though I'll talk to Cook about preparing more substantial fare now that you're back. I'm sure the tray will be sitting outside the door, along with your boots."

Still, she did not move. She was, instead, watching him the way the French had watched Michael for months after he'd shown up at their gates, professing a mostly sincere disgust of all things English.

Michael fetched the tray—his boots could wait—
and brought it to the bed, setting it down beside
Brenna, and taking a place at the foot of the bed.
Butter, honey, a basket of scones wrapped in snowy
linen, and a pot of tea were arranged just so.

"The staff knows how to welcome the laird home."

Her chin came up. "The staff takes its direction
from the lady."

Michael buttered a flaky, warm scone, set it on a
plate, and passed it to her.

"I was once assigned the job of keeping track of an
enemy patrol in the mountains." An English patrol,
which detail he did not share. "Those fellows were
part mountain goat. They went up this track and
down that defile, and I was supposed to follow without letting on I was in the area."

Brenna paused with the scone two inches from her
mouth. "Because they would have captured you?"

They would have shoved him off the bloody
mountainside and told him to give their regards to
Old Scratch.

"Something like that." He possessed himself of her
hand, helped himself to a bite of her scone, and resumed
his tale rather than laugh at the consternation on her face.

"I eventually figured out that the way to execute
my assignment was to get above them. You shouldn't
waste good food, Brenna."

He saw the temptation to smile flirt with the corners of her mouth, and saw her battle it aside as she
took a bite of scone.

"So when darkness fell, I began to climb. Gets cold
in the mountains at night. Colder."

Brenna paused in her chewing. "Would you like some tea?"

"Please. So there I was, clinging to the side of some damned French mountain, or possibly Spanish—there being little distinction when a fellow's teeth are chattering and he has to piss—darkness falling, and me waiting for the moon to rise. Then the clouds came in. Sound can travel in odd ways in terrain like that, so I could hear the patrol below me, hear them laughing about the idiot thundering along behind them, smell the meat cooking over their campfire."

Brenna stirred cream and honey into his tea and passed him the mug.

"It was a long night?"

"It was an interminable night, and that was before it began to sleet."

He took a sip of pure heaven, the kind of heaven that had both tormented and comforted his memory on that mountainside.

"Is that how you feel now, Michael? As if you're clinging to a mountainside in hostile territory, bitter weather coming in, night coming on, and the enemy laughing at you from behind their loaded guns?"

He passed her the mug of tea and took the last bite of her scone.

"I meant no disrespect to you when I complimented the kitchen staff, Brenna."

She did not give his mug back, but cradled it in her hands.

"I anticipate criticism. It's freely handed about here, for decisions made, not made, made too late, made too soon. I did not know what you'd want for breakfast, where you'd want breakfast, and a wife should know these things. I forgot to ask, and then you were asleep."

Cold, dark mountainsides were apparently in ample supply in the Scottish Highlands, and Michael dared not belittle her concerns. An angry cook or a vindictive laundress could cause much suffering among the objects of her ire, regardless of pesky male nonsense like a war to be waged.

"For breakfast, I would like my wife's company. I care little about what's served, provided she shares it with me, but hot tea and fresh scones will never go amiss with me."

Brenna took a sip from the mug and held it out to him, then busied herself slicing, buttering, and drizzling honey on a second scone. She put half on her plate, half on his, and passed it to him.

The day gained a measure of hope.

Michael had found a ledge on their marital mountainside. A small, narrow ledge, but one they could share.

❧

Brenna fetched her husband's boots rather than linger over the last cup of morning tea in hopes he'd tell her another story.

"You have your da's way with a tale," she said, passing him the mug of tea and taking the tray to the corridor. "I could listen to that man spin a yarn time after time, the same story, the same ending, and yet, I hung on his every word. Winters grew longer when he passed away."

Michael unrolled his shaving kit on the windowsill

and set up his folding mirror. "Angus has some of the same ability, particularly when the whisky's on hand."

Yes, he did. The same rumbling burr that drew the listener in, despite all sense to the contrary.

Brenna poured warmed water into a green porcelain basin and set it on the windowsill. "Do you shave every morning?"

"Mostly. Beards itch." And yet, he'd threatened to grow one—for her?

"I thought they were warm."

"A decent wool scarf is warmer. Will you weave one for me, Brenna, my love?"

He was flirting. She would get used to it, though flirting back was probably a hopeless cause. "Mind you don't cut yourself."

Now what was she to do? Get dressed with her husband in the same room? *He* had no difficulty strutting around in nothing but his cotton underlinen.

"Will you wear the Brodie plaid today?" he asked as he dabbed lather onto his throat and cheeks. "I'll kit myself out in the laird's regalia, unless you think that's overdoing the clan pride."

"It is not possible for a mortal Scotsman to overdo clan pride," Brenna said as he drew the razor along his jaw in a movement that ought not to have fascinated her. "I'll wear the plaid, and so will everybody else who owns a scrap of the tartan. At least it isn't raining."

"Or sleeting."

To see a man shave was intimate. To see him moving around in only one old, worn, comfortable item of apparel, and to start the day with him held the same odd closeness.

"You don't snore either, Husband."

He smiled at her in the little mirror and went on scraping lather and whiskers off his face.

While Brenna blethered on. "You don't kick, you don't move about much, you don't talk in your sleep. You do, however, give off a lot of heat."

"Which ought to recommend me to your continued keeping September through June. Should you be getting dressed, my lady?"

She was a baroness. Did other baronesses watch their husbands make odd faces at a shaving mirror each morning?

"Soon. I dress quickly."

But she ought to be doing something, so Brenna sat on the foot of the bed, pulled the ribbon off the end of her braid, and unraveled the single plait she usually slept in. She didn't bother retrieving the brush from the vanity, because the vanity sat near the window.

Michael set the razor aside, wiped off his face, and began reassembling his kit. "You've pretty hair, Brenna Brodie. You always did."

She had red hair, and lots of it. "You missed a spot."

He looked disgruntled, as if she'd said the wrong thing, but he'd look mighty silly Trooping the Colour with that bit of lather on his chin. Brenna rose from the bed, took the towel off her husband's shoulder, and dabbed at the spot near where the dimple in his chin appeared when he smiled.

"There. Your fizzog at least is presentable."

Michael Brodie was what the old women would call a braw fellow, tall and muscular, but lithe. Dancing in his kilt over crossed swords, he'd be—

"I'm tempted to kiss my wife." His voice had gone thoughtful, and Brenna couldn't mistake the heat in his eyes. Nor could she quite understand it.

"Because I've wiped soap off your chin?"

His smile was unnerving, all male, all happy to *be* male.

"Because you bear the scent of flowers, because your unbound hair makes my hands itch, and because it's early morning on a beautiful day. I don't have to kill anybody today, and I don't have to prevent anybody from being killed."

Such was a soldier's definition of a beautiful day.

Brenna closed her eyes rather than look upon his smile. "Kiss me then."

A wife expected to endure her husband's kisses—at least—and he couldn't tarry at it too long, because he was soon to be out in the bailey, greeting his staff.

"Such bravery," Michael said, and Brenna heard a smile in his voice. His arms came around her, slowly, not a pillaging embrace but more of a stealthy reconnaissance. She did not—could not—relax.

"You might offer your husband a hug of a morning."

He was still smiling, but a feeling other than patient resignation stole up from nowhere and wrapped Brenna more tightly than her husband's arms. She had seen plenty of flirtation and carrying on in the great hall and in the tavern in the village. When Lachlan's mother had been alive, she'd been in her husband's arms frequently, holding his hand, touching his hair or his sleeve. Even Davey MacCray's wife sat in his lap, kissed his cheek, and carried on with him when he wasn't too drunk.

While Brenna understood none of it.

"You put your arms around me," Michael

whispered. "You lean on me, and you know I rejoice to take your weight against me, because the feel of you in my arms alone gives me pleasure."

He was instructing her in the basics of marital affection, and Brenna was grateful for his guidance. Pathetically grateful. She looped her arms around his trim waist and swallowed past a lump in her throat.

"Lean, Brenna Maureen. Lean on your husband."

His arms were around her loosely. She could whirl away and grab her hairbrush; she could scold him for keeping her from her appointed tasks. He wanted more from her than a simple hug. He wanted trust, courage, good faith, and hope.

Michael's hand stroked over Brenna's unbound hair, a patient, soothing caress that landed like the blow of a claymore on her heart.

"Michael, I don't know—"

His hand caressed her again, smoothing down her hair, gently, slowly. Then again.

She leaned.

❧

Something was amiss with the Baroness Strathdee.

Michael had come to this conclusion as he, Angus, and the baroness had worked their way down the line of maids, footmen, laundresses, gardeners, and other retainers standing at attention in the morning sunshine.

Brenna knew each of the thirty-some souls by name, but had limited her participation in the ritual to the occasional terse comment.

"Jeannie Fraser, make your curtsy. Thomas Brodie,

son of Ella and Daniel Brodie, make your bow to your laird."

And when the inspection was complete, Brenna had excused herself with unceremonious speed.

"I am puzzled by something," Michael said as Angus ambled with him toward the stables a short while later.

"Life is a puzzling proposition most of the time. Whisky helps. Ale is seldom a bad idea. A good night's rest can have a fine effect on a man's outlook."

He peered over at Michael, as if inspecting him for evidence of that last.

"Why do we have so many working at the castle, if Brenna lives there alone?"

"It's a big place, the castle, and your mother was the one who trained Brenna how to run it. The ladies have their standards, and a prudent man doesn't interfere if he can help it."

"I'm not a prudent man, I'm the laird. You tell me we're barely scraping by, and my wife has nigh three dozen people to do her bidding." And yet, Michael would not on his least charitable day have accused Brenna of idleness.

Neither, apparently, would Angus.

"You ride a fine beast," Angus remarked as they walked into the long stone barn. "Is he English?"

"German," Michael said, pausing outside Devil's stall. "Found him at Tattersall's, though he was said to be too crazy to ride."

"He doesn't look crazy, but then, the worst of 'em seldom do. Like old Davey MacCray. Sweet as the day is long until he gets to brooding."

"I'll take Boru out," Michael said to a groom. "It's Patrick, isn't it?"

"Pat will do, Laird."

The boy had the lanky grace of the born horseman, and the red hair common to plenty of Brodies. He soon brought out a rangy gray wearing Michael's saddle, and a glossy black gelding as well.

"Who's this?" Michael asked, letting the black sniff his glove.

"Campbell," Angus said. "So when I put the crop and spurs to him, I'm striking a blow for the clans."

Boru was not as elegant as Campbell, but several inches taller, and more heavily boned. "This was my father's favorite mount?"

"Aye." Angus swung up. "Bastard will jump anything he's faced with, including things he shouldn't. Where are we off to?"

"Let's ride the banks of the Dee."

"You don't want to start on your tenant calls? They'll be expecting you."

Michael climbed aboard the gray and gathered up his reins. He should call on his tenants, all three dozen of them. He really should.

"Give the women a day to sweep their hearths and bathe the children. After nearly ten years, another day won't matter much."

Angus looked like he wanted to argue, but instead delivered a stout whack to Campbell's quarters and cantered out of the stable yard.

When Michael returned two hours later, he'd satisfied himself that Brenna was riding a safe, sane, and even trustworthy mount, and he'd satisfied himself as well that the River Dee still sounded beautiful on a summer morning, and still reflected sunlight more brightly than any jewel.

"How many tenants did my father have?" Michael asked as he and Angus handed their horses off to young Patrick.

"Too many," Angus said, slapping his crop against his boot. "When snow is a possibility any month of the year, the land isn't intended to support huge tribes of people. The English have grasped this concept more clearly than we do ourselves. The hardier breeds of sheep are the answer, though some still debate it."

Memories abruptly punctuated the soft morning air, of Michael's father roaring at Angus on this same topic.

"We seem to have plenty of sheep."

If the sheep, one of God's least intelligent creatures, could eke out a living in the Highlands, then a stout Scotsman with his wife and family would be even better suited to the challenge—or so the old laird had bellowed.

"We could have more," Angus said as they crossed the bailey. "But that discussion can keep for another day. I delighted to see you in proper attire this morning, lad. The neighbors would probably find it a fine sight too."

Two years in London refined certain instincts that all the battlefields in the world could not.

"Are you suggesting we hold a ceilidh in honor of my arrival?"

Angus turned a guileless smile on his nephew. "A party, ye say? A celebration? With fine food and drink, and dancing into the night? Everybody sporting about in their plaids? The children hiding under the tables, and the pipers drinking like lords? Now why would I go and suggest such a lot of bother as that?"

He tromped off, swinging his crop as if he were conducting an orchestra, whistling some tune designed to get a man's toes tapping.

Even the army had understood the need for an occasional celebration, though Michael wasn't sure what Brenna would make of the notion. He found her in the solar, a room his mother had tacitly declared the province of the ladies.

"Greetings, Wife. What mischief are you up to on this bonny day?"

"Ledgers," she said, not rising. She'd changed out of her finery and was once again in a high-waisted smock, the hunting-plaid shawl around her shoulders. "Have you any idea when the rest of your baggage will arrive?"

"Any day." Michael advanced into the room, which he'd neglected on his ramblings yesterday. In an otherwise dark, solid edifice, this room was light and airy, its ceiling a good ten feet, its windows plentiful.

The air bore the scent of lavender and roses, and the walls held framed memories. "We were handsome children."

He studied a painting done of him with Brenna and two of his sisters, Bridget and wee Erin. "I'd forgotten how hard it was to sit still for this. You girls made it look easy."

Brenna set aside her quill pen.

"I loved to hear your mother reading. She could have read sermons to us instead of those old fairy tales, and I would have held still by the hour. Your da once told me he'd fallen in love with her brogue."

Because Brenna sat at an escritoire, Michael could not appropriate a place beside her, so he peered over her shoulder.

"You've a tidy hand. What are all these figures?"

"Expenses."

Something in her manner suggested the topic was sensitive, and yet, a man needed to understand the finances of his own household.

"Can you explain them to me?"

"Of course."

"I meant now. We could take this ledger and a picnic, find a shady spot by the river, and catch a nap." The plan struck him as a brilliant combination of work, play—and wooing.

"Or you could pull up a chair. When I'm done with the ledgers, Cook wants menus from me, because plain fare will not do now that *his lordship* is home. I'd like to take your measurements too, and cut out some kilts for you, though the ladies from the village are happy to help stitch them up. I should also write to your sister Bridget and let her know that you've arrived safely, because I doubt you'll think to do it, and somebody needs to take a basket to Goodie MacCray, because this time, I don't think old Davey's bellyache is a simple matter of too much drink."

She might as well have laid into him with Angus's riding crop, so acutely did guilt assail him—also resentment.

"You have to do all that today?"

"I was planning on doing it before luncheon."

"Show me," he said, taking her wrist in one hand and her infernal ledger in the other. "Show me your ledgers, and then I'll take old Davey his basket while you do your menus, but I swear to you, Brenna Brodie, if you expect me to eat haggis, I'll trot right back to London."

His offer of help did not appear to please her. "I don't know what you like to eat. I was hoping Cook might recall."

"I will eat anything, up to and including boiled shoe leather, but not the damned haggis, neeps, and tatties. I suppose haggis is your favorite dish?"

"I'll eat it. You really don't like potatoes? Even with salt and butter?"

"I have no grudge against them, and I will eat turnips, but I got sick once, eating haggis as a boy, and cannot abide—are you laughing at me?"

"Some Scot you are. Next you'll be sticking out your pinkie finger and wearing satin breeches."

She was smiling, though she tried to bury her smile in the ledger in her lap. Because he treasured her smiles, Michael dredged up more complaints.

"I've worn satin breeches, I'll have you know. A fellow hardly dares show up at Carlton House in anything less. My shoe buckles would have blinded you, and my stockings were of clocked silk."

"You poor dear. If you're done whining, I can explain my figures to you."

She nattered on about dry goods, larders, cellars, and such other topics as would make a quartermaster's head spin, and yet Michael did manage—over the teasing of her rosy scent and the pleasure of admiring her cleavage—to pick up on a few details.

Such as the fact that nobody worked at the castle full time, but rather, a position was usually shared by at least two people, the better to spread the coin.

Angus had failed to elucidate this scheme, suggesting he did not himself grasp it. "You set back something each month for every employee?"

"I do. In coin."

"Does Angus know of this?"

She closed the ledger and cradled it against her chest.

"I don't ask Angus about the crops and livestock, he doesn't ask me about the household accounts. He is not the laird here, but I am the lady."

And wasn't that a fine way to run an estate, with the left and right hand in ignorance of each other?

Though she had a point.

"Angus believes we're teetering on the edge of ruin. He won't come right out and blame it on my absence, but I gather certain decisions should have been made in the last five years by the laird, and I was...away, so they didn't get made."

Brenna set the ledger aside and folded her hands in her lap.

"What aren't you saying, Brenna?"

"Angus thinks Scotland should be overrun with sheep."

"Scotland *is* overrun with sheep, so is England, and I suspect Ireland and Wales aren't faring much better, but I'll tell you this: wool had much to do with why Wellington's armies were successful."

"You didn't fire wool bullets, Michael."

He got up to pace, abruptly impatient with her,

her ledgers, and the way she could keep some part of herself in silence even in the midst of a conversation.

"Wool is light in weight, it keeps a body warm even when it's wet. Even the finest wool is hardy as hell, and it doesn't stiffen up and hold the wet like leather. On the Peninsula, officers were quartered in the old convents and town halls, the churches and what have you, but the men bivouacked on any patch of dry ground they could find, often without even tents to protect them."

Brenna rose too, and Michael was reminded that his dear, sweet little wife had acquired height in his absence.

"Wool is a fine product," she said. "Every croft in the shire has a loom, and we weave and knit as much to sell as we do to wear, but Brodie land can support more than a bunch of bleating sheep. You've bottom land, pastures, decent fields marled for year upon year that can grow a good crop of oats. How many more of the clan do you want to see replaced by sheep?"

In one corner of his mind, Michael marveled that he was arguing with his wife, and delighted that she trusted him enough to disagree with him. Another part of him admired the way her bosom heaved when she was in a taking and had forgotten to wrap herself in her damned shawl.

"I don't want to see any of the clan replaced by sheep. How many tenants did my father have?"

"Forty-six families when he died, and that was down from fifty-eight when he married your mother."

Why hadn't Angus given him those numbers?

"You haven't told me why you're withholding wages from the people who work here at the castle."

She turned away from him, picked up her ledger, and set it atop a stack on the escritoire.

"I save a bit back for each one, so when the damned sheep have eaten every last holding and garden on Brodie land down to the roots, my people will have a little something to build a future on."

He had more questions for her, questions he would not ask—yet. Why so few MacLogans among the employed? How did she choose to whom to give employment when so many needed it? Why did she call them *her* people and not *our* people, while the bottom land was *his* not *ours*?

"Can we afford to throw a party?" The inquiry was genuine, in light of their discussion.

"Of course. A celebration will be expected now that you're home. Choose a date, and I'll confer with the staff."

Her tone was mild, as if they hadn't been nearly shouting at each other two minutes earlier, and yet, Michael had the sense he'd disappointed his wife—again, some more.

"A week from Friday. That will allow everybody to sleep off their drunk before services on Sunday."

Brenna resumed her place at her escritoire, opened the ledger, and dipped her pen in the glass inkwell.

"Next Friday, then. Cook will have Davey's basket ready by now."

She was dismissing him, as effectively as if Wellington himself had muttered, "That will be all, Colonel Brodie."

Wellington was hundreds of miles to the south, God be praised, so Michael stayed in the doorway, studying his wife. She was pretty, tidily swathed in her hunting tartan, and angry as hell. He was not sure how he knew this, but he would have bet his horse it was so.

He would not ask her what he'd done wrong, lest he fall prey to that female conundrum that started with: "If you have to ask…"

When he repaired to the laird's bedchamber to take off his riding boots, he saw Brenna's riding habit hanging on the door of the wardrobe, and insight struck, rather like a serving of a bad haggis.

He'd not only gone riding without his wife, contrary to a previous invitation, but he'd borrowed her mount without even asking her permission first.

Four

"HE SAYS HE'LL EAT BOILED SHOE LEATHER," BRENNA reported to Cook. "I am not sure he was jesting."

"Army rations," Cook snorted. "As like to kill a man as the enemy's fire. He'll probably like a beefsteak now and again, if he's been among the English. Some eggs and bacon to go with his bannocks and scones in the morning."

Beef was an extravagance, though not quite a luxury. "We can slaughter a cow next week," Brenna said. "For there's to be a celebration Friday next, and roasts will be expected. Send the fellows out after some game early in the week, and let Auld Henry know we'll tap a barrel of the aged whisky."

But what to serve Michael for his meals?

"Have ye a headache coming on, Miss Brenna?"

Cook was an ageless fixture at the castle, a force to be reckoned with, whose scones and pastries were as a light and insubstantial as she was solid and phlegmatic. If she had a name other than Cook, Brenna had never heard it, nor had she once heard the woman raise her voice.

"Not a headache." A husband. The human equivalent of a skittle ball knocking the pins of Brenna's routines in all directions. "I didn't eat enough at breakfast."

Or at dinner the previous evening.

Cook shoved away from the kitchen worktable and fetched a tray bearing a rolled sweet bread of some sort and a dish of butter.

"Can't have it bruited about that I let our Brenna get peckish," Cook said, heaving herself onto the bench across from Brenna. "Master Michael was never a difficult lad. I'd go on as you did before, and let him accommodate himself to life here as best he can."

Brenna accepted a slice of bread with raisins, nuts, and spices spiraling out from its center. "You mean with the menus?"

Cook scooped out a bit of butter and passed it on the knife to Brenna.

"I mean with everything. Angus will keep him busy calling on the tenants for the next few weeks, and the old laird never bothered much with how the household went on. We kept him fed and his sheets clean, and that's all most men fret over. That and having a decent fire somewhere in the house come winter."

She helped herself to a slice of bread, her big hands curiously dainty as she dabbed butter on the bread.

"This is good," Brenna said. "I like the walnuts, but the cinnamon comes dear."

Cook took a contemplative nibble. "You were naught but a girl when her ladyship turned this castle over to you, Miss Brenna. Woe unto your husband if he criticizes a good effort made on his behalf in his absence. I daresay you've done better with the castle than that old man has done with the land."

Her ladyship would be Michael's mother, who as the daughter of an earl had been born a lady, and whose title was preserved by the household as a courtesy and a point of pride long after the lady had left the earthly realm.

"I don't interfere with Angus, and he doesn't interfere with me." Which arrangement had worked adequately for years, but Michael's return would upset that balance as well.

"You mustn't fret," Cook said, patting Brenna's hand. "Master Michael's a canny lad, and he knows times have been hard. You ask me, he picked a poor time to go a-soldiering. Not enough the damned English must run off every crofter in the Highlands, but they must send our boys away to make war in the King's name too."

"You can't blame the English for a crofter deciding life in the New World holds more promise than an endless succession of Highland winters." The Corsican was also not England's fault—or Michael's fault.

Cook took another bite of her bread, and in the very way she chewed, conveyed a respectful difference of opinion with her employer.

"I'll keep to the menus we agreed upon, and Master Michael can let us know how good Scottish fare suits him. Boy never did fancy haggis though."

"No haggis, please. He specifically asked we spare him the haggis."

"Yes, he did," a masculine voice called from the direction of the pantries. Michael emerged from the corridor, his kilt swinging about his knees. "When Cook makes so many other wonderful dishes, a man need not aggravate his belly with haggis."

He plucked a bite of bread off the tray.

"This looks good. Mrs. MacCray sends her thanks for the basket and says Davey's on the mend. Davey says he's sure to be dead by Sunday if somebody doesn't get him some decent whisky." Michael took the place beside Brenna, which trapped her against the wall. "What mischief are you two getting up to?"

"No mischief a'tall," Cook said. "I'll just be fetching that hamper."

She bustled away, moving with surprising speed for such a large—and generally dauntless—woman.

"I believe I'll finish this loaf," Michael said, buttering himself another slice. "Spoils of war, and all that. Would you like some?"

"No, thank you. What hamper is Cook talking about?"

He dipped his damned bread in Brenna's tea.

"We're picnicking, you and I. Rambling down to the riverbank, spreading a blanket, and wasting some time. I've missed the sound of the river when the water's low."

Brenna moved her mug closer to him, for she was certainly no longer inclined to drink out of it herself. She'd promised herself not to berate him, and had managed well enough earlier, but that was before he'd pilfered her tea and threatened her afternoon. "Did you enjoy riding my horse?"

He paused with a bite of bread poised over her tea. "I'm apologizing. That's why we're having a picnic, because you're entitled to be put out with me for taking your horse without asking."

"You are pleased, I take it, to be able to put matters right with a bit of 'wasted' time?"

The canny lad had become a canny man, just not canny enough. He set the rest of his bread down.

"I would like to relax and be private with my wife, to enjoy a pretty day and a pretty patch of ground while we share a meal. I am sorry I didn't ask before I rode your horse, but I wanted to assure myself he was a safe mount."

They were sitting side by side on the same hard bench, and yet Brenna felt as if she and her husband could not possibly be the same species.

"The time to have investigated the beast's sanity was five years ago, Michael, when your da came to grief. I would not have taken Boru as my mount were he not steady and sound."

Frustration seemed to fill the kitchen, even as Cook disappeared into the butler's pantry, humming a tune in a minor key.

"Did you forget we were to ride out, Michael?"

Following on her question, an astonishing thought tried to elbow its way past her indignation: Was he as *ashamed* of having forgotten they were to ride as Brenna was ashamed on those rare occasions when she failed to execute a task entrusted to her?

"I didn't recognize most of the staff this morning, and that unsettled me." He picked a walnut out of the bread and put it on the plate. "Where did they all go?" he asked softly.

The question was rhetorical, and yet the bewilderment was genuine and not that different from what Brenna felt when she considered she did not even know what to feed her husband.

"We'll picnic," Brenna said, "though as apologies go, a simple 'I'm sorry' will win you more forgiveness than will wreaking havoc with my schedule."

She maneuvered herself off the bench, leaving her husband among his spoils of war.

"If we're to share a picnic, where are you off to?"

"I'm fetching my shawl. The sun's out now, but we're in the Highlands, and you know the fair weather cannot last."

❧

Michael put aside the sweet bread he'd been eating and resisted the urge to follow his wife so they could finish whatever argument they'd just *not* had.

"You never did care for cinnamon," Cook observed, removing the tray.

"The Spanish put it in everything—their meat dishes, their desserts, their coffee and chocolate. Perhaps I've developed a taste for it."

"Don't be barkin' at me because your missus is out of charity with you. She treasures that horse." Cook didn't retreat to her pantries or larders after firing that shot, but lingered, wiping at a spotless table with a spotless rag.

"You're a female," Michael observed. "Translate that last exchange between me and my wife."

Cook had sneaked him biscuits when he'd still been in dresses, and she'd explained to him certain curious aspects of female biology that neither of his parents had seen fit to enlighten him about. If he had an ally at the castle, it might be she.

Heaving a sigh such as would prove her gender

if nothing else did, Cook lowered her bulk to the opposite bench.

"You've been gone a long time, Michael Brodie."

He'd been gone so long that even Cook showed the passing of the years. Her hair had been red, and now was faded to the sandy blond that befell a redhead in later years. Her face was lined, and she sat carefully, as if hips and knees protested silently against too many Highland winters.

On the strength of his childhood memories of her kitchen, Michael felt entitled to some honest grousing.

"A fellow doesn't end up with a barony hanging around his neck because he's dug a few ditches and marched about whistling some military airs. I wasn't exactly having tea with the regiment for ten years."

"Neither was she."

When Michael wanted to upend the table and bellow that planning menus and stitching samplers were not the same as surviving for years behind French lines, something in Cook's eyes stopped him.

"Tell me." Because his wife might never make the attempt.

"Directly after you left, your mother took your wee sisters to Ireland."

"Because my grandda, the earl, had more conse-quence than my father. I understand that."

"You don't understand as much as you think you do, laddie. Because Brenna was your lawfully wedded wife, it fell to her to manage the household. Nobody else could put up with your da's rages and sulks."

The warning—about Brodie males and their tempers—was neither subtle nor appreciated.

"As my wife, Brenna should have expected to take on that role."

"Ye daft mon, she was sixteen years old when you left."

And…chubby. Also quiet. "I assume Mother provided some instruction?"

"Yer darling mother visited in the summers, though whether it was out of regard for your father, for the appearances, or for Brenna, I do not know. She was a good woman, was Lady Catherine."

A good woman who'd essentially deserted her husband and taken her daughters with her.

"You're saying Brenna faced a challenge."

"You never were stupid, Michael Brodie. Brenna faced a war. Your parents were too absorbed with their own dramatics, and everybody from Goodie MacCray to Angus Brodie assumed you'd left to get away from your bride."

This was, unfortunately, not far from the truth, though Michael hadn't expected his departure to be blamed on Brenna.

"People must gossip about something, and many young fellows join their regiments before the appointed day."

"One and twenty is young, is it?"

So what does that make sixteen?

"I was due to report in a matter of weeks. Brenna knew that when we married. The whole shire knew it."

If he'd been a little boy, Cook's sad, patient expression would have had him searching his conscience for sins to confess, and his pockets for crumbs. When he remained silent, she shoved to her feet.

"You'd best be off on that picnic, hadn't you?"

Michael rose as well and snatched a wicker hamper from the counter. "Yes, I had best be off, while the beautiful weather lasts."

∽✖∾

The meal would have been ambrosial to a soldier on the march—some sort of fowl, more of the cheese Brenna was so proud of, rye bread, and ale—but Michael could not appreciate it.

"The food doesn't agree with you?" Brenna's question was gratingly casual.

The company did not agree with him, but he'd asked for this picnic, so he'd make use of it. "The food is fine. Would you like to walk for a bit?"

"Honestly? No. I'm of a mind to take your measurements."

"I'm not of a mind to have them taken." Though taking his measurements would mean Brenna had to touch him, or nearly touch him. She had consumed her food at the very edge of their shared blanket, and let the murmuring of the nearby River Dee serve as their conversation. Any passerby might have thought from their lack of talk that they'd been married for years.

Which they had, goddammit.

She hiked her knees and wrapped her arms around them, putting Michael in mind of a citadel raising its drawbridge and dropping its portcullis.

"What was it like, after I left?" He didn't want to know, but he suspected this was part of the general apology he owed her.

"So we're to talk?"

"Married couples often do." They often wrote letters

to each other when separated too. She spared him that observation.

"When you left..." She stared at the river, as if trying to recall the second line of an obscure ballad. "It was a relief, in a way."

"Like it was a relief to leave my home and family and everything I knew?"

Some fool who'd had too much ale in the village had said those words, some fool who could not abide the sadness he'd seen in Cook's old eyes, or the careful lack of emotion in Brenna's.

Her smile now was *kind*. Possibly forgiving, even.

"Your da explained it to me. He said young men are restless. They need to at least see the world even if they can't conquer it, and a wife is sure proof a fellow will never get his chance at that big, wide world."

"I wish somebody had explained it to me."

"I think you figured it out. What was it like, in Spain?"

She would be hurt if he brushed her question aside, and yet, he was reluctant to answer it.

"First came Portugal, then Spain, and then France. They were successive circles of hell on one level, and yet, the land was beautiful, and there's much about war that makes a man feel alive." For a while, and then it made him wish he were dead, and then it made him dead inside if not in the absolute sense. "Cook says you took over the running of the castle from the time I left."

She brushed her hand over the grass. "I needed something to do, and the castle needed running. Your father adjusted, eventually, to your mother's being gone for most of the year, but I don't think he ever got used to being without your sisters."

"Neither did I."

Brenna stroked her hand over the grass again, and because Michael did not want to behold her patient green eyes, he lay back on the tartan blanket and folded his hands behind his head.

"They were too little to be sent away, and Erin was not well."

He stared up at a brilliant blue sky full of puffy white clouds, not very different from the sky over Spain, Portugal, France, or Ireland, and yet, a feeling like homesickness swamped him.

Brenna stirred on the blanket several feet away.

"Erin rallied a bit, in Ireland. The softer weather probably gave her a few more good years. Your da wrote to them often."

While Michael had not written often at all.

"I didn't want them to go. A fellow expects to see his sisters married off, eventually, but they were children, and in a sense, I felt responsible for them. I feared I would never see Erin again, and I was right."

He closed his eyes, the sun being too bright, and the sound of the river too soothing.

"Was that part of what sent you off to the regimental offices with your funds in hand? Your mother and sisters were leaving, and your father wasn't stopping them?"

"Aye." Though nobody had said as much openly. In preparation for Michael's wedding to Brenna, all had been good cheer and bright—false—smiles.

He dozed off then, which was a mercy, because he'd failed utterly to interrogate his wife regarding the early years of their marriage. She hadn't been lying when she'd said his absence was a relief, but Michael had the sense she was presenting the only facet of the truth she could bear to look on herself.

When he opened his eyes again, it was to see that Lady I-Want-to-Take-Your-Measurements Strathdee had also surrendered to the arms of Morpheus. She was curled on her side, her tartan shawl wrapped around her, a four-leaf clover in her fingers.

They had passed a night in slumber, but that had been in pitch darkness. In the bright sunshine of a pretty summer day, Brenna asleep was an intriguing picture. She looked less severe, less busy, and less formidable—also tired.

What had sent her looking for lucky clovers?

Michael extricated her little treasure from her fingers and folded it in his handkerchief, then considered what a man was supposed to do, when he'd endured as much talking as he could possibly stomach in the course of one picnic and he found himself on a blanket with his pretty, sleepy wife.

Brenna had been dreading the business of measuring her husband for his new kilts, and so, of course, she dreamed of his knees, which somehow managed to be handsome, for all they were *knees*. She dreamed of the way sunlight caught the red in the hair on his arms, and of the way his back curved down from broad, muscular shoulders.

And between one thought and the next, her awareness became filled not with adult masculine muscle and contours, but with a particular combination of panic and nausea familiar to her from long acquaintance.

She tried to sit up and strike out in one motion, though something prevented her from rising. "Get off me! Get off me *now*!"

She flailed about wildly, and had just recalled that a stout kick in a certain location would win her free, when reason intruded.

"Brenna Maureen, cease!"

Michael had flattened her to the blanket with the simple expedients of his weight applied to her person and his hands manacled around her wrists. "You'll unman me, you daft woman."

"Get off me." She'd meant to crack the words over his idiot head, but they'd come out as a whisper.

"Nothing I'd like better." He rose up, first on his hands and knees, then to kneeling, his expression suggesting he feared for her sanity.

Brenna scrambled away to sit up and wipe the back of her wrist over her mouth. "What were you about? Did you try to kiss me?"

"Yes. Yes, I did try. On the cheek. You looked so pretty, and there's nobody about, and a man should kiss his wife every now and again, because she sure as hell isn't showing any signs of kissing him."

For all his faults, and for all the errors and omissions he had committed, Michael wasn't wrong about this. He was also sporting a red patch along one side of his jaw.

"I'm sorry if I struck you. I don't like kissing." While she positively loathed the seething dread suffusing her every limb and organ.

And yet, if she'd asked her husband to rejoin his regiment, he could not have looked more confused. "I kissed you last night."

"On the—" Brenna touched her finger between her brows. "Here, and I was awake."

Michael settled beside her on the blanket, sitting tailor fashion, his bare knees much in evidence. "You don't like kissing, or you don't like my kisses?"

"Kissing isn't sanitary."

"For God's—" He peered over at her, likely to see if she'd spoken in jest. "You're serious." Another look, full of consternation. "Kissing is *just kissing*, Brenna. It's harmless. It's sweet and tender and arousing and—"

If he kept up with that litany, Brenna would soon cry, but he fell mercifully silent.

The river babbled by, and a breeze riffled the grass. The scent of horses in the next field graced the air, and Brenna's shawl—woven with a goodly complement of lamb's wool—was soft beneath her fingers. She concentrated on those simple realities while her breathing gradually slowed and despair edged out panic.

"So no kissing you awake of a morning," Michael said. "In case you're interested, I would not object if you sought to take a comparable liberty with my person."

As if she could. "I'll remember that."

They gathered up the remains of the picnic, Brenna carrying the blanket and Michael the hamper. In a fit of contrariness Brenna could not explain to herself, she wished Michael might take her hand as they walked.

And when he didn't, she wished she might have the courage to take his.

❧

"You'll be pleased to know, Uncle, that a party is being planned."

Michael wasn't pleased. Roughly twenty-four hours ago, his very own wife had nearly kneed him in the ballocks, and not entirely by accident. The notion still upset him.

Angus pulled a pipe from between his teeth. "A gathering, ye say? Imagine that. Best start sobering old Davey up now. If he arrives drunk, then we'll no' be dancing after midnight. Man plays a mean fiddle, and he's the best piper in the shire, drunk or sober."

The first of the tenant calls lay ahead of them, and for Michael, another difficult night beside his difficult wife lay behind him.

"I'm sure Brenna will see to Davey's state of sobriety. Tell me about these cousins of hers."

Angus slipped his pipe into his pocket, a mannerism that had fascinated Michael as a small boy. He'd waited in vain for the day when his uncle's jacket caught fire.

"They're hard workers."

When a man could say nothing else complimentary about another fellow, he offered that very observation. Among the English, "he can hold his liquor" was a similar sort of damning with faint praise.

"What are their names?" Because this was another of the many topics Brenna had been unforthcoming about—or perhaps Michael hadn't had the fortitude to ask her directly.

"Three remain, two having gone for the fair woods of Pennsylvania. The oldest is Hugh, and the other two take their direction from him. The middle one's Neil, and the youngest is Dantry. Stubborn, the lot of them. Typical MacLogans. They think to raise cattle, and yer da gave them good bottom land to do it."

"Cattle? Up here?"

"Aye."

Many a female would have said Angus was in his prime, and yet he had the elderly ability to put contempt in a single syllable.

"There's demand for beef."

"Let the Lowlanders raise their beef. Cattle require fencing, and fodder in winter, and they take nigh a year to produce a single calf. Cattle produce no wool, and a good sheep hide will answer most any need for leather."

Michael turned the topic rather than listen to another panegyric to the ovine.

"Other than a profane interest in cattle, have you any complaints against the MacLogans, or will they have any against me?"

Campbell tried to snatch a mouthful of grass, for which Angus whacked him smartly on the shoulder with his crop, sending the animal dancing sideways.

"The MacLogans keep mostly to themselves," Angus said when he'd brought his horse under control. "Hugh lets Lachlan help out around the castle, because he knows Brenna will give the boy a few coins and will teach him to read, though you ask me, reading isn't always a good thing. Letters put ideas in a fellow's head, and there's no dealing with a female who reads anything other than her prayer book or her recipes."

Brenna read. Michael had found her with a book more often than not when she'd been a girl.

"Has Hugh MacLogan only the one child?"

"He also has a daughter."

Again, the way Angus said only a few words suggested having a daughter ranked along with raising cattle and allowing a son to learn to read, though clearly, the worst transgression was—as it had been for centuries in the Highlands—having the wrong last name.

"Hugh, Dantry, and Neil. The boy's name is Lachlan. They're interested in raising cattle, and they've good land to work with. What else?"

Angus drew up at the foot of a track that lead off to a pair of whitewashed stone crofts. "You forgot stubborn, contrary, and independent."

"Now that's odd," Michael said, nudging Devil down the track. "Those are the very same qualities that distinguished many a Highland soldier when the fighting was at its worst. We stormed walled cities, climbed mountains, marched on nonexistent rations, and beat the damned Corsican's men clear back to France—all on the strength of stubborn, contrary, and independent."

None of which, in Michael's mind, had to necessarily result in the sort of close-minded, judgmental pontificating Angus was in a mood to dole out. The idea that Brenna had endured years of Angus's tiresome sermonizing added another dreary dimension to an already dreary day.

"You'll see," Angus muttered. "Can't tell a MacLogan a damned thing. Never could. The lot of 'em are contrary and half-daft."

Because Michael knew little about raising cattle, he didn't try to tell his tenants anything. Hugh MacLogan had Brenna's red hair, her height, and the lanky build of many a crofter. Hard work and Highland weather had planed him down to muscle and bone. Being a MacLogan on a Brodie holding likely accounted for a lack of small talk and smiles.

"You don't interbreed the Highlands with the Angus?" Michael asked as he and Hugh walked along a stone wall between two pastures. Country-fashion, they traveled opposite sides of the wall, each man stopping occasionally to replace a tumbled stone from whence it had fallen.

"They have different purposes, the Angus and Highland," Hugh said. "Though the Angus are tough for all they gain weight more quickly than the Highlands." He slapped a sizable rock back onto the top of the wall as if it weighed nothing.

"MacLogan, is there a reason you keep glancing back at the crofts? Do you expect Angus will steal your chickens?"

Something crossed Hugh's craggy features, something between disgust and despair. "He's your uncle."

"Yes."

"Ask Brenna why I might want to keep an eye on Angus Brodie."

A girl child with hair as red as her father's came scampering out of the croft. At the sight of her, Hugh turned back, though he and Michael hadn't walked half the perimeter of the pasture.

"You've no wife," Michael said. "Who looks after your daughter?"

Hugh stopped and hefted another rock. "We do. She's sensible, is my Annie, and a good girl."

The good girl scampered directly to Angus's fancy black gelding, which brought Angus from his perch on a nearby stone wall, pipe in hand.

"Hugh, are we in a hurry?"

"Yes."

Another red-haired fellow had emerged from a cow byre halfway up the hill, and he, too, was apparently in a hurry to reach the crofts.

"One of your brothers?"

"Dantry. Boy has a temper and a mortal dislike for sheep."

And Angus was in a mood to sermonize. Michael nearly tripped over a loose stone at his feet, but didn't stop to stack it back where it belonged.

❦

"Tell me about your cousins."

Brenna fussed as she tied a ribbon around the bottom of her braid, because this was not a topic she could have anticipated. "What do you want to know?"

Michael turned down the covers on their bed, sat on the edge, dusted the soles of his bare feet together, and scooted back to arrange himself against the pillows. He was again wearing only his drawstring breeches, which Brenna took for a measure of husbandly consideration.

"Do the MacLogans typically raise cattle? I know little about cows, though I enjoy a good cut of beef."

He wanted to talk about cows, while Brenna wanted to talk about kissing.

Or the lack of it.

"My uncle Seamus MacLogan had a fold of handsome Highlands. Ferdie and Amos MacLogan emigrated to Pennsylvania, where the winters aren't so harsh. They think the Aberdeenshire blacks will do well there."

"Hugh plans to export cows?"

Brenna blew out her last candle and draped her night robe over the foot of the bed. "You must ask him about his precious cows when Angus isn't on hand to scowl and fume and pace about."

"I tried that. You're leaving the window open?"

"It's a soft night. I like the fresh air." Needed it, in fact. Brenna climbed onto her side of the bed. "Hugh is shrewd. If he thinks there's a market for cows, then you can bet he has a reason for it."

Angus had reasons for criticizing anything Hugh or his brothers put their hands to, and Brenna did not want to discuss those reasons any more than she wanted to discuss cows.

"When did your cousins come into Brodie tenancies?"

"The spring after our marriage, as a condition of the settlements." Brenna lay on her side, facing her husband, though she could not see him well.

He shifted about, making the bed heave and rock. "You read the settlements?"

"You didn't?" In the pained silence following her question, Brenna realized she had insulted him without meaning to. "I'm sorry. That came out wrong. I know you read the settlements, because you signed them, as did I. I've had occasion to refer to them from time to time, while you could not."

He was silent, and the darkness abruptly took on an oppressive quality. No breeze stirred in through the window; no moonlight illuminated the bedchamber.

"Brenna, if you had three wishes, would one of them be that you had never married me?" His tone was gentle, not accusing.

"Michael, you've not been home three days. What are you asking?"

His hand settled on her cheek, which caused her to flinch—but only flinch.

"You startle whenever I touch you. Even in sleep." His fingers traced her jaw, bringing her a whiff of vetiver and despair. He could not have asked her that fanciful, brave question about wishes in the broad light of day.

"You surprised me, Husband, yesterday by the river. I'm not keen on surprises." The way Michael had probably not been keen on French victories.

He withdrew his hand. "So if I tried to kiss you now, you might let me survive with my manhood intact?"

She could not guarantee that. "The conception of children doesn't require kissing."

"You've made a study of this?"

She had, in fact, to the extent that asking old women for specifics was a study, though worse than despair, she now heard mockery in Michael's tone.

"Maybe I could kiss you." Brenna's suggestion was unplanned and not at all likely to succeed. "You mustn't expect much. I haven't the experience you do."

Michael rolled across the mattress, so the warmth and bulk of him pressed against Brenna's side.

"The vast majority of my experience was gained before I married you, Baroness, and I would not object had you no experience at all. I am available to be kissed at your earliest convenience."

He was eager to mash his mouth against hers, eager to slobber all over her. "Maybe you should just swive me and have done with it."

"Brenna Maureen, you would sound more enthusiastic about selling Boru to the English. I'll kiss your cheek now, despite your woeful lack of interest."

He kissed her cheek so quickly, Brenna barely had time to tense up in preparation—and then he rolled away.

"Good night, Wife. I will dream of your kisses."

Brenna shifted to her side, so they were again back-to-back in the big bed. That kiss had been nothing. No slobbering, no enduring his tongue down her throat, no…nothing.

And he had warned her.

Brenna fell asleep wondering at Michael's question: If he had three wishes, would one of them be that he hadn't married her—or might he wish that his wife could someday kiss him with the enthusiasm any soldier home from the wars deserved from his lady?

Five

FROM THE WARMTH OF THE BIG BED, MICHAEL WATCHED as his wife began her day. Brenna was inherently considerate, making little noise as she brushed out her hair and laid out her clothes. She was also inherently decent, too decent to admit she regretted marrying him.

Because what, after all, could they do about it now?

He struggled up against the pillows. "I've been thinking." And thinking, and thinking.

Brenna's hands did not pause as she organized her hair into a thick braid.

"Good morning. What have you been thinking about?" She remained facing the mirror, which of course meant she could keep surveillance on Michael in the mirror's reflection.

"I never wooed you. We never wooed each other."

She whipped a green ribbon around the bottom of her braid, tied a knot, and yanked the ends tight.

"My da wanted a place to stash me. Your da needed a bit of coin. Wooing wasn't necessary. I was eight years old when the betrothal contract was signed, for pity's sake."

The way she batted the brush at the end of her braid suggested the topic—like many topics—annoyed her.

Michael rose, retrieved their tray from the corridor, and placed it on the hearth. While Brenna tidied up the bed, he poured a mug of tea, added cream and honey, and brought it to her.

"Wooing," he said, extending the mug to her. The cup was the same one she used every morning—blue with pink roses. He wanted to tell her to leave the damned bed for the maids, except Brenna was a woman who needed to move about.

And he'd yet to see a maid in this wing of the house.

"Explain yourself," Brenna said, accepting the cup but not taking a sip.

"We are stuck with each other, why not make the best of it?"

He caught bewilderment in her expression before she took to studying her tea. "Did you put honey in this?"

"I did."

She took a drink, then set the mug back on the tray and resumed making the bed. "We could get an annulment."

Must she sound so hopeful?

"Not likely. We've spent three nights in the same bed, we've had years and years to repudiate our vows, and I, at least, was an adult when we went through a ceremony the import of which I well understood. Under Scottish law, you were of age as well." Though under English law, she'd been too young by years. "Based on the betrothal contracts, the union also had your father's blessing while he was alive."

Brenna lifted her tartan shawl from the foot of the bed and wrapped it around her shoulders.

"I suppose an annulment would cost money." She sat on the bed, as if the weight of this realization took the wind from her domestic sails.

Michael had money. Ten years of officer's wages carefully invested, a knack for lucky wagers, and a parting gift from Sebastian St. Clair had left Michael quite comfortable. The Strathdee barony also came with an income, though now wasn't the time to share that news with his reluctant wife.

Wearing only his linen drawers, Michael took a place beside her on the bed they'd yet to put to its happiest use.

"I realized something when I was dreaming of your kisses."

"Bother your dreams," she muttered, though she also smiled, as if him dreaming of her kisses was not *entirely* a bother.

"I realized that I love you."

She was off the mattress and headed for the door before he could snatch her hand and bring it to his lips.

"Michael Brodie, that is not amusing, and if you think I'll fall for sweet words from a man who would rather make war than be married to me—"

An interesting and appallingly female way to view service to King and Country. "Listen to me, Brenna, before you go flouncing off in a cloud of righteous fury."

"I've never in my life *flounced*," she shot back, turning to face him.

She looked coldly affronted—she was good at

looking coldly affronted—and yet, Michael's every instinct told him she was hurt, perhaps even scared.

And had been for some time.

"I recall the day you came to live at Castle Brodie. You had no doll. I thought girls were born clutching dolls, because even the poorest crofter's daughters seemed to have something with yarn for hair that they called a doll. You had a storybook."

She settled on the hearth, looking brittle and cold in her nightgown and shawl. "When you're an only daughter with four older brothers and no memories of your mother, a good story can be a comfort."

Was that why she taught young Lachlan to read?

"I worked harder on my lessons after you came to live with us. I understood that you were to be my wife one day, and I could not have you more learned than I was. You were reading French by the time you were ten years old."

"French isn't difficult."

"Not for you perhaps." Michael rose, moved the tray, and took a place beside her. Under his linen-clad backside, the stones were hard and cold, but at least Brenna hadn't bounced to her feet. "For me, it was gibberish, but command of that gibberish saved my life on many occasions."

"Was that why you ended up in France? You spoke the language well?"

"Most of Wellington's officers were fluent in French, which was fortunate when French deserters came our way."

She hugged her knees. "Were you a deserter, then?"

"I was not, not to the people who counted, and

part of the reason I did not come home to you immediately is that I made enemies on both sides of the war. I did not want to risk them following me here."

Brenna turned her head, so her cheek rested on her knees.

"That's all you can say? For two years, the entire shire whispers about why Michael Brodie turned his back on his wife, his clan and his holdings, when he might have come home to a hero's welcome, and that's your explanation?"

He wanted to give her more, because the entire shire hadn't merely whispered. They'd muttered, speculated, gossiped, and insinuated too. In nine years—in nine hundred years—that aspect of human nature would not have changed.

He also wanted to kiss her. Huddled in her shawl, her toes tucked under her hems, Brenna looked young and unhappy.

"I made the acquaintance of torturers, Brenna. Men who excelled at inflicting suffering, men who could cherish a grudge like a Papist would cherish a piece of the true cross. The barony is at least in part an effort to provide me with safety by recognition."

She studied him, and he bore it, though her pensive expression made clear she was not thinking about kissing.

"Tell me about this love you think you have for me."

He silently thanked her for the change in topic, though in its way, love was no more easily discussed than torture.

"I knew from the day I first beheld you that we

were to be wed. Even a boy of thirteen understands what that involves."

"A girl of eight does not. I knew you had a nice smile, and when you teased me, it wasn't mean."

"You were mine to protect, not mine to annoy."

She jostled his shoulder. "Such a wee knight, you were."

Any affection from Brenna was precious, and Michael basked in her approval, even if it was for a boy long grown—a boy who'd had decent instincts and a loving heart.

"You liked me," he said. "You were quiet about it, but you liked me."

Elsewhere in the castle, people were stirring. A door banged, sheep bleated in the outer bailey, and somebody upended a bucket of water onto the stone steps below the bedroom window.

"You were partial to shortbread," Brenna said. "Scottish girls are born knowing how to mix up a batch of shortbread, whether they can lay claim to a doll or not."

"I'm still partial to shortbread, and I'm still partial to you."

The analogy was simple. Brenna appeared to consider it.

And then reject it. "You hardly know me. I hardly know you."

He slipped his hand into hers, lest she hare off to domesticate in some safe, distant corner of the castle.

"That's not true, Brenna Maureen MacLogan Brodie. I know you're fluent in French and you dance beautifully, and this is fortunate, because your singing voice is atrocious. You mutter in your sleep, cannot stand the sight of a weed in your flower beds, and think Sir Walter's novels are ridiculously sentimental."

"How can you know that?"

"Because for eight years, we lived under the same roof, day in day out. I watched you read, knit, and embroider your way through Highland winters. You watched me try to grow a beard when I was seventeen."

Her smile said she'd forgotten about that. "You'd grown so tall, but your voice still cracked when you were excited."

He wanted to kiss her while she was thinking of that gangly, awkward boy. "We are not strangers, and I do love you and have for years. I'm thinking I'll kiss you now."

She didn't pull away when he bussed her cheek, and he didn't press his attentions on her any further than that one chaste peck.

She did, however, clutch her infernal shawl more tightly.

"I suppose you think this settles matters between us, because you've rediscovered a boyhood affection for the woman you're now married to?"

So huffy—while she studied the toes peeking out from under her hem.

"A few shared memories settles nothing, because if our marriage is to amount to anything, you must rediscover an affection for me. That's where the wooing comes in."

"I'm to endure wooing now in addition to kisses?"

"You're a quick study, Brenna Maureen, and yes, you must resign yourself to being wooed. I've participated in many a siege, and I'm confident my skills are up to the challenge of wooing you. I still favor your shortbread above all others."

He winked at her, and one instant too late realized that likening his wife to a walled city in enemy territory was perhaps not the wisest analogy.

"You're confident," Brenna said, rising from their perch on the hearth. "Have your years on the Continent prepared you for the task before you? Will you bring a rifle to bed with us, Michael?"

He opened his mouth—then shut it. Wooing Brenna would involve something other than vulgar innuendo, though he wasn't sure exactly what.

"No, I will not bring my rifle to bed." He would stop wearing his underlinen to bed too. "I am puzzled about one thing, though."

Brenna paused before disappearing behind the privacy screen. Her braid trailed down her back, her feet were bare, and she looked reluctantly intrigued—also dear. "What could possibly baffle the Great Wooer of Castle Brodie?"

Michael stood and prowled toward her, abruptly needing for the discussion to be serious.

"A marriage is a committed union of two souls, Brenna Brodie, not the desperate attempts of one soul to attach the affections of the other. So I'm wondering: How will *you* woo *me?*"

‿✦‿

"Walk with me, Elspeth Fraser." From the way Elspeth stopped, then continued as if she hadn't heard him, Hugh MacLogan concluded that his invitation lacked a certain graciousness.

"You might as well," he said as she resumed striding along and he fell in step beside her. "A wee thing like you wouldn't be able to outrun a fellow like me." Unless, of course, the fellow was sporting a cockstand behind his sporran such as might trip him onto his ignorant, randy arse.

"I'm about to explain something to you, Hugh MacLogan, and you'd best pay attention, because what I have to say will stand you in good stead should you ever decide you want to woo another female."

"I'm listening." He could listen to her scolds all day and far into the night, though he'd rather listen to her sighs and bury his nose in the glory of her wheat-blond hair.

"When a man approaches a woman, and he wants to gain her notice, wishing her good day will generally get matters off to an encouraging start."

Matters had got off to an encouraging start the day he'd laid eyes on her, only to proceed exactly nowhere in the intervening two years.

"Good day, Elspeth Fraser."

She smacked his arm and muttered something that might have been, "Ye thrawn, glaikit mon."

Ann had called him the same thing more than once.

"I've a question for you, woman, if you're done handing out lessons in flirtation and violence."

As they approached the wooded hill upon which the castle sat, she walked faster. "Simple civilities are not flirtation. What did you want?"

He wanted to flirt with her but didn't know how. More than that, he wanted her to flirt with him.

"How is Brenna getting on with her long-lost husband?"

Elspeth stopped as they gained the shelter of the trees and turned blue, blue eyes on him. He loved her eyes, loved the way they conveyed her intelligence and humor, her heart—and her temper.

"Why is it any of your concern?"

"Brenna is my cousin, and I don't know this baron. He's been gone so long nobody really knows him, and we haven't an explanation for much of his absence."

"Why don't you ask Brenna?"

Off she marched through the trees, as if that question settled the business. He caught up with her in four strides, because her legs were that short.

Though they'd likely fit around his waist well enough.

"If I were to ask Brenna, I'd have to present myself at the castle, which would cause talk. Brenna would tell me all goes well with her husband, when the man hasn't the sense to call on his own tenants without Angus Brodie glowerin' at his side."

Elspeth's steps slowed. "I've seen them ride out together, Michael and Angus. Brenna has too."

He walked along beside her in silence while the birds sang and the breeze soughed through the pines. The morning was pretty, the girl was pretty, and the fellow…had never been pretty. Not in his looks, not in his manners, not in his speeches.

"I'm worried about Brenna," Hugh said, the same sort of thing he might have blurted out to his Ann, or whispered to her in the dark at the end of the day. "What sort of man leaves his wife to contend with things at home, when the war's long over and the Corsican growing fat and bald on some faraway island?"

Elspeth was worried too. Hugh caught that in the single fleeting glance she flicked in his direction.

"Michael's reasons are for Brenna to determine. They're married, and they've been sharing a bed since the day the laird returned."

Interesting, and exactly the sort of thing Hugh would not have known how to inquire about.

"And?"

Any man who'd been married to the mother of his two children knew sharing a bed might be a result of exhaustion and convenience, and did not necessarily guarantee the couple in the bed enjoyed wedded bliss.

Elspeth caught her toe on something, a root, a rock, and stumbled a bit, but Hugh was too preoccupied with the glints of red in her hair to grab for her elbow.

"And Brenna seems fine," Elspeth said, catching herself and marching on. "Her baron watches her when he thinks she's not looking, as if he could see the girl he married in the woman she's become."

Hugh scanned the path for more promising obstructions and saw none. "From what I could gather, the girl he married was no prize, through no fault of her own."

"I should hit you again," Elspeth said on a weary sigh, "but I don't want to bruise my knuckles."

They'd come to a clearing partway up the hill, one that sported a bench. The lady wasn't even breathing hard.

"Sit with me a moment."

She looked around the clearing, as if hoping for a wild boar or some other distraction to come along, not that boars had frequented the woods in centuries.

"You neglect your manners on purpose, don't you, Hugh MacLogan?"

If only that were the case. With others, he was polite enough, but with her...

She sat, and through some female trick, managed to do it truculently. "None of your dirty rhymes, Hugh MacLogan."

He took the place beside her, though a gentleman was supposed to ask.

"Dantry's our poet, unless you'd like a few verses of old Rabbie Burns." Who could, indeed, be naughty— brilliantly naughty. "Would Brenna tell you if her husband were making a nuisance of himself?"

"You mean if he's pestering her in bed, and because she's his wife, she has to allow it?"

Yes, he'd meant exactly that, among other things. "Aye. Brenna deserves more careful handling than that."

Her posture lost some of its starch, as if, all odds to the contrary, Hugh might have stumbled upon a sentiment with which Elspeth agreed.

"Are you in love with your cousin, Hugh? Because if you are, that's no help to her now. Brenna is loyal, and in some ways more proper than a duchess. If her husband exercises his privileges, then you've nothing to say to it—and neither does she."

As Hugh watched a shaft of sunlight burnish Elspeth's hair to the hues of a crackling fire, he realized several things: First, Elspeth was worried about Brenna too, and that was not good. Second, Elspeth completely mistook familial concern for something else. Third, nobody could see them as they enjoyed a moment of privacy in the woods.

"Elspeth Fraser, I have no amorous feelings toward my cousin and I never have. Brenna would gut me like a rabbit if I so much as winked at her wrong. You, however, are not my cousin, not married, and not armed with anything more than a sharp tongue."

Elspeth's brows had just drawn down in puzzlement when Hugh leaned over and kissed her on the mouth.

❧

"No woman ever knew less or cared less about wooing a man than I do," Brenna said, whipping around when she reached the end of the parapet. "I am married to a ridiculous man."

Elspeth saw in Brenna the same tension she often saw in her employer. Many people thought bitterness drove Brenna—and some would concede she had good reason to be annoyed—but Elspeth suspected Brenna was haunted by a vast bewilderment about human interactions generally, and her marriage in particular.

"You are married to a clever man," Elspeth said. Over at the loch, two red-haired kilted fellows were making their way down to a beach shielded on three sides by trees.

"I want none of this sentiment Michael seems hell-bent on introducing to our marriage. He's the laird. Why can't he harass the tenants, waste money in Aberdeen or Edinburgh, occupy himself with making and drinking whisky, and disappear to London for months at a time?"

The question was so plaintive, it distracted Elspeth from the men pulling their shirts over their heads a quarter mile to the east.

"You used to like your husband."

Like a bird in flight dropped by an arrow, Brenna plopped onto the stone ledge that lined the interior side of the crenellations.

"I may still like him, but I cannot understand this affection he claims to hold for me."

Dantry MacLogan was not as muscular as his older brothers, being the youngest, but Neil was a fine figure of a man. Not as fine as Hugh, though.

"You are not so hard to like, Brenna."

Brenna rose and came over to stand next to Elspeth. "Where's Hugh?"

Brenna did not see that the MacLogan brothers were shedding their clothing, only that they were missing a sibling.

"One of them always stays within shouting distance of Annie, or they take her with them if they have to leave the property."

"Smart of them." Brenna turned her back to the stone wall before any truly interesting male parts were in evidence. A silence spread, during which two kilts were draped upon the rocky beach and Elspeth watched naked men dive into a loch cold enough to wake the dead and kill the living.

"They could send Annie to you," Elspeth said. Because how was Elspeth to further her acquaintance with a man when he spent most of his time hovering around home and hearth?

"No, they could not. I had to argue for an entire summer to pry Lachlan loose from them, and then only on certain terms."

The silence took on a pained quality—a more pained quality. "Hugh has stopped bathing in the loch."

"How am I to woo my dratted husband?"

Elspeth hurt for her friend, even as she wanted to pitch her over the parapet. "You start by listening to him." As she had not listened to Hugh when he'd surprised her on the path. "You pay attention to him, and you're good at paying attention, Brenna."

Though a woman who could turn her back on the fine specimens on the beach without even a glance was not a woman with a natural advantage when it came to wooing a fellow.

"I can do that," Brenna said. "I can also bake short-bread. I don't recognize that coach."

Because Brenna was not preoccupied with the bathers, she'd seen what Elspeth had not noticed. A heavy traveling coach, luggage lashed to the roof and the boot, was heading for the castle along the road from the east.

"Michael's baggage?" Elspeth suggested.

"Maybe."

The coach clattered over the drawbridge spanning the dry moat. Footmen and grooms came out to meet it, as did Michael and Angus.

"Is *he* spending more time at the castle?" Elspeth asked.

The breeze dislodged a strand of Brenna's hair and whipped it against her mouth. "Yes. With Michael."

The coach came to a halt, the sweat on the horses and dust on the carriage testifying to a long journey.

"Tell Angus he's not welcome."

"Angus is Michael's family. I cannot tell my husband to refuse his uncle the castle. Michael would think me ridiculous."

"You tell Angus. Tell him his every wicked deed

will be laid at Michael's feet if he doesn't keep himself away from you and your husband."

An older woman, plump and plain, climbed out of the coach. Michael hugged her, then Angus bowed over her hand.

"You told me, Elspeth, to listen to my husband, and I will certainly make the attempt, but what's to say he would ever listen to me? He loves Angus, he trusts Angus, and Angus is making himself appear indispensable."

Elspeth did not point out that all of those factors had applied between Angus and Michael's father, too.

"You have company, Lady Strathdee. Best go welcome them."

Brenna left, and when Elspeth resumed spying on the beach, the bathers were nowhere to be seen.

❧

"I'm not coming out."

An odd feeling skittered down Michael's spine as he beheld his sisters' old nurse standing in his very own bailey. "That is a child's voice."

A tired, unhappy child's voice.

"So it is," Prebish said, still beaming at him as if he were her long-lost son—which, in a sense, he was, or as good as. "Miss Maeve, come ye out and make a proper curtsy to your brother."

The odd feeling curled more tightly around Michael's vitals, despite the pleasant lilt of Prebish's County Mayo brogue. "You brought Maeve?"

He was going to kill his sister Bridget, or the King's mail, because either a critical letter had been lost, or Bridget hadn't done him the courtesy of writing.

As Michael had neglected to write regularly to his own wife?

"I'm not coming out. Scotland is cold and bumpy, and all they have to eat here are scones, bannocks, and fish."

And there was Angus, watching Michael with thinly veiled curiosity.

"Ye could haul the little blighter out by her heels. Begin as ye intend to go on, I always say. Children need to know who's in authority."

How would Angus, a confirmed bachelor, know what children needed?

Before Michael could raise that salient point, Brenna came down the castle steps, skirts swishing and no smile in evidence. Michael climbed into the coach.

"Hello." His youngest sister was young indeed. He'd never met her, but she was the image of Erin at her age, all big blue eyes, freckles, and coppery braids. "I'm Michael."

"I know. It's your fault I had to leave Ireland."

The girl looked exhausted, rumpled, and stubborn. Exhausted and rumpled were easily remedied.

"How do you figure it's my fault? I had no idea you were coming."

Which was the wrong thing to say. Maeve gave him a look his mother often gave his father, and not when they were in charity with each other.

"Bridget is having a baby, and she said you're a baron now, so here I am, and my backside *hurts*."

He could haul her bodily from the coach, because the way her arms were crossed and her chin was jutting suggested nothing less would pry the child from her tantrum. Because her backside was not the only part of her aching, Michael shifted to sit beside her.

"Did Bridget give you a letter for me?"

"No. She was crying."

A little catch in the girl's voice portended tears looming much closer than County Mayo, so a change in tactics was in order.

"Are you hungry?"

"I am full of scones and cold tea, and I nearly retched halfway up from Aberdeen because of the stupid roads."

Which was worse? A nauseated child or a tearful child, and why was it his business? Michael was on the point of reaching for his sister when a form darkened the coach door.

"Well, thank goodness you're here, then." Brenna climbed into the coach and took the seat opposite. "You look like you could use a trip up to the parapet."

"No more trips. I hate trips."

"Come here," Brenna said. Her smile suggested great mysteries lay on the opposite bench, which for Michael, they rather did. "Look up. Way, way up."

The girl switched seats and gawked out the window as Brenna pointed at the battlements. "Bridget said I'd live in a castle, like a princess."

Live? As in grow up here? Next to where resentment stirred, Michael felt a curious pleasure, to know Bridget had entrusted their youngest sibling to his permanent care.

"I'm Brenna, and I live in that castle. So does your brother Michael."

"Brenna the Baroness," the child said, still craning

her neck to see the stone walls soaring over the bailey. "The castles in Ireland are mostly falling apart."

Brenna slipped an arm around the child. "This castle is in excellent repair, though it hasn't any princesses. It does have a wonderful big kitchen, though."

"I hate scones."

"You are tired," Brenna observed, and three words had never held such compassion. "Coach journeys are the worst."

Maeve leaned against Brenna's side. "They're long." Her weary, wistful tone suggested even nine years on the Continent couldn't have been as long.

"And bumpy," Michael added. Both females glanced over at him as if they'd forgotten he was in the coach.

"Very," Maeve said.

Now what to say? Michael did not want to bodily overpower a small child with half the footmen, Angus, Prebish, and Brenna looking on, and yet, he wasn't about to humor the girl much longer. She was his responsibility, after all.

"What's needed here," Brenna said in a considering tone, "is shortbread."

Maeve peered up at her. "Shortbread? Not scones?"

"Shortbread," Brenna said. "Have you ever had it with lavender in it?"

"Is it purple?"

Of course it wasn't purple, but it was delicious.

"I haven't had lavender shortbread since I went to Portugal," Michael observed, casually, of course.

"Then I think it's time we made some," Brenna said. "Though that will require a trip to the kitchens."

"Are the kitchens up there?" The child pointed aloft at where, oh joy, Elspeth Fraser and two other maids appeared to be watching the drama below—or watching the footmen.

"No, those are the parapets," Brenna said. "That's where I go to think. We can take our shortbread up there and feed crumbs to the birds."

Lucky birds.

"I like birds. We had lots of birds in Ireland." As if she were a bird, the child fluttered out of the coach without another word. Michael followed then turned, intent on assisting his wife from the coach. When he extended a hand to her, she hesitated then placed her fingers against his palm. That inspired him to haul her down the steps so she careened into his chest.

What he should have done was express his gratitude that she'd handled the child so well. Perhaps he should have kissed her knuckles or beamed a husbandly smile of relief at her.

"Save me some shortbread." He growled the words right in her ear, nothing husbandly or beaming about them.

"A small bite," she said, smirking up at him.

The last of the resentment Michael felt to have a child thrust upon him—and a cranky, stubborn child at that— evaporated in the pleasure he felt at his wife's smirk. He set her on her feet and swung the child up to his back.

"Come along, Maeve Brodie. You're old enough to learn to make your own shortbread."

Because a man could never have too many women mixing up batches of shortbread in his castle.

They left Angus in the bailey, his expression bemused.

Six

"COME ALONG," MICHAEL SAID, PICKING UP THE PLATE of shortbread with which the evening meal was to have concluded.

Brenna did not like his tone, but she would wait to tell him that until they were in the privacy of their rooms. He came around the table and held her chair for her, so she added that to the list of items they'd discuss in private.

"I don't recall either of my sisters having a sense of self-possession to match Maeve's," Michael said as they climbed the stairs. "It unnerves one."

"A girl without parents faces a choice. She can either cower away from life, wondering which loved one will be taken from her next, or she can meet life head-on."

Michael paused on the landing, and by the flickering light of a mirrored wall sconce, Brenna caught him studying her. She plucked a bite of shortbread off the plate and marched up the steps.

"Maeve is bright," Brenna added. "She'll manage." Or she wouldn't, and there was nothing Brenna could do about it. The thought ached bitterly.

"She's young, to be shuttled back and forth like this."

"She's likely the same age I was when I came to the castle." Brenna shoved the shortbread into her mouth lest she make more irrelevant observations.

"Nearly. She will be very pretty." His tone suggested a brother's wary concern, rather than a stupid man's glee that another pretty female would be larking about the realm.

Brenna waited while Michael opened the door to their sitting room. "So it's a good thing her brother is a baron, right?" she asked.

"It's a good thing her brother's a big fellow with a stout right arm. In ten years, I should also be able to dower her adequately, if we can enforce a few economies." He closed the door behind them and set the shortbread down. "Would you object very strenuously if I put my arms around you right now?"

Men were a fickle lot. Brenna placed her uneaten bite of dessert back on the plate. "Not *very* strenuously." Not at all, in fact.

Michael enveloped her in a simple sturdy hug. He smelled of good things—the outdoors, cedar, and clean wool—and his embrace offered the same sanctuary it sought. "We've had an eventful day."

Brenna's fingers drifted through the soft hair at his nape.

"Another eventful day, but guests are a pleasure, and your wee sister should know her only brother."

Something about his embrace shifted, and then he drew away.

"Maeve is not a guest. Prebish had a letter for me from Bridget, all brisk and sensible. The good Lord has finally seen fit to bless my sister's union with the probability of a child, and the baby must claim Bridget's focus."

He accepted that reasoning? "Balderdash. A woman can love more than one child, particularly her little sister and her own baby."

Michael took a lit candle down from the branch on the mantel. "She can, but Bridget's husband does not approve of Maeve's forwardness, and isn't about to take on the expense of tutors, governesses, a pianoforte, and the other necessities of a young lady's upbringing."

Brenna felt cold without her husband's arms around her, and yet, a fire this time of year would be an extravagance. "Are we to incur those expenses?"

"We'll find a way to manage them."

He disappeared into the dim recesses of the bedroom. Brenna had no choice but to grab the plate of shortbread and follow him, because the discussion was not finished.

"This castle is no place for a little girl. She'll have no playmates."

"You managed. In a house notably devoid of girls your age, you managed just fine. Besides, Hugh's Annie is about Maeve's age, and there are bound to be other girls in the village Maeve can play with. This isn't England, where the lord in his castle doesn't associate with his own people."

Brenna put the shortbread on the night table, when she wanted to pitch the entire plate at her husband.

"I did not manage. I *endured*, and I had no choice. Hugh will never let his Annie spend time under this roof."

As if nothing were amiss, as if Brenna's words

mattered not at all, Michael unknotted his cravat and draped it over the open door to the wardrobe.

"When a man doesn't pay his rent, he'd best not disdain the hospitality of his laird's home."

"*What?*"

He pulled his shirt over his head. "Angus says if the tenants paid timely, we'd not be short of cash. Your cousins are among the delinquent accounts."

Brenna took his shirt from his grasp.

"They pay, Michael. What is your uncle going on about? Every family pays, though many pay in kind, and some need a little extra time."

He sat to pull off his boots, the candlelight illuminating the powerful musculature and bones of his back. "I can't pay taxes with blankets and bread, Brenna. Angus was very clear about that."

Angus. Of course, Angus was clear.

She hung her husband's shirt up, needing to turn her back on his casual nudity and on the fatigue his posture revealed.

"You're to evict the slackers and run more sheep?"

"Brenna, please come here."

Please. He held out a hand to her, as if in entreaty, though he'd issued an order. She put his boots in the hallway first, for show, then approached the big rocker where he sat wearing nothing but his kilt.

"Here," he said, patting his bony knee. "I was in the middle of a rousing argument with Angus when Maeve's coach pulled up. He tried to resume hostilities before dinner, and I am not capable of having any more differences of opinion with my family just now."

This could not end well. Angus was Michael's

family, but Brenna was his family too. She crossed the room on dragging feet, uncertain what exactly Michael had in mind.

He rose, scooped her against his chest, and sat. "I tried to tell Angus that diversifying our sources of income is smart. If all we have are sheep, then one year some stupid blight or disease can come through and wipe them all out."

"Or a fancier breed with finer wool can become more popular," Brenna said, finding her husband's lap an oddly comfortable place to be. "The tenants work hard, they've been loyal when you were not here, and Angus is set in his ways. He'll say his way is the only way to avoid ruin, but his way is what has brought matters to the present pass."

More than that, she could not say, especially not when cuddled against Michael's bare chest.

"I told Angus I will make no decisions for the present. He ranted and stomped and lectured, but I can recall him carrying on with my father in a similar vein. Angus needs a wife."

God pity any woman foolish enough to marry Angus Brodie.

"Can we also delay a decision regarding Maeve, Michael? She may not settle in here well, and she really will be lonely." To posit the decision as one they shared was presuming, but for the child's own sake, Brenna could not afford to waver.

Michael's cheek rested against Brenna's hair. "Bridget has made a decision, and my place as head of the family is to provide for my younger sister."

"See if she settles in," Brenna said, unwilling to let

Michael think the battle over. "A small child can be very disruptive, and she's not yet been here a day."

"While I've not yet been here a week."

A moment of thoughtful silence passed, while Michael set the chair to rocking slowly and Brenna held a growing list of problems at bay: Maeve could not stay at Castle Brodie, taxes could not be paid in blankets and bread, and Angus could not stop bullying and annoying what few tenants remained.

And that was the least of the problems Angus Brodie could cause.

"Promise me something," Michael said.

Another softly worded order. "I've already made promises to you, Michael Brodie, and I've kept them."

He kissed her temple, and without bothering to warn her.

Neither did Brenna bother to object.

"I'm glad you kept your vows. If I haven't said that previously, I'm saying it now. I want another promise, though, and I'm happy to give it back to you."

He did not tell her he'd also kept his marriage vows, though he didn't lie to her about it either, which was something.

"What promise?"

"When we come up here, to our private rooms, can we agree to leave our differences at the door? Can we set aside a few rooms of our castle to be free of strife and carping?"

Our castle? He'd been home less than a week, and it was *our* castle? She wished it could be so, but how could it be *ours* when it had never been hers or even his?

Though she wanted Maeve's situation to be *our* decision.

"I cannot give you such a promise, Michael, for if I never take issue with you before others—and I will try very hard not to—then where are we to air our differences?"

"Shrewd," he said. "Also a valid point, so I will make this promise instead: I will promise to listen to what you have to say, not only in these rooms, but especially in here. I will listen with an open mind."

The words were not complicated, but their effect on Brenna was. She felt grateful, humbled, and despairing, for he'd guessed so easily that in her life, somebody to listen to her had been a critical lack.

If only he'd offered to listen to her on their wedding night nine years ago. "I will make you the same promise, Husband."

"That will serve." He gave her bottom a brisk pat—and when had his hand found its way to her fundament?—then rose and set her on her feet. "Let's get you undressed, and I have another question for you."

"You are a font of interrogation," Brenna said, moving behind the privacy screen lest she behold him unfastening his kilt.

"I'm essentially a new husband," he said as Brenna tugged her dress over her head. "We new husbands are curious fellows. My question is this: Have you given any more thought to how you'll woo me?"

❧

"Auld Angus must be nervous to have the laird underfoot at last," Dantry MacLogan said.

The diffidence of his tone suggested Hugh was to oblige him with a reply. Neil, the quietest of the three, could be counted on to referee if the discussion became *physical.*

"I think it's Brenna who's nervous," Hugh observed. "More nervous, poor lass." He stopped fussing with the fire—peat took its own time to catch—and peeked in on the children, both sleeping soundly.

"What has Cousin got to be nervous about?" Dantry took down a cribbage board and a worn deck of cards from the mantel.

The deck sported thistles and unicorns, which had always put Hugh in mind of the hardship and beauty that was Scotland. "Neil, will you join us?" Hugh asked.

Neil, ensconced before the fire in the household's only rocking chair, shook his head. The children said he told the best stories, but Hugh's theory was the bairns were that impressed to hear their older uncle speak at all.

Hugh took a seat at the table where they'd eaten their supper two hours earlier. "Cousin has a husband on her hands she likely never thought to see again. He'll go poking his lordly nose into every nook and cranny, and be listening at the keyholes of a night. The wrong keyholes, if I know Angus Brodie."

"Which," Dantry said, taking a seat at the table, "we do, to our sorrow and shame."

"Our damned inconvenience," Hugh rejoined, shuffling the deck as quietly as it could be done. "Thank God we've most of us paid our rents. Angus was that close to burning out Alexander MacIntosh. Now the man will have a chance to bring in a crop and sell off some fall lambs."

"Unless the laird burns him out anyway."

The silence that rose as the cards were dealt was sorrowful. The worst of the landlords burned their people out in autumn, when the crop was harvested, the livestock was fat, and winter was bearing down.

As Hugh's preoccupation and fatigue resulted in a gradual loss to his youngest brother, Dantry got around to the real point of the conversation.

"Lachlan is tired of cleaning boots and pots. The boy is ready to work in the stable, and he's old enough."

He would also make more than the few coins Hugh allowed Brenna to pay him.

"The stables are Angus's province," Hugh observed. "No son of mine will be working for Angus Brodie, and no daughter either. Play your hand, Dantry, and stop agitating."

"A little more coin couldn't hurt," Dantry said, tossing out an eight of clubs.

"Fifteen two," Hugh countered, with the seven of diamonds. "If Lachlan can work the stables, he can work the fields with us."

"A pair is twenty-two," Dantry countered, playing the seven of clubs. "Working the fields brings in no coin, Lachlan will be more bother than help, and every groat makes a difference."

"Twenty-nine for six points," Hugh said, laying down the seven of hearts. "And a go, for seven, and last card is eight."

Dantry sat back, staring at the pile of cards on the table. "You're not being practical. Angus has refused in-kind payments when he wants to make a point. The lease specifies rent in coin, and—"

"The stables are the laird's province," Neil said, getting up and heading down the hallway. "Not Angus's. Angus could end up being the one turfed out, and it's about damned time. The man needs a dirk between his ribs."

The rocking chair moved in his absence, coming to a standstill eventually, as Hugh gathered up the cards and passed them to Dantry.

"Remind me never to cross our brother," Hugh said. "And no more about Lachlan working where Angus Brodie has a say. I'm the boy's father."

Either Dantry was holding decent cards, or he recognized unassailable logic when it threatened to turn emphatic. Neil's door closed quietly, and the rest of the game was played in silence.

⤮

Michael was learning to study Brenna's expressions because, in the details of her physiognomy, she hinted at her emotions. A certain angle of her brows suggested curiosity, another skepticism, another suppressed ire.

But a man could study only those expressions he could see, so Michael rounded the corner of the privacy screen and beheld his wife in her shift, stays, and stockings. He slipped past her to the basin in the washstand in the corner.

"I did not enjoy the climate in Spain," he said. "The days were blisteringly hot much of the year, while the nights were bone-chillingly cold. The French mountains were uniformly cold, but that's at least predictable. Do you make this soap?"

In the mirror above the washstand, Brenna's eyebrows suggested utter bafflement.

"I do. We do, the women and I."

She watched him brush his teeth and wash the parts that counted. When Michael reached under his kilt to tend to the parts that also counted if one shared a bed with his wife, she turned away and started taking down her hair.

Her hands shook, and Michael felt like a bully—like a hopeless bully.

"You never did answer my question. How shall you woo me, darling Brenna?"

"Don't *ever* call me that." A hairpin went skittering to the floor.

"Darling is a bit of a stretch, I admit," Michael said, picking up the pin. "We are not the darling type, I'm thinking." He set the pin down near her hairbrush. "Perhaps we could exchange hints about this wooing business."

"You are ridiculous. Can you not allow me some privacy?"

He lounged back against the wall, which was cold against his bare shoulders, but he did not leave the small space behind the privacy screen.

"I woke up with you today, Wife, but within twenty minutes, you'd flown away to confer with Cook—again—or Elspeth or Goodie MacCray or the birds on the parapets. I hardly had a chance to speak with you, because Maeve has been dropped in our midst and my dear uncle has chosen today to take the gloves off, so to speak, and give my conscience the drubbing it deserves, and then dinner was—"

"Angus Brodie has no right to pummel your conscience," Brenna said, whirling and marching up to him. "That man has done nothing but prosper in your absence, and if Castle Brodie still stands, it's despite him and his overbearing ways, not because of them."

Better, much, much better to see the fire in Brenna's eyes and the determination in the angle of her chin. Michael eased forward and did his best to loom over her.

"He said I'd neglected my wife. Angus said you could not be blamed for growing headstrong in my absence. He said the kindest thing I could do was take you in hand sooner rather than later."

Brenna's hand snaked out, as if to slap Michael for conveying that sentiment. He made no move to stop her. He was too glad to see uncomplicated rage pouring from her in every line of her posture.

Her hand slowly returned to her side, but she remained before her husband, a pillar of feminine outrage in shift and stays.

"Your uncle has no business commenting on any aspect of our marriage. Not now, not ever."

"Exactly what I told him." Michael pulled a stray pin from bright red curls near Brenna's right ear and presented it to her, like a flower. "He didn't take it well."

She blinked at the hairpin, then snatched it from his hand. "Thank you."

Michael had the sense she was not thanking him for the hairpin, and left her a bit of privacy, the better for him to ponder her reaction. Angus was an interfering old besom who'd been allowed to run tame on the property for too long. Of course, he'd have marital advice for his only nephew. Angus was at best an indifferent rider, but he'd barked orders to the stable lads left and right, half of which, Michael had quietly countermanded in Angus's absence.

Angus also had decided opinions about raising cattle, though he'd no cows of his own, when all over the shire, the larger holdings typically kept a fold of Highlands, at least.

Angus would need some reminding of his place, was all.

Just as Brenna needed reminding of hers.

"Are you hoping I'll fall asleep before you join me, Brenna Maureen?" Not Brenna darling, not ever that, apparently. Michael spotted the tray of shortbread and popped a bite into his mouth.

"Yes," came the response from behind the privacy screen. "Go to bed and warm up the covers like a good husband, why don't you? You've had a long day, so don't wait up for me. I insist."

He held the plate over the top of the privacy screen but resisted the urge to peek. "All that wifely concern can leave a lady peckish. Have some shortbread." He felt her take a piece, as delicately as a mouse purloins the cheese without springing the trap, which might be a first step in the direction of somebody wooing somebody else.

"Shortbread counts as wooing," he informed her, setting the plate on the night table. "At least it does if you put lavender in it. Now you must give me a hint, Brenna my dear, and tell me something I've done that counts as wooing in your eyes."

She stirred around behind the screen then emerged, wrapped in a nightgown, night robe, and her hunting tartan. Her hair was in a single thick plait down her back, and her feet were bare. She looked wary, tired, and uncertain.

And he craved her. Craved her in her layers of night-clothes and her layers of pride. He craved her body, and even more, he craved her trust. She was home to him in a way he could not explain, not with words.

"That kilt is dusty. You are in want of your drawers," she said in the same tone she might have reminded him to get his elbows off the table. "I know they're clean, because we did laundry today." She crossed to the wardrobe as if to search out his prodigal drawers, but Michael moved up behind her and wrapped his arms around her shoulders.

"I am in want of my wife. Come to bed, Brenna." He led her to the bed, unwrapped the plaid from her shoulders, then waited while she handed him the night robe. "In you go."

She climbed onto the bed and hitched up against the pillows, pulling the covers to her chin as Michael moved around the room, blowing out candles.

He came to the last lit candle, the one on his side of the bed, and made a decision.

"Will you sleep in your kilt tonight?" Brenna asked, smoothing a hand down the quilt.

Michael turned his back to his wife, unpinned the wool, and let the kilt fall to the floor. "No, I will not."

He faced her, held still long enough to let her have a good look, then blew out the candle.

"Is a display of manly attributes your daft notion of enticing me into your arms?" How casual her voice sounded, when Brenna's heart was thumping like a trapped hare's. She shifted to organize her pillows, and her foot brushed up against a hairy male shin.

"In Spain, we slept in our clothes, night after night, for two reasons. We had to be ready to fight, of course, because sneak attacks by the French or the peasants were a possibility at any point." His recitation took no apparent notice of Brenna's accidental contact with his shin. "Then too, an officer caught out of uniform was subject to torture, as if war wasn't torture enough."

She'd gone still like a trapped hare, too, because not only was Michael naked—gloriously, fascinatingly naked—but he'd also strayed closer to Brenna's side of the bed.

"I see." She saw nothing, for the moon wasn't up yet, and clouds had made for an early sunset, though she caught the scent of heather, vetiver, and lavender from her husband's person.

"What did you do with your busy self today, Brenna Maureen? I catch the occasional glimpse of you, but you're always barreling around some corner, like the King's post making its last mile of the day."

"Summer is a busy season." A toe nudged up the length of Brenna's calf. Just that, a glancing nudge. If he could ignore these little mishaps, so could she. "Getting Maeve unpacked took some time, because the child has her own ideas about how her things should be put away."

Based on the amount of luggage the girl had brought, Bridget had indeed sent Maeve away permanently.

"You left Elspeth to humor the girl, and then what?"

"I oversee the laundry, as much to catch up on the gossip as to make sure the clothes are clean."

The mattress bounced as Michael swatted at his pillows. When he'd subdued them, he was closer still.

"Fraternizing with your troops. Every good officer learns the knack of fraternizing without being familiar. I love the scent of these sheets."

The compliment pleased her for its very casualness, despite Michael's proximity.

"We hang them in the sun when we can, or spread them over the lavender bushes. Michael, is there a reason why you must neglect your own side of the bed?"

"Yes, there is. What was the gossip?" He abandoned any pretense of stealth, slipped an arm under Brenna's neck, and drew her against his side.

"Goodie MacCray's youngest thinks Neil MacLogan is handsome, which, the ladies agree, he is, though his conversation is lacking."

"Perhaps he expresses himself more clearly through deeds."

Such subtlety. "Michael, what are you about?"

"I'm giving you a hint." He gave her temple a kiss too. "In case you were puzzled about exactly how I want to be wooed."

Brenna was not puzzled. She was tired, she was worried about the addition of Maeve to the household, she fretted over Michael's remarks earlier about rents being unpaid, and she...liked the scent of her husband's shoulder.

He and his wooing would drive her to Bedlam. "I don't suppose my husband would care for another piece of shortbread?"

His chest bounced, as if he chuckled. "I know better than to risk getting crumbs on our newly washed sheets."

Michael's fingers traced the hair back from Brenna's brow, the caress beguilingly tender.

Though not the least bit threatening. "You want *affection* from me, Husband?"

Michael didn't immediately answer, and as the silence drew out, Brenna felt uncertainty shading toward despair. She was twenty-five years old and had no instincts, no internal compass, when it came to the most basic marital matters.

Worse, she likely never would. This lack was a particularly miserable way to be broken, invisible and yet intimately obvious. She braced herself to roll away, but Michael's arm gently dissuaded her.

"I do want affection from you." Michael's tone said this conclusion surprised him. "I want it desperately."

And yet, he lay there, his arm around her, his desperation apparently checked.

Or perhaps he was uncertain too?

His fingers swept slowly across her brow; his chest rose and fell.

"When you were in the army, there was no affection, was there? You fought, you marched, you besieged, you tortured, and there was no one to take your hand or lie down with you on a chilly summer night. No one to know you favor lavender in your shortbread."

The nights had been cold, he'd said. Brenna would learn to listen to her husband more carefully. She tucked a knee across his thighs, wondering what was so delightful about war that men endured it for a day, much less for a decade.

"I had the memory of your smiles," he said. "I had the old songs. I had hope."

Hope was not a cuddly bedfellow. Hope was a nightingale, perched on the windowsill in the dead of winter, tempted to seek death rather than endure another moment of uncertain captivity.

Brenna reached up in the darkness and cupped her husband's jaw, bristly with a day's growth of beard. "I'll give you a hint too, Michael."

He caught her hand and ran his nose over her wrist, then held her fingers in his. No kissing, no clutching, nothing but a joining of hands. "I'm listening."

"When you tell your uncle"—Brenna wasn't going to say his name in this bed, not ever—"when you tell him that our marriage is none of his business, and never will be, you're doing a fine job of wooing your wife."

They fell asleep entwined, the cool breezes wafting in through the open window, while under the covers, husband and wife were snug and warm.

❧

Scotland was cold and bumpy. Ireland was wet and bumpy. One had shortbread, the other soda bread, but other than that, Maeve could not find significant differences.

For in neither country had she anybody to play with.

"I'm like a princess in a tower," she informed the fat orange pantry mouser, which was batting at daisies blooming in the shelter of the garden wall.

Bridget had had a walled garden in Ireland, all neat and trim, the walls low. Here, the walls were high and thick, serious about keeping out both bitter wind and prying eyes. The flowers were the stubborn varieties, nothing delicate about them.

"Does your brother know you're hiding in here?"

The man stood in the only door to the garden, the breeze catching his kilt.

"You're Uncle Angus. Bridget said I'm to stay away from you because you have a wicked temper."

White brows shot up. "I've a temper? As I recall, our dear Bridget was easily vexed herself, and over mud, dogs in the house, and other infractions which the sovereign has disgracefully neglected to make hanging felonies." He wasn't smiling, but his blue eyes said he was teasing.

"You know Bridget?"

"I'm her uncle too, child. Were you aware there's a tiger in your garden?"

More teasing, and Maeve liked it. "That's Preacher. Michael says he brings the mice their eternal reward."

"Aye, and he brings the lady cats something else entirely." Uncle crossed his arms and got comfortable against the worn jamb of the garden door. "How is Scotland suiting you so far?"

He was the first person to ask her this question, and the way he watched her suggested he would listen to her answer, not be off about some grown-up errand even as Maeve considered her reply.

"I don't know yet. The shortbread is nice. Brenna makes it with lavender, and Michael said it's his favorite."

"It's not your favorite, is it, princess?"

Had he overheard her? The notion was both unsettling and pleasing. "Lavender is for soap."

"And lemon drops are for little girls." From his coat pocket, he withdrew a sack, one Maeve recognized might contain sweets. He shook it, the sound tantalizing. "Come sweeten your day, little Maeve. You've certainly sweetened mine."

More teasing. Maeve rose from the grass and advanced on him. He wore the same plaid as everybody else around the castle except Brenna, and he was tall, though not quite as tall as Michael. She had to reach up to get at the sweets, which meant Uncle was still teasing her.

"Thank you." She popped the little candy in her mouth, and it did taste of lemon and sugar—also of bitter smoke. She did not spit it out, because that would be rude, and Uncle Angus seemed nice.

"I used to come here to sketch on a pretty day, but you're bored, aren't you, child?"

Nice, and he paid attention. Maeve watched the cat disappear among the daisies. "Brenna said I might take this garden in hand, but it's a wreck."

"A pretty wreck," Uncle Angus said. "Like our Brenna."

Maeve didn't know what to say about that. "Preacher likes it here."

"Come winter, Preacher will like it much better under your covers. Have you met Lachlan?"

The daisies rustled, but no desperate little squeak suggested Preacher had put an end to a hapless rodent.

"I haven't met anybody except Michael and Brenna. Prebish is resting, and Elspeth is busy."

Uncle snapped off a daisy and held it out to her. This was clever of him, a grown-up trick, because daisy stems were tough. "Do you know where the stables are, child?"

Maeve nodded, twirling her flower and watching the now-still daisies. "I saw them from the parapet. You can see everything from up there."

"Take yourself to the stables, and you'll find a boy named Lachlan who's about your age. By Highland standards, he's a cousin-in-law of sorts to you, and he's horse mad. Ye ken?"

Bridget's husband had been horse mad. Kevin's house was full of pictures of horses, he wore riding clothes until teatime, and in spring, he stayed in the barn all night if a mare was close to foaling. When he talked about his horses, he sounded like he was reading poetry.

"Lachlan's my cousin?"

"Not quite, but he's Brenna's cousin, which counts nearly the same in these parts. He's a good lad, and I'm sure he'll introduce you to the horses and the stable cats if you ask him."

"I like horses and cats, but I wasn't allowed to have a pony in Ireland. Ponies are expensive."

Bloody damned expensive, according to certain grown-ups whom Maeve had been allowed to overhear more than once—purposely, she suspected.

"Find Lachlan, but don't tell him I told you where he was. He's truant from the kitchen, and I wouldn't want to get the lad in trouble."

He winked at her and strode off, his kilt swinging the same way Michael's did. A flash of orange caught Maeve's eye, and there, eight feet above the daisies, the cat sat on the top of the wall.

"I'm going to the stables to find my cousin." Though in Ireland, she'd had a sister, and Bridget had seldom been good company. Maeve had a brother here…somewhere.

The cat sat atop the wall, its expression as dour as a preacher's. When the beast started washing its paws, Maeve felt well and truly ignored—and free to find her cousin.

It occurred to her, as she tried unsuccessfully to snap off a lovely white daisy, that if Uncle had remained rooted in the doorway, her only escape from the garden would have been over the walls. She spat out the lemon drop, brandished the daisy before her like a sword, and charged off toward the stables.

Seven

THE GARDENS AT THE BACK OF BRENNA'S CASTLE WERE
like her: tidy, contained, and modest, also more
appealing the longer Michael studied them. Pansies
did well here, and Brenna used their vivid colors for
contrasting borders. She'd found a variety with the
same blue as Maeve's eyes, and used it to edge a bed
of something white and frothy.

As white as the sun-bleached sheets on Michael's
bed. He mentally pitched that analogy aside, but a
heavy tread on the other side of the hedge stopped
him from rising from his bench and getting on with
his day.

"Shouldn't you be up on your parapets, Brenna
MacLogan?" Angus's voice held a note of cajolery, but
also a touch of something unpleasant.

And the lady's name was Brenna Brodie, and had
been for nearly a decade.

"Stand aside, old man. Where I go is no concern of
yours." Michael hadn't heard Brenna's approach, but
he *heard* her lifting her chin.

"This was my home long before you appeared,

young lady, and it will be my home until the day I die. You'd best watch your tongue."

While Michael debated intervening, a silence stretched. An orange cat—a tom from the dimensions of his head—came strutting along past the roses.

"You had best watch yours, Angus Brodie. I heard you tell Lachlan nobody would miss him if he wanted to enjoy a few minutes of a pretty day." Brenna's accusation might have been of murder most foul, for all the venom in her tone.

"He's a boy, Brenna MacLogan, a species you will never understand, else you'd not have allowed Michael to waste ten years of his life soldiering on the bloody Continent."

Michael rose, because that was the outside of too much, but a crunch of gravel on the other side of the hedge suggested Brenna was marching herself right up to Angus.

"Do you forget, Angus Brodie, that Lachlan's mother limped her entire life as a result of a mishap in the stables? Do you forget that the boy works for me, not you, and that his father will punish him if his few minutes in the sun take him rambling down to the stables again?"

Michael sat back down.

"The boy loves horses," Angus said, though some of the pugnacity had ebbed from his words. "Ann Brodie loved horses despite getting her toes wrinkled. The boy feels closer to his mother in the stables, and scrubbing pots and polishing boots will hardly support him when he's a man grown."

The discussion was becoming interesting, and

apparently to the cat as well. The beast hopped up beside Michael on the bench and head-butted Michael's ribs.

"It's for his father to say where the boy spends his time, not you, and not me," Brenna added. "For now, Lachlan works in the castle."

Michael only caught the sound of her fading steps, because he listened very hard, hard enough to hear the cat purring mightily—in his lap.

"Presuming beast." The damned thing weighed a ton and looked mortally disgruntled to be set on the ground.

In the exchange regarding Lachlan, who had been presuming and about what? Brenna had the right of it—the child's father would make any and all final decisions—but in Angus's side of the argument, Michael heard the echoes of the uncle who'd taught him the sword dances and his first few simple card tricks.

Little boys needed to explore the world, not scrub dirty pots all day.

"Has yon beast corrupted you into lurking behind hedges now?" Angus asked when he'd rounded the end of the hedge.

Michael rose and fell in step beside his uncle. "Yon bright sun has encouraged me to linger in my own garden. When did you and Brenna stop getting along?"

Angus was silent for a moment. The cat leaped out in front of them from among some yellow pansies, then sat on its sturdy fundament and yawned.

"She was a good girl," Angus said, "the sweetest little thing, and so quiet. When your mother left, she changed, or started changing. I am sorry to say it didn't help when you left, either."

"You expected her to stop me from joining up?" Michael posed the question casually, but Angus's accusation had been grossly unfair, not that he could know that.

"Women have their ways, especially plump, pretty young women."

The moment was ripe for difficult questions, but Michael disliked discussing his wife this way. That Angus recalled her as plump and pretty was vaguely disquieting, particularly when Brenna was no longer that young woman.

"Brenna has no guile," Michael said. "I love that about her."

Angus knelt to pet the cat, the movement slow and a little careful, bordering on elderly, though Angus wasn't fifty years old. "This one loves the ladies too, every chance he gets."

Michael did not love the ladies; he loved his wife, though he suspected Angus took that point well enough. Because Michael could not ask the most difficult questions, he asked something else.

"Do you ever get lonely, Angus?"

The cat, in the manner of many felines, went in a blink from purring and rubbing itself against the hand that petted it, to swiping at the same hand with a paw sporting a full complement of extended claws.

Angus casually knocked the cat into the roses. "Bloody beast." He got to his feet ungracefully. "You ask if I'm lonely. To live in the Highlands is to have some acquaintance with loneliness."

Michael spared a glance for the cat, who righted itself and bounded off for another flower bed.

"A man could say the same thing about the Spanish plains or the French Pyrenees. Loneliness isn't a function of geography." Nor was it a function of marital status, something Brenna had divined that Michael had not. While he'd been marching off to war or holed up in the French mountains, his wife had been lonely.

So had he. Brutally lonely. Not homesick, or not purely homesick, but lonely. The realization required some pondering.

"I travel into Aberdeen from time to time," Angus said. "It's a fine city."

Aberdeen was a fine city, with as many brothels as any other port town.

Angus was his only living adult relation, and so Michael persisted, because there was no one else to ask. "But in winter, when we're stuck up here for weeks at a time, sometimes months? When the smell of wet wool is in every room and you'd sell your soul for a bit of birdsong. How have you managed all these years?"

How had Michael's father managed, when those winters meant his wife was off in Ireland, his daughters too?

"You can't sell your soul," Angus said as they reached the stables. "You can only condemn it or hope it merits salvation. This is my home. I'll not leave it."

Which stirring declaration had nothing to do with the question on the floor.

"I might ride out with my wife this afternoon."

"You do that," Angus said. "I'll scare up Hugh MacLogan and tell him his boy's too old for the scullery. With a bit of training, the lad will make a fine addition to our stables."

Angus talked about Lachlan as if he were a yearling with good bloodlines.

"Leave that to me," Michael said. "My wife is aggravated enough to have Maeve underfoot without any warning. It won't hurt Lachlan to scrub a few more pots, and he does a good job with a pair of boots."

Something flitted through Angus's eyes, a sort of crafty, commiserating humor. "Aye, I'll leave it to you then. This is your home too." He strutted off in the direction of the village, something about his gait putting Michael in mind of the tomcat.

"It's not my home *too*," Michael said to nobody in particular. "I own the bloody place."

"Are you talking to yourself?" Maeve appeared from the depths of the stables, Lachlan at her side. The boy looked a bit defiant, but knew enough to hold his tongue.

"I was. I assume Lachlan gave you a tour of the stables, for which I thank him."

"He did," Maeve said. "You have the biggest horses I've ever seen. Lachlan said we might be allowed to clean some harness, but Herman Brodie is off looking at a mare, so maybe some other day."

Herman Brodie, stable master for the past fifteen years, was probably off looking at a mare of the two-legged variety.

"You two wash your feet at the pump before you

go back inside the castle. But first, I've been meaning to ask you both something."

Maeve and Lachlan exchanged a look, which Michael did not begrudge them. Everybody needed allies, whether he or she scrubbed potatoes and pots, was newly arrived from Ireland, or owned the damned castle.

"You, Lachlan, are in the kitchen for much of the day, and I need to learn a certain recipe. Do you know your letters?"

"Some." The boy's ears turned red, suggesting "some" amounted to his name or a vague approximation of it.

"We'll get Maeve to help us, then. I want that shortbread recipe," Michael said. "The one with the lavender. You can winkle it out of Cook, and Maeve can write it down, but you must tell no one." That last part had both children smiling. "Can you do this?"

"We can," Maeve said, her grin impish.

"Yes, Laird. Must we do it today? Cousin made a big batch just yesterday."

Laird. Lachlan was the first to address Michael as laird, and from the child, the title bore respect and something...something Michael liked, something that eased the homesickness and the loneliness both.

"No rush. The important thing is to be casual about it, so nobody notices what you're up to."

"We can do that too," Lachlan said, grabbing Maeve's hand.

"Before you scamper off, Lachlan, I need a word with you. Maeve, you'll find pencil and paper in the desk in the library." At least, there's where it had been for the first twenty years of Michael's life.

Maeve waved to them and skipped away, reminding Michael that Brenna used to skip all over the bailey, when she'd first arrived to Castle Brodie.

Lachlan watched Maeve skipping up to the castle, the way Michael might have watched a plate of fresh, warm shortbread on a cold winter's day.

"I know I'm not supposed to go to the stables, Laird."

Loneliness was not the exclusive province of adults.

"You're certainly not supposed to lark about the stables in your bare feet. Shall we sit?" Michael gestured to a worn bench in the sun outside the barn doors. "Taking a few minutes to show Maeve around is hospitality. We pride ourselves on our hospitality in this shire."

The boy scuffed dirty toes in the stubby grass under their bench. "Maeve likes horses." While Lachlan clearly liked Maeve, or liked having any child to associate with during his long day.

"She's my sister," Michael said, which earned him a curious glance. "You have a sister."

"Our Annie. She has the same name as my ma did."

"Why don't you wear your boots if you're sneaking into the stables?"

"Boots are for winter, and I don't sneak."

Michael knew that—about the boots—but he'd forgotten it. When every penny counted, something as dear as a pair of boots shouldn't be wasted on summer weather. Soldiers were equally protective of their footwear, and a regiment's cobbler was never allowed to volunteer for the most dangerous missions.

"A man who's working around horses has to wear his boots whenever he's in the stables. I don't care what Herman says, or Angus, or your own father. I'm the laird, and these are my stables."

Lachlan scuffed both feet. "Yes, Laird."

Which in the dialect of little boys meant "Go bugger yourself."

"Lachlan, if I ask your father to let you work in the stables, I'll provide the boots as part of your pay, but I can't have Brenna wroth with me for stealing her best kitchen help."

Understanding dawned in Lachlan's solemn blue eyes. "We none of us like to make Annie upset. When she cries is the worst. Only Uncle Neil can manage her when she cries."

"Uncle Neil's a good man." Whom Michael would probably not recognize if he sat down with him at the same table in the pub. "We must not rush you from the kitchens, and I do need that shortbread recipe."

"Aye." The boy looked down, though a grin had appeared.

"Away with you, and don't forget to wash your feet."

Lachlan shot off the bench, but only as the boy reached the bailey did Michael realize he'd had an audience. The marmalade cat sat in the barn doorway, having a casual wash.

"You'll not be tattling on me to my wife, cat, or I'll tattle on you to all of yours."

The cat paid him no mind. No mind whatsoever.

❧

"Hold still." Brenna spoke around a pair of pins.

"How long does it take to tuck up some damned wool?" Michael groused. "A man wants to find his bed at the end of the day, not serve as his wife's pincushion."

This was the fellow she was supposed to woo? "Turn a bit."

He obliged, which meant Brenna had a fine view of the backs of his calves. Hairy, muscular, male…they were interesting, those calves. She took a pin from her mouth and fastened another few inches of hem.

"What did you find to do with yourself today, when you weren't serving as my pincushion?"

"I made the acquaintance of our boot boy, Hugh's son. I also made the mistake of allowing Herman Brodie to accost me on a sunny afternoon, and nothing would do but I must introduce myself to every equine on the property, including all five foals born to us this spring. Then, of course, we had to have a pint of summer ale, or two."

Or six. He'd sent word up from the village not to hold supper for him.

"Turn again." She took the last pin from her mouth. "If you found Lachlan in the stables, the boy will hear about it from his da." Though why hadn't Brenna thought to look for Maeve in the stables? What girl raised in an Irish squire's household wouldn't be horse mad?

"Are you staring at my arse?"

"I will never, not if I live to be ninety-four years old, understand the male mind." Though she might take up admiring her husband's backside. She pushed the last pin through soft wool and sat back. "I am not staring at your blessed fundament. We're done here. Take off your kilt and mind the pins."

He stepped away. "You were taking overly long about that last part. If you did want to stare at my arse, I'd hardly be offended."

Brenna made to rise, only to find her husband assisting her.

"You are tired from riding all over the shire with Herman, and you likely didn't get a proper dinner at the pub. I am tired from trying to figure out when you're teasing, when you're flirting, and when you're merely making conversation."

He kissed her nose. "So stop trying to figure it out and talk to me. What occupied you this lovely day? I know you did not go riding with your husband."

Out of habit, Brenna never lit many candles after dark, but one had to see clearly to deal with hems and measurements and such. Now that she was looking at Michael's face rather than his knees, feet, or calves— all of which were interesting—she could see he was not happy.

"Was I supposed to go riding with you, Husband?"

"Yes, you were, but Herman kidnapped me, and I suspect Angus put him up to it. Ouch, damn it."

He'd stomped over to the privacy screen, which made the kilt swish about his lordly knees, and likely impaled those same knees on a half-dozen pins.

"I'll be back." Brenna left him swearing in French and possibly Spanish behind the privacy screen, and took herself down to the kitchen. Bread, butter, cheese, and a few strawberries went onto a tray, along with a pitcher of cold lemonade.

When she returned to the laird's chambers, Michael was in a dressing gown—thank heavens for small mercies—and standing near a branch of candles on the mantel.

"I'd forgotten you keep a journal," he mused.

"Some years more than others." Some years, not at all.

"You don't seem concerned I might read it."

Brenna set the tray on the desk near the windows.

"You're a great one for conversation. Why would you read my journal when you might instead plague me with talk? Come eat."

He set the little book on the mantel and took the seat at his desk. "Lemonade?"

"You favored it as a boy." She pulled a chair up on the other side of the desk, when what she should have done was set the food out in their sitting room. "I can take the tray to the other room—"

Her husband regarded her with a smile that was both approving and male.

"You recalled that I enjoy lemonade. Please sit, Wife. The other room is bound to be chilly by now, while our bedroom is cozy. I hardly recognized anybody at the pub."

Brenna took a seat, still trying to understand that smile, and what it meant when the laird didn't recognize his tenants.

"Herman didn't handle the introductions?"

Michael made himself a sandwich of buttered bread and cheese, the soldier in him apparently happy to eat with his fingers.

"It was odd. Nobody came over to greet us, though some tipped their hats or otherwise acknowledged us. Angus showed up and pointed out this tenant or that new bride."

"Have some strawberries."

Michael paused, his half-eaten sandwich in his hand. "You have some strawberries. What aren't you telling me, Brenna Brodie?"

"Angus showed up. Do you think your tenants would barge in on a conversation between you and Angus?"

Another bite disappeared, though he chewed more slowly. "You're saying my tenants avoid Angus."

Everybody avoided Angus, but Brenna could hardly tell her husband that.

"He's the steward, and he doesn't usually come around unless trouble's afoot or rents are due." She stuffed a strawberry in her mouth rather than say more. The berry had appeared perfectly ripe, but turned out to be one of those fruits that looked much better than it tasted.

"Makes sense. You aren't having a sandwich?"

"I had a decent meal." With Maeve, who had tried hard not to let her disappointment at Michael's absence show. Brenna appropriated a sip of Michael's lemonade, the better to keep that sentiment silent as well.

"Herman says the yearlings are ready to take in to Aberdeen for sale. I've half a mind to go along."

He wasn't asking her permission to leave—or was he? "You must do as you see fit. Angus usually accompanies the livestock going to sale."

Something flickered across Michael's face, something a wife of nine years ought to be able to read.

"We'll send Angus. A change of scenery will do him good, and he, at least, won't be tempted to take ship for the New World."

Brenna did not mutter *if only he would*, because

Angus was the devil she knew, and inflicting him on others all unsuspecting wouldn't be honorable.

"Will you have another sandwich?"

"I would have my wife feed me some strawberries." He sat back, his blue dressing gown gaping open, a smile lurking in his eyes. "If she's willing."

The food had calmed him, or maybe the small talk had. Brenna chose a medium-sized berry and held it up to his lips.

"Whom did you recognize in the pub?"

He took the berry from her fingers with his teeth, carefully. "I know the old people, mostly. They were old when I left, and they're ancient now. Vera MacDonald still holds court from the inglenook. Another berry, please?"

Brenna chose a larger specimen, though the largest berries were seldom the tastiest. "Who else?"

"William Campbell, Thomas Miller. A few others by sight, but not by name. These are good."

"More lemonade?"

This time, he took the berry from her fingers then trapped her hand in his. "This is wooing, Brenna." He kissed her knuckles, while a warmth that had nothing to do with the cozy fire spread up from Brenna's middle.

"You're not so hard to woo, then."

Because Brenna was studying the empty plate, she wasn't expecting it when her husband came half out of his chair, leaned across the desk, and gave her a strawberry-flavored kiss on the mouth.

"Neither are you. Let's to bed, shall we?"

Brenna took a sip of the lemonade, set the last glass

on the night table, and then put the tray in the corridor while Michael banked the fire.

❧

The end of their evenings had become routine, and that pleased Michael inordinately. Most people tidied up at the end of the day, tended to their ablutions, and shed their clothes before climbing into bed. Soldiers tried to maintain a semblance of the same mundane order, though battle doomed those efforts to periodic failure.

Brenna used the wash water first and emerged from behind the privacy screen in a dressing gown made from the dark Brodie hunting plaid. Michael was coming to think of the pattern—soft blues, green, and black, with red-and-yellow accents—as Brenna's personal tartan.

"Did you leave me any warm water, Wife?"

"Of course not. You'll have to go wash in the loch," she said, filling the warmer with coals. "The young men in these parts pride themselves on being able to wash in the loch when it isn't frozen over."

He'd washed earlier, when Brenna had retreated to the kitchens, but he washed again, because his wife had not only left him warm water, but she'd scented it with lavender.

"Bathing in the loch isn't necessarily about getting a young man clean," he said from behind the screen.

"It's about flirting with lung fever?"

"It's about flirting with the young ladies who might be peeking from the battlements or the bushes. Then too, the cold water can douse a fellow's most mischievous preoccupations, at least temporarily."

That provoked a silence. Michael peeked over the screen as he used his tooth powder and saw Brenna untying the sash of her dressing gown. While he watched, she let the garment fall to her hips, an unconsciously graceful unveiling of her naked back, down to the swell of her hips.

Perhaps bathing in the loch had something to recommend it, even when a man no longer considered himself young. Michael's teeth should have been sparkling by the time he put aside his toothbrush, blew out the last candle, and shed his dressing gown.

Because he'd banked the coals, the room was nearly pitch-dark. Brenna's voice came floating through that darkness.

"Would you like a sip of lemonade?"

"Yes, please."

Lemonade and tooth powder was not a pleasant combination, but accepting the drink let Michael touch his wife's hand, and then wrap her fingers around the glass when he was done.

"You never did tell me what you got up to today, Baroness."

He punctuated his observation with a casual toe run up her calf. He loved her calves. They were sturdy, dusted with fine red-gold hair, and yet, elegant too.

"I lost Maeve for a time." Her tone said this was both a worry and a transgression—on her part.

"And I've lost you. If you're going to hoard your report for when we're abed, you'll at least cuddle up when you deliver it."

He waited. Brenna was in bed without a stitch

of clothing, and whether and when to build on that display of courage had to be her decision.

She surrendered with characteristic grace, tucking herself against his side.

"You spend the afternoon swilling ale with the fellows, and expect me to throw myself into your arms when you come toddling up the hill, half-seas over?"

While she groused and got comfortable, Michael wrapped an arm around her shoulders.

"I had two pints. Where did you find Maeve?"

"I didn't. She came skipping back up into the great hall just as I was about to send Lachlan for you, except I couldn't find the boy either. Hugh doesn't like having his son take the laird's coin, but somebody has to teach the child to read, and a position in the kitchen was all I could think of."

"Nobody teaches our children to read?"

"Their parents do, when they have time, but Lachlan's a boy, and his menfolk are busy. I figure if I can teach Lachlan, he'll teach Annie."

In Michael's absence, Angus had been a sort of self-appointed steward, and Michael was grateful for that, but Brenna had apparently become the laird.

"Maeve can read quite well. I expect she already has some French too. What else did you do today?"

He half cared what she'd got up to, but mostly he wanted to hear her voice. Brenna recounted a feud among the footmen regarding days off, a discussion at the herb woman's in the village over who ought to lead some infernal committee at the kirk, and an inventory of goods and stores in anticipation of the upcoming gathering.

Her recitation was probably the longest speech he'd had from her, and she'd give it to him only in the dark.

"You resist a natural urge toward cuddling," Michael observed when she'd paused. He caught her leg behind the knee and hiked it across his thighs. "Though you do give an admirably detailed recounting, if a man is persistent enough in asking for it. You mustn't worry about Maeve wandering on a pretty day."

She nuzzled his shoulder, though her gesture had the feel of a horse nose-butting a preoccupied groom.

"Michael, the child could get lost. She could come to harm, and no one would know where to look for her. She could fall from the battlements."

"Nobody sober has fallen from the battlements in five hundred years of Clan Brodie history. You used to disappear for hours when you weren't much bigger than Maeve."

Sometimes, he'd followed her, telling himself a fellow ought to guard his future wife, but mostly he'd simply been curious about her disappearances. Angus had caught him a few times and accused him of spying.

"Maeve is a visitor," Brenna replied. "She can't know to stay away from the village drunk, or that the Miller's billy goat is a menace to all in his pasture."

"The goat's damned stench ought to warn her of that, and Davey MacCray is no threat to anybody except himself. Shall I have a word with Maeve?"

Was that what this was about? He did not take issue with Brenna's characterization of his small sister as a visitor, because the main point was valid: Maeve did not know her way around. Exploring was a child's natural inclination, but the line between exploring and getting lost had more to do with when sunset fell than with a child's common sense.

"Please. A very direct word."

"You didn't have that word?" Brenna could be direct, though Michael was coming to realize she didn't enjoy confrontation. Dreaded it, in fact.

"You're her brother and the laird. If I rebuke her, she'll resent me. If you rebuke her, she'll listen."

Probably right. Recruits listened to the general who'd never fought the enemy hand-to-hand, while ignoring the advice of the battle-hardened sergeants.

"You think I'm laird here?"

Her arm fell across his midriff. "I know it. You'll know it soon too."

Because the loch was a half mile distant—and because he was in bed with his wife and not a stitch of clothing between them—Michael captured Brenna's hand in his and laced their fingers.

"I do not like this business of being laird."

He hadn't been teasing, and the tension he felt suffuse his wife suggested she knew that. "You'd rather go back to murdering in the King's name?"

"Protecting," he said, enunciating each syllable. "I took it upon myself to protect a certain delicately placed fellow—Sebastian St. Clair—and my task proved infernally difficult. But no, I do not want to rejoin the army, so stop fretting that you'll waken and I'll be gone." *Again*. He kissed her fingers—in long overdue apology? "I have to wonder though, what's the point of coming home from war if I spend all day missing my little sister, a girl I've never even seen before this week?"

The tension in Brenna's body shifted, to a listening sort of attentiveness. "You missed your sister today?"

"We crossed paths, but she was more enamored of Lachlan, of the cat, of the very beams of sunshine in the bailey than of her older brother. And that isn't the worst of it." He was whining, and he'd waited until he had the cover of darkness to do it. Some brave soldier, he.

"What was the worst of it?" This time she didn't nuzzle his shoulder, she sniffed at him.

"I bathed, I'll have you know."

"What was the worst of it, Husband?"

She was laughing at him, and while his pride winced, some other part of him, maybe the part that was learning to be a husband, thought that was a good thing.

"I've come home from war, and supposedly I'm laird here, but all I do the livelong day is listen to people complain about things I must address, while I stand around looking patient and missing the hell out of my wife."

Brenna was cuddled up along his side, so he felt her silent laughter, felt her try to fight it, and felt her lose.

And then he felt something else: he felt the wife he had missed all day, the wife he loved in some fashion, the wife naked in bed with him, hike up on her elbow and press her lips to his. A solid, mouth on mouth, hint-of-lemonade kiss, which by exercise of self-discipline alone, Michael allowed to remain a simple kiss.

She did it again, a quick in-case-he-missed-the-first-one kiss, then subsided against him, her arm wrapped across his middle, her leg across his thighs. As if her bare, warm breasts hadn't briefly brushed against Michael's chest, as if he was supposed to think after being teased so cruelly.

"Good night, Husband. I'm sorry your day was such a trial. Tomorrow will be an improvement, I'm sure."

Brenna fell asleep wrapped in her spouse's arms, while Michael thought of frigid lochs, tooth powder, and lemonade. She was right, of course. Tomorrow would be better. Any child knew, and most husbands did too, that kisses made everything better.

Eight

KISSING WAS NOT DIGNIFIED. KISSING ACCOMPLISHED nothing. Kissing was a stupid, messy, uncomfortable inconvenience invented by men, because men were not concerned with anything save their own base impulses.

Some men.

"Are you angry?" Maeve posed the question while admiring her own needlework.

"No, I am not angry." Though Brenna had been stabbing at her embroidery as if trying to commit murder-by-needle on the heather and thistles adorning Michael's handkerchief. "How are your stitches coming?"

Maeve held up a hoop, upon which simple chain stitches outlined an orange cat.

"Preacher will be vain, to know you've immortalized him with your sewing," Brenna said. "Will you embroider him a butterfly to bat at, or some grass to sit upon?"

Maeve budged closer on the sofa of Brenna's sitting room. "I knew I wanted to have Preacher on my handkerchief, but I'll have to sketch the rest."

Brenna put her hoop aside and ran a hand over Maeve's coppery braid. "I know the perfect place to sketch. Come with me."

They stowed their hoops, gathered up a lap desk from the bedroom, and repaired to the battlements.

"Over here," Brenna said, "we're out of the breeze, and we have a fine view of the loch. There's Cook, gathering some herbs from the kitchen garden, and you can watch Herman Brodie shoeing Bannockburn."

"Herman calls the horse Banshee."

Herman called the horse other things too, things a child would delight in overhearing.

"You can sketch your cat an entire garden, a herd of mice, or a flock of butterflies. Be sure to think about what color each flower or butterfly would be."

While Brenna could sit in the sunshine and come to terms with a revelation.

"Butterflies," Maeve said, opening the lap desk. "I don't like that Preacher kills the mice."

"He's a cat. Cook adores him for killing the mice."

"No, she does not." In the way of children, Maeve was handling each pencil in the desk, evaluating them one by one for some quality known only to her little-girl fingers. "She feeds him scraps and leftover cream, and he has no need to kill mice."

Such were the insights gained by a child who'd already realized Cook was an ally to the young and the hungry, both.

"So don't draw him any mice to terrorize. Draw him butterflies he cannot catch."

Butterflies, like the butterflies that had risen up in Brenna's belly last night, when—too late to check herself—she'd realized she was about to kiss her husband out of his pout.

"Preacher shouldn't kill things if he doesn't have to. It's not nice."

Maeve fell silent, absorbed with her sketching. She sat beside Brenna on the bench in the sun, the stones of the castle wall warm at their backs, while Brenna let the familiar peace of the view settle over her. Beyond the village, partway around the loch, one of her cousins was mending a wall while wee Annie "helped." Cook had gone back inside, and Herman's farriery had progressed to a second great back hoof on the plow horse.

Why had she kissed her husband?

"Have you ever been to Ireland, Brenna?"

"No, I have not." And that hurt. Brenna hadn't been invited to go to Ireland. She'd been told Michael would have expected her to stay and mind his castle. "Tell me about Ireland."

Maeve considered the tomcat sitting in the middle of the blank page. "Ireland is rainy. How many butterflies in a flock?"

"As many as you please." An entire bellyful. Far below the parapets, Angus emerged from the dower house and started on the path toward the stables. "Do you miss Ireland?"

"I miss Bridget. Kevin yelled a lot, and Bridget yelled back at him." Several butterflies, enormous in relation to the cat, took shape on the page.

"Late for dinner, muddy boots, reading at breakfast, that kind of yelling?"

"Yelling about me too. Kevin said Michael is head

of my family, but how can somebody be the head of your family when you've never seen him?"

Angus always swaggered; Brenna did not imagine that. He was swaggering into the stable yard now, his kilt flapping because he'd eschewed a sporran. She hated when he did that, and suspected he knew it.

"You ask a fair question, Maeve. Michael is my husband, but I didn't see him for years."

She should not have said that, especially not to Maeve, but the horse, Bannockburn, had seen Angus coming up the path and lifted its great head to the consternation of the groom holding the lead rope. Brenna had been distracted by Angus's ability to unsettle another, even another of a different species.

"Did you miss Michael while he was gone?"

"Desperately." Though she hadn't told him that. Not yet. "I miss him right now."

Maeve paused in her sketching. "Grown-ups are silly. I like Michael. He doesn't yell, and he doesn't smell like dogs or muddy boots."

"Fine qualities in a man, to be sure." He also cuddled wonderfully, and had the patience of a saint. In the stable yard, Angus had begun pointing and gesturing, as if he'd explain to a seasoned stable master how to trim a hoof on a beast that stable master had likely foaled out.

"Michael likes shortbread, and I like shortbread. Lachlan does too. I think that's enough butterflies."

"That is so many butterflies, Preacher will dive for cover among the pansies. What colors will you make them?"

"Too many colors. I can't embroider this." Maeve

set the sketch aside and appeared to take an interest in the goings-on below. "Herman names each big horse for a Scottish victory."

"Fortunately for Herman, we don't have that many heavy horses." Though Michael coming home had been a victory of sorts. A victory without a name.

"Uncle Angus is yelling. He was nice to me yesterday."

All the pleasure Brenna took in the bright, pretty day, all the preoccupation she'd felt with the doings of the previous evening, evaporated.

"Maeve, I want you to listen to me."

This earned Brenna a cautious, sidelong glance. "I can hear you fine, even with Herman and Angus both yelling."

The men were distant enough that their words were snatched away by the breeze. Brenna spoke slowly, so her words would find their target.

"Avoid Angus, and never be alone with him. If he tries to make friends, then don't anger him, but slip away as soon as you can."

"Bridget said Angus has a sorry temper."

Bless Bridget. "That's part of it. I'll tell you one other thing. If you ever need to get away from him, you come up here. He's afraid of heights. He doesn't even like to be in the minstrel's gallery in the great hall."

Which realization, had given Brenna significant satisfaction.

"I had hiding places in Ireland, for when Kevin and Bridget got mad at each other when I was little. Prebish told me I was silly, because Kevin would pick Bridget up and carry her to their bedroom. They'd stop yelling then."

The horse tried to yank its leg away when Angus picked up a front hoof. More yelling ensued as the beast capered around on the end of its lead rope, and then was taken back into the stables.

"Bannockburn likes carrots. He doesn't like yelling," Maeve observed.

"He's a good fellow." Brenna wanted to say more, wanted to make sure the child had absorbed her warning, but Maeve went back to sketching butterflies, so Brenna rose to stand by the parapets.

Herman caught sight of her and waved. Angus did not wave, but resumed lecturing the stable master, or trying to.

Angus was afraid of heights, and Brenna was not. She loved the view, loved the fresh air and the drenching sunshine. Loved seeing the land—part settled, part wild, all beautiful—and the village at peace down below the wooded hill. She had been afraid of kisses, though.

Had been.

She offered Herman a jaunty wave, resumed her place by the child, and filled her mind with thoughts of butterflies and kisses.

❦

"How does one go about kissing?"

Brenna's question stopped Michael mid-reach toward his shaving kit. She stood in her dressing gown on the threshold of the space behind the privacy screen, watching him at his morning ablutions.

"One goes about kissing tenderly, joyfully, and if he's a fortunate man, frequently." Also carefully, if he was Brenna Brodie's husband, and gratefully. "Shall I demonstrate?"

As he unrolled his shaving gear, Michael's heartbeat picked up. He was discussing kissing with his wife, in their bedroom, in the broad light of a beautiful Highland summer day.

And Brenna looked as determined as a line of infantry preparing to storm a broken siege wall.

"You may. Demonstrate, that is. Briefly."

Michael was also in his dressing gown, which was fortunate, because it hid a reaction to her words that might not aid his cause. He took a steadying glance out the window at the cold, dark loch, at the whitecaps whipped up by a cool, brisk breeze.

"Come with me." He led her by the wrist into their sitting room, locked the door to the corridor, then regarded the challenge before him. "You want to learn how to kiss?"

"I've said as much." While her ramrod posture said she was done talking.

Ah, but in her silence, Michael detected uncertainty and longing, both of which told him his Brenna had been a faithful wife in even this minor regard. She hadn't kissed; she hadn't permitted anybody to kiss her while her husband was off soldiering.

Michael tugged her over to the desk near the window, the better to count the freckles dusting the bridge of her nose.

"This might take some patience on your part, Brenna Maureen. I'm out of practice, though I suspect the knack will return to me in time."

She wrestled her wrist free of his grip. "You're out of practice?"

"One hasn't much call for kissing when at war." Murdering in the King's name being ever so much more enjoyable. He patted the desk. "Sit."

Brenna perched on the edge of the desk. "You truly didn't have much occasion for kisses while you were gone?" She offered her question while arranging the folds of her dressing gown over her knees, then closing the placket more snugly over her middle, then adjusting the drape over her calves.

"I missed you. That left no time for kissing anybody, save the occasional horse. Oh, and a cat, in London. Shameless fellow by the name of Peter. Hold still."

The fussing stopped. "You start off your kisses by giving orders?"

He started off his kisses by sending up a prayer that he'd get this right. He'd kissed Brenna before, fumbling overtures on their wedding night, and casually since returning home. This was a kiss she'd invited, asked for, even. Michael's entire marital campaign might flounder and sink on the strength of the next few minutes.

"Give me your hands."

She gave him a cross look.

"Give me your hands, please, dearest, lovely wife."

She surrendered the requested appendages.

Michael kissed each palm for luck, then placed them where his neck and shoulders joined. "A firm grip is best, so your fellow doesn't wander off midway through the festivities. If you think he's entertaining such a notion, you can grab him by the hair instead."

"Like this?" She seized him above his nape in a beguilingly firm grip. No wandering off allowed.

"Exactly. Once you've got him in hand, so to speak, you look him over, and don't be shy about it. Men can be dense, and shy glances won't penetrate their—are you laughing at me?"

"You daft beast, you wouldn't know anything about how to kiss a man, would you?"

The question flummoxed him, utterly. He stepped closer, between her legs, and dropped his forehead to hers.

"I want to do this right, Brenna. I want to kiss you so a feeling more blessed than the sun beaming in that window fills your heart and lightens your every step. I want to share a kiss with you that means this desk stays in the family for generations, because long ago, Great-Great-Grandda Michael came home from war and kissed his Brenna while she sat upon this desk, laughing at him."

A kiss that would assure her he'd never leave her side again.

Her grip on him became more fierce. "Such expectations are a kiss in themselves."

Her lips grazed his, soft as sunshine. Michael resisted the urge to take her in his arms, resisted the need to wedge his body against hers.

"Again, please, Wife. Kissing wants practice."

She repeated the gesture, this time kissing her way across his mouth, corner to corner. "You taste like tooth powder."

While she tasted like hope. "What do I feel like?"

More kisses came his way, and he endured that torture until her tongue touched his upper lip. This necessitated—much as life necessitates breathing—that he tuck one arm around her shoulders.

"You're all bone and muscle and braw determination," Brenna said, her breath feathering across his chin, "while your mouth is wondrous soft."

He dipped his head to brush that wondrous soft mouth across her lips, like one fellow might gently slap a glove across another's cheek in a moment of high drama. "You're softer. Marvelously soft."

While part of him was growing marvelously hard.

⁂

"Something tells me you aren't where you're supposed to be, child."

Maeve was caught, and Uncle Angus, standing in the door of the stall, looked infernally pleased to have found her. Grown-ups were entirely too big sometimes.

"I'm allowed out of the castle, as long as somebody knows where I am." Though Lachlan likely did not qualify as a somebody, and "outside" certainly was not an adequate description of her whereabouts.

"You were peeking at Wee Bannockburn, weren't you?"

To be accurate, she was marveling at the size of the droppings in Wee Bannockburn's stall. Wee Bannock, a huge dapple gray, was the biggest horse Maeve had ever seen, and Lachlan claimed he had the biggest droppings in Aberdeenshire.

Boys were always interested in things like horse droppings.

"My uncle in Ireland would like him. Bannock's a fine lad."

In the next stall over, Bannock munched at a pile of hay taller than Maeve.

"Your uncle would like the damned beastie better at pasture, which is where a horse belongs come summer." Uncle Angus came into the stall, which caused the horse to sidle away from the hay.

"Bannock doesn't like it when you swear."

Uncle Angus bent at the knees and hoisted Maeve to his hip. "If you're going to sneak out of the castle, get your boots dirty, and come to table smelling of horse, you should at least get a decent look at your friend, and Bannock doesn't give a—Bannock doesn't care a whit about my language as long as he can get at his hay."

Maeve was too big to be carried like this, and Uncle smelled of pipe smoke and whisky. The scent wasn't entirely unpleasant—some people had whisky with their breakfast even in Ireland—but it was an old man smell. And yet, the view from Uncle Angus's hip was better than trying to peer between the slats at the horse, or getting her pinafore dirty climbing over the boards.

"He's busy with his hay. You can put me down now."

"You're not that heavy. Have you seen the foals in the back paddock?" He walked with her into the barn aisle and didn't put her down until they were in the saddle room. "We'll find a bite of carrot, and you can pet their wee noses. Perhaps I'll sketch them for you one day soon."

Admiring horses from a distance was one thing, but Maeve knew as well that horses—especially young horses who had yet to learn their manners—could nip when fed treats.

"Maybe we're not supposed to spoil their lunches."

The door to the saddle room was closed, which meant nobody would see them taking the carrots, and yet, Maeve felt vaguely uneasy. Like when Bridget fought with her husband. Like when Maeve hadn't really told anybody where she would be.

"Them wee beggars would eat every blade of grass in the shire," Uncle said, producing three carrots from a sack. "Come along, Maeve, and meet the horses you might someday ride. This excursion can be our little secret."

He took her by the hand, and Maeve went, because all misgivings aside, meeting horses she would ride was a wonderful offer, one she could boast of to Lachlan.

Though she likely would not be telling Brenna or Michael about this outing. Uncle Angus had said it was to be a secret. She let Angus take her hand and lead her out to the paddocks behind the barn.

❧

A soldier occasionally left important parts of himself on the battlefield—a hand, a foot, an eye, the ability to hear out of one ear. Casualties were more often intangible, however—a sense of humor, the ability to sleep through the night or tolerate thunder.

Michael knew of no veteran who'd lost the ability to ask a simple question, and yet, sitting in the pub among his own people, a pint of fine summer ale before him, Michael couldn't seem to find the words.

"You were married."

Across the scarred table, Hugh MacLogan studied the outline of a thistle gouged into the table. "Aye. For five years."

For a widowed Highlander, this amounted to a speech, so Michael was encouraged to try again. "You had a wedding night."

MacLogan stuck a finger in his mug and licked foam from the end. He was being courteous, a casual interest in ale being less rude than staring at the poor sod with the unconsummated vows.

"Aye. *We* did."

Somebody two tables down let forth a magnificent burp, which sparked a spate of admiring comments about the burper, his mother, and his digestion in general.

"I have not yet had—Brenna and I have not had the pleasure of a wedding night."

Michael spoke softly, lest the state of his marriage become common knowledge. The people in this tavern would not understand why their laird had neglected his lady. Despite his glib reasoning before Brenna about not wanting to leave her with child, Michael had never examined too closely why he'd left without consummating his marriage.

"That explains a few things," MacLogan observed. "Snug's in want of use."

The snug would be more private, so Michael joined his cousin-by-marriage in the nook at the end of the bar.

"Your ale didn't agree with you?" MacLogan asked as he slid onto the bench.

Michael retrieved his drink from their table, then took the opposite bench. "The ale is quite good."

He'd sounded bloody English with that pronouncement. MacLogan was laughing at him too, but the bastard was silent about it—damned Scottish of him, to laugh only on the inside and make a man squirm with his confessions all the more.

"You're looking to me for marital advice, *Laird*?"

Such delicate irony. "I'm looking to you for advice regarding your cousin, whom you've spent more time around in the past decade than I have."

"Right. Here's some advice, then: treat Brenna right or I'll kill you. Dantry will dig your grave, and Neil will dance upon it. Fine dancer, is our Neil. He might even pipe you on your way."

More courtesy. "Precisely because you *do* care about her, I'd appreciate any insight—" Bloody damn. Abruptly, Angus's wifeless state did not loom as such a trial. "Brenna's skittish as hell."

"Maybe she wouldn't be so *skittish* if her husband hadn't turned his back on her for nigh ten years. Just a thought."

Michael stalled by taking another sip of his ale. A barmaid, sturdy, buxom, and dark-haired, sauntered toward the table, but something in MacLogan's expression must have dissuaded her.

"Brenna is entitled to be exceedingly vexed with me. I was gone too long, I didn't write enough, and I should be made to pay in the coin of her choosing for as long as she pleases."

"Damn right. With interest."

"She wants our marriage to work, though. She's said as much, and yet, she doesn't...I can't...."

Behind them, a series of greetings indicated more custom had arrived for the noon meal.

"Brenna has her reasons," MacLogan said. "If she's said she'll have you, then you're as good as had, but you'll have to talk to her if you want to know her secrets. Her lot hasn't been easy, and her trust is worth earning. If she does part with those secrets, just recall it's you she protected with her silence. Dantry! Neil! The laird's buying a round for the house."

A cheer went up, and Michael lifted his mug in acknowledgment. A few pints of ale was a small price to pay for confirmation that Brenna was not merely reticent with him; she was secretive.

Michael turned to greet MacLogan's brothers, the smile freezing to his lips. Dantry was still growing into his muscles, though he had his brother's height and red hair. Neil, however, was big, had dark auburn hair, and was by no means a stranger to Michael.

Even though Michael had seen Neil MacLogan in his nightmares for nearly ten years, he stuck out a hand in greeting anyway. Neil was Brenna's family, and thus Michael's family too.

❧

Brenna floated through her day, occasionally touching her fingers to her lips and wondering how married people got anything done. A few kisses—a few wonderful, lingering, marvelous kisses wrapped in her husband's strong arms—and Brenna had gone daft.

This was how Hugh had felt about his Ann, how—once upon a time, long ago—Goodie MacCray had felt about Donal. A feeling more blessed than sunbeams, even more blessed than the fresh breeze whipping off the loch and setting the Brodie pennant to flapping against the flagpole above one corner of the parapet.

The feeling had grown even better, when Michael had framed her face with his hands and touched his mouth to hers, slowly, deliberately. She'd peeked and found him watching her, his concentration ferocious and tender all at once.

That kiss—her pleasure in it, Michael's lips curving against hers when she'd grabbed him by the hair and kissed him back—proved so much was possible for them that Brenna would never have dreamed they could have.

A kiss like that was a foundation, upon which hope and joy and—

Brenna's mental effusions evaporated, between one feathery, lovely thought and the next, for out behind the stables, Angus Brodie walked in from the paddocks, carrying a child on his back.

A girl child.

Since Michael's return, Brenna had lapsed in her vigilance. She hurried down through the castle and across the bailey, too sick with dread to castigate herself for that now, and too angry.

She forced herself to emerge from the stables at a dignified pace. "Maeve Brodie, you are old enough to walk."

Angus sauntered along, making no move to put the girl down. His hands were laced under the child's bottom, while Maeve's arms were around his neck.

"It's a long way in from the yearling paddocks, Brenna. You'll not begrudge a wee child a piggyback ride, now will you?"

Damn him. He manipulated and implied and finagled until his actions were above reproach, kindly even, and Brenna was cast in the role of villain or incompetent.

Sometimes both, if Angus was in a particularly nasty mood.

"Put the child down, Angus. She told no one where she was going, and she knows better. I'm frequently on the parapets, and can see disobedience and foolishness when it goes skipping across my bailey of an afternoon."

The girl wriggled down and stood beside Angus with her hand in his. The sight nearly caused a reappearance of Brenna's noon meal.

Maeve hung her head and scuffed her boot heel in the dirt. "I'm sorry, Brenna. I wanted to visit with Wee Bannock, and——"

Because Brenna had once been a small, lonely girl in Castle Brodie, she could finish the sentence: and Uncle Angus promised me some treat, some special outing, that my young conscience could not withstand. Brenna saw that the outing had not taken untoward turns, either, which was a relief so vast it would fill the loch.

Brenna saw as well when Angus gently squeezed the girl's hand, a signal to Maeve not to implicate Angus in her first failed attempt at truancy.

"I know better," Maeve said, dropping Angus's hand. "I'm sorry."

She would know better still before the day was over.

"To the castle with you, Maeve, and wait for me in the solar. You are not to go in through the kitchens, either."

Where Cook would fuss and cluck, Lachlan would sympathize, and Michael might interfere, if his business in the village were concluded.

Angus at least waited until Maeve scampered off before he marched up to Brenna and stood breathing pipe smoke and lemon drop at her.

"You have no say where that child is concerned, Brenna."

"She cannot be wandering off. She's new here. She could get lost, hurt, or *worse*."

He gave her a strange look, part humor, part convincingly honest regret, and part glee, because he no doubt knew what proximity to him did to Brenna's insides.

"You honestly believe I'm the worst thing that could happen to a wee lass who's wandered to the foals' pasture of a summer's day, Brenna? You wound me, and all over a few silly moments years ago, which your female imagination has inflated past all reality. Allow me to remind you of some relevant facts: my father and brother were laird here, your husband depends on me for guidance when it comes to the estate, and if I take a notion our best bottom land cannot be wasted on cow pastures, then your cousins—the last of your clan to stand with you in this shire—will be on the next boat out of Aberdeen."

For Brenna to counter with scathing indignation would only please him. To kick him where she should have kicked him fifteen years ago would enrage him.

"Am I supposed to choose my cousins over that innocent child, Angus? For I will not." She had contemplated killing him on many occasions now that she'd grown older. The notion comforted far more than it appalled. With Angus gone, Maeve would be safe, and Brenna's cousins could raise their cows.

Though Michael would not understand, and the justice of the peace might have something to say about it.

Perhaps Angus saw the speculation in her eyes. Saw that the adult woman was gradually weaning herself from the fears of the young girl.

"You daft woman, have you told your husband about the money you lost us all those years ago? Told him how bitterly we've struggled thanks to your arrogance and incompetence? Why don't you worry about that, instead of a little walk to the paddocks, which—must I remind you?—are also visible from your parapets, among many other places?"

He shook his head, his attitude not so much disgusted as *disappointed*, for which Brenna purely, cleanly hated him.

When he'd stomped off, kilt swinging for want of a sporran to hold it decently in place, Brenna stood for long moments, breathing her rage into submission.

Rage could be a fine thing. Rage had kept her alive when she'd been so ashamed she'd dreamed of flying off the parapets to a place where nothing hurt, and young girls didn't have to endure behaviors they shouldn't understand.

She'd been angry at Angus for years, angry at the old laird and his lady, and then angry at Michael too, though he, of all of them, was blameless. She would be angry a bit longer, despite Michael's return, and despite his marvelous kisses.

As Brenna gathered her tartan shawl about her and pondered the scold she'd visit upon Maeve, Neil MacLogan emerged from the trees, silent as a cat. If he ever smiled, he'd be the handsomest of Brenna's cousins. He wasn't smiling now.

"Were you spying on me, Neil?"

"Was he bothering you?"

While Brenna's animosity toward Angus was consistent and fortifying, Neil's antipathy toward the older man was a seething, dangerous presence in the back of his eyes. The sight was far more attractive to Brenna than it should have been.

She started walking in the direction of the stables, much of her joy in the day contaminated by a few minutes in Angus's company.

"He made a fool of me. I came down here prepared to tear a strip from him for leading Maeve astray, when all he'd done was carry her in from the foals' pasture." He hadn't had to pluck the child from the castle, hadn't had to entice her in the least. Angus was nothing if not patient and observant.

Neil fell in step beside her. "You won't let me kill him."

This was also true. "He doesn't need killing, he needs watching." Constantly, unceasingly.

"He seems to understand that."

"Maybe he's getting old." People outgrew their wickedness, or were cut down by it. The gallows seldom ended a long life.

For the length of a paddock, Neil kept his silence, and it was too much to hope that he'd drift off without sharing more of his thoughts.

"Don't tell yourself he's getting old, Brenna. Age won't stop Davey MacCray from craving his liquor, and Angus is the same way, only worse. He watches and waits, like an ugly sea beastie under his rock, until somebody lonely, invisible, and hurting wanders by or is late on their rent, and then he devours his prey."

Brenna had never asked what Neil had seen, what he'd heard in the village. This was as honest as he'd been with her, and it was more than honest enough.

"I won't let this happen again, Neil. You need not warn me."

And still, Neil prowled along at her side, big, dark, and quietly, lethally angry. Nobody built a stone wall as sturdy as Neil MacLogan did, or as quickly. Brute strength was part of it; he also had sheer, unrelenting focus too.

"I heard him threaten you, Brenna. Heard him threaten *us*." Neil used the Highland version of us, *us MacLogans*. The sole remnants of the clan in these parts, which included Brenna, apparently, at least in Neil's thinking.

"You've paid your rent, and Michael's here now. Angus can't throw you off the property merely because he's peevish with me."

Neil stopped her before they gained the barn. Inside, some unhappy horse kicked rhythmically against the wall, a usually docile beast turned violent for the sheer, bored hell of it.

"If Angus thinks he can't come after us cousins, then he's all the more likely to come after you, Brenna. He'll whisper his lies into Michael's ears, bring up the past as if it happened yesterday, discredit you and find ways to turn your husband from you. When that happens, you come to us."

She should have appreciated such an offer—Hugh

had never been as explicitly supportive—but instead, Neil's words scared her.

"Michael is a good man, and he's my husband." Though if she had to choose between Michael and her cousins? Between Michael, and Lachlan or wee Annie?

Neil shocked her then, twice. First, he shocked her by smiling, a slow, sweet smile devastating in its sadness. Second, he kissed Brenna on the cheek.

"I was a good man once too, Brenna Maureen MacLogan Brodie, and you *are* a good woman."

He sauntered away, into the barn, and soon the horse stopped its kicking, while Brenna remained between the paddocks, wondering how in the world she would tell her husband—before Angus did—that she'd betrayed her people to the tune of hundreds of pounds they could ill afford to lose.

Nine

AN EXTRA ROUND OF ALE MADE THE TAVERN A MERRY place at midday, though Michael knew better than to linger. He'd be toasted into standing for another round, and then another. Somebody would alert Davey MacCray that the pipes were needed, and soon nobody's afternoon would be productive and everybody's wives would be wroth with the laird.

He walked out into the bright afternoon sunshine, a Gaelic blessing ringing in his ears.

A kiss from his wife, a toast from his people, and life was good.

"Showing the flag before the troops, are ye?" Angus fell in step beside him, and the glow of the day dimmed. Angus would have been tolerated among the good spirits inside, much as Michael had been tolerated among his French and English confreres, but never welcomed.

"Angus, good day. I wanted to discuss cows with Hugh MacLogan, and a pint or two seemed in order." He'd *meant* to discuss cows with MacLogan anyway.

"A bit of fraternizing on the laird's part makes

sense when he's been off to war. A henchman's role is different."

Angus had apparently appointed himself to the role of trusted delegate. They gained the trees at the bottom of the hill, and in the shade, even the summer day bore a slight chill.

"My return will change things, Angus. I appreciate that you've taken an interest in the estate in my absence, but you've earned the right to pass that burden to me now." Such diplomacy. Michael's former commanding officer would have been proud of him. Of course, St. Clair had also excelled at the delicate art of torture.

"I will pass the estate burdens to you, gladly. Particularly if you think cattle can thrive in a land that knows much more of winter than any other season."

Michael said nothing. The Highland cow had been a staple of the crofters for centuries and gave birth happily in blinding snow, which was not at all the point.

"How are the plans coming for your wee party?"

"I'm on my way to discuss that very topic with my lady wife." And perhaps to cadge a few more of her fierce, sweet kisses.

"You're wise to keep your hand in. Brenna's a good girl, and she'll want very much to impress you, but you mustn't let her be too extravagant. Folk will take it amiss."

Angus fell silent as the path up the hill reached its steepest point.

"We're to celebrate my return, but not too lavishly?" Though hadn't this celebration been Angus's idea in the first place?

"Aye, that's it exactly. Ever since— On second thought, Brenna won't want to appear unthrifty, so likely I'm worrying for naught." Angus made a great production of huffing and puffing, when Michael damned well knew his uncle was healthy as a mountain goat.

Also crafty as a fox. Michael took the bait anyway. "Ever since what?"

"Brenna will tell you in her own time. We had a spot of trouble a few years after you left, and people in these parts have long memories. Brenna was little more than a girl, and she doesn't deserve to be held accountable for ancient history, but she's a MacLogan. They were never a very trustworthy bunch."

As if the Brodies had never shifted allegiance? Never made pacts with the various devils who'd taken a hand in Scottish politics? And in what corner of Scotland had less than a decade ever qualified as ancient history?

They crested the hill, the view of the village below and the fields and loch beyond steadying Michael. It was good to be home, and unlike those fellows in the pub, Angus gave his loyalty freely and did not expect Michael to still be earning it when his grandchildren were climbing this hill beside him.

"Why don't we stop by the dower house, and I can retrieve some of the ledgers you've stored there?"

"Those dusty old things?" Angus snorted. "You aren't so very anxious to return to your bride, are you, then?"

"I'm very anxious to return to my bride, but if I have those ledgers to study, then I also have an excuse to remain at the castle, rather than hare all over the shire trying to look busy."

Which seemed to be what Angus's day consisted of, come to think of it.

Angus's smile made him look very like Michael's father. "She's training you already. Good for our Brenna, I say. Come along, then."

The dower house sat just outside the bailey, the location chosen by Michael's mother. His father had groused and stomped about the castle, complaining about the expense, but he'd spared no effort to please his wife.

"You'll wait here," Angus said as they reached the door. "A bachelor household isn't always prepared for company, and it's a fine day to enjoy the fresh air." He winked and disappeared into the house, so Michael took a seat on the front steps.

It *was* a fine day to enjoy the sunshine, and even if Michael had wanted to see the inside of the house that his mother had fitted out down to the last teacup and table runner, Angus was entitled to his privacy.

Michael could visit the dower house anytime, and Brenna awaited him at the castle—Brenna and her kisses.

❧

"I've missed you, Wife."

Strong arms encircled Brenna's waist from behind. Her inclination to struggle was checked at the last instant by two things: Michael's vetiver-and-lavender scent enveloped her at the same moment she would have raised her foot to stomp on his arch, and Michael's mouth landed on the slope of her shoulder.

Already, she knew him by his kisses.

"You miss me after a few hours in the village?"

"I miss you after a few minutes in the village. Let's go to our rooms." He growled his suggestion against her neck and let Brenna feel the rising evidence of his arousal against her backside.

She wanted to go to their rooms, though they'd have plenty of privacy here in her solar. Wanted it badly, but alas, not for the same reasons he did. And yet, she made no effort to leave his embrace.

"You randy pestilence, I have work to do."

"So do I. We can do it together, in bed. I've ever been enthusiastic about reading in bed."

To be teased by one's husband was a lovely addition to the day—provided he was teasing, and Brenna could not be certain he was.

"You've been swilling ale, Michael Brodie. Shall I read you temperance pamphlets in bed?"

"I've been missing my wife." He turned her by the shoulders, and with no more warning than that, covered her mouth with his.

Maybe the ale had made him a bit clumsy; maybe the altercation with Angus had left Brenna more off balance than she knew. In an instant, Michael shifted in her mind from a teasing husband to a menace she could not control, a menace she'd faced many times without warning, and in circumstances she could not flee. When Michael's arms tightened around her, she struggled in earnest, the only thought in her head to get free.

"Brenna, calm yourself." Michael had her loosely by the upper arms, his green eyes full of concern. "I seek only your kisses."

She could not break his hold, could not—

"Wife, you'll do yourself an injury. Please cease your thrashing and—"

His pleading tone penetrated her panic, and Brenna abruptly went still. "I'm sorry. You startled me."

Michael's hands dropped, slowly, the way a canny groom backed out of a stall when a green horse had turned aggressive.

"Do you want to hit me, Brenna?"

His tone was cautious, full of bewilderment, but also holding a note of self-doubt, and that tore at Brenna's composure in a whole new way.

"I will never intentionally strike you, Husband. Will you sit with me?" Because her knees were weak, and the last thing she wanted, the very last thing, was for him to leave her alone just then.

He held out a silver flask to her, one engraved with the Scottish thistle. "Ladies first."

Brenna helped herself to a bracing tot of fine potation, watched as Michael did the same, then took a seat on her sofa. That shared nip of good whisky restored something to her, and Michael's taking the seat beside her restored something more.

"Do I need to kill somebody, Brenna Maureen? Somebody who presumed in my absence to pester you with attentions you'd not encouraged?"

His trust in her was every bit as startling as his embrace had been.

"You're sure I was so loyal?"

He grabbed her hand and kissed her knuckles. "I love you."

"Husband, your flask please." For the day had

indeed taken a disconcerting turn. Several of them. "What has that last declaration to do with anything?"

She wished she'd had warning he was about to gift her with this pronouncement, so she might have anticipated his words. He'd said them once before, and she hadn't known they were coming then either.

He passed her his flask, and Brenna had to disentangle their hands to uncap it. The second sip tasted every bit as fortifying as the first.

"More for you?"

He shook his head and set the flask on the table before them. "Did you tat that lace?"

The table runner was russet blond lace, not particularly intricate, but pretty. "The first winter you were gone. Why did you say...what you just did?"

"I *love* you, Brenna Maureen, and I *know* you. I know you are loyal to your bones, and that you are deserving of my loyalty as well."

Brenna did not have a strong head for drink, and she had even less ability to withstand the inebriating effects of her husband's forthright speech and affectionate manner.

"You've implied you remained faithful to me when you went soldiering, and I thank you for that."

The words were inadequate, because as handsome as he was, as charming as he could be, Michael had had offers. Brenna knew he'd had many offers.

"Faithful and loyal are not the same thing. You are my wife. You deserve both, and while I was keeping my breeches buttoned, you were without benefit of my protection here. This brings us back to my earlier question: Who needs killing? Please tell me the bastard has taken ship for the New World, lest I mark my return here with a bit of homicide, upon which the fellow's relatives and the justice of the peace would surely frown."

Abruptly, entire casks of the finest aged whisky were not sufficient to fortify Brenna against the confusion of the moment. She had never, not once, foreseen that Michael might invite her confidences this way, much less that she'd want to surrender them.

For which Angus would, inevitably, have his revenge.

"There's nobody you need to kill. I've lived at the castle without family, more or less, since your father died, and I'm skittish, is all."

The word had his brows twitching down. "I do not care for this skittishness, my lady. Do you know how to defend yourself?"

"I know a man is vulnerable behind his sporran."

"I told you that when you were fifteen." This recollection seemed to settle Michael, though he reached for Brenna's hand again, and this time kept his fingers entwined with hers. "I've learned more tricks since then, the camp followers being extremely resourceful women when needs must."

Brenna stroked her fingers over his knuckles. He'd scraped his middle finger sometime this morning, and pinched some heather, guessing by the scent of his hand. "They used these tricks on you?"

"They did not, but among the soldiers—some of the soldiers—the attitude toward the women was that their lot was not so difficult. The most trying fate to befall a wife was that her fellow might be struck down in battle, in which case, she could choose from every other worthy in the regiment and be married again the next week."

"Were they married, these sentimental fools who viewed women with such compassion?"

"Some were." He leaned forward to move his flask off the table runner, but did not turn loose of Brenna's hand. "War can bring out the worst in men, as well as the best. I was glad you were not there, Brenna. I missed you badly, but I was glad I'd spared you that life."

Brenna didn't take that gladness away from him. Maybe someday, but not on this startling, disconcerting, bewildering day.

"You brought ledgers here. Was that the reading in bed you mentioned earlier?"

"Ledgers are a way to catch up, though an imperfect way. Will you show me yours?"

Subject safely changed, for which Brenna could only be glad. "Of course. Anytime you please." Though she hoped he didn't intend to read her ledgers in bed.

"Right now, I please to have a different discussion with my wife."

And maybe someday she'd learn to recognize when Michael was teasing, and when he was in deadly earnest.

"About?"

"Did you know that a man's eyes are nearly as vulnerable as his ballocks? That you can put him on the ground by striking the backs of his knees?"

Brenna fell in love with her husband at that precise moment, or realized she'd already fallen. As Michael prosed on about where exactly to strike a man's ribs so he might gasp for breath, Brenna became a bit breathless herself.

Michael's flask sat at a corner of the table, his ledgers were in a haphazard stack on her desk, and his hand was wrapped around hers. He would kill to protect her or avenge her honor, he offered her undying loyalty, and he knew precisely how to cheer a lady up when she'd made a complete hash of her husband's flirtations.

She loved him, and because she loved him, she would never call upon him to wreak the vengeance he so enthusiastically contemplated.

"So you don't dine at the castle, even now that the laird has come home? And you being his closest kin?"

Davey MacCray sounded reasonably sober, for which Angus was grateful. Drunk, Davey could be merry or mean; sober, the man maintained a shred of discretion.

Angus took his time tapping his pipe into his hand, letting all and sundry know he answered because he chose to, not because he owed the village drunk a reckoning.

"The laird and his lady are newly reunited after years of separation. Do you think they'd want me underfoot at such a time?"

A chair scraped back across the common, pretty young Dantry MacLogan getting comfortable for some eavesdropping.

Davey gave a humorless laugh. "Nobody wants you underfoot, auld man. You should learn to play the fiddle, and then you'd serve a purpose other than cantering about on your fancy black horse and tormenting the crofters with your greed."

The barmaid came around, topping up tankards— another pair of eager ears. Davey patted her fanny, which earned him a clonk on the side of the head with the pitcher. Something about the exchange made Angus feel more of an outsider than Davey's taunts ever could.

"How do you know I didn't win that horse in a card game?"

Davey took a considering sip of his ale and revealed the performer's inherent sense of how to grab an audience's attention.

"Are you saying you diced for that horse?"

"I'm asking a question." Because Angus hadn't won the blasted animal in any card game, and as sparsely populated as the Highlands were, gossip yet managed to travel from village to village and tavern to tavern with astonishing speed.

"And we all know"—Davey gestured with his mug toward the room in general—"that when Angus Brodie asks a question, we are bound to answer, lest we find ourselves strolling down to Aberdeen, our worldly goods upon our backs and winter hard upon our heels."

Coming here for a pint without Michael was a mistake, but Angus had wanted to gauge the mood in the village and had been thirsty for some summer ale.

"Your sons chose to leave the shire, Davey MacCray, very likely to get away from your drunken temper."

And now, no chair scraped, no barmaid swished

by. The room went quiet, suggesting Angus had made another mistake.

"Did you need to burn them out, Angus?" Davey asked softly, contemplatively. "Did you *need* to burn out two families, two hardworking young men just starting out with their wives and children? So you could run more sheep on their land and afford your fancy horse?"

Davey's boys had been gone for three years, three years that had seen a substantial increase in Davey's consumption of spirits.

"Your sons did not pay their rent. Honorable men pay their rent."

Davey took another sip of his ale, the quiet becoming so dense that Angus found it difficult to draw a full breath.

"When I see you on that fine, fancy beast," Davey said, "I do not think about being honorable, Angus Brodie. I think of my wee granddaughter, forever scarred in her mind and on her arms by the flames you had the King's man set. I think of my wife, crying herself to sleep for months after the boys took ship, boys who would have made a go of it, had you shown the least lenience with their rents. I think of Herman Brodie, coming back from selling the yearlings and telling us you spent good coin on a horse you didn't need—a gelding, not even fit for breeding stock. I do not regard honor for a moment when I contemplate these doings of yours."

Davey had the poet's ability to threaten murder without mentioning death, and yet Angus was more weary than worried.

"You're a drunk, Davey MacCray, and if your woman cried, it was because she was left behind by her own sons. What I spent on that horse was a pittance compared to what the laird's own lady cost this village, coin she has never repaid."

The quality of the silence changed, as Angus had known it would. Brenna's famous misstep had paid all manner of interest over the years, and at the appropriate time, Angus would put it to greater use yet.

Michael liked his wife, which couldn't be helped—he saw Brenna through a boy's adoring eyes, and in some ways, Brenna was still the girl he'd left behind. Angus could permit the liking up to a point, but he could not allow it to become trust.

Never that.

"Another round for my friend," Angus said to the serving maid. "Hatred works up a man's thirst, almost as much as an honest day's work can."

He left his half-finished ale on the table, mostly as a display of arrogance—it was superior ale—and rose to leave. Neil MacLogan had come in at some point and sat with his brother Dantry. He'd grown into a fine-looking man, had Neil, and that was just a pity all around.

"Gentlemen." Angus nodded. He paused by the door to button his coat, the night having turned damp and cool. Neil MacLogan rose, and for the first time, Angus felt a prickling of unease.

MacLogan did not approach him, but rather went to the table Angus had vacated and picked up the crockery mug Angus had been drinking from.

Angus slipped out the door as the sound of a mug

smashing to pieces on the hearthstones shattered the chilly night air.

~⌇~

A woman's ledgers revealed a lot about her. What she kept track of, how often she made entries, the accuracy of her tallies, and even the nature of her penmanship all merited study.

As did the nape of her neck.

"When will you allow me to dress your hair, Wife?" Michael stood behind his spouse as she sat at her vanity, his hand itching to take the brush from her. Another lady might have allowed it, might have regarded such high-handed behavior as the opening moves in a romp that left them both winded and spent on the bed.

Not his Brenna. She kept track of every penny; she made journal entries daily; her hand was always tidy.

"You've enough hair of your own," she said, tying off her braid with a green satin ribbon. "Why not see to it?"

He'd given her a ribbon of that exact color for her thirteenth birthday. Had saved up to buy it for her, had fretted over the perfect shade of emerald.

"Why don't I ask my wife to brush my hair? I'm particularly tired tonight."

She glanced at him in the mirror, though the view was likely of his bare belly. "You don't tie your hair back at night, so it will just become messy. I'll brush your hair out in the morning."

He put his hands on her shoulders—slowly, gently, lest he surprise her—and bent low to address her left ear.

"One of the many traits I admire about you, Lady Strathdee, is that if you say you'll do something, the thing is as good as done."

She didn't flinch away, so Michael had to be the one to straighten and busy himself banking the fire. As the Baron St. Clair's combination valet, man of business, and self-appointed bodyguard, Michael had dwelled in a household full of London servants. He hadn't realized how much he craved the sort of privacy he had with Brenna in their chambers.

"Did you find anything of interest in my ledgers?"

He'd found confirmation that a careful girl had become a meticulous woman, one who ran a household with efficiency and common sense.

"I found that reading over numbers makes my eyes cross, and I found out why quartermasters were invariably difficult. Window open or closed?"

She'd want it open. Brenna was a lady who craved fresh air.

"Open, but wait until the candles are blown out," she said, rising. "The nights will soon be getting longer, and I'm not sorry for it."

A husband could only be cheered by that pronouncement. He waited until Brenna had warmed the sheets and pillows before unpinning his kilt. In a state of breezy undress, he opened the window and lingered for a moment. "No moon tonight."

Perhaps his wife had coughed; perhaps she'd snickered.

"Come to bed, you daft man. You'll catch your death by that window."

A zephyr off the loch blew out the candle on the

sill, but Michael made a slow tour of the room, blowing out the others.

While Brenna watched him. She did not peek at his semierect cock; she frankly studied it, and his chest and belly and flanks too. A woman who kept tidy ledgers could be expected to take inventory.

"You are a handsome specimen, Michael Brodie." Brenna's tone rendered this observation something less than a compliment, not quite a complaint.

"I'm a tired specimen," he said, climbing in beside her. "Will you cuddle up, Wife?"

She answered him by draping herself along his side, her head on his shoulder.

"You want to have relations," she said, sounding as prim as a Presbyterian minister winding up for his second three-hour sermon of the day.

"Aye. With you. Eventually." Often too. "How are the preparations for the gathering coming?"

He'd thrown her off stride with that question, which wasn't what he wanted to ask her. He'd wanted to ask if she'd take his cock in her hand and relieve his sexual frustration, except she likely did not know how. He wanted to ask her to use her wide, lush, prim mouth to pleasure him, and to tell her—to hell with asking—to sink her fingernails into the muscles of his tired arse as she did.

The room was cooling down as the night air wafted in. Michael tossed back the covers so his left side was available to the chilly breeze while Brenna nattered on about some damned thing or other.

"...and heaven only knows if Davey will show up sober or drunk," Brenna was saying. "He's always worse this time of year."

Her hand caressed Michael's chest, her nails drifting through the hair trailing down the center to
his belly.

"Why is he worse?"

"His sons left in high summer. Angus would not
allow them to pay rent after harvest, like everybody
else. They'd taken possession of their crofts in high
summer, and Angus said the rents were annual.
Without a crop ripe to sell, they could not make rent,
and so they emigrated. Angus had their crop harvested
by the remaining tenants."

The chilly breeze barely registered against Michael's
lusty inclinations, but something cool in Brenna's tone
did distract him.

"You are angry about this." Michael was angry
about it too, if the situation had been as Brenna said.
Angry, furious, and heartsick.

"Angus wanted the land for his damned sheep, so
he burned Davey's boys out. If Davey hadn't run into
the flames to retrieve the youngest, the girl would
likely have perished."

This went on all over the Highlands, had been going
on all over the Highlands for decades if not centuries.

With one difference. "If they could not afford to
pay the rent, how could these families afford to take
ship, Brenna? How is it they did not join the hordes of
Highlanders starving in the cities or trying to live off
kelp and salted mackerel on the coast?"

"They could afford passage to Baltimore."

Nowhere in Brenna's careful ledger had she tracked
the funds that would allow such an undertaking, and
yet, Michael was sure she'd provided these families

what they needed to leave the shire, and likely to find a decent start in the New World.

"Angus should not have burned them out," Michael said. "My father never burned out anybody who was making an honest effort. Never. If the old laird made an example of the rare slacker, he made sure the family was provided for first. We don't burn out our own because they've fallen on hard times."

Angus would have known that.

"We should not speak of upsetting matters when it's time for sleep," Brenna said. "You had best kiss me to take your mind off burnings and mayhem."

Daft, dear woman. "You think a kiss good night will settle me down?" The topic under discussion had settled him down—some.

"Perhaps a kiss good night will settle *me* down."

Michael seized on this opportunity, because the nights were, indeed, getting longer.

"Brenna Maureen MacLogan Brodie, if you've a mind to kiss your husband, you needn't go mincing about, hinting and suggesting. I am yours to kiss at your whim and pleasure. God knows, you did without my kisses long enough. I'd never begrudge you such a small thing now."

He expected her to roll over in puzzled silence. He expected he'd have to go sit in the windowsill until his ballocks froze to the size of raisins. Perhaps a swim in the loch—

The covers rustled. A warm female breast brushed over Michael's arm. Soft fingers feathered his hair back from his brow, and the merest touch of lips graced his mouth.

"I don't know how to ask, Michael. I don't know what to ask *for*."

A man should be honest with his wife, particularly when she demonstrated such courage.

"Brenna, kiss me, please. I'll go mad if you don't kiss me right now."

He went mad anyway, waiting for her to gather yet more courage, to touch her lips to his once more. She was shy and careful and *naked*.

Very, very naked, though Michael had no idea when she'd managed that feat of marital magic.

Michael lay on his back, heart pounding, as Brenna learned the shape of his mouth with her own. She licked, she sucked on his top lip, then the bottom, then went a-plundering over his brow to take his earlobe between her teeth.

"I am so proud of you." Michael was proud of himself too, for not closing his hand around the luscious weight of her bare breast.

Brenna swung a leg across his thighs and mounted him. "Because I give our people safe passage across the sea?"

"That too." He closed his eyes, lest he be enthralled by the glints of gold and scarlet the firelight found in her braid.

She hiked the covers over him, including his chilled left side, then leaned down, grazing his chest with lovely, warm, soft breasts. "You're becoming aroused. You desire your wife."

Not a sermon this time, but curiosity and more pride. She was pleased to be tormenting him, and he'd soon be hard as a pike staff.

"Shall I arouse you too, Brenna Maureen? A husband isn't worth the name unless he pleases his lady."

Her answer was to sit up, so the evidence of his arousal was snugged against her sex. "Give me your hands, Husband."

Michael gave her his hands and a bit of his heart. She settled one of his palms over each breast, experimentally, and his cock leaped.

"Touching me did that to you?"

"Aye."

"Touch me some more."

Ten

BRENNA'S BREASTS HAD BEEN HER SALVATION: HER breasts and her height. Women had breasts; girls did not. Girls were small, flat-chested, and invisible. A tall, shapely woman was noticed, and in that notice lay measures of freedom and safety.

These realizations had come upon Brenna slowly, dimly, as she'd seen that for one man, her developing breasts had not been objects of curiosity or desire, but rather, disappointment—disgust, even. She'd loved her breasts ever since.

"Brenna Maureen." Just that, her name, but uttered like a prayer, while Michael treated her breasts to a slow, warm caress that could only be called reverent. "Kiss me, please."

She loved her breasts, and loved Michael too. Loved that for all he'd gone for a soldier, he would never force her, never tell her to hush and be still while he stole from her what should only be freely given.

He levered up to nuzzle her jaw, asking for kisses when he might have demanded them.

"I won't break," Brenna whispered, brushing her mouth over his. "I'm not that fragile."

She wasn't that fragile *any longer.* As Michael's tongue delicately traced her lower lip, Brenna realized that all his years away had served a purpose. Ten years ago, even five years ago, she could not have been a true wife to her husband.

But she could be now.

"Tell me," Michael said, closing a thumb and forefinger over her nipple. "Is that what you want? More? Less?"

"Both," she said, bracing herself on her elbows. "Both breasts at the same time. And your kisses."

For a man who'd been years without female company, Michael was good at making love. He could fondle her breasts with both hands, kiss her, and shift about beneath her in such a fashion that Brenna lost track of the specifics and surrendered to a general pleasuring.

For long minutes, she kissed him while he stroked her breasts, teased her nipples, and undulated that male part of him against Brenna's increasingly damp sex. Brenna sat up, the better to grab a much-needed deep breath. "Perhaps we should close the window, and some of these covers are—"

Michael drew a finger down the midline of her brow. "Stop weighing and measuring. Every knife, fork, and spoon will still be in its appointed drawer come morning."

Brenna's wits had abandoned their assigned drawer, and for once, this made her happy. "I want to make love with my husband, and he has yet to explain to me—"

Michael's thumb glided up the crease of her sex. "When I make love with you for the first time, it won't be with the candles out, under the covers, not even moonshine to illuminate your passions."

"Our passions," Brenna managed, but he'd touched her again with his thumb, a slick, sweet pressure and retreat that flung her entire mental store of silver high into sparkling beams of sunshine. "I want to see you too."

She would *need* to see him. Need to see that it was her Michael and no other with her in the bed.

"I'm right here, Brenna." He caressed her breast with just the right balance between assurance and entreaty. "Close your eyes."

"No."

By the light of the dying fire, Michael's smile bloomed, naughty, approving, and tender. "You disobey the husband you vowed obedience to?"

"In this bed, I obey no one but myself."

And his thumb, oh, his thumb. She obeyed that single part of him, moved into his touch in a rhythm that came from him like a gift, not a command at all.

She accepted that rhythm and made it her own.

"Brenna Maureen, dearest wife, I could not love ye more."

She wanted to hold the sight of Michael's fierce, tender smile close, wanted to cling to it, a final reassurance of the rightness of what she felt, but the pleasure was too much. She went soaring, into a brilliant, magical darkness of bodily joy, into a marital benediction for the trust she'd placed in her spouse and in herself.

Brenna did not recall closing her eyes, did not make a decision to moan softly as the pleasure took her, did not intend to collapse on her husband's chest as the bright, trailing streams of ecstasy faded like so many stars falling through her body.

And she most assuredly did not give herself permission to cry.

"Hush, now," Michael whispered, his hand drifting over her hair. "Settle yourself, and we'll talk."

Few men would have made that offer—few would have known it was needed.

Brenna used a corner of the sheet to swipe at her tears. "No words, Husband. Hold me."

Fundamental fairness suggested she ought not to be issuing orders if she wouldn't take any. She batted that sensible thought away and touched her tongue to the pulse in Michael's throat. This made him smile. She could *feel* that it made him smile, so she did it again.

Her husband held her; he kissed her temple; he stroked her hair. Never did a man put right so many wrongs without needing a hint how to go about it.

Brenna sorted through words and gestures that might communicate her vast appreciation for his consideration and generosity, but none accommodated both her full heart and her flagging courage. With her last waking shred of awareness, Brenna hoped falling asleep in Michael's arms would convey the many tender sentiments her silence did not.

❦

Never had torment and bliss so neatly intertwined to choke a man's selfish impulses and leave him aching in body and pleased with himself in spirit as he lay beneath his sleeping, sated wife.

Brenna had gone off like the fireworks displayed in such abundance in the victory celebrations, and yet, Michael wasn't entirely sure what foe had been vanquished in their bed.

Time and distance had gone down to defeat, surely, for nine years of separation might easily leave husband and wife with unbridgeable differences.

Fear had suffered a loss as well, fear that their marriage would limp along, a convenience and a convention rather than a covenant.

Brenna had also surrendered something to him, and he something to her—his heart, at least—and yet, Michael drifted off with a sense of having come upon a greater wilderness than he'd anticipated.

One he would explore, hand in hand with his lady wife.

They awoke to a brilliant sunny morning, some little brown bird singing its fool feathers off at the windowsill. Michael slid a hand over the warm female flank snuggled up to him. "Good morning, Lady Strathdee."

Her ladyship mumbled something, suggesting she didn't share the bird's, or her baron's, charity with the day.

Michael brushed Brenna's hair aside and spoke right against her ear. "Brenna Maureen, it's a beautiful day. Wake up and kiss the husband who loves you."

He nudged her with his half-erect cock, a reminder of what he had planned for her in the broad and beautiful light of day, and a distraction from the words she'd likely find a bit awkward the first thousand times he spoke them to her.

"Go away."

"I've married a shy woman." Though, bless her, not at all shy about giving orders in bed. "Perhaps a cup of tea will restore your courage."

A tousled head emerged from the pillows. "Tea won't help with that."

Trust would help; tea wouldn't hurt.

"Keep the bed warm for me, Wife." Michael tossed the covers aside and paraded to the door, returning with the breakfast tray and more than the beginnings of a morning salute.

Brenna's expression, however, was less than tantalized, and she was a lady who did enjoy her tea. Michael set the tray across her lap and sneaked a kiss to her cheek.

"Brenna, are you yet a maiden?"

The question needed to be asked. The way she stared at the teapot, at a loss for words, at a loss even for an expression, assured Michael it did.

"Why do you ask?"

Rather than climb in beside her, Michael perched at her hip and brushed her hair back from her cheek.

"A woman can be faithful and loyal to her husband, and yet, there are those who would trespass against her chastity. I went to war, Brenna. I saw what men will do when their morals have died on the battlefield. I wasn't here to protect you. If you came to any harm, the fault lies with me."

Those words needed to be said too.

She unwrapped the teapot and lifted it, as if to pour, though her hand shook. Rather than risk a scalding, Michael didn't interfere.

"I am yet a maid, as much as you left me a maid when you went to war," she said, setting the pot down and wrapping it back up in its white toweling. "Your absence did not put me at risk of harm."

She stirred cream and honey into the mug of tea, while Michael weighed her words. His wife was being kind, sparing him an accurate accounting. Perhaps she hadn't suffered the loss of her maidenhead, but somebody had trespassed nonetheless.

She offered him the tea. He wrapped his hands around hers and held the cup to her lips instead.

"Will you tell me, someday, Brenna, what burdens I left you with? I know it wasn't easy, and the telling won't be easy either, but a husband and wife should be able to talk about anything."

She held the cup to his mouth. "Will you tell me about France?"

Michael took a swallow of hot, sweet fortification. The covers had dipped, exposing the curve of a lovely, pale breast. He twitched them back up as Brenna returned their tea to the tray.

"Why would you want to know about privation, misery, cold, bad rations, and a lot of stinking, drunken—"

Her smile was slight, the first pale glimmer on the eastern horizon of humor. "It's the same thing. I want to know about you, and if that means accursed Frenchmen and sore, stinking feet, then that's what it means."

She had him, because he'd reveal every dingy, craven, weak corner of his soul to gain his wife's trust. Almost.

"France was complicated," Michael said, offering

her the tea. "Nobody warns a fellow that war is a great seductress. The handsome uniforms are the start of it. The sprightly tunes come into it too. Then you wake up one morning before you've even taken ship, and your job that day is to attend the execution of a deserter, or some poor blighter who took the King's shilling a few too many times. Every single man marches past the bullet-riddled remains, eyes right. You get a sense that this is serious business, that your part in it—even your small, bumbling part—matters greatly."

Brenna set the tray on his side of the bed. No more taking tea, then.

"And the battles?"

"The battles." God, the battles. Out on the window ledge, the bird was no longer warbling its joy for all the world to hear. "Even in the battles, there's seduction. You march about for weeks, and you hear rumors. We'll engage the enemy this week, perhaps tomorrow. There are skirmishes and raids, to get your blood up, and still, you do not *fight*."

How easily he'd forgotten this corrosion of the nerves, this gradual peeling away of the civilized man to expose the beast who could kill joyously.

Brenna took his hand. "But then you do battle."

"You fight. You fight past the limits of your endurance. You fight amid carnage of indescribable violence. The sieges were the worst, and there were many sieges."

He had gone to France gladly, to get away from the sieges. When Brenna drew him down against her, he went unresisting into her embrace too.

"You lost friends."

"No, I did not. In the space of his first battle, a soldier learns not to make friends. One has comrades, fellows, camp mates, drinking companions, all of whom can be killed in an instant, all of whom he would die to protect, but one avoids friendships."

And that habit apparently took a long time to shed. Brenna's arms came around him. Michael closed his eyes.

"These men who aren't your friends, whom you would die for, are they why you stayed away so long?"

The answer was complicated; the scent of Brenna's soft, soft skin was not. Heather, lavender, and a kind of safety of the heart enveloped him. Michael pillowed his cheek against her breast and sorted through the truths Brenna deserved to hear, and the ones he must not burden her with.

"In large part, yes, loyalty to my duties kept me away. In the company of his mates, the soldier feels alive. He feels that he's pulling his share of the most important load he'll ever bear. The misery proves that, you see. The worse he's wounded, the more urgently he wants to return to his unit, the more bitterly he feels entitled to engage the enemy again. It's like a drug—not the privation, not even the violence, but the responsibility. The feeling that every single soldier matters vitally."

Soldiers did not talk about this. Officers didn't even talk about it, and yet, generals and nations depended on it. Men sought that sense of responsibility even at the risk of their own lives, because within it lay assurances that a fellow, for all his shortcomings, was unassailably honorable.

False assurances though they were.

Brenna's arms came around him. "You were responsible, in France?"

"I was tasked with protecting one man, and he was devilishly difficult to protect. Many wanted him dead, even after the war ended. Especially then."

But had Sebastian St. Clair been more important to Michael than his home? Than his wife?

He would tell her the rest of it, the part about him being a coward and a fool and a bad husband—but not just yet.

"I run one castle," Brenna said, her embrace becoming fierce. "This castle is an entire world to me. I feel as if how I go about my duties here determines not only my own worth, but the course of the planet. If my ledgers did not balance, if I could not find a good price for our wool and lace, something awful would have happened to you. This is not rational, and yet, if harm had befallen you, it would have been my fault. All I could do to protect you was tat lace, add my figures, and save my coins."

He'd wanted her trust; she'd given him her troth long ago, and he'd gone larking off to play hide-and-seek with death in the frigid mountains of France.

"We have years," Michael said, kissing her throat. "God willing, we'll have years to protect each other and save our coins together. You brought me home safely, Brenna. You and your ledgers and your bargaining over wool. I'll never leave you."

The words eased something in him, set at rest the part of him that hadn't yet come home to stay, but was instead in readiness for Brenna to send him away.

He kissed her mouth, kissed the tea-sweetness of her lips, and secured a hand around the rope of her braid.

And those other reasons he'd stayed away, someday he might confide even those, when they were silly, distant overreactions she need not be troubled by.

Brenna got a nice firm hold of his hair and kissed him back. She was a fine, bold kisser, his wife, also patient, and clever with her tongue. The confidence of her kiss told Michael that now, right this very morning, he would make love with his wife.

And she with him.

"We need to move the damned tray," Michael muttered as his hand went questing among the bedclothes for the treasure of her breast. "I'll not be soaking the covers with tea and—"

Honey had possibilities.

Brenna's fingers glossed down Michael's ribs and wrapped right straight, directly around his burgeoning cock.

"You said we'd make love in the sunshine, Michael Brodie. Said our passions would enjoy the broad light of day, and the sun's well up."

She gave him a firm pull on the word *up*, and joy blossomed along with arousal.

"My wife heeds my words. I am the most fortunate of husbands." In so many ways. Michael lifted away and set the tray none too gently on the floor, then straddled his lady. "I'm going to kiss the hell out of you, Brenna."

Love the hell out of her too.

"Enough announcements," Brenna muttered, grabbing him behind the neck. "Get under these covers."

They started kissing and yanking at the covers and laughing, and then kissing some more as Michael got himself tucked in with his wife. He crouched over her, at which point she went still.

And silent.

"I'd rather you were laughing," Michael informed her right breast. "Or hauling me about, giving me orders. Perhaps I shall tickle you."

Her hands landed in his hair, so gently as to do nothing more than tug at his heart. "You're daft. I can't kiss you when you're intent on—when you're focused elsewhere, in case you hadn't noticed."

"I can kiss you."

Her stillness took on a different quality, a bodily listening, as Michael acquainted her breasts with the pleasures a man's mouth might bring them. He kept his cock from touching her, kept all of him from touching her, except for his mouth.

The bird hadn't resumed its fool chirping, which was fine, for the moment wanted all of Michael's concentration.

"Michael, stop." She panted this command, her hands stroking over his chin and jaw.

"Brenna, you can't mean—"

Oh, but she did, for some idiot was knocking softly but insistently at the door.

Michael raised himself up over his wife. "What the hell is it?" he bellowed, while Brenna mashed a smirk into his chest.

"Company, milady, milord," Elspeth Fraser's voice replied. "They arrived very late last night and said not to disturb you, a Lord and Lady St. Clair, from

London. We thought you would want to join them at breakfast."

⚜

Brenna's fury bewildered her.

"Did you invite these people?" she asked her husband.

He crouched back, his hair in disarray Brenna had caused, and his cock...

Brenna had plans for that part of her husband, and those plans did not include making polite conversation over breakfast with a pair of English interlopers.

"The last person I would expect to see this summer is the Baron St. Clair and his new wife."

And yet, Michael was apparently curious, possibly even pleased, to spend more time with this man who'd nearly cost Brenna her marriage. The longer Michael was home, the higher that toll loomed in her awareness.

"I suppose we'd best welcome them." She put not forbearance, but martyrdom in her tone, which caused her damned husband to smile.

"We'll have many sunrises, Brenna Maureen. I promise you that."

He'd promised to love and cherish her too. A lump rose in her throat for no discernible reason. She hated the Baron St. Clair, and his lady wife had much to answer for as well.

Michael hopped off the bed. "Come, love. Our first guests deserve nothing less than our cheeriest smiles."

He had the most interesting backside, beautiful even. Brenna smiled at that instead. "May a woman have a cup of tea before producing this cheery smile you seem to think is in order?"

Michael shrugged into his dressing gown. "She may share a cup of tea with her husband. I can't think what St. Clair is doing in Scotland, much less here in Aberdeenshire."

"Maybe he's passing through on a tour of the Highlands." In which case, the fool Englishman might have at least sent a note. Brenna left the bed and went to the window, letting the chilly breeze blow the last of the sleep from her mind.

"You resent this interruption," Michael said, his arms wrapping around her middle from behind.

"I hate this interruption," Brenna said. "The moment was right, and I wasn't sure we'd have any right moments."

Michael stood behind her, tall and solid, the waning evidence of his arousal snugged against Brenna's backside. "Will you ever tell me who treated you ill, Brenna?"

For years, Brenna had trotted about in her thoughts, like a kitchen dog turning a spit, wondering how things would have been different had Michael not left her.

"The fool made a nuisance of himself long before you married me, Michael." Cook had once muttered something about devils who preferred lamb to mutton. Brenna couldn't quite manage that much honesty.

The man at her back went still, and the breeze off the window had gone from refreshing to chilly. "Long before I married you, you were but a child."

"Girls grow up early in the Highlands. He hasn't dwelled at Castle Brodie for years. I'm happily married now, and we've guests waiting."

Only an invasion by this particular Englishman could have served to change the subject. Michael's arms dropped away.

"We do, but we'll revisit this topic, Brenna Maureen."

He disappeared behind the privacy screen, while Brenna stole a quick cup of tea for herself and made a second one to share with her husband. In a very short time, he was dressed and ready to descend to the breakfast parlor, while Brenna…

Dithered.

"Leave the damned bed for the maids to make," Michael said. "Shall I brush out your hair for you?"

"The maids do not come into this room, the footmen either," Brenna said, taking her turn behind the privacy screen. "I allow them into the sitting room, and they leave the coal and wood, the washing water, and the trays there."

As Brenna patted her face dry with a towel Michael had already used—vetiver was a lovely scent in the morning—her husband watched her over the top of the privacy screen.

"You're not a chambermaid, that you should be making beds and replacing candles."

"I like my privacy," she said, untangling her braid. "Sometimes you are entirely too tall, Michael Brodie."

He moved off, and Brenna heard the wardrobe opening. "You are particularly pretty in green, and today should be nearly warm. Will this cotton frock do? And this is a lovely cashmere shawl."

Brenna dealt with her hair, wondering why Michael had to be so eager to leave their bed and have breakfast with his Englishman. She allowed her husband to do up her hooks, her resentment mounting when he didn't even bother to tease her with a kiss to her nape.

"You look quite fetching," he pronounced as Brenna slipped into her shoes. Even his compliment irritated her.

"I care not for any man's estimation of my appearance, save yours. Your English friends are welcome, Michael, but their timing is horrid."

His smile was the sort of flirtation only a husband could turn on his wife. "Anticipation is a pleasure unto itself, my love. The sun shines at midday and afternoon as well as morning, you know." He turned to survey himself in the mirror. "Will I do?"

He smoothed his fingers over his hair, putting Brenna in mind of the bachelors who stood milling about the punch bowl at the infrequent local gatherings.

Brenna's husband was not eager to meet these guests; he was nervous of them. The knowledge came from the slight worry in his eyes, the brevity of his smile, the way he tugged at his handsome dark green paisley waistcoat.

"You'll do wonderfully," Brenna said, kissing his cheek. "My plaid shawl will serve for this occasion. The English are known to exalt appearances over practicalities, but we Scots are more prudent."

She passed him her dark green hunting plaid and held still while he draped it around her shoulders.

When Michael offered her his arm at the head of the stairs, she wanted to roll her eyes, because they were putting on a display for the dratted English invaders. Instead, she took her husband's arm and even allowed herself to lean on him, just a bit.

❧

A commanding officer looked after his men, though Sebastian, Baron St. Clair, had long since accepted that one subordinate regarded St. Clair's welfare his over-riding concern—despite any orders to the contrary.

"Who's the girl?" St. Clair asked his host as he and Michael Brodie—Strathdee, for God's sake—ambled toward the stables.

"What girl?"

"The little red-haired sprite who poked her head into the breakfast parlor, hung about in the doorway waiting to be noticed, then flounced away in a snit."

Michael came to a halt as an enormous draft horse was led by, silky feathers swirling about its enormous feet with each step.

"I didn't see her. That would be my sister Maeve. Your baroness is in good looks."

Sebastian might have bristled, to have his former valet, bodyguard, and factotum complimenting Milly's appearance, but for two things. First, Milly *was* lovely. Any man with eyes in his head could see that, and she grew lovelier by the day.

Second, Michael Brodie offered his compliment as small talk and only small talk. Milly could have sported three hideous heads, horns, and a tail, and Michael would have noted that she was in good looks.

Such was the effect of reuniting this soldier with the wife he'd never mentioned in all the years Sebastian had known him.

"Are we to engage in a footrace, Michael?"

"Perhaps." He marginally slowed their pace toward the stables. "I'm entitled to revenge for your sneak attack, St. Clair. 'The note must have gone astray'? Even your dear wife wasn't fooled. She'll have a few words with you in private for your rudeness."

Yes, she would have a few words with him in private. This penchant for private discussions was part of the reason her ladyship was in a nominally delicate condition.

"I was worried about you," Sebastian said, and he managed this disclosure with a feigned casualness learned on the battlefields and perfected in discussions with his wife. "You repair to the North, and I get not so much as a note confirming your safe arrival. Rude of *you*, some might say."

"I've been preoccupied."

Many a man had enjoyed similar preoccupation; few were so fortunate as to enjoy it with their very own wife.

They gained the stables, where the early morning activity of mucking, feeding, haying, and scrubbing water buckets had given way to the more placid tasks of bringing in the stock that had pastured overnight and turning out those who'd pasture by day.

"The light is different this far north, but the smells of a stable are the same," Sebastian remarked.

Michael stopped before the stall of a handsome, nervous bay. "You're different too, St. Clair. Millicent agrees with you. Marriage agrees with you."

"As it does with you."

Michael stretched his hand out to the horse behind the bars, and the beast spared him a glance but did not leave its pile of hay.

"My wife already knows how to manage me," he said, dropping his hand. "She grew up here from the age of eight, and had many years to study her prospective husband."

And yet, Lord and Lady Strathdee did not appear to be a settled couple or like people long familiar with each other. "Did you ever take leave, Michael?"

"I would have used every bit of it coming and going, and other than my own home, there was nowhere I wanted to go."

Sebastian's specialty had been interrogation, but it took no expertise at all to see that Michael was not only preoccupied, he was worrying a problem.

"Nonetheless, you love that woman to distraction. Was it really *that* important that you find your way to my command, Michael? You could have taken a position at the Horse Guards, for example."

"Patrick, mounts for his lordship and myself. We'll ride the Dee, and we won't need a groom."

A stable boy moved away toward the center of the barn, where a saddle room was most likely to be found. Michael took off in the opposite direction, toward stone-fenced paddocks out behind the barn.

"I was under orders," Michael said. "I took those orders seriously. I also had reasons to avoid my home, or I thought I did. I was an idiot."

Had Michael not taken his orders seriously, Sebastian would likely be dead.

"Did your idiocy have to do with that lovely redhead fluttering her eyelashes at you from over her teacup?"

"When did you start mincing along like some footman showing off new livery, St. Clair? I've yearlings to check on, and at this rate, winter will arrive before

I see them. And yes, my idiocy had everything to do with Brenna, and nothing at all."

An oak spread over one corner of a paddock, creating shade for a bench some wise soul had built likely centuries before. The scene was restful—horses lipping grass in the lush paddocks, birds flitting about between the barn and the branches of the oak.

While Michael was in a pucker over something. In years of privation at a French garrison, and more years of duels and difficulties in the wilds of London, Michael Brodie had never once been in a pucker.

"Do you know why I have arrived to your doorstep, Michael? Why I have brought my new wife, whose health is supposed to be delicate—though she scoffs at such a notion—hundreds of miles north, risking your wrath and handily earning your baroness's displeasure?"

"You surely did that—earned Brenna's displeasure."

Sebastian gestured toward the bench. "Shall we sit?"

Hospitality meant Michael must accommodate his guest's request, and the interrogator in Sebastian also knew that constraining the movements of a restless man meant words might escape that the man would otherwise keep inside.

Michael sat, his gaze going to the battlements where a pennant flapped in a crisp breeze.

"That flag did not fly from the time my father died until the day I arrived back here. That's the tradition, and Brenna would not have it any other way."

Sebastian took a place beside him, the stone making for a cold, hard seat, though Michael didn't seem to notice the discomfort.

"Why did you stay away from your home so long? You adore that woman, and in this environment, you move differently, you speak differently, you even look different." And Michael apparently cared not one whit why a commanding officer had traveled hundreds of miles with an expecting wife to enjoy the frigid summer air of Scotland.

Keen green eyes assessed Sebastian, the first direct look Sebastian had endured from his host. "Different, how?"

"More yourself. More a laird of Clan Brodie. You belong here. You didn't belong in London, and neither of us belonged in France."

Even mention of the country seemed to blight the pretty morning, but it felt good to say the words to the one person who could understand them.

"You belong with your Milly, and I belonged with my Brenna, though I handily forgot that bit of truth."

"A soldier's guilt at this late hour, Michael?"

Across the paddock, a pair of leggy chestnut yearlings began the sort of mock battle that honed the reflexes, built strength, and occasionally resulted in the ruin of a good animal.

"My wife told me this morning—as you were barging into my very breakfast parlor—that some fellow had made a nuisance of himself to her long before her marriage, though at some point, the blighter apparently emigrated."

"The lot of a female is seldom easy." Sebastian did not allow himself to reflect on what his Milly had endured, lest he take to kicking Michael's venerable granite wall.

"She was sixteen when I married her, and she confirmed that her troubles antedated our vows."

"Ladies can be very attractive at sixteen." Though Sebastian had never been drawn to youth in such abundance.

"You miss the point, St. Clair. When I went off to war, Brenna was apparently not troubled by any more fools. What sort of man pesters a very young woman—and Brenna's womanhood was yet developing when we married—but leaves her alone once she has no man on hand to protect her?"

The implication was disgusting, though the legal age of sexual consent was twelve. Michael was a friend, so St. Clair offered what comfort he could.

"The kind of man who desists once a lady's spoken for?"

"Brenna was engaged to marry me from the age of eight. She was a sweet, quiet, retiring little dumpling, and never gave anybody a bit of trouble."

Sebastian had watched the sweet, quiet lady over breakfast, and suspected she was capable of causing a good deal of trouble—now. He'd have to compare notes with Milly, though, when she'd finished her reconnaissance in the lady's solar.

"Your wife will tell you of her past when she's ready. You spoke vows years ago, but you're newly married. One has to unlearn the habit of silence, as you well know."

"Her cousin said as much, and warned me my wife's silence was a kindness. I am not owed any kindness by the wife I abandoned for years."

Soldiers were an interesting lot. They offered their lives for generals and kings who would not break bread with them; they fought harder battles upon coming home than they'd faced on foreign shores.

And never talked about any of it.

"You fought to keep that wife safe, Michael, and all the wives and children. Nobody broke up more domestic squabbles at the garrison than you, most of them without my having to say a thing. Your wife might like to know that about you."

"I think not." Michael rose and regarded the two yearlings rearing and squealing at each other when they might have been grazing or napping in the sun. "Talking to one's wife becomes a habit too, and there are some things Brenna doesn't need to know about why I left, and why I stayed away as long as I did."

Sebastian got to his feet, movement being a good idea after a man had done days of penance in a traveling coach.

"Perhaps you should trust your wife with those confidences, Michael. She might surprise you with a few more of her own."

Michael marched off, the yearlings continued their mock battle, and the Brodie pennant whipped and snapped above the battlements in a stiff, chilly breeze.

Eleven

"I WANT TO GO HOME," MAEVE DECLARED. EXCEPT, where was home? "When I was in Ireland, Bridget didn't yell at me for walking out to the paddocks, and Kevin gave me carrots and apples to give the horses."

Preacher was not impressed by this declaration. He continued to sit beside Maeve in the saddle room, licking the daylights out of his left paw. Preacher could eat mice; he did not have to brave a breakfast room with strangers in it—English strangers, who talked very oddly indeed.

"I hate Scotland. I shall run away."

The door to the saddle room opened, and Patrick, a red-haired groom, stood in the door. Patrick had a lot of freckles and he smiled. He had extra names for the horses, the same way Uncle Kevin had.

"The faeries have left a wee gift in my saddle room, and a great, fat banshee."

Preacher left off washing his paw and strutted out the door, and Maeve was sad to see him go.

"I'm not supposed to be here. I didn't tell anybody at the castle where I was going except Lachlan."

"Then you might scamper right back and no one the wiser." Patrick looped two bridles over his arm, suggesting somebody other than Maeve was going riding.

"I'm waiting for Uncle Angus." The idea came to Maeve on the moment, though in truth she'd been thinking to snitch a carrot to appease the hunger in her belly.

Patrick set the saddle he'd lifted right back down on its rack. "What in the world would ye want with that auld bugger?"

No smiles accompanied the question. "Uncle Angus is my friend. He introduced me to all five yearlings and said we could come visit them again, *anytime*, and he would sketch them for me too." He'd also teased Maeve about making a sketch of *her*, because she was such a bonnie wee lass.

The way Patrick glanced at the open door made Maeve wish even more that she'd never left Ireland, because something she'd said was creating a problem. Brenna's scold yesterday suggested everything Maeve said, did, wished, and forgot to do was always going to be a problem.

"Don't scold me. Uncle Angus is nice."

Patrick swore, the same curse Uncle Kevin used when a horse came up lame. Something about the Almighty and bullocks.

Patrick draped the bridles over the saddle and appropriated a place beside Maeve on the trunk. He smelled good, like hay and horses, and he had the long, bony wrists Maeve figured must come from being a groom.

"Wee Maeve, ye stay far away from Angus Brodie,

ye hear me? He's a cranky auld mon who has no patience for others, and thinks only of himself."

Patrick looked like he wanted to say more, but Maeve was glad he didn't. She liked Patrick, and she liked Uncle Angus.

Sort of.

"You shouldn't say mean things. Nobody is supposed to say mean things." And yet, everybody did.

"I'm saying a true thing, child, and this is also true. The laird is showing off his yearlings out back to the English lord. If ye get up to the castle straightaway, nobody will know ye came down to visit Preacher before brightening Cook's day with a visit."

Cook was nice, and Patrick was trying to be nice now too.

Maeve hopped off the trunk and left the barn, but the queerish feeling in her tummy wasn't entirely hunger. Nobody wanted her here, nobody liked her, and where she might have felt at home—in the barn, with the horses and cats—she wasn't supposed to go.

Preacher fell in step beside her, probably hoping to dart into the kitchens when Maeve slunk into the back hallway.

"I hate it here, and I'm planning to run away. You can come with me."

Except Preacher seemed very much at home at Castle Brodie, as did everybody else except—in some way Maeve couldn't put into words—Uncle Angus.

❧

"Is all to your liking, Lady St. Clair?"

The Scottish baroness was the soul of civility as

she sat plying her needle, though Milly had enjoyed warmer welcomes from her cat.

"Our rooms are very comfortable," Milly replied. "Breakfast was lovely, and you have a beautiful home." Though visiting the lady's lovely home now might have been the stupidest decision Milly had ever made—or allowed Sebastian to make.

"You're tired," Lady Strathdee said, putting her hoop aside. "Travel can be wearying. Perhaps you'd like to take a nap?"

What Milly would like to do was find her husband and cling to him, though he would pester her with well-intended questions, and Sebastian was very good at getting answers to his questions.

"I am tired," Milly said. "Sebastian and I haven't been married long, and though his company is a delight, in the confines of a traveling coach for days…"

Her hostess's smile bore the first hint of understanding. "Michael was gone for years, and though I am very pleased to have him home, he makes a deal of noise, tracks mud into Cook's kitchen, and renders the beginning and ending of the day a busier undertaking altogether."

"As does St. Clair," Milly said, picking up the lady's hoop and admiring a scene of a golden hart in clover. "I lived with my maiden aunts before joining the St. Clair household, and becoming Sebastian's baroness is an adjustment in many ways."

The solar was a lovely place, full of sun because of its location at the top of the keep, comfortably stuffed with pillows and cushioned chairs, and feminine in its green, cream, and gold color scheme.

"You weren't—" Lady Strathdee fell silent and rose, crossing to a desk that sported a number of ledgers. "You didn't *expect* to become a baroness?"

Milly suppressed a wince, while her hostess tidied up the ledgers, though they'd already been in two neat stacks.

"I still wake up every morning, having to recall that St. Clair has done me the honor of taking me to wife. Are you truly glad Michael has come home?"

The question might have provoked a retreat into Scottish reserve, which made the English variety look tropical by comparison, but instead, Lady Strathdee smiled.

"You used the word adjustment. I'd say it's more like my entire life has been upended, though it badly needed upending in some ways."

Another twinge hit Milly in a low, female place, but she'd been having queer pangs and twinges since she'd met her husband. "Shall we ring for tea?"

"Tea for you," her ladyship said with a significant look at Milly's raised waistline. "Michael said I'm to cosset you."

She tugged a green-and-gold brocade bellpull and got a look in her eyes that put Milly in mind of Sebastian on the scent of some answers, so Milly went on the offensive.

"How has your life been upended?"

Her ladyship took the seat at the desk, looking elegant and confident. "Michael sent no word he was coming north, though we knew he'd returned to England and remained with his commanding officer in London. We heard all manner of rumors, none of them pleasant."

Milly heard the sound of cannon swiveling on well-greased hinges. "That must have been difficult."

Her ladyship opened a ledger. "I was accustomed to his neglect by then. Michael was not a reliable correspondent." She ran her finger down the page, fine russet eyebrows knit as if the tally puzzled her.

"But he's back now, and not likely to leave anytime soon." Another twinge came, this one worse than the last.

"He's back," her ladyship conceded. "Nine years is a long time to roam. Castle Brodie has changed in those nine years."

Lady Strathdee—Sebastian said her name was Brenna—had changed in those years. Any woman would change between the ages of sixteen and twenty-five.

"Give it time," Milly said. "I love my husband to distraction, but I still find some matters difficult to discuss with him."

"My lady, are you well?"

Truly, Brenna Brodie had accurate aim. Milly was saved from an immediate reply by a knock on the door, heralding the arrival of the tea tray. Tea in Scotland apparently included scones, butter, strawberries, and honey, which—unlike the ham, bacon, and eggs at breakfast—had some appeal.

"I am—"

Milly's hostess put the tray down on the low table before the settee and crossed her arms. She was a tall woman, and wrapped in her dark plaid shawl, she put Milly in mind of a widow or a maiden aunt who'd seen enough of sorrow to withstand a few inconvenient truths.

"I am afraid I'm losing this baby." Mostly, Milly was afraid, afraid Sebastian would be upset, afraid this meant they'd never have a child, afraid this looming tragedy was her fault.

"Oh, my lady." Her hostess unwrapped the plaid shawl and swirled it around Milly's shoulders. The scents of heather and lavender came with it, soothing scents that eased the lingering upset caused by the smells at breakfast. "Shall we fetch his lordship?"

"No, please do not tell Sebastian." Because Sebastian would blame himself, and God knew what that would do to their marital intimacies. "I've been somewhat uncomfortable since I learned I was carrying."

Milly found a cup of hot, fragrant tea in her hands, with no idea how it had arrived there.

"Are you bleeding?"

Thank God for Scottish practicality. "Spotting. A little, but I didn't bring any cloths."

"Cloths we have. Spotting isn't necessarily a fatal sign. I've read every pamphlet and treatise I could find on the subject. The French have some good books, and we've a very competent midwife in the village."

The tea helped, and Lady Strathdee's brisk pragmatism helped too. Milly suspected notifying Sebastian would not help at all, though withholding this from him hadn't exactly been easy either.

"Can you send for the midwife and have her visit while the men are out riding?"

Her ladyship split a scone, applied butter and honey, and passed it to Milly on a plate adorned with porcelain roses. "I can send for her. Best I go fetch her myself."

Though Milly wasn't sure she even liked Brenna Brodie, she didn't want to be left entirely alone either. She wanted Sebastian, and that would not do.

"She won't heed a summons from you? Your husband is laird, isn't he?" The scone was ambrosial, and yet Milly knew she must not bolt her grain.

"You shall call me Brenna. I know you English like your manners and such, and we've just met, but I've only ever been Brenna. This baroness business—"

"I'm Milly, and baronessing is quite a lot of uphill work, even when one is madly in love with one's baron. Why won't the midwife come?"

Old hurt flattened Brenna's lovely mouth. She withdrew a silver flask from a skirt pocket and uncapped it. "Shall you?"

"No, thank you." Though Milly's estimation of Highland hospitality rose further.

"The midwife has reason to hate me, and in the seven years since that reason arose, has shown no sign of relenting in her ill will, nor is she alone in her lack of regard for the lord's wife."

Milly nibbled on her scone, and wondered what it must be like, to be lady of the manor, newly reconciled with your lord, honor bound to try for some heirs, and on the outs with the only midwife in the shire.

"Have some tea. Did you flirt with her husband? Dress her sons down for swearing in the churchyard?"

"I cost her her sons. She's not likely to assist me in bringing mine into the world."

Her ladyship—Brenna—showed no sign of making herself a cup of tea, so Milly fixed one for her. "You killed her sons? I find this difficult to believe."

And yet, clearly, Brenna believed it, or something every bit as bad.

"It has to do with money," Brenna said, accepting the cup of tea. "It all has to do with money. I was eighteen and trying to make the point that I was the laird's wife, though Michael had been gone for two years. I asked my cousins to escort me into Aberdeen with the wool harvest."

Aberdeen was a good sixty or seventy miles to the east and no easy journey.

"Drink your tea," Milly said, finishing her scone and deciding that she'd share the next one with her hostess.

Brenna held the teacup before her, like a chalice or a serving of woe.

"We traveled to the coast easily enough—the weather held fair—and we got a fine price for the wool, because we'd so much to sell at once. I was very pleased."

Milly set half a buttered scone on a plate, drizzled it with honey, and passed it over. "And then?"

"And then as I was riding home, I went ahead of my cousins. They were in want of one more pint to celebrate our success, while I sought to get home and brag on my bargaining abilities. Angus had scoffed at me, of course. I was too young, I was a woman, nobody would take me seriously, and the city was a dangerous place."

"I do not like this Angus fellow. Who is he?" Milly liked Scottish scones though, liked them quite well.

"Nobody likes Angus except Michael. Angus is the devil incarnate, the self-appointed land steward for the Brodie holdings, and my husband's only surviving male family."

Brenna's tone was defeated, and Milly's dislike for Uncle Angus blossomed into loathing. "Eat your scone and tell me what happened." Though Milly could guess all too easily.

"I was set upon by thieves, and every groat, every last coin, and my purse as well, were taken from me." She tore the scone to sweet, buttery crumbs, then licked her thumbs and fingers. "I rage when I think about all the money stolen from our people, but I cry when I recall that purse. Michael gave it to me when I turned fifteen. He made it himself—nearly cut off a finger working the leather—and I don't know how I'll tell him I lost it."

"You didn't lose it. It was stolen from you."

Wool was the lifeblood of the Highlands, though. Sebastian took a keen interest in agricultural trade, enough that Milly understood what the loss of a year's revenue would do to an entire village.

Brenna dusted her hands together. "No, it was not stolen from me at all. Thievery is an odd crime. If nobody witnessed the theft, and you are one of those shifty MacLogans whose own husband hasn't a care for her, then you *lose* the village's livelihood. It is not stolen from you. In the space of a muttered aside at the tavern you are transformed from a victim to a victimizer."

Milly set her teacup down with a bang. "They accused *you* of *stealing* the money?"

Brenna nodded, her gaze going to the tidy stacks of ledgers on the desk.

"I made it worse. I do not get on well with Angus, so I kept my books separate from his, and what extra I had from time to time—from selling piecework, Cook's extra preserves, spices from the kitchen gardens, and so forth—I've used to help those in need. Guilt money, they call it in the village, and they're not exactly wrong."

"I still do not see how you're responsible for the midwife's difficulties."

Though Milly already had a sense that Scottish logic was subject to the more compelling sway of clan loyalties and old hostilities.

"Mairead and her boys put everything they had into sheep, as Angus nigh insisted they do. Nobody here trusts the sheep, but raising sheep is all Angus knows. Sheep are easy, biddable, stupid, without defenses—"

Brenna stared off into space, as if an insight befell her that would require much study under solitudinous conditions.

"So the midwife's family lost a lot of money," Milly said, because all of the pieces of the puzzle were still not on the table.

Brenna rose and returned to the desk, where one ledger yet lay open. She was apparently one of those people who enjoyed numbers, something else Milly could like about her.

"I gave both of Mairead's sons passage to Canada. They were hard, hard workers, and they deserved better than to slowly starve in Aberdeen, looking for work and finding none, while their mother did nothing but worry and grow old fretting over them."

"You lost money too, I take it?"

Brenna ran a finger down a page of her ledger, as if answers lay in these neat columns and tidy figures. "The Brodie lands lost money. That would be in Angus's ledgers. Angus has certainly not let me forget that we'd have much more coin were it not for my carelessness."

"Bad enough that criminals are forever blaming their victims," Milly said. "Worse yet when the family who should protect you takes the same position."

Her ladyship took another nip from the pretty little flask.

"I like you, Baroness St. Clair, and I am very glad you've come to visit. Let's get you up to your chambers, and I'll fetch Mairead Dolan if I have to drag her here by the hair."

"I feel better," Milly said, surprised to find it was the truth. "Perhaps all I need is rest." And to talk with her husband.

"Then rest you shall have," Brenna said, rising. "Travel is fatiguing under the best of circumstances, just ask wee Maeve."

They chatted their way up to Milly's rooms, about the small child who'd recently come to visit from Ireland, about the difficulties of getting acquainted with a husband who'd left not twenty-four hours after his wedding.

As Milly parted from her hostess at the bedroom door, she considered that Sebastian had arranged this journey north on the strength of a mere hunch, a conviction clothed as a whim, that Michael Brodie needed an ally.

Sebastian hadn't been wrong. Michael Brodie needed an ally badly, as did Michael Brodie's baroness.

⟡

"We'll take them shopping," Michael announced, snagging St. Clair by the arm. "What fellow doesn't gain his lady's approval when he takes her shopping?"

St. Clair came peaceably, which was fortunate, because Michael knew not what else he could propose in the face of St. Clair's worries.

"Milly might not have the energy for shopping," St. Clair said. "She spent much of yesterday abed, and my baroness is not a woman to idle about."

My baroness—how casually St. Clair referred to his relatively new wife.

Michael led his friend across the cobbled bailey, finding St. Clair's anxiety both endearing and irritating— for it matched his own.

"*My baroness* says travel is fatiguing, as does my wee sister. Your lady needed a day to recover, and now a frippery or two will put her in charity with you, or allow her a bit of revenge for being dragged the length of the Great North Road and beyond. You never fretted like this over your garrison in France."

St. Clair wrestled free of Michael's hold, and abruptly, a pretty Scottish summer morning became fraught.

"I fretted. I fretted nigh incessantly over the damned men, their damned families, the damned supplies and lack thereof, the damned prisoners, *you*—"

St. Clair's role in France had been difficult and complicated, while Michael's had been difficult and simple: Michael's job had been to watch over St. Clair.

He'd been damned relieved to turn that responsibility over to Millicent St. Clair.

"And you're fretting over me still?" Michael

hazarded. What else could explain this impromptu journey of hundreds of miles, without an invitation, and the lady in an interesting condition?

The clip-clop of heavy, iron-shod hooves ricocheted off the walls of the bailey like so many pistol shots.

"That is an enormous horse," St. Clair remarked as Bannockburn was led out of the stables.

"Named for an enormous battle—or for breakfast," Michael replied. "You need not fret over me, St. Clair. My Brenna has taken over the post and does a better job than you ever could. Come along, and you can buy me a frippery to restore my good graces."

St. Clair belted him on the arm—a goodly smack but not too hard. "You never once said you were married."

And thus they reached the foundation of St. Clair's worries. Michael resumed walking rather than air more linen where any boot boy or lady's maid might come by.

"I never said I wasn't married. What color hair ribbon shall I buy for my Brenna?"

St. Clair laughed, which was the object of such a ridiculous question between former soldiers. A hint of that humor lingered in the baron's eyes when Michael announced to the ladies that a sortie would be made to the village after lunch.

"To the village?" Rather than offer him an approving smile, Brenna's question was careful. The way she patted her lips with her serviette was careful too.

"We'll stop at the tavern and enjoy some of the finest summer ale in the Highlands," Michael said with a wink—while the ladies exchanged a glance that was also careful.

Reinforcements arrived a heartbeat too late from St. Clair. "I've a notion to stretch my legs, and a ramble to the village would suit—if my lady is up to the exertion?"

Brenna rose so quickly Michael barely stopped her chair from toppling. "We'll take the carriage."

For a ramble down the hill?

St. Clair's lady was on her feet as well. "I'll need to change my shoes. Sebastian, Michael, if you'll excuse us?"

The ladies departed, though neither had finished her meal.

"What was that about?" St. Clair asked, helping himself to a chicken leg from his wife's uneaten portion.

Michael scraped the last bite of mashed potatoes from Brenna's plate. She had Cook flavor them with butter, cheese, and chives, an improvement over the army's version of the same offering.

"Probably consulting each other on the preferred color of hair ribbon." Though all Brenna's ribbons were green, and Michael had never noticed what color Baroness St. Clair preferred.

When the ladies assembled on the front steps, Brenna pulled Michael over to the climbing trellis of pink roses. "This will be a short outing, Husband."

"You are not pleased with the prospect of spending some coin on yourself?"

She gave him the sort of look that in an instant conveyed both incredulity and expletives.

"The baroness is in a *delicate* condition, ye daft mon. She canna be haring all over the shire at her fellow's whim."

Milly St. Clair had been dragged the length of the *realm* at her husband's whim, suggesting Brenna's anxiety was ill-placed.

"I want to spoil you a bit," Michael said, plucking her a rose and getting stuck in the thumb with a thorn for his troubles. "I want to show you off and assure the world we're in charity with each other." Because they were—in charity with each other.

He was almost sure of it.

And he wanted to buy her a hair ribbon that wasn't green, but he passed her the rose and kept that silliness to himself.

"What am I to do with you?" Brenna said, sniffing at the rose.

"Does that mean you love me too?"

She smacked him across the cheek with the little rose, but smiled as she did, and then climbed into the waiting coach without allowing him to assist her.

⋐⋑

The ladies bought hair ribbons, they bought muffins, and they each dropped a coin in the poor box when Michael suggested they sit for a moment in the churchyard to take advantage of the shade.

The day was the sort of summer day Michael enjoyed most—warm in the sun but almost cold in the shade—and yet, the outing was not going according to plan.

The baker had not added that free, thirteenth muffin intended to curry a customer's favor. The apothecary's thumb had hovered a quarter-inch above the scale when he'd weighed out the ladies' peppermint tea.

Michael's raised eyebrow had kept that thumb from adding a larcenous bit of weight to the scale.

"Let's have that ale," St. Clair said, rising from his bench and offering his hand to the baroness.

The doting looked good on a man who was a caretaker at heart. When Michael offered Brenna his escort, she put her hand on his arm gingerly, like a debutante at her first ball.

Perhaps they needed more practice with the business of procuring fripperies, because the visit to the village felt *off*.

"Why do you buy only green ribbons for your hair?" Michael asked as they ambled toward the tavern. "The truth, Brenna, or I will kiss you right here in the churchyard."

His threat provoked a snort. "That churchyard has seen more souls made than saved, according to Goodie MacCray. I'm your wife, perhaps I'll kiss you."

He kissed her cheek without breaking stride, and the outing became cheerier.

"I thought you liked green ribbons in my hair," Brenna said quietly, as if St. Clair, who was nigh plastered to the baroness's side, might have been eavesdropping on this great confidence.

For it was a great confidence.

"I like your hair in a green ribbon. I also like it unbound. I especially like it in complete disarray and spilling down your back while I love you."

"Hush." She bussed his cheek before he could kiss her again, and that would have put Michael in charity with the entire world, except the tavern went quiet as he ushered his lady and their guests to the snug.

"Let's try this summer ale you've boasted about," St. Clair said, assisting his wife to the bench along the wall. St. Clair scooted in beside the baroness, and for all the bonhomie in his words, his eyes were hard.

Whatever was amiss, St. Clair had picked up on it too.

"I'll place our order at the bar," Michael said. "Ladies, if you'll excuse me?"

As Michael wended his way between tables, he assured himself that an English peer was not likely to meet with a warm welcome in the wilds of Aberdeenshire. The '45 was as close in memory as Davey MacCray's most recent ballad, and in Michael's childhood, he'd known old men who'd claimed to recall the battle in all its tragic, gory detail.

While every family in Scotland could recall the hardships and butchery following Culloden.

"Two pints of summer ale, and two ladies' pints," Michael told the barkeeper.

No polite banter followed, no small talk about the weather. When Michael left coins on the polished oak surface of the bar, the barkeeper hesitated a moment before scooping them into a pocket.

"My thanks," Michael said, and because he took a moment to thread his fingers through the handles of four mugs, Michael overheard Dora Hennessey's muttered aside to one of the Landon sisters.

"Had to bring her fancy coach down the hill, didn't she? Had to throw her coin around on frivolities and go strutting about with her English friends."

He tarried, as if his hands were too clumsy to manage four mugs, but it was his mind that felt clumsy.

The parsimony of the baker and the apothecary, the odd looks at the lending library, the absence of greetings from anybody passing by the churchyard—this rudeness was not a function of prejudice against the English in general, but rather, was animosity directed solely against Brenna.

His dear and beloved Brenna, whom he'd left behind when he went off to war.

Michael marched over to the biddies hunched over their tea along the far wall, like a pair of broody hens unwilling to leave their nesting boxes.

"Ladies, Brenna thought you might enjoy a summer ale. She's ever so considerate, is our Brenna. For example, she insisted the coach be brought out for Lady St. Clair's use, knowing how limited a woman's energy can be when she's traveled far in a certain condition."

He thunked the two smaller mugs down on the table, when he'd rather have upended them and smashed the crockery.

"Th-thank you, Laird," the Landon besom managed.

"Thank my wife."

Michael stomped off, growled an order for two more lady's pints to the barkeeper, and rejoined his party in the snug.

When he saw the ladies across the room were sending him wary looks, he kissed his wife's cheek and saluted with his mug.

Twelve

"THEY WENT TO THE VILLAGE WITHOUT ME." MAEVE'S lips quivered as she made this announcement. She stomped over to the bread basket, mostly because that would keep her back to Cook.

"Aye, and you're supposed to be working on your penmanship with Miss Elspeth," Cook said. She was beheading carrots, which as far as Maeve was concerned, was a fine fate for carrots—except then they'd likely show up in a stew pot or on Maeve's plate.

"Elspeth went to the village too, and told me to read myself a story, as if it's bedtime."

Cook's cleaver paused. "You've no one to read you a story of a night?"

Bridget used to, sometimes, but then Kevin would come by, his hair neatly combed back, his fingernails spotless, and declare it was time to blow out the candles. Bridget never argued with him, not for one more page, not for one more paragraph.

"I can read to myself."

Sure enough, Cook scooped up all but two of the carrots and tossed them into a huge stew pot. Next she'd deal with the turnips and potatoes, because neeps and tatties went with everything here in Scotland.

"Would you care for a piece of shortbread, wee Maeve?"

"No thank you." Shortbread would not make Maeve's brother like her, much less love her, much less pay attention to her. "I'm off to find Preacher."

"You can look in the stables, I'm thinking." Cook held out the two carrots, and damn—damn was a very bad word, but Elspeth said using it in your mind wasn't wicked—damn if that didn't make Maeve feel like crying too.

"I'm not supposed to go to the stables without telling somebody."

"I'm somebody," Cook said, slapping the carrots gently into Maeve's palm. "The laird and his lady are off for a ramble through the village. You might as well pass a little time with Bannock, aye? He strikes me as a lonely sort of horse, working all the time or alone in his stall with nobody to play with."

Cook winked. Maeve did not know how to wink back, but Cook had a point: Bannock probably was lonely. Maybe Preacher had known that and had gone to visit him.

"I won't be gone long," Maeve said. "I'll go right to the stables and come right back."

"Sure you will, and maybe by then you'll have an appetite for some shortbread."

Probably not. Maeve headed for the stables at a fast trot, lest she run into Lachlan, who'd remind her she wasn't to be in the stables at all. Preacher was nowhere to be found, but Bannock was in his stall, munching hay, which seemed to be what Bannock liked to do best.

"Wee Bannock!" Maeve called, which provoked one hairy, horsey ear to flick. "I've brought you a treat, Wee Bannock!"

The beast did not even look up, and why should he? Maeve wasn't tall enough to reach through the bars of his stall and show him his treat.

"Bannockburn is a lucky lad," said a male voice from behind her. Maeve was abruptly hoisted up to Uncle Angus's hip. "He gets treats and a visit from a pretty lass."

Angus smelled good—of horses and hay—and he hadn't been asked to go to the village either.

"I brought carrots for Bannock, but I'm really only looking for Preacher."

"And you found me instead." Angus bussed her cheek, a tickly, scratchy sort of kiss that made some of Maeve's anger slip from her grasp—some of her hurt. "Perhaps we need to get Bannock's attention?"

"He's eating. He won't pay attention to anything until he's done eating." Michael was the same way, and Kevin had been fond of a good meal too.

"He's a gelding," Angus said, which Maeve knew meant the horse was tamer than a stallion. "We can't blame him for his priorities, but neither will he mind if you want to perch for a moment on his back."

To sit on Bannock? The tallest horse in the stables, maybe the tallest in the shire—*in all of Scotland*? This was ever so much better than a visit to the village.

"He won't mind?"

"He won't even notice," Angus said, opening the

stall's half door one-handed. "You must not pinch the poor lad with your legs or bounce about on him too hard. All that comes later."

Angus's smile was the sly smile of somebody who knows he might be getting in trouble but wasn't too worried about it.

"I'll sit quietly. Kevin used to take me up with him when he hacked out sometimes." Maeve had forgotten that, probably because it was one more thing to miss about Ireland.

Bannock was even bigger up close than he appeared from several feet away. His withers were higher than the top of Uncle Angus's head, his feet were...no wonder people wore boots in the stables.

"Up you go," Angus said, hoisting Maeve upon the horse's broad back. "Catch a bit of his mane to let him know you're up there."

The ceiling was much closer to the top of Maeve's head, and the sense of being atop the world both scary and fine. She petted Bannock to let him know she appreciated the view, and because petting any animal was a cure for much that ailed a girl.

Kevin had said that too, and abruptly, the lump was back in Maeve's throat.

"When you're a bit bigger, perhaps you'd like to ride Bannock right through the middle of the village." Angus took a carrot from her and passed it to the horse.

For a fellow like Bannock, a foot-long carrot was no more than a tea cake. He munched his treat and went right back to his hay without a pause in his chewing.

The horse honestly did not seem to know or care that Maeve was on his back. "May I get down now?"

A flash of orange streaked straight up one of the supports at a corner of Bannock's stall. The great horse dodged right, toward Angus, and Maeve nearly slid off Bannock's back. She clutched at his coarse mane for dear life until Angus's arms came around her.

"I've got you, child. The daft horse merely took a fright." Maeve was wrapped around Uncle Angus, piggyback, but frontwise. She'd fallen off twice while hacking out with Kevin, but never from such a great height, and she clutched at her rescuer desperately.

"Preacher made him jump."

"Preacher is a menace," Angus said, holding Maeve very tightly, her legs about his waist. "But you're safe. Bannock meant no harm, but he hasn't claws or fangs like that cat. When he's afeart or can't puzzle things out, Bannock knows only to run and hide."

Still Angus held her, tightly enough that Maeve could feel the rising and falling of his chest. This close, he smelled not of horse and hay, but of pipe smoke and wool.

"You can put me down now."

"Soon." Angus walked with her from the stall, closing and latching the door before striding down to the saddle room with Maeve plastered to his front. When he lowered himself to a bench, Maeve ended up straddling his lap.

She scrambled off, struggling a little to loosen his hold. When she stepped back, Angus was breathing a bit heavily and twitching at his kilt.

Maybe Bannock had spooked Uncle too?

"You're wearing the hunting plaid," Maeve said. The only other person she'd seen wearing it was

Brenna. "The pattern makes it so nobody can see you in the woods."

"The better to get closer to your prey. Are you all right then, wee Maeve?"

Angus was the only one to ask that question, though he was also the one who'd put Maeve on Bannock's back.

"Maeve, the coach's coming up the hill." Lachlan stood in the door to the saddle room, his expression carefully blank. He should envy Maeve her freedom—though the boy was wearing a handsome pair of new boots.

"I'm coming," Maeve said. "'Bye, Uncle Angus!"

Even though nobody was ever supposed to run in a stable no matter what, Maeve scrambled to Lachlan's side and took his hand. "I went to find Preacher."

"Of course ye did, ye daftie. Does Preacher eat carrots now?"

Maeve slowed and dropped Lachlan's hand—they were clear of the stables, and the coach had to take a long way around the hill to get up to the keep. "The carrot is for me," she said, breaking it in half. "And for you."

Lachlan did not believe her, of course, but he was a friend—as much as a boy could be a friend—and so he munched his half without comment.

Bannock hadn't cared that Maeve had brought him a carrot, hadn't cared that she was sitting up on his back, and hadn't made any effort to keep her safe when Preacher had gone streaking by.

Maeve took a bite of carrot and tried not to cry.

❧

"I was trying to woo you," Michael said, and from his tone, Brenna suspected he regarded the outing as a miserable failure, when the opposite was true.

"And you have," Brenna said, pulling off a half boot. "You've shared your day and your friends with me, and you've bought me a brown velvet hair ribbon I shall treasure until my hair turns gray." He'd also taken her by the hand and the arm, held doors for her, whispered to her in public, and kissed her in the churchyard—and none of it had been anything less than his honest enjoyment in her company.

Every woman deserved to be kissed in at least one churchyard, just as every woman deserved to be wooed, and thank heavens, her husband grasped this.

Michael settled beside her on the bed and took her half boot from her, his unhappy sigh suggesting he was not placated by her answer. Several doors down, the Baroness St. Clair was napping, and her husband offering whatever assistance with that endeavor a devoted—and worried—spouse might lend.

Brenna's husband was worried too, and that she could not abide.

"This boot is worn at the heel, Brenna Maureen. Why can't you allow yourself a decent pair of heels?"

Michael's patience was worn at the heels too, and yet, Brenna had not yet decided how to answer the questions he was about to ask.

"I would have sent them to the cobbler before winter." Where they would have sat, unless Brenna had Elspeth take them, and claim them as her boots.

Or perhaps not—not all the villagers swilled Angus's poison.

Michael's arm came around Brenna's shoulders, as heavy and well fitted as an ox's yoke.

"What happened in the village, Brenna? I had all I could do not to dump my ale over the heads of those vicious old biddies."

Wouldn't Brenna have enjoyed that sight—for about half a minute.

"I'm glad you did not. They're idle gossips and hold me accountable for you being gone so long." And for their cousins emigrating, and for the wool harvest being thin some years, and the winter early. Angus was nothing if not tireless.

Michael kissed her temple and brought a hand up to massage Brenna's nape. "You've put up with such gossip for years now, and it's my fault."

Though afternoon sun poured through the window, fatigue hit Brenna like a wet plaid. Fatigue of the body and of the spirit.

"That feels lovely." She kissed his cheek for good measure.

"I will get to the bottom of this, Brenna."

He probably would, and then this happy little mutual wooing of a marriage would be reduced to ashes. "Must you get to the bottom of it this minute? It's idle gossip, nothing more."

Idle gossip, veiled looks, subtle delays in service, and so much more that Michael, with his soldier's instincts, would not miss. Desperation seeped through Brenna's fatigue, and she cuddled closer to her husband.

"Why did the baker give you the smallest twelve muffins he could find?" Michael asked.

And no extra muffin or biscuit to curry goodwill—Michael would have noticed that too.

"Because the castle is well provisioned," Brenna said. "Other households need the biggest muffins far more than we do. Are you inclined to nap with me, Husband, or will you natter on about a bunch of pinch-penny Highlanders?"

He wouldn't natter on, he'd interrogate his wife until years of unfortunate history came tumbling out and Brenna was forced to defend herself and make explanations that could lead nowhere—or worse than nowhere. Angus would see to that.

Michael's nose pressed gently against Brenna's ear, and his vetiver scent wafted into her awareness. "Do you want to nap with me, Brenna? *In the broad light of day?*"

The sunshine was soft, the bed beneath them was soft, and Michael's tone was softer still. His questions now were not bent on uncovering old miserable truths, but rather, on inviting Brenna to share a future with him, to trust him as a wife trusts her husband on their wedding night.

Sorrow and *love* tangled up inside her. Love for the soldier who'd come home to her when he might have wandered endlessly, love for the man who'd announced his regard for her without any promise of reciprocity, love for the husband who'd ruin everything with his protectiveness and tenacity.

"I want to love you," Brenna said, skirting an outright declaration like the coward she was. "It's a beautiful afternoon, and I want to make love with my husband."

Even as a slow wicked smile lit Michael's features, Brenna knew she was borrowing joy against the day when truth intruded like a blight on a marriage that should have taken root years ago, and blossomed by now with many children and many shared memories.

"I want that too, Brenna Maureen," Michael said, tugging at the laces of his boots. "I've wanted that forever."

Based on Michael's expression, the trouble in the village, the guests down the hall, the entire universe had left his awareness, save for his focus on Brenna and what would happen in their bed in the next hour.

Someday, he might look back on this hour and conclude Brenna had consummated their vows to distract him from the answers he wanted, and that was a pity, for it wasn't the entire truth—but it wasn't untrue, either.

❧

Brenna would look back on this day and conclude her husband had manipulated her, but Michael could not bring himself to change course. She hated confrontations, suffered her way through each one, and Michael could gain permission to make love with his wife on this difficult afternoon because she dreaded explaining the situation in the village more than she dreaded his attentions.

Hang the bloody villagers, hang the nip-farthing crofters, hang everything—Michael would make such glorious, tender, ravenous love to his wife that she'd have no choice but to trust him with her secrets.

St. Clair, a former professional interrogator, might

scoff at Michael's tactics. The Baroness St. Clair would likely applaud, though.

Desiring Brenna was simply a gift; wooing her a delectable challenge. Getting the woman out of her clothes might be impossible.

When Michael was free of boots and stockings, he rose, which put the front of his kilt at about Brenna's eye—and mouth—level.

"Shall you undress me, Wife?"

She set her footwear tidily beside the bed and scooted back against the pillows.

"I think not. A grown man can undress himself if he's properly motivated."

Michael considered her suggestion as he arranged his boots beside hers. Brenna wasn't being entirely shy, though she was being entirely Brenna.

Making him work for his pleasures, which he was more than happy to do.

"Watch, then, and plan our afternoon while you do," he said, unbuttoning his waistcoat. The better to entertain his wife—and the better to stop himself from falling upon her like a beast—he moved away from the bed, making a proscenium of the hearth rug.

The waistcoat he tossed in the direction of the privacy screen.

"Michael Brodie, for shame."

Brenna wasn't teasing, though she was watching, so Michael hung the blasted waistcoat on the back of the rocker and got busy with his neckcloth. The knot had become Gordian at some point in the day's rambles, but he managed to wrench it open without strangling himself.

When he would have whipped the damned thing out the window, Brenna arched one fine, eloquent eyebrow.

That eyebrow promised that husbands who were cavalier with their clothing would suffer retribution at the hands of their wives. Michael *folded* his neckcloth and laid it *tidily* over the back of the rocker as well.

"Am I to be the only one sporting about unclad?" Michael asked as he took a seat on the hearth and started on his cuffs.

"The breeze is fresh. When you're done dawdling, I'll consider your question. One doesn't want to suffer an avoidable chill."

Because his head was bent toward his wrist, Michael permitted himself a smile.

"I am available to assist my wife," he said, which was, at last, the blessed, damned truth. He pulled his shirt over his head, draped it *neatly* over the waistcoat, then rose, clad only in his kilt.

Brenna remained on the bed, crossed-legged and barefoot, but otherwise fully clothed. She gave nothing of her mood away, not in her expression, not in her posture, not in her silence.

"Brenna, have you changed your mind?" Asking the question nigh killed Michael, but never, never, even by persuasion or innuendo would he prevail on his wife for favors she was reluctant to grant.

She regarded his chest, her brows knitting at a particularly bewildered angle, and that's when insight struck: Brenna wanted to be in charge of this situation, but had no idea how to go on. She needed to be in charge, in fact, but had never traveled the path they would follow.

Whoever had betrayed her youthful trust, whoever had trespassed against her person, had left scars where a woman's natural sense of her own urges and pleasures should lie.

Michael would deal with the rage such a conclusion provoked—later. For now, he had a wife to bed. Wearing his kilt and what he hoped was a reassuring smile, he climbed onto the bed and took her hand.

"Brenna, I love you. I want very much to please you, and right now, I'm a bit nervous of my prospects." More than a bit, though determined, nonetheless. "Can you meet me halfway?"

Even his cock was rethinking those prospects, which was probably divine providence, because Brenna's hand suffered a minute tremor.

"Meet you halfway?"

"I am your willing slave in all that might transpire in this bed, but a slave needs instructions, hints, the occasional command. A husband needs them even more." A husband needed them desperately, because so much that was wondrous, sweet, and nourishing to the soul might be lost if Michael misread his wife in the moments that followed.

Those delicate, lovely brows rose on the word *husband*.

"You are not my slave, Michael Brodie, and I will never be yours. Not your slave, your plaything, your wee pleasure, your little secret—"

She closed her eyes, as if willing herself to put aside the ire gathering in her words.

"I am your husband," Michael said, kissing her knuckles. "I would like to become your lover, and I would adore having you for mine." He would like to be so much more to her too—her friend, champion, partner, confidant, most loyal opposition, lady's maid, companion, and favorite pest, for starters.

Brenna took the hem of his kilt between her fingers and thumb and rubbed the wool slowly back and forth. "I know nothing of being a lover. I know something of the swiving part."

She spoke with regret and rubbed the wool the way a child grasps a favorite blanket for reassurance.

Perhaps Michael should have waited for the dark of night, not to spare Brenna's sensibilities, but to spare himself the sight of her bewilderment. He spun a half-truth as delicate as the dust motes wafting about on the afternoon sunbeams.

"This part of being married is not complicated, Brenna Maureen. We touch, we kiss, we pleasure each other, we join our bodies and pleasure each other yet more. If God is generous, we conceive a child, the first of many, and then we sigh and hold each other and wonder at all the loveliness we've shared."

And Michael would wonder, too, at all the years they'd missed. For as surely as desire hummed softly through his veins, so too did regret. He'd made decisions any soldier would be proud of, and served in a difficult position loyally and well.

Those same decisions were something any husband—any lover—would regret for all his days and nights.

"So kiss me," Brenna said. "We've kissed before, and I think I have the knack of that much."

Her posture was wary, her eyes downcast, and yet she still stroked her fingers over the hem of Michael's kilt. Michael kissed her palm, and without giving up her hand, stretched out on his back.

"Let the kissing begin," he said. Let the loving begin, for Brenna did love him. She had to have some form of tender regard for him, or she would not take these steps with him.

He'd amused her, though, and that was good. "I'm to do the work?"

"A little guidance to your husband shouldn't be too much to ask." Brenna had been guiding the entire castle for years, navigating past financial difficulties, clan jealousies, Angus's backward notions, and Highland winters. Appealing to her sense of responsibility earned Michael a considering look that turned into a shy grin.

Brenna swung a leg over his thighs and straddled him. "Fine, then. Here's a place to start."

The place she chose to start was a soft, sweet kiss to Michael's forehead, a benediction, followed by a teasing brush of Brenna's lips across his—a warning shot.

Michael tucked his hands under his own backside to stop himself from plunging his fingers into Brenna's hair, freeing her braid, and using it to tug her down to his chest. Instead, he leaned up to keep his mouth on hers when she would have pulled away.

"More kisses, Husband?" she asked, her mouth so close to his, Michael could feel her words brush over his lips.

"All of your kisses. Everywhere. Kiss me with your mouth, Brenna. With your hands, with your hair."

He wanted her breasts kissing his bare chest too, but the blasted woman was still in possession of every stitch of her clothing. She wrapped a hand around the back of his head and proceeded to divest him of every stitch of coherent thought, until Michael's chest heaved and he had to sit hard on his hands.

"We can do this without removing your clothes," he whispered to the lavender-scented warmth of his wife's throat.

"Without—"

Befuddled. A quick peek told him that's what that particular angle of her eyebrows meant. He'd befuddled her with this kissing.

"Your clothes." Michael allowed himself one hand to stroke over her midline. "Your blasted clothes, love. I want my hands on you, but if you're too shy—"

"I'm not shy," Brenna said, sitting back and getting to work on her bodice buttons. "I'm modest—there's a difference when a woman has a husband."

The difference was too subtle for Michael to fathom as one button, then two, then twelve slid through their buttonholes, revealing a corset cover embroidered with vining pink roses.

"You dressed to go into the village with me," he said, tracing a rose. "May I?"

"You may."

He allowed himself the use of two hands for the purpose of unlacing her stays, a tedious, seductive process that did not require them to leave the bed, because his Brenna had worn front-lacing undergarments today, as if she'd anticipated the direction their afternoon might take.

Anticipated—or *hoped*.

"You do beautiful needlework, Brenna Maureen."

He offered the compliment to distract Brenna from his hands, gradually loosening her bindings. "Perhaps you might embroider one of my dress shirts next winter."

Brenna covered his hands with her own. "That's loose enough."

She rose from the bed, wrestling skirts, bedclothes, stays, and probably a load of modesty as well. Standing beside the bed, she let it all go—every stitch, so the sunbeams from the window illuminated her bare skin, turned her hair to gold and fire, and caught the beautiful turn of her back, waist, and hips.

"I've dreamed of you like this," Michael said, holding up a hand to her. "Longed to see you thus. You gift me, Brenna Maureen, with more than I deserve."

She put one knee on the bed and leaned over him. "Such blather. Pure husband-talk." Her hand twitched his kilt aside. "Married-man nattering." She kissed his chest. "I like it, but mind you limit such nonsense to the bedroom."

"Brenna, my kilt."

She was naked, they were to make love, and she was scolding him. If only she'd take off Michael's damned kilt, his happiness would be complete.

"Aye, it's a lovely kilt. I'll make you one out of the hunting plaid, though. It's a prettier pattern."

"You're planning a sewing project, when I want to ravish you."

Needed to ravish her, and yet, his hands were tucked back under his arse, lest he affix those hands to her breasts, her derriere, and all points in between.

She straddled him, naked as God made her and twice as luscious. "Not ravish, Michael. Love. You want to love me, and I want to love you."

Likely to silence his assurances that he did love her, Brenna kissed him again, so Michael told her with his mouth, his gusty sighs, and his nose tracing her jaw and ears and collarbones, that he loved her dearly.

"May I use my hands, Brenna?"

"I've certainly been using mine," she said, sitting back. She cupped his jaw with both of those hands and ran her thumbs over his cheeks, where a midday beard made his skin rough. "Men have such different textures." Her palms flowed down, over Michael's chest, her nails scraping his nipples lightly.

"I feel that," he rasped. "I feel it right down to my—soul."

Her smile became that of the enchantress, the siren, the woman in league with passion and wisdom as she did it again, and again.

And again. "Brenna—"

"I said you might use your hands, Michael. On me. If you were of a mind to."

He had no mind. He had only a throbbing cock and a bone-deep conviction that he'd expire of wanting in the next minute—and be glad of such an end.

"I'll get even, Brenna Maureen. I'll get so even—"

He left off trying to form words and instead palmed both of her breasts gently, learning the shape and weight and warmth of them. Brenna watched him, and her breathing changed, became deeper.

"You're beautiful," Michael said. "Your breasts are so... I must—" He touched his tongue to her nipple, the way he might have lapped dew from ripe, low-hanging fruit on a bright fall morning. "I love—"

Brenna cradled the back of his head against her palm and offered herself to his mouth. He obliged; he obliged willingly and joyously. Kissing, nuzzling, lapping, and when Brenna's damp sex brushed over his hard cock, suckling.

"We've kissed," Brenna said. "We've touched. We've pleasured each other."

Michael nuzzled the underside of her breast, where the scent of lavender blended with desire. "And?"

"And please join your body to mine."

Her coronet had come loose, her thick red braid teasing at Michael's belly. He took up the end and brushed it over her nipples.

"You do it. I'm otherwise occupied."

For this was important, that Brenna put her hands on her husband and take him into her body of her own volition.

"You like my breasts."

Michael left off toying with those treasures to study his wife's face.

"I adore them, but more, I adore that you'll share them with me. To touch you thus is a precious privilege." He kissed each breast, hoping Brenna would exercise a few privileges of her own.

She remained still, poised above him, naked and rosy, her hair tousled and the afternoon light slanting across her face. Some sentiment quivered through her, some difficult, passionate declaration.

"What, Brenna Maureen? You can tell me anything."

She brushed a thumb over his mouth. "I *cannot* tell you."

Though clearly, she wanted to. For nine years, Michael *could not* come home. "Then keep your words, and give me your loving."

To emphasize his suggestion, Michael let his hands fall away from Brenna's breasts, so the moment was entirely in her keeping, the decision hers, just as the decision to remain at war had been unilaterally his.

Brenna did not disappoint. She took his shaft in her hand, seated him at the opening to her body, and settled over him enough to start their joining.

"Is that how it goes?" she asked, bracing herself on her hands.

"Exactly like that, and even more, if you'd like. All of me, if it would please you." He could barely form words, so desperately was he fighting the urge to thrust. "You might move a bit, get comfortable."

Her experiments nearly cost him his back teeth, so hard did he clench his jaw. What she lacked in experience, Brenna made up for in courage and curiosity. In no time, the infernal woman had a rhythm, gliding over him easily, with a sweet sort of eagerness which would soon part Michael from his reason.

"You said we'd pleasure each other more," she reminded him. "Is this the more part?"

Lucifer's bones. "Soon, love. Maybe this will move things in the proper direction." He added an undulation of his own to her efforts, not half of what his body wanted to do, not a quarter. "Do you like that?"

Her expression acquired a degree of concentration

she didn't turn on her ledgers or her embroidery, and neither did she answer him.

Not in words. Her body replied in a resounding affirmative though. Her hips took on a focused, questing sense of purpose, her breathing became labored. Michael added a touch more power to his thrusting as Brenna rose over him on straight arms.

"Michael?"

"Here."

"Look at—look at me."

He looked at her, at her breasts gently heaving with her exertion, at the pale, smooth skin of her torso, at the way blond curls kissed damp auburn where their bodies joined.

"Look at—" She used her hand fisted in his hair to shift his focus to her eyes, and abruptly Michael understood. He locked gazes with her, let her see all the desperation and homesickness and love in him, gave her irrefutable visual assurances—as pleasure came for them, overtook them, and swamped their every faculty—that she was with her husband, and he was with her.

And no other.

When the cataclysm ebbed, Brenna hung over him, heaving like a steeplechaser who'd won over a muddy course against a tough field.

"Let me hold you," Michael said, but he made no move to drag her against his chest, because these moments were every bit as fraught as what had come before. "I'd like very much to hold you, I mean."

He'd like very much to see her eyes, to know if the past few moments had been the true start to their marriage, or the end of all its hopes.

"Brenna? Love?"

Her breathing eased marginally, and she slowly, slowly raised her head.

To reveal a face transfigured with the sort of joy a man didn't expect to behold in the mortal realm.

"What I wanted to say earlier?"

Michael couldn't help but smooth her hair back. "My lady, you've said sonnets and ballads and volumes." He did not need to hear her say she loved him, for her sentiments were beyond dispute.

She caught his hand, kissed his palm, and beamed down at him.

"What I wanted to say, Michael Brodie, was *welcome home.*"

His expression likely matched hers then, for joy, for fatuous pleasure in simply drawing breath, for she'd given him the words, which, especially from her, he had very much needed to hear.

Thirteen

ABERDEEN ALWAYS HAD THE SCENT OF THE SEA ON IT, like a siren's perfume, sometimes faint, sometimes strong, depending on the whims of the weather. The fresh, briny fragrance called to a man, promising that distant shores held adventure, magic, and beauty such as a cold, granite city of the North would never allow him.

Neil MacLogan viewed periodic trips to the coast as a test, not because he wanted to leave his family and sail away, but because he wanted to murder the man he followed.

Angus strode down one of the twisting side streets leading back from the docks, eagerness making him heedless even in the sharp, bright sunshine of a summer afternoon.

Twenty paces behind, Neil followed silently, patiently, knowing exactly where the bastard was headed. Another right turn, three houses down, to a tidy, nondescript dwelling sporting geraniums in the window boxes, for God's sake. The gray stone steps were scrubbed, as if a prosperous merchant's wife presided over a hardworking staff within. The windows gleamed like blank eyes, though behind each one, curtains were drawn closed.

And always would be.

Angus glanced up the street, then up at those windows, his expression containing an eagerness that made Neil's gut clench. Between two cheery pots of geraniums, a half-dozen tin soldiers lay scattered on the stones, their skirmish ended by whatever heinous responsibilities some boy had been called to within the house.

Angus raised a hand to knock, then instead smoothed a palm over his hair, the gesture as nervous as a suitor with a ring in his pocket.

"Knock on that door, and you will not live to see the sunset," Neil commented pleasantly. "In fact, you probably won't last until teatime."

Angus's hand lowered slowly. He turned as if he might not have heard Neil's soft promise.

"Fancy a taste of fresh game yourself, MacLogan?"

The words were taunting, but in Angus's eyes, Neil saw fear, which wasn't half as gratifying as it should have been.

"Are you afraid I'll beat you to death?" Neil asked, gathering up the soldiers. "Afraid I'll tell Michael what a sick old pervert you are and let *him* beat you to death?"

"If I'm a pervert, so are half the schoolboys in English public schools, and you along with 'em," Angus replied, but he began walking back the way he'd come, briskly, because nobody lingered on that tidy stoop admiring the geraniums for long.

Neil dropped the soldiers in a pocket and fell in step beside him.

"What young boys do among themselves behind locked doors is a far cry from what you're about. Attempt to visit that brothel even once more, Angus Brodie, and I will tell Michael exactly what passed between us all those years ago."

They turned a corner, so the afternoon sun was obscured by taller roofs. This wasn't a geraniums-and-scrubbed-stoops sort of street, it was more of a sailors-looking-for-a-tavern thoroughfare, with more foot traffic.

"You'll not say a word," Angus muttered. "A few moments years ago are hardly worth remarking, and Michael would wonder why you kept silent so long."

On two previous occasions, Neil had made similar threats, and Angus had come back with similar taunts. The victim was too ashamed to disclose abuse; this was a tenet the Anguses of the world relied on to protect their freedom.

"I am not the only person whose silence allows you to swagger around above the ground, old man. You would have seen my family thrown off their property had I accused you, and Brenna needed us close by."

"You'll never say a thing," Angus retorted. "You might not have wanted what you got from me, but you didn't protest, and your brothers would spit in your eye if they knew what you'd done."

No, they would not. Neil knew that for a fact.

"I could not protest. Those who've complained in recent years have lost their holdings, but Michael is back now. If I were you, I'd take a notion to see more of the world, old man."

They'd reached the doors of a decent-looking establishment trading as the Boar and Hound. Angus stopped and spat into the gutter.

"The castle is my home, and I'll not leave it. You, on the other hand, had best be sure your rent is paid in coin—and to the last groat. Whisper so much as a hint of your lies where Michael can hear them, and it's you who'll be taking ship—if you're lucky."

"My truths, not lies. If I take ship, I'll take certain little parts of your anatomy with me," Neil said. "That is a promise, Angus Brodie."

He bowed, courtly as any titled baron, and turned on his heel, back the way they'd come, for a certain set of soldiers needed to be returned to their rightful owner.

⌇

Michael Brodie was a god, a genius, a man whose children Brenna would cheerfully, cheerfully bear by the dozen.

"You're quiet," he said, his hand trailing over Brenna's shoulder. "Have I loved you to sleep?"

He'd loved her to freedom, to relief so vast it filled every corner of Brenna's soul, to peace and joy and ferocious insights she'd ponder for years when she had the privacy to do so.

"You want to chat now, Husband? Is that what comes after the pleasuring?"

Michael's lips brushed over her ear. "So you were pleasured. A husband likes to hear about these things. I was pleasured too."

Brenna could not doubt that, could not for a moment fail to sense in him the same repletion and wonder filling her heart.

"Kind of you to tell me. That was not pleasure, Husband."

His hand on her shoulder paused; then he took to rubbing her earlobe between his thumb and forefinger.

"Did I get it wrong, Brenna? Shall I try again, do you think? Practice makes perfect, and we have hours before supper."

He was teasing her. She bit his nipple, gently. "It wasn't only pleasure. We're married now."

"Aye."

Bless the man, she did not have to explain.

"How do you like being married to me, Brenna? Be honest."

He meant she was to be brave, to trust him, which was not a command she could entirely obey—though neither could she entirely ignore it. Not now, not after *this*. Some of the rosy joy dimmed, the way a sunset loses its fiery glory as night approaches.

"I love being married to you, Michael Brodie, but it's difficult too."

"Because I take up space in your bed? Can you not see some advantages to that arrangement?"

His gentle levity had tears threatening.

"I can see the advantages, but being married, it becomes harder to know—that is, certain things aren't easily shared."

He kissed her forehead this time. "Just tell me. We'll sort it out. We're getting better at sorting things out, and we'll get better still."

Brenna had dwelled for years in high, cold mountains, but Michael was assuring her she need not dwell there alone. The generosity and folly of his assurances washed through her, bringing despair and hope in equal measures.

"In the village, things were awkward." They were awkward in the bed too, as Michael's male member slipped from her body, leaving dampness in odd places.

He patted her bottom. "Cuddle with me, and we'll discuss this." As casually as if they were trading places at a card table, Michael scooted out from under her, grabbed a handkerchief off the night table, and passed it to her.

"Is this why men always carry a handkerchief?" Brenna asked, putting the little square of cotton to use on parts now curiously tender.

"It's why I'll always carry two," Michael said, holding out an arm.

He'd known she needed a handkerchief, and Brenna knew he needed to hold her—they were *married*—so she cuddled down against his side and prepared to offer her trust to go along with her body and her heart.

"Your people don't like me."

"Our people, or they don't like us."

Generous of him. "They like you, Michael, or they'll recall they once did, and will like you again soon, but they don't like me, for the most part."

And that hurt—it still hurt.

Michael brought the covers up over her shoulders, wrapping her in warmth, vetiver, and another scent that was intimate, masculine, and Brenna's to treasure.

"Is their resentment because you send their sons and

daughters to Canada and America? Surely that's better than starving down in Aberdeen on a diet of mackerel and seaweed?"

"The emigration is part of it, but not all. They hate Angus for the evictions, and well they should."

"I nearly hate Angus for the evictions," Michael said, rolling to his side so he faced her.

She could roll to her side so she faced him, or she could remain on her back, staring at the ceiling.

"This room has cobwebs, there in the corner by the window. Do you see them?"

"I see my wife, trying to say hard things and worrying what my reaction will be. I love you, Brenna. That's my reaction."

She should tell him she loved him, for she did. The conviction was amazing—also terrifying. Brenna shifted, so her back was to Michael's chest, her hips tucked into the lee of his body.

"The people, our people, think I stole the entire proceeds of a year's wool harvest from them."

Michael's arms came around her, one under her neck, the other around her waist. "I would pronounce that accusation ridiculous—you would not steal from the devil himself—except you mean it seriously. When did your great larceny occur?"

He was trying to hide it, but Michael was angry. She loved him for being angry on her behalf, she who'd never thought to love a man for anything.

"Two years after you left. I wanted them to take me seriously, wanted to prove I could bargain with the merchants as the lady of the shire ought. My cousins accompanied me, and a few of the tenants.

The tenants went home ahead of us to tell of our good fortune—I'd done a good job, you see. We were set for the year, and perhaps a bit more."

"You're still doing a good job."

She could manage this recitation because his arms were around her, because his strength was at her back, and because in the comfort of their bed, he'd allowed her the courtesy of turning her face to the shadows lengthening along the wall.

"I had the money with me, right with me, and when we stopped at the inn in Aboyne, my cousins wanted to linger over another pint. I was impatient and wanted to get home so I could brag on my accomplishments."

She managed that last with more sadness than bitterness, an accomplishment in itself.

"Go on." Michael's embrace had not changed, and his words were merely pleasant, like the kiss he dropped on her nape.

"I was set upon by a half-dozen thieves. All wearing kerchiefs over their faces and hats pulled low. They knew exactly what to take, including my horse. The horse was eventually found wandering near Hugh's land, still in its bridle and saddle."

"But your reputation had been sent galloping straight into the sea," Michael said. "Were the thieves caught?"

"By the time my cousins got me back here to report what happened, there was no point wasting time searching. Aboyne is miles away, and night was falling."

"Tracks don't sleep," Michael said, arms tightening around her. "When the welfare of an entire village is at stake, somebody should have at least asked questions and alerted the authorities."

"Angus took care of that. He suspected the merchants were responsible, that they'd given me a good price because they knew they'd only be paying it temporarily."

In the ensuing silence, Brenna wished she'd been brave enough to face Michael as she told her tale, for then she might have had a clue as to his reaction.

"What aren't you telling me, Brenna? This isn't all of it."

His tone bore a hint of commanding officer, or exasperated husband. Because she could not—could never—tell him *all of it*, Brenna scraped together one more handful of courage.

"Angus put his theory forth only after the villagers had concluded I'd taken the money myself. Hugh, Neil, and Dantry couldn't vouch for me, because they'd seen nothing. Without witnesses, I could not be tried."

"And neither could you be exonerated," Michael concluded. "Then you produced funds sufficient to send half the youth of the shire across the ocean."

How clever he was.

"Stupid of me." She was so tired of feeling stupid.

"Stupid, indeed. Why should you confirm their verdict with generosity you might have squandered on your own finery? Far better to hoard up your wealth while our people starved. They were so willing to convict you without evidence, they deserved to starve."

He'd been angry before; he was furious now.

Brenna could feel the heat coming off of him, feel the tension thrumming through him. Because he was enraged, she could let her own anger go and acknowledge the weary sorrow beneath it.

"If I protest my innocence, I'll only make it worse," Brenna said. "I understand that, and it was a long time ago. We manage. They may not like me, but at least when you're about, they'll respect me."

Michael heaved a great sigh against Brenna's back. "I haven't been about, though, not for years. Would you feel any better if I told you your sacrifice indirectly contributed to vanquishing the Corsican?"

Brenna did roll over then, only because Michael allowed it. If he'd chosen to pin her to the mattress, he had many times the strength to do it.

"I could not have been a proper wife to you nine years ago, Michael. It's enough for me that you had a hand in vanquishing the Corsican. Let the past go, and I'll do likewise."

The hair behind his left ear stuck up at a funny angle. Brenna smoothed it down, then added a few more caresses now that she could pet him as much as she liked.

Because they were married, and because she'd asked him to take a vow of sorts with her.

"I'll let the past go when the people you've spent nine years looking after let it go."

Not the answer she'd needed, but pure Michael.

He shifted over her, right directly over her.

"If we're careful, do you suppose we might bring each other pleasure again? This talk of robbery and judgment inspires me to seek closeness with my wife."

She let him change the subject, because she had no choice. "Or maybe the sight of my breasts does that?"

His smile was slow and precious, full of possession, admiration, and pleasure. "Possibly. Show them to me again, and we'll find out."

❧

"The people in the village resent me for being gone so long." Michael offered this observation by way of apology to St. Clair, who studied the countryside from the parapets.

While Michael studied his wife in the bailey below, picking flowers for the bouquets in a great hall nobody used.

"The people in the village didn't insult you, Michael, they insulted your wife." St. Clair was too good a friend—and too careful a commanding officer—to trade a half-truth for a platitude. He at least had the courtesy to stare out across the loch while he delivered his verdict.

"How could you tell?"

St. Clair was observant, which was what had made him such an effective and feared interrogator. He was also kind, a secret the baroness had apparently unearthed all on her own.

"Resentment is in the eyes, mostly, in the silences, and the postures that speak of defeated anger that won't die. The average crofter has been nursing a grudge handed down to him by his grandfather since the '45, and your wife is begrudged the very air she breathes."

"Not quite that." But for some in the village—the

tavern keeper, the biddies, the shopgirl selling hair ribbons—it was a near thing.

"The minister mentioned that were it not for the generosity of 'the castle,' there'd be nothing in the poor box." St. Clair offered this casual observation while studying the loch, which was quiet today. A perfect, flat mirror of sky and clouds.

"The selfsame minister who'd best be preaching about forgiveness, reconciliation, and Christian charity," Michael said. Above them, the pennant whipped against the flagpole, and in an hour, this vantage point would be chilly. For now, it was beautiful, and a good place to plan a strategy.

"You'll take up the cause of your lady's popularity?"

"I'm to blame for the disrespect shown her," Michael said, something he ought to have told Brenna, though she would have argued with him. "If I'd been here, she would not have been robbed of a year's worth of wool proceeds."

St. Clair hiked himself up to sit on the stone parapet, as if a drop of several stories weren't at his back. "My dear wife mentioned something about this."

Interrogators were supposed to be brute animals, torturers without souls, but St. Clair approached his calling differently. He arranged matters so one was motivated to confide in him. Michael had seen him do it time and again, and each time, had felt a sense of sympathy for the poor bastard unburdening himself of his secrets.

Among whom, he would now number, and be grateful for the privilege.

"While I was scampering around the mountains

of southern France, playing nursemaid to a lot of French recruits, Brenna was trying to establish her authority here. She bargained with the merchants down in Aberdeen for the year's wool harvest, and was robbed of the proceeds on her journey home. Every crofter who ever raised a sheep has reason to resent her endlessly."

"For a Scot does hold his coin very dear," St. Clair murmured.

"And his children dearer," Michael added, because to all appearances, Brenna had used that money to send young people away from their parents. "Would you please get the hell down from there? Your baroness would take it amiss if you were to slip."

"Somebody climbs higher than this to get yonder pennant waving in the breeze," St. Clair said, hopping down.

"I used to climb up there," Michael said, eyeing the flagpole. "The view is magnificent, but the slates are slick as ice when it rains. Rather like French mountainsides when a winter storm blows through. I'm off to talk to Elspeth."

Down in the bailey, Brenna stuck the pad of her thumb in her mouth, as if she'd pricked it on a thorn. Even at this distance, the sight did things to Michael's composure.

"What has the fair Elspeth to say to things, other than that Hugh MacLogan is a doomed man?" St. Clair asked.

"Noticed that?" St. Clair noticed much and had probably noticed Michael ogling Brenna from four stories up.

"She watches him the way I watch my Milly and you watch your Brenna. What will this conversation accomplish?"

"Elspeth likes Brenna. I want to know why, and then I want the rest of the village to know why." Elspeth was in a position to drop hints, make casual observations, and otherwise counter a steady tide of judgment and scorn.

"Hard to invade an enemy camp with only one foot soldier," St. Clair said. "Good God, those fools are going swimming in that lake."

"It's a loch, and they aren't fools, they're single Highland gentlemen in want of wives."

Down past the woods surrounding the castle's hill, Dantry and Hugh peeled out of their kilts and shirts, leaving their clothes in a heap on the stony beach.

"You'd think they'd take their boots off first," St. Clair said.

"You'd think that if you were married. I'll talk to those two, as well." But not to Neil if he could help it.

St. Clair turned to rest his elbows on the stones behind them, while Michael remained facing the bailey. "Why question your in-laws?"

"They were with Brenna when she was robbed, or they should have been. Nobody called in the authorities. Nobody did a systematic investigation. Nobody followed tracks. Nobody did anything except blame my wife for being the victim of a crime."

First Hugh, then his younger brother, dove head-first into the frigid waters.

"Makes my stones shrivel just to watch them," St. Clair muttered.

While Michael wanted to make somebody else's balls shrivel for what had been done to Brenna—but whose?

"How is your baroness?" Michael asked, because Brenna had told him, as they'd drowsed in each other's arms after a second, thorough, sweet loving, that Milly St. Clair had suffered some ill effects from her journey.

The closeness of that confidence, the intimacy of it, brought a pleasure related to, but different from, the loving.

"My lady is in need of rest," St. Clair said, shoving away from the stone wall, turning, and climbing back up to resume his seat. "If you think you'll be sending us on our way anytime soon, I am bound by concern for my lady to disappoint you."

Well, of course. Michael had stuck by St. Clair against all odds, and now the favor was being returned.

"I could not have the Baroness St. Clair's welfare on my conscience," Michael said. "My wife's situation is burden enough. Matters here could get messy."

"So what will you do?"

"Two things. First, I will enlist what allies Brenna has—Elspeth, the parson, the MacLogans, a few others—to restore her standing in the community."

St. Clair rose and traversed the parapets until he reached the conical roof over the staircase. "And second?"

Michael looked away, because the damned fool was about to scramble up on the roof until he could touch the flagpole, as Michael had many times in his boyhood—his foolish boyhood. The very top of the roof was a flat space maybe two feet across, the flagpole anchored in its center.

"Second, I'm going to do what my uncle should have done years ago and move heaven and earth to clear Brenna's name."

In a half-dozen nimble steps, St. Clair was up to the flagpole. "The view is unbelievable," he said. "You are a wealthy man, Baron Strathdee, if you are lord of this vista."

All Michael wanted was to be lord of his own castle and of his lady's heart. "I am a wealthy man, and you are not a mountain goat. Getting down is trickier than getting up."

St. Clair traversed the slope of the roof, arms outstretched like a circus performer. He'd trod a similar path in France, disaster on all sides and no margin for error, and as in France, he came to a safe landing and made it look easy.

"One is left with a question, my friend," St. Clair said, his cadence ever so slightly French.

"I know," Michael said. "I bloody goddamned know: Why didn't Angus make any effort at all to bring to justice those who stole from my wife, and from the entire village?"

Hugh and Dantry had apparently had enough of the frigid pleasures of the loch, for they both climbed onto the shore and used their shirts for towels.

"You suspect Angus?"

"I'm supposed to suspect her cousins," Michael said. "They had motive and opportunity. They were the ones who allowed her to be unescorted on a road not always well traveled. The horse she was riding was found near their holding, and they made no defense of her either."

"Complicated," St. Clair said, a wealth of pity in a few syllables. "Perhaps your uncle conducted no investigation because he did not want to deprive Brenna of her only close family."

"Or perhaps he did." Because Brenna had counted six armed brigands after her money, surely enough to overpower her, as well as Neil and Hugh.

St. Clair's eyebrows rose in an eloquent reconfiguration of the available facts. "You suspect Angus of stealing from the entire village and maligning his niece-by-marriage into the bargain? Of casting suspicion on her cousins too? For what purpose? He has no need of coin, he has a Scotsman's loyalty to clan, and he's *your* only close family."

That last part, about being Michael's only close family, was what hurt the most.

"Somebody took the trouble to get Brenna's horse up here from Aboyne, left the saddle and bridle on so there'd be no mistaking the animal, and made sure the beast was found near the MacLogan holding. That makes no sense."

"If thieves are desperate enough to steal from an entire village, then they sell the horse, saddle, and bridle down on the coast," St. Clair concluded. "Unless they're trying to implicate the MacLogans."

An unhappy, speculative silence spread, broken only by the pennant snapping and whipping in the breeze.

"I expect Angus back from Aberdeen tomorrow," Michael said. "I thought I'd search his quarters before then."

"Not by yourself," St. Clair said in a tone that

suggested pulling rank was yet within his abilities. "You're distracted, you'll miss the obvious—"

The door scraped open, revealing Elspeth Fraser looking flushed and unhappy.

"You've missed him," Michael said. "MacLogan and his brother are already scrubbed as clean as soap and cold water can make them."

Elspeth put Michael in mind of that quote about a woman being little but fierce, and she wasn't having any of his teasing.

"Never mind the daft MacLogans. I cannot find Maeve, and was hoping she'd taken herself up here to sketch."

"She's not with us," Michael said, "and she's not with Brenna, and evening will soon descend. St. Clair and I have been up here for a good half hour, and we haven't seen her leave the castle. Find Lachlan, search the stables, talk to Cook, and, for God's sake, hurry."

⁓

Dinner was a quiet business, with the Baroness St. Clair carrying most of the conversation. She quizzed Brenna on how wool was woven, the various Brodie plaids, and the accoutrements necessary to create a formal Highland dress ensemble.

While Brenna was so upset, she barely tasted her lamb and potatoes, and Milly St. Clair took over the duties of hostess for her.

As a friend would have.

"You might consider wearing the colors of Clan Sinclair," Michael said. "Brenna can show you the plaid, and it wouldn't take long to have a kilt made up. Sinclairs have been in Scotland for centuries."

"You've sewn kilts, then?" St. Clair asked over a bowl of trifle.

"I've been measured for my share." Michael's reply was served with an indulgent smile in Brenna's direction, a husbandly smile, and yet it would do him no good.

They were doomed to have a rousing argument, and Michael likely knew it.

Brenna rose without giving Michael a chance to hold her chair.

"In the interests of allowing all and sundry to get a good night's sleep, I'll suggest Lady St. Clair and I withdraw at this point. We'll be in the solar, gentlemen."

"You're preoccupied," Lady St. Clair—Milly—observed as they made their way down the corridor.

"I'm furious." One could be honest with friends.

"Maeve's a little girl, and far from home. Of course she'll explore, and she came to no harm."

These were the arguments Brenna anticipated from Michael. She did not want to hear them from her friend.

"She came to no harm this time." Because Angus was in Aberdeen, because Elspeth had known to keep a close eye on the child.

Because Michael had raised the alarm the instant he'd realized Maeve was missing. Brenna didn't want to be fair about that, but in the disagreement she intended to have with her spouse, she'd have to acknowledge that much.

"We are tired," Milly observed as they reached the

third floor. "Would you be very offended if I sought my bed and left you to the company of the teapot?"

"You are well otherwise?" This mattered to Brenna, that Milly be in good health. It mattered very much.

"Fatigued, but otherwise thriving. I suspect Sebastian will abandon the port with unseemly haste."

"And Michael will join me soon enough as well."

Milly stifled a yawn, then fussed the drape of Brenna's tartan shawl. "You were terrified for that child."

Brenna was terrified for all the children, though in Angus's absence, she'd relaxed her guard.

"The little ones can so easily come to harm." Saying the words provoked an ache in Brenna's throat, an ache where tears ought to be and never had been.

"Go to bed," Milly said, kissing her cheek and enveloping her in a brief hug. "Things always look better in the morning. We'll sew Sebastian a fine kilt and make a laird of the Western Isles of him."

Things did not always look better in the morning. Sometimes, for years, things looked just as bad in the morning as they had the night before. Sometimes they looked worse, because sleep had been interrupted by an unwelcome visitor or bad memories.

Brenna resisted the inexplicable urge to hug Milly back desperately tight, and took herself off to prepare for battle with her husband.

Because the night was mild by Highland standards, she did not bother lighting the fire, but tended to her ablutions and then climbed into bed to await her spouse. He arrived quietly less than thirty minutes later, while Brenna feigned sleep and kept her face toward the wall.

The mattress dipped, the sound of two male feet rubbing together whispered in the darkness, and then Michael raised the blankets and climbed in beside her.

"You're not asleep, Brenna Maureen. If you're too upset to talk, we can have our discussion in the morning."

He was brave, and he was braced for a fight.

"I do not want to argue with you in this bed." She did not want to argue with him at all, but argue, she must.

"Not argue, discuss. We're getting better at sorting things out together, you'll recall. Maeve's situation requires sorting out." His tone made it plain that Brenna's reaction to Maeve's situation was what he intended to sort out.

And yet, beneath the covers, Michael's hand sought Brenna's. He linked their fingers, even as Brenna lay with her back to him.

"She cannot be kept safe here," Brenna said. "If any harm befell that child, I would never forgive myself." Michael wrapped himself around her, and while Brenna tried to find some resentment for his presumption, all she located was relief.

"She was picking flowers, Brenna, and teasing the cat. This hardly qualifies as courting disaster."

Maeve had been picking flowers in the walled garden, a place Brenna avoided for the memories it held.

"She can pick flowers in Ireland. For all we knew, she might have gone down to the village or wandered to the river."

"The river is about two feet deep in most places this time of year. I'll teach the child to swim if that will ease your worries."

Nothing would ease her worries. She turned so she

faced Michael in the gloom. "You can't teach her not to wander off, not to be curious. She has a solitary nature, and you can't teach that out of her."

"We'll hire a governess."

Brenna had had a governess, and even governesses had half days, and retired to their own chambers at night. "That's an unnecessary expense."

"We can afford it. The yearlings were prime horse-flesh, and I've some funds too, you know."

Brenna did not allow that shiny lure to distract her. "We'll spend the yearling money entertaining the shire Friday next."

Michael pulled her into his arms, where Brenna fit with an ease only recently gained.

"What is this about, Brenna? Will you deny us our marital pleasures because any child you bear might someday come to harm? Children do, you know. This one will fall from a pony. That one will come down with measles."

Brenna was worried about measles and broken bones, but she was terrified of Angus. In her husband's arms, the ramifications of Angus's continued presence at the castle spread through her like symptoms of influenza.

Neither her daughters nor her sons would be safe. No tutors, governesses, or nannies would be vigilant enough, because the compulsion that drove Angus never slept, never paused in its desire for gratification.

And yet, she could not allow that beast to be unloosed on some unsuspecting community on the coast or farther away, where she'd be powerless to protect anybody.

Michael dipped his head to nuzzle her cheek. "Brenna, are you crying?"

"I am tired." Weary unto death of coping, of managing, of holding inside fear and fatigue as well as a rage that would commit murder did she allow it to. "I am so tired."

He gathered her closer. "Rest. We'll talk more."

"The child must leave, Michael."

And thus did Angus win, again. Any dream Brenna had harbored of a happy married life dissipated in the darkness, because she would choose the safety of children she'd never meet above that dream.

How she would deny herself and her husband the pleasures they'd found in their marriage she did not know, but deny them, she must.

"Two governesses, then, and a nursery maid," Michael murmured. "She shall be as a princess, never alone, wrapped in cotton wool every waking hour. Go to sleep."

As Michael's breathing became regular, and the scent of vetiver wafted through Brenna's senses, a thought stole through her rage and sorrow—a radical, frightening, powerful thought.

What would keep the children safe, all the children, was the truth.

About Angus.

About Angus and Brenna.

If Michael believed her, then the truth would effectively hobble Angus, assuming Michael allowed his uncle to live.

If Michael did not believe her, then her marriage was over.

As it would be, quite possibly, if he did.

Fourteen

"THE POST IS FULL OF LETTERS FROM AFAR," MICHAEL observed over a mug of summer ale.

The posting inn was the heart of the village, both geographically and otherwise, and a dozen people were scattered about the common, sipping their pints and waiting to see if any of the letters Martin Dingle sorted were for them.

"Post is usually from all over—it being the post," Dingle muttered, making two tidy stacks of about a dozen epistles each.

"Let's see who's been mindful of their correspondence," Michael said, scooping up the nearer pile.

By interfering with His Majesty's mail, Michael was arguably committing a felony. By interfering with *Michael*, Dingle could provoke a confrontation that would split the room—and the village—asunder and require direct opposition to the laird whom the shire had waited years to see returned home.

"Here's one for you, Goodie MacCray," Michael said, holding a thin missive up to the window as if he might see the contents the way a candled egg revealed what lay within the shell. "Maybe you'll let us know how your boys are doing?"

He wasn't about to bring the letter to her. The blasted woman could walk eight paces to hear how her family fared. She pushed to her feet, tugged a plain wool shawl about thin shoulders, and snatched the letter from Michael's hand with her thumb and forefinger.

"How are they, Goodie? Are they starving on the streets of Aberdeen? Are they so hungry their wives are doing the unthinkable to keep them in neeps and tatties?"

His tone was light, while the room had gone silent as a tomb.

Michael's people were a canny lot, and clearly, the laird was in a mood.

"They prosper," Goodie said. "Eagan has a farm, and he and Meg are expecting another little one this fall."

"Delighted to hear it." He swiped another letter off the counter. "And here's a thick packet for you, Mairead. Maybe it includes a bank draft?"

He subjected it to the same scrutiny, holding it up to the light, shaking it, drawing as much attention to the letter as if he were a magician preparing to perform sleight of hand for his rapt audience.

Mairead rose, slowly, her gaze glued to the epistle in Michael's hand. Whatever was within, she needed it badly.

And that was fine, because she had something Michael needed badly too.

"How fare your sons, Mairead? I've been meaning to ask." He tapped the letter against his palm, the way a headmaster might tap his birch cane before administering discipline to a miscreant.

"They're in Pennsylvania."

"Pennsylvania? Not the wilds of Illinois? The woods of Kentucky? How are they managing in Pennsylvania?"

A masculine voice came from the door. "They're managing wonderfully." Hugh MacLogan came striding into the common, kilt flapping. "Dingle, pull a man a pint, if you please. Mairead's boys are both married, and they're farming not far from my brothers. If we get to exporting beef, we expect they'll sell some for us."

"So our crofters' sons are now contemplating international trade? How things have changed while I was off larking about in service to the King."

For good measure, Michael passed out three more letters, and all the while Hugh sipped his ale and watched from the snug. By the fifth letter, little old Vera MacDonald had caught on.

"My granddaughters are all married and raising their bairns in Boston," Vera said as she hobbled up to get her letter. "Wee Sara can draw anything, and she sends me the sketches of each child. It's not the same though," she said, jutting her chin in Michael's direction. "It's not the same as seeing them, hugging them, hearing their prayers each night."

She was half Michael's size and close to three times his age. She'd been a child when the '45 had turned Scotland into an oppressed province of the Crown, and she knew the value of survival.

"Madam, if you'd like passage to Boston, your laird and his lady can arrange it for you, just as your lady has arranged it for anybody else with the gumption to make a new life in a new land."

He'd surprised her, but better than that, he'd challenged her, and Vera did not disappoint.

She cackled, revealing four teeth optimally situated to holding a pipe. "You'd miss me, Michael Brodie. There'd be no one to tell the stories on your grandfather and his da. No one to tell Dingle when he's mixed a nasty batch of ale for rushing the process."

She shot Dingle an admonitory glower, though the poor bastard probably hadn't served a bad batch of ale for thirty years or more.

In the snug, Hugh tried to hide a smile behind his ale.

"We'd muddle on," Michael said. "We'd muddle on without anybody who misses their family too much to stay here with us, and we'd be happy to help them arrange their travels."

He slapped the rest of the letters down before Dingle, shot a look at Hugh, and headed for the door. When he'd gained the sunshine of a pretty summer morning, he stood for a moment, listening.

The murmuring started up within two seconds of the door swinging shut, and that was good. Let these people comprehend that they either stood with their laird and his lady, or they stood in line for a ticket to the New World.

Michael's next stop was the minister's cottage, where he'd suggest some sermon topics that deserved consideration over the remainder of the summer.

"What was that all about?" Hugh MacLogan asked. MacLogan hadn't emerged from the posting inn that quietly, but Michael had been that intent on his list of homilies.

"I'm angry," Michael said, striding off. "Mad enough to knock heads about, pitch those ungrateful biddies off their...tenancies, and relieve the parson of his living."

"It's a fine day to be in a temper," Hugh remarked. "Anything in particular set you off? You're not known to be hotheaded but then, any fellow who was at war as long as you were might have a few quirks."

"We're going the wrong way," Michael said, stopping in the middle of the High Street. "The minister lives south of the inn."

"Do you feel a confession coming on?"

"I'm more in the mood to cast the moneylenders out of the temple," Michael said. "Brenna told me about being robbed all those years ago, and the small-minded, ungrateful, worthless fools who are my people have held her responsible for every sick calf and dropped stitch since."

For though Brenna hadn't said as much, Michael knew the Scottish temperament, and knew how badly a scapegoat could suffer when the regiment was feeling mean and no enemy obliged their destructive appetites.

"So you'll change their minds about Brenna by threatening to cast them off their land? Interesting approach."

Hugh was a brave man, and like many truly brave men, he was casual about his courage. Given the state of Michael's temper, one might even call MacLogan cavalier.

"I'm none too happy with you, either," Michael

said, changing direction to head for the trees. "What the hell were you thinking? Allowing a young woman, alone, to take off on horseback when you knew she was carrying a year's worth of profit in her purse?"

Now Hugh's expression shuttered. "I don't get free of this place that often."

For no good reason, Michael wanted to hit the man. "Everybody in this shire has lost the gift of plain speaking. What the hell does leaving the village have to do with abandoning Brenna and jeopardizing her safety?"

"I wanted to bring my Anne a token, and Aboyne is a market town."

More indirection. Michael contemplated howling at the moon, except the sun was well up.

"Aberdeen is a damned trading port, and you couldn't find your lady a hair ribbon there?"

"Hair ribbons in Aberdeen would come dearer than hair ribbons in a market town."

Michael started up the incline toward the castle, and MacLogan showed no inclination to leave him in peace.

"You mean to tell me you allowed Brenna to risk the roads without escort because you were pinching pennies over a bloody hair ribbon?"

Hugh paused in the shade of towering evergreens. "You needn't shout. We were thirsty, the barmaid was friendly, and Brenna was in a tearing hurry. I didn't know she had the coin in her purse, I thought it was in her saddlebags, and those we'd brought in with us. Brenna rides well, and we thought we'd catch up to her within the hour."

They'd reached the clearing with its ancient bench. Michael contemplated wrenching the thing from its location and using it to bludgeon MacLogan.

"Why didn't you make any effort to defend Brenna? Why no investigation? Why has she been pilloried for this year after year?"

MacLogan appropriated the bench, the dappled forest shadows nearly camouflaging him in his work kilt, boots, and plain shirt.

"Because for once, I agreed with Angus."

Michael kicked at some ferns encroaching on the path, then felt rotten for it. "Explain."

"Angus said any defense of Brenna would only make her look more guilty and raise more questions. The fact of the matter was, she chose to go on alone, she chose to take the risks of continuing unescorted, and she chose to take the money with her as well. She was a woman grown and in a position to make her own decisions."

"Did your wife console you with that logic as well?" MacLogan looked so miserable, Michael concluded Anne MacLogan had railed at her husband at length over that very same pile of tripe.

"I regret that decision now, Laird, but when I've raised the issue with Angus, I'm admonished to let sleeping dogs lie."

"Somebody's lying. Brenna did not steal that money."

"How can you say that? You weren't here."

"MacLogan, if you believe Brenna stole from her own people and used the money for her own comfort, then you and yours are welcome to leave as well. I'll pay your passage anywhere, provided you leave before the summer is out. *Brenna Brodie did not steal that money.*"

Something crashed through the bracken above them, a deer likely, startled out of its midday nap—not that Michael was yelling. Quite.

MacLogan scooped up some rich, black dirt and let it fall through his fingers. "If you clear off everybody who doesn't like your wife, who will pay your rents? Who will work your lands?"

"Wrong answer, MacLogan. Perhaps you'd best start packing. Brenna will miss you."

MacLogan rose and dusted his palms together. "Brenna is no thief, and I'm her kin. If she was robbed when I was tasked with keeping her safe, the responsibility is mine. I've said as much to her."

"You needed to say as much to the village, *and you have not.* Not in years of allowing your cousin to suffer from being the victim of a crime."

MacLogan tilted his head up, as if a stray beam of sunshine might find its way to him despite the dense canopy overhead.

"I'll say as much now, and Neil will too, but, Laird, what good will it do you to send from your home every tenant and relation who thinks your wife guilty?"

MacLogan was a good man, maybe even better than most, but he was a man who'd gone for years without a woman in his life, without a woman in his heart.

"When Brenna faces rejection and judgment on every hand, it isn't a home for her. It's a place to live, a place to work herself to exhaustion, a place to fret over and lay fires in the winter. She's making camp between battles and sieges, not making a home. Castle Brodie is not a home for her until she's loved and respected here, rather than merely tolerated. I love her and I respect her, and I will see others treat her appropriately or escort them to the property line."

MacLogan studied the trees for a moment, then dug in his sporran. "Read this."

"What is it?"

"A letter from my middle brother. He talks about the markets, and the best place to land cattle if we're thinking of exporting. His choice is Baltimore, but you've seen something of the world. Your opinion might be worth hearing."

A man could not export beef from Aberdeen if he'd taken ship himself. Michael stuffed the letter in a pocket, admitting to himself that he was relieved MacLogan would not tuck tail and run for the coast.

"I'll read it. Where are you off to?"

"I've a notion to pay a call on our minister. Give my regards to Brenna."

He ambled off, intent on his confessions—or something—leaving Michael with a letter in his pocket and a towering need to kick somebody's kilted backside.

Anger wouldn't sway anybody's opinion of Brenna—MacLogan had been right about that—and Michael wasn't exclusively angry. He was also worried, maybe even scared.

Brenna had let him hold her last night, but nothing more than that, and while they'd exchanged a few civilities over the issue of Maeve's safety, the topic had become a lit grenade launched in the direction of their fragile marital trust.

Michael had no idea why this might be so, and Brenna wasn't about to pass along any clues.

Which made it all the more imperative that he search Angus's quarters sooner rather than later.

∞

What few people were left in the Highlands managed to generate as much drama as a garrison of French soldiers and their families, *and* the entire population of greater London.

"Take it," Sebastian St. Clair said, holding an ivory silk handkerchief out to the Baroness Strathdee. He used neither his commanding officer voice nor even his Baron St. Clair voice. He used his devoted nephew and doting husband voice, which provoked the lady to a fierce glower.

Michael probably adored that glower on his Brenna, though he'd be horrified to see the lady in tears.

"My thanks, Baron. Good day."

She would have stormed off with his little flag of truce, but Sebastian could not allow that. He fell in step beside her.

"What had you barreling out of those trees like a fox who's heard two packs in full cry?"

"I've things to see to," the lady said, her pace picking up to that of a whirlwind. "If you'll excuse me."

"Alas, that I cannot do," he said, taking Michael's wife by her wrist. She wrenched free with a speed and strength Sebastian might have expected of a seasoned fighter.

"What are you about, Baron? You are a guest in my home, and every courtesy must be shown you, but I'll not tolerate bullying."

She stood her ground, when she might have made a grand, offended exit.

Sebastian liked this woman, and Milly liked this woman, which mitigated in favor of leaving the lady in peace. Michael, however, *loved* the Baroness Strathdee. Brenna Brodie had been the emotional ballast keeping her husband sane even across international borders and roiling seas, though she apparently failed to grasp this herself.

Because Michael loved his Brenna, Sebastian was doomed to interrogate her. "Michael would kill me if I bullied you, and thanks to me, he knows all manner of clever ways to ensure I suffer terribly in the process. Let's stroll a bit, shall we?"

She sent a look back toward the trees, one of longing and hurt, and yet, she would not be rude to a guest. "A short walk only."

Michael had stomped down the postern path at roughly the same velocity as Michael's wife had emerged from the woods.

"I was a torturer, you know, in service to France."

He took perverse pleasure in admitting his prior profession before polite company, enjoyed watching lords and ladies squirm when he said what they all murmured behind perfumed gloves and painted fans.

The admission held no joy now, but rather felt like reciting the sentence an innocent accused would endure if convicted of a serious crime.

Brenna Brodie snorted. "Are you intent on torturing me now? It's already been tried, and yet I'm still enjoying excellent health, aren't I?"

"You were crying, my lady." Her admission about

already having been tortured upset Sebastian. One lost the knack of detachment when one was ferociously loved, and for the queer pang in his heart, he had Milly to blame.

Or thank.

Somebody had abused the Baroness Strathdee's trust at length, though Sebastian did not believe she regarded her husband as her betrayer. Not yet.

"Do you suppose I should be confiding in you, my lord?" she said, churning along into the castle's back gardens. "My husband is home after nine years away with little contact. We're bound to encounter the occasional rough patch."

Sebastian tried to snap her off a white-and-yellow daisy, but daisies were tough and fibrous, and he ended up half pulling the thing out by its roots. His bungled gallantry had done the unexpected and made the lady pause.

"Here," she said, producing a folding knife from a skirt pocket. "Daisies want trimming."

She smiled too, mostly with big green eyes that had recently been crying. The effect was lovely, if conducive to more pangs of a half-French heart. Sebastian took the knife and trimmed dirt and roots from the flower stem.

He presented the blossom to the lady. "Do you know what daisies stand for?"

She took it, but didn't do anything so foolish as bring it to her rather definite nose. "They stand for a bit of cheer and a deal of weeding. For some they stand for provocation to sneeze. Thank you."

"They stand for innocence."

Well, hell. This drawing-room trivia had the tears welling again. She tossed the flower back among its kin.

"I must be——"

He took her by the arm, gently, lest she draw his cork and shout down the castle walls, because Brenna Brodie was that sensitive to a man's mishandling of her.

"You promised me a short walk," he said, steering her in the direction of a thriving if somewhat raggedy hedge.

She remained trenchantly silent, which lack of resistance alarmed the husband in Sebastian and appeased the interrogator. Women were not as likely to break under torture, but kindness and attentiveness could lay siege to their carefully constructed defenses, particularly when offered from an unexpected quarter. For this lady, based on Milly's disclosures, kindness from any quarter would be unexpected.

"Let's sit for a moment, shall we?" Sebastian pushed open an old wooden door and led the baroness into a walled garden. She went unresisting and even allowed him to settle her on a sunny bench.

"I hate this place." She directed her sentiments to his handkerchief, which was hopelessly wrinkled as she spread it in her lap. "I hate this garden."

"Hating is a great effort."

"Hating can keep one safe."

What harm could befall a woman in a sunny, walled garden right up against the castle's solid granite walls?

"You don't hate your husband," Sebastian observed, coming down beside her. "My wife says you're besotted with each other." Which had been a relief beyond imagining, because most of Michael's long absence from Scotland had been on Sebastian's behalf.

"I am besotted." More daisies grew here, more innocence, along with pansies in a riot of cheerful colors.

"A woman usually announces such a thing with a hint of joy, a coy smile, some wonderment. What has upset you, my lady?"

She didn't flinch at his question, wasn't surprised by it. Her answer, however, was a surprise to Sebastian, who'd heard many unusual answers in his time in France.

"My husband *loves* me. He truly loves me. He defends me to my own relations when he has no proof that I'm blameless."

When Sebastian had come to the conclusion that Milly loved him, the world had at once come right and gone spinning off its axis.

"You can't do anything about his love for you, you know. Michael is stubborn and loyal to the bone. He might be suffering simple infatuation, though. The joy of homecoming, marital pleasures, that sort of thing?"

Michael Brodie was head over ears for his Brenna. A career prying truths from reluctant sources hadn't been necessary for Sebastian to see that.

She swiped at her cheeks with her knuckles. "He loves me. It isn't infatuation, it isn't a homecoming rut, it isn't…anything simple. I heard him giving Hugh MacLogan a verbal birching, confronting my cousin about things that happened years ago, and now my husband must campaign over old territory, and it's all—"

Sebastian's handkerchief suffered a mauling in the baroness's fist.

"I learned something about your Michael when we served in France," Sebastian said, his insides feeling rather like the handkerchief looked. "Michael is a born protector. Despite being on the wrong side of the battle lines, Michael chose to remain where fate had cast him, right by my side, even as France fell and our peril increased. Michael's instincts are as formidable as my own when it comes to human nature. I would be quite, quite dead were it not for Michael's tenacity."

"*Fate* cast Michael into the French mountains?"

"Fate in the form of some generals, whose orders could not be denied. Nothing less would have kept him from you." Though from the lady's question, Sebastian concluded that Michael was the recipient of some blind faith from his wife, and blind faith was not usually given in small increments.

She held the folded handkerchief against her eyes, a small, temporary blindfold. "Michael will ruin everything with his tenacity and protectiveness. If he goes poking at hornets' nests, all manner of horrors will result. I've managed here for years, made do, got by, and seen to the castle. Now…"

Now she ran out of the woods crying, and let a stranger lead her to exchanging confidences in a garden she hated.

"Now you love him, and everything is at once simple and complicated."

Sebastian wanted to take her hand, wanted to give her some human contact to tether all of her difficult emotions, and yet, if he did, she'd probably vault over the walls after she'd laid him out flat.

"Michael is a good man," she said, which Sebastian took for agreement with his conclusions. "A very good man."

He could remain silent—an interrogator's best friend was a taut, well-timed silence—but a small, solid, everyday sort of truth seemed more appropriate. "You are a good woman."

"Michael is determined to see me thus. He's stubborn, is Michael Brodie."

She adored his stubbornness, for it matched her own.

"You love him," Sebastian said again, for she wasn't about to admit as much to him. "So what will you do? He wants your good name restored, wants you to have the respect you deserve. He's willing to confront all and sundry on their small-mindedness to accomplish his goal."

The lady also wielded the tactic of silence well. The garden was sheltered from breezes, but its walls could be breached by an enormous marmalade tomcat who strolled along his personal parapets, tail held high.

"Michael adores his uncle Angus," the baroness said after a few quiet moments. "Angus is quite fond of Michael as well. Always has been."

Foreboding prickled over Sebastian's arms. Puzzle pieces were trying to snap into place, but he kept them on the fringes of his awareness, because the picture they'd form might result in somebody having to kill somebody else.

"Did Angus appropriate a husband's rights in Michael's absence?"

If so, he'd see the man quietly transported to Van Diemen's Land, or some such sunny clime, his ballocks packed among his underlinen.

"He did not, but you are a canny fellow, Baron. I think I'd best leave you here with Preacher to enjoy the flowers and the sun."

She rose and tucked Sebastian's handkerchief into the pocket from which her knife had appeared. The better to give her space, Sebastian remained on the bench.

"What will you do, my lady?" *And will you allow me, Milly, anybody, to aid you?*

The cat leaped down onto the place the baroness had vacated beside Sebastian and nudged at Sebastian's elbow with its head.

"I'll have these damned walls brought down," the lady said, striding off toward the door. "I'll need some time to plan, and the mess will be considerable, but that won't be my fault either. Enjoy the sunshine while it lasts, Baron."

❦

Brenna's emotions were shifting, and like cargo broken loose in the hold of a seagoing ship, the potential for damage was great. Among the feelings careening around inside her was a determination that Maeve not fall into the trap that had ensnared Brenna.

And the way to keep Maeve safe was not only to impose reasonable discipline on the child, but also to make sure the girl knew she was valued and held dear.

"You're quiet," Maeve remarked as they wandered past beds of pansies under sunny midday skies.

"Pansies symbolize thoughts," Brenna said. "I'm thinking."

Maeve was a child, so her question was inevitable. "What are you thinking about?"

About how the castle, the grounds, and even Brenna herself felt different when Angus was sixty miles away and Neil's responsibility. About how a little girl should be able to play safely in her own back gardens. About how another girl, abandoned by family and overlooked by kin, and even set aside by her husband, hadn't been safe.

Though in some regard that made no sense, Brenna felt safe now.

"I'm thinking about how much I'd miss you if you went back to Ireland."

Maeve's smile was shy. "I'd miss you too. Let's put our blanket here."

"A fine spot." Far finer than that damned walled garden. Brenna was already planning what she'd do with that space when those walls came down. A propagation house, maybe, or a larger conservatory. Michael might have some ideas—assuming he did not return to France or London or wherever he'd been when Brenna had needed him.

"Will you tell me a story?" Maeve asked. "Preacher likes stories too."

The idiot cat had trailed them from the kitchen and now sat on a corner of their tartan, as if he'd lent them the blanket from his personal surplus and awaited their thanks.

"You can tell me about Ireland," Brenna said. "I've never been, though I hope Michael will take us there for a visit."

Michael, who was still somewhere in the village, wreaking havoc in the name of restoring his wife to the good graces of people whose opinion never should have mattered as much as it did.

"Why are you smiling?" Maeve asked, flopping to the blanket with a child's abandon. "I heard you yelling yesterday. At Elspeth and Michael and Cook."

The tone was casual, but to a little girl, the lurking question was important.

Brenna lay back beside the child, something she would not have done had Angus been on the property—damn him—unless Michael had been with them. Vigilance was that much a habit.

As was silence—another stout cable snapped in Brenna's emotional cargo hold—though habits could be unlearned.

"Your brother was a soldier for years. A little yelling won't bother him." Hopefully, a lot of yelling wouldn't bother him either.

"Bridget and Kevin yelled, and they laughed too."

"Maybe it's like that when you love somebody. You can yell when you need to, but you laugh too." Because laughter was needful. Michael understood that, maybe all soldiers did.

Maeve crawled off the blanket, searching through the grass. "You love Michael?"

"Very much, though lately I forgot that." Just as she'd forgotten the heavenly scent of a flower garden approaching its peak, and the glory of a Scottish summer sky on a sunny day.

"Let's look for lucky clovers," Maeve said. "How can you not know you love somebody? I love

Cook. I love Lachlan, though he's only a boy. I love Bridget and Kevin. Why do all these clovers have only three leaves?"

Maeve did not yet include her brother or Brenna on her list of people she loved, but she would, and soon.

"The three-leaved variety taste as good as the others, and for Bannock and his friends, that's lucky enough."

Maeve stuffed a clover in her mouth, chewed, and made a face. "I'm glad I'm not a horse."

"So am I. I'm glad you are a little girl who has joined our household and will brighten all of our days with her presence. I'm especially looking forward to the winter holidays with a child in the house."

Maeve shot her a bashful smile, and just like that, something snapped into place in Brenna's heart. These were the words nobody had given her, ever, though Michael was trying to give them to her now. These were the words that might have protected her from Angus and from so much else that was painful and wrong in a small child's life.

"Did you have whisky with your nooning?" Maeve asked, munching a white clover flower this time.

"Something like that. I'm tired of expecting everybody to turn their backs on me. You won't run away from us, will you, Maeve? It would break my heart, and Michael's too."

Brenna was careful not to look at the child as she issued this challenge. If she wanted people to stop turning their backs on her—and she did, some people in particular—then she had to stop acting in a manner that invited their rejection. Michael might get the attention of the villagers and make them rethink their opinions, but it was up to Brenna to make them *see*.

"Prebish and I traveled forever and ever to get here," Maeve said. "If I ran, I'd run back to Ireland, but I wouldn't know how to get there."

"Good. If you ran, I would be wild with worry for you, so don't do it. Ever."

Maeve must have liked her clover flower, for she popped another one into her mouth. "Not even when I've been bad?"

"You could never be so bad that we'd want you to run away," Brenna said. "Will you eat all of Bannock's treats?"

"Bannock isn't allowed in the garden," Maeve said, grinning. "He'd leave meadow muffins."

Naughty talk, the simple, fun kind of naughty talk a child ought to enjoy. Damn Angus, though he was surely damned already, and had been for years.

"If you were planning to knock down the walled garden, Maeve, what would you do with the space when the rubble was cleared away?"

The cat curled up on a corner of the blanket, Maeve ceased searching for lucky clovers, and a game of what-if ensued—what if we planted roses? Spices? Bright red tulips?

While Brenna played a game of her own: What if my husband and I have a child? What if I can find the courage to tell him I love him too? What if his love is mine to keep?

And what if it isn't?

Fifteen

"Now I know how to get you to picnic with your husband," Michael observed, brushing Brenna's fingers aside and tying the ribbon at the end of her braid into a snug bow. "All I have to do is set half the village to scrubbing, dusting, and cleaning the ballroom's chandeliers and windows, and you'll flee the premises." He used Brenna's braid to tug her closer. "I think the noise disagrees with you so badly, you might even have joined me for a walk along the Dee or an afternoon on a shady blanket."

The preparations for the celebration at week's end had turned Brenna's day upside down and left her too tired for any confrontations with her husband as they prepared for bed.

"I would have gone with you, Michael. I'd have stolen away with you and spent the day anywhere quiet." Provided Elspeth spent the day with Maeve, and Cook kept Lachlan from straying. Brenna slid her arms around Michael's waist and leaned into him.

"You were like that as a girl," he murmured,

wrapping her in a loose embrace. "You had a knack for finding quiet corners, for going unnoticed."

Until Angus had found her in those quiet corners, and now the damned man seemed to be lurking in a corner of Brenna's very mind.

"Why the sigh, Wife?"

"I'm tired, Husband." Some distraction was in order, because a tired woman might say things she dreaded saying to a patient, affectionate husband. "You looked very braw without your shirt today. The ladies made little progress cleaning the ballroom as long as you were working with the fellows on the stair railing."

"Sawing oak is sweaty work." He hitched her closer. "We can't have our guests tumbling into the ballroom when a railing gives way, and I gather the ballroom hasn't been used much since Mama took the girls to Ireland."

"I like the scent of fresh-cut oak." Brenna had also liked the scent of her husband's exertions, liked the taste of his kiss after he'd taken a wee nip, liked the look of him, a few flecks of sawdust in his hair, muscles bunching and rippling as he'd traded good-natured insults with the other men.

"I had fences to mend," Michael said. "I waxed a bit pontifical when Dingle handed out the mail yesterday."

Brenna might have stepped back, except Michael's arms prevented it. "Elspeth told me." As had Hugh, and even Cook had reported a second- or third-hand version of events. "Do you fear I'll scold you for scolding them, Michael?"

He kissed her on the mouth, the gesture tasting of husbandly fatigue laced with exasperation.

"I'd understand if you needed to scold me, but Brenna Maureen, these people can't have it both ways. You're there to post their bail when they lack opportunity here in Scotland or can't pay their rents, and for solving that problem, those left behind resent you. Have they seen the privations faced by the families trying to eke out an existence in the cities? Do they ever stop to wonder how they'd fare without your generosity to protect them?"

Had Michael ever wondered how Brenna had fared without him?

He had. Between nuzzling his throat and kissing his chin, Brenna realized that his scolds were not so much for the village as they were for himself.

"Michael, it's late. We're tired, and while I appreciate your indignation on my behalf, you must be patient. To many people, grudges can be as dear as children."

Some of the bewilderment seemed to seep away from him as his embrace shifted and became more intimate.

"As dear as grandchildren," he said, his hips snuggling in low against Brenna's belly. "*You* are full of dearness, Brenna Brodie."

This small moment at the end of a long, busy day was full of dearness. Michael shared his frustrations with Brenna comfortably, with the same ease as he hung his waistcoat over the back of the reading chair each night or draped his cravat over the door to the wardrobe.

"You are full of blather," she said, her mouth landing on his in what she'd intended as a reciprocal end-of-day kiss.

Except Michael was ready to change the subject,

apparently. He was done grumbling about stubborn grudges, done letting the past intrude on the present. Instead, he took her end-of-day kiss and turned it into a Start-of-Something-Else-Entirely kiss. The shift resulted in Michael's entire body becoming subtly alive against Brenna, as if her nightclothes had melted away in response to the change in his focus.

Brenna kissed him back, a challenge for a challenge, which provoked him to smile against her mouth and gently swat her bottom.

"Into bed with you, Brenna Maureen. You need your rest."

"I need my husband."

He'd stepped away, toward the privacy screen, and paused while turned partway from her.

"Brenna?" His posture said he was braced for her to deliver that scold, but he was hopeful too, that she might take him up on that Something-Else-Entirely kiss.

"I want my husband," Brenna said, surprised both to hear the words coming from her own mouth and that they were such a relaxed, casual statement. Surprised as well that she'd guessed accurately.

The combination of desire, affection, and loneliness roiling about inside her was...a need for Michael. A perfectly acceptable, even commonplace need of a wife for her husband—and that, too, was dear.

"Unless my husband is too tired?"

"Never," Michael said, dropping into the reading chair and getting to work on the laces of his boots. "I'll never be too tired to love you, Brenna Brodie. Never too tired to listen to you or hold you or walk the banks of the Dee or"—he wrestled the second boot off—"throw you onto that bed."

"Set those boots in the corridor," Brenna said. "You'd make a racket loud enough to wake our guests if you pitched me onto the bed."

He managed it quietly enough, Brenna's soft "oomph" being the only audible evidence of his exertion.

"Hang the boots," he said, unfastening his kilt. "I wasn't sure we were to risk having children, not after last night's"—Brenna tossed her night robe to the foot of the bed—"discussion."

His kilt came undone in the next moment. He draped it over the chair so he stood by the bed wearing a puzzled smile and shadows cast by the firelight. Bless the man, even in the dim light, his interest in Brenna's invitation was abundantly evident.

"I don't know about children," Brenna said, drawing her nightgown over her head. "We can talk more about children, and we probably should. What I know is the day has been long, and even when I was in the ballroom arguing with Goodie MacCray about how many candles should go on each chandelier, and you were teasing Hugh about wanting to show off for Elspeth, I felt an ache, Michael. For you. Twenty paces between us, half the village looking on, work to be done, and I felt an ache."

The mattress dipped as Michael sank one knee on the bed.

"Did you now? An ache? For me? Even when there was work to be done? Where did you ache, Wife?"

In her heart. "Inside. In wifely places."

He flopped to his back beside her. "Come here, and tell me about these wifely aches."

"I am married to a great, silly man," Brenna groused, shifting to hike a leg over her husband. "One who teases when I confess to him that I've a need of him. One who tosses me about like so much laundry in my own bed—"

Michael's hands, large and warm, settled on her breasts. "Go on. I am ever willing to listen to your confessions, dear heart."

The banter went out of Brenna as she realized she hadn't had to ask Michael to love her in this position. He'd learned already that she couldn't be comfortable on her back beneath him, not yet.

"I love how you do that," she said, her spine melting with his caresses. "You seem to know—"

He stroked her gently, finishing with a slight pressure to her nipples. "I need you too, Brenna. That's what I know."

Lest he say more, Brenna kissed him. His words ceased, and yet he did say more. Said he loved how freely she offered him her breasts, how aroused she became for him, and how snugly their bodies fit together when he eased his way into her damp heat.

And with his sighs and caresses, he told her he treasured both the pleasure they shared and he treasured *her*.

"Stop holding back," he whispered. "You don't need to hoard your satisfaction away, as if the supply is limited, Brenna. I will always be here for you."

Oh, why must he say those words now? Tonight they were man and wife, sharing a simple and profound intimacy, but tomorrow they might find themselves again separated, and by nothing so easily explained as war on the Continent.

"Will you always be here?" She panted the question, because the dratted man had shifted beneath her, the angle of his thrusting taking on a diabolical effectiveness.

He gathered her close, so close she could not see his face, and that was a mercy.

"I love you, Brenna Brodie, and I'm home to stay."

His words, low, hoarse, and passionate, drove her past all restraint, so that tears and pleasure deluged her in the same procession of endless sweet, awful moments. When she lay battered and drifting on Michael's chest, he kissed her cheek and withdrew from her body in a slow, hard slide.

"Michael?"

"Hush. Hold me."

She could not hold him, hadn't the strength, hadn't the wits. Instead, she cuddled close as, a few slow, undulating moments later, he groaned softly beneath her, and a wet warmth slicked their bellies.

The scent of spent lust joined the lavender of the bed sachets and Michael's vetiver soap, a married bouquet, and not an entirely happy one.

As they lay breathing in counterpoint, Brenna took Michael's earlobe into her mouth, a small comfort against the sense of emptiness his withdrawal had left. She knew why he'd done it. He loved her, and he was home to stay, but her welcome—despite their present posture, despite vows, despite all the tenderness she felt for him—was still in doubt.

When she ought to have told him she loved him, Brenna fumbled for the handkerchief on the night table instead.

A woman who truly loved her husband would find

a way to share not only her body with him, but the truth as well.

❧

"You've been seen taking carrots to the stables, my girl, and now half my carrots are missing. What am I to put in today's stew, I ask you?"

Cook's great arms were folded over her chest, her apron sported streaks of dried blood, and no hint of a smile suggested to Maeve that this was anything other than the start of a birching or worse.

"I don't steal," Maeve said, knowing Lachlan lurked in the pantry and could hear every word. "I don't even like carrots." What's more, Cook had freely given her the only two carrots she'd taken to the stables.

The scullery maid scrubbing sand into the bottom of an enormous pot over at the sink shot Maeve a pitying look.

"Maeve, everybody knows you nip out to the stables without permission, and Wee Bannock could put away half a bag of carrots in nothing flat. If you admit you took the carrots, I'll not go to your brother about it."

Her brother? The brother who could not be bothered to do more than quiz Maeve about her day if he happened to glance her way at supper? The brother who seemed to spend all his time mooning after a woman he'd been married to since before Maeve had been born?

"I do not steal," Maeve said, "and I do not lie, and I do not like carrots." Besides, Uncle Angus kept a bag of carrots in the saddle room, but Maeve didn't say that. Uncle had told her the stash of carrots in the stable was one of their secrets, and secrets must be kept.

The scullery maid went back to her scrubbing, but from the butler's pantry, Maeve heard something scrape and clank as if one of the boxes that held the cutlery had been shifted.

"Are you saying that Lachlan took the carrots?" Cook asked. "Or young Kelsey over there? Are you saying *I* took carrots from me own kitchen, Maeve? Lying is not an attractive habit for a wee lass to fall into."

Maeve would never eat shortbread again, not if this fat, unfair old woman was the one to make it.

"It's your kitchen, and that means you should know where your carrots are. I did not steal them, and I want to go home to Ireland."

Whatever Lachlan was doing in the butler's pantry, he wasn't minding it very closely, because a loud clatter suggested he'd made a mess in there.

Cook drew in one of those offended-grown-up breaths through her nose, growing larger as she inhaled. The strings holding her apron closed disappeared at her waist as hips and ribs met on the tide of her indignation.

"This is my kitchen, young lady, and that saucy talk will not be allowed."

"Whose saucy talk is holding up my luncheon?" a man's voice asked from the back hallway. "I cannot have Cook's sweet temper tried, or the castle will go hungry."

Michael came sauntering in, his kilt flapping against his knees, his hair sticking up like somebody had messed it. He was smiling, which was good, though he wouldn't be for long.

"Maeve snatched a bag of carrots," Cook said, her accusation full of the tsk-tsk tone any child would loathe. "When I confronted her, she denied her misdeeds, refused to apologize, and told me in my kitchen I should be able to keep track of every wee thief who comes darting through the root cellar."

"That's not what I said!"

Michael's smile vanished as if snatched away by piskies.

"You'll keep a civil tongue in your head, Maeve Brodie, particularly when addressing your elders."

Where else would she keep her tongue but in her head? "Cook is lying. I did not take the carrots, and it *is* her kitchen."

Cook—blast her to the Bad Place—shook her head in dismay, though Maeve had spoken nothing less than the truth—three truths in fact.

"Go to your room." Michael said this in the same tones Kevin used to talk to a hound who'd made a mess on the carpets.

The hounds knew to slink away, tail tucked, but Maeve wasn't a hound, and she hadn't piddled on any carpets.

"I haven't done anything wrong!"

Michael crossed the kitchen and stood over her, looking about ten feet tall.

"You compound your errors, Maeve, when you take that tone with me. Apologize to Cook for your disrespect, and we'll discuss your thievery later."

Maeve nearly countered that *Cook* should be apologizing to *her*, and that when Michael respected

his youngest sister enough to spend two minutes with
her outside the dining parlor, then Maeve would listen
to his orders.

Lachlan saved her from a slap or worse, for
when grown-ups made up their minds, they became
unreasonable. Maeve had ended up in Scotland on
the strength of just such stupid, stubborn, grown-up
thinking. Had she tried to argue with Michael further,
a birching would surely have come her way.

But the sound of crockery smashing in the butler's
pantry turned all heads in the direction of the hallway.

"I didn't take the carrots," Maeve yelled, darting
toward the back door. "You're all mean. You're
unfair, you don't listen, and *I want to go home*!"

She pelted past Lachlan, who stared in dismay at the
shards of porcelain all around his feet, pelted past the
look of horror he aimed at her, and scampered up the
winding stairs that would take her away from the only
place she'd felt comfortable in the entire stupid castle.

"You're raising a little girl," Michael observed as he
and Hugh ambled across the bailey.

"Aye. My Annie. She's the spit and image of her
dear ma." Hugh's tone said he took vast comfort from
the girl's resemblance to her departed mother.

While Maeve's look was unique, not fair like
Michael, not dark like Erin and Bridget. In the
kitchen, the child had been a small red-haired pillar
of righteousness, chin quivering with outrage, her
meager stores of childish self-restraint flung on a pyre
of righteous self-defense.

He'd been reminded of Brenna as a girl. For all her quiet, Brenna had been stubborn, and still was.

"How do you know when Annie's lying?" Michael asked, because Cook had been certain the carrots were missing, and in fairness to Cook, Maeve had been the logical suspect.

"Annie doesn't lie. Young children usually have to be taught to lie. What is this errand we're about, Laird? I have work to do."

"Let your brothers do it. We're searching Angus's quarters." Saying the words did not make the job any more appealing. Hugh paused in their progress across the bailey and made a pretense of surveying granite walls that had stood for centuries.

"Are you turning me into a thief? I'll not do it."

"We'll take nothing that belongs to Angus, but I've been asking myself who benefits from discrediting my wife? Who stood to gain the most from turning the entire estate against her?" Who had subtly undermined Michael's respect for Brenna from the very day he'd returned home?

"Anybody would benefit from a year's profit on the wool," Hugh snorted. "I don't like Angus, and my brothers purely hate him. Neil in particular can't abide the man, but even Neil would balk at searching a fellow's private quarters."

No, Neil would not. Left to his own devices, Michael suspected Neil might burn Angus's home cheerfully, with Angus locked inside it.

"Have you ever asked Neil why he hates Angus?"

"I have not, though Annie had her suspicions," Hugh said, striding off at a rapid clip. "If we're to riffle

Angus's linen, then let's be about it. I assume you've sent him off on some errand?"

"I sent him down to Aboyne to lay in some supplies for the coming festivities, and his household help has a half day today," Michael said, catching up to Hugh. "I'm exercising a landlord's reasonable right of reentry to inspect my property. Angus believes in upholding the law. What did you mean about children being taught how to lie?"

They passed over the drawbridge, the boards solid beneath Michael's boots in a way stone could not be.

"Annie is a good girl. She'd rather admit she's misstepped than lie and have the weight of a guilty conscience dragging around wherever she goes. As long as my punishments are reasonable, she'll tell me readily enough when she's done wrong. If I flew into a rage, hurt her, or kept every transgression hanging before her eyes like some martyr on a cross, then she'd learn to lie well."

Hugh's parenting methods comported exactly with what Michael had found to be the case with adolescent recruits in both French and English armies. Minor crimes weren't worth lying over, and yet, in a sense, Lachlan had lied by remaining silent in the pantry rather than coming forward with what he knew.

While Maeve had been telling the goddamned truth.

"This is a lovely property," Hugh said as they approached the three-story stone dwelling Michael's father had built as the dower house. "Needs flowers, though."

Granite could be pretty. Much of Aberdeenshire was built of granite, a soft gray available in local abundance. Stone didn't burn; it didn't creak and shift with the endless freezing and thawing of the changing seasons.

And yet, it was cold to look at and cold to dwell in. Michael led the way through a wooden gate painted white and streaked with mud.

"Cook accused Maeve of stealing carrots."

"Oh, that makes nothing but sense," Hugh said, closing the gate behind them. "Show me a child who steals vegetables, and I'll show you a child wrongly accused."

"Cook has no children, so your reasoning might not occur to her, but Maeve does like to visit the stables." Alone, when she'd been told not to.

When her brother ought to be the one taking her there.

"The old carrots are reserved for the stables," Hugh said as Michael fished a heavy iron key out of a pocket. "The carrots that get tough and hairy before they're dug up. Cook ought to know that."

Michael hadn't known that. Lachlan, Maeve's timid young champion, had had to explain it to him after Maeve had pelted off in high dudgeon.

"I'm surprised Angus even locks his door." Michael had to use a bit of force to get the tumblers to turn. "Doesn't he trust his own people?"

"He shouldn't," Hugh replied, following Michael through the door. "We sure as hell don't trust him."

Lachlan had known that too. He'd explained to Michael, through tears and a boy's ineffective attempts to sweep up shattered porcelain, that Angus appropriated the good carrots for the saddle room whenever he pleased, and—Lachlan had added, chin jutting—"nobody crosses Angus Brodie. Not even when he needs crossin'."

Even Brenna didn't cross Angus, and what did that say?

"Shall we stand about here, breathing old pipe smoke, or have a look about?" Hugh asked.

The place reeked of pipe smoke, and not in the pleasant lingering fragrance Michael associated with the winter evenings of his boyhood.

"Somebody needs to air this damned place out. No dower property should reek of pipe smoke."

Based on the front hallway, the house was tidy enough. The floors were clean, the rugs freshly beaten, the corners and windowsills free of cobwebs, and yet, an unlived-in quality persisted.

"Unless you're planning on dying in the near future," Hugh said, fingering a dark wool cloak hung on a peg, "this house won't have to serve as a dower property anytime soon. Even the clothing stinks of that damned pipe."

"Then we'd best not linger here, or we'll bear the stench ourselves."

Though Michael wanted to head right back out the front door rather than snoop through his uncle's belongings.

"What are we looking for?" Hugh asked, heading for the back of the house.

They were looking for a truth nobody had wanted to find.

"Angus probably keeps ledgers and diaries, that sort of thing. My uncle is not stupid. He won't leave a confession in plain sight, but he might leave enough evidence that I can piece together what happened."

The first parlor, the most spacious and traditionally the most formal, was largely as Lady Catherine had left it. Furniture upholstered in the Brodie plaids, a thick Axminster carpet, and a large fieldstone hearth would make the room cozy in winter. Cutwork and embroidery were framed on the walls, some of it done by Lady Catherine, but much of it less sophisticated.

When Michael moved closer to study one framed, lacy little circle, Hugh remained in the doorway.

"Anne hadn't the patience for cutwork. Said it would ruin the eyes."

"Brenna did this one." The patterns cut into the paper weren't as delicate or as intricate as Lady Catherine's pieces, but Michael recognized the paisley motif. "She did this one too."

"A parlor isn't supposed to have bare walls. Angus himself did that painting, unless I'm mistaken."

The painting hung over the fireplace, four children and a marmalade kitten, an unraveling ball of yarn causing much merriment for all involved.

"Preacher's grandsire, perhaps," Michael said, studying the kitten. "I can't recall sitting for this, but Angus was always quick with a sketch. He caught Bridget to the teeth."

And Erin. Small, pale Erin, who'd been near Brenna's age but never her match for energy.

"Don't suppose there's much to find in here," Hugh said, still not setting foot in the room. "If I committed a grand crime, I'd hardly leave the evidence in the most public room of the house."

"Angus isn't in here much." Michael turned his back on the portrait, surveying the rest of the room. "The pipe smoke is barely noticeable."

"How about we look in his office?" Hugh suggested. "I'd love to get a peek at what he pays himself."

"I know exactly how much he pays himself." Michael closed the door to the parlor, but had the sense he was leaving behind something noteworthy. Not evidence, perhaps, but something that might point to evidence.

They spent an hour in the office, and found every ledger book and tally sheet neatly organized and filed. Rental agreements, some of them going back to the time of Michael's grandfather, were arranged alphabetically, and expired agreements kept in the drawer below those.

"Then what are these?" Hugh asked, peering into the bottom drawer while Michael investigated Angus's desk. "We have the agreements in force now—and they don't fill an entire drawer—then the leases for all those holdings either vacant or back in your control, and then—"

He scraped the bottom drawer open farther.

"Uncle has a mistress," Michael said, running his finger down a column of figures in a green ledger book. "Down in Aberdeen. A Mrs. Fournier."

Hugh lifted the half-dozen leases from the bottom drawer and brought them to the desk Michael occupied near the window.

"You sound pleased for the old bugger."

Relieved, in fact. "You're a widower. Don't you crave the company of a friendly woman from time to time?"

Hugh peered at the figures marching down the page.

"I can't imagine getting *that* lonely. Even if she's French, comely, and creative, that's a bloody lot of companionship he's paying her for, and I doubt Angus gets down to Aberdeen more than four times a year."

The sense of matters out of place grew stronger as Michael considered the figures. Mrs. Fournier was growing wealthy on the strength of Angus's infrequent visits. On a steward's salary, she was an extravagance, affordable only if Angus had investments somewhere yielding interest.

But then, how did a man make investments on a steward's salary, particularly when he was using much of his income on a woman? How did he maintain his household accounts, put some by for his dotage, pay the help who served him day-to-day?

"What have you found there?" Michael asked.

"A few more leases," Hugh said, pushing the stack across the blotter. "My own among them."

With Neil's name scrawled across the top in pencil. Each lease had a name similarly annotated, in faint pencil, and not the leaseholder's name.

"You're the only family still here. The rest of this stack have left."

"Neil nearly went into a decline when old Deardorff and his boys cleared out," Hugh said, peering at the top lease. "Jack Deardorff was the closest thing Neil had to a friend, though they seldom socialized."

"I recall Olin Deardorff." Michael traced Jack's name—Johnson Andrew Deardorff—in a corner of the Deardorff lease. "He hated the winters and played a mean fiddle." He'd also never liked Angus, not even when Michael had been a boy.

"That he did. Angus would be happy if I were to clear out," Hugh said, "but nothing we've found suggests he robbed Brenna at gunpoint and made off with a year's profits." Hugh scooped up the leases and put them back out of sight in the bottom drawer. "Do we keep looking?"

"I don't want to."

"I do," Hugh said, studying a bookcase full of tomes on art, drawing, architecture, and sculpture. "I want to find something that will let you hound the bastard from the shire the way he's tossed so many off their holdings, meaning no disrespect to my laird's uncle, of course. I never knew Angus took his art so seriously."

"He has talent," Michael said, rising from the desk. "My father admitted that much, but studying on the Continent thirty years ago was out of the question. Money was tight, the auld laird not convinced of the value of book learning beyond what it took to read the Bible, and France was falling into bloody disarray." The office held no paintings, no drawings, and no feminine cutwork or framed embroidery.

And that was also a relief.

"If I were harboring evidence of a crime committed years ago, I'd not keep it in the rooms where tenants, company, or family might visit me," Hugh offered with studied casualness.

"Neither would I." Michael closed the ledger book with a snap and reshelved it in the same position from which he'd removed it. "You take the family parlor. I'll have a look around upstairs."

Hugh's expression went blank, pityingly blank, for it was a sorry day when a man had to search through his uncle's personal effects for evidence of a crime against family.

Sixteen

"I TOLD HIM." LACHLAN'S VOICE HELD HOPE AND PRIDE.

Maeve didn't so much as turn to face him. "You told who?"

"I told the laird you didn't take the carrots." Lachlan scrambled up onto the bench beneath the parapets. "You're not supposed to be up here alone."

Boys were stupid. Cook was stupid. Older brothers were stupidest of all.

"You're up here with me, so I'm not alone, and Brenna said I could come up here."

If Maeve were honest, she'd admit she was glad to see Lachlan, even if he had kept silent while she'd suffered many injustices.

Lachlan picked at a bit of moss growing from a crack in the stones.

"Brenna probably said you could come up here when Prebish was about, or Elspeth. If you fell off the parapets, your head would split open like a tomato. You shouldn't come up here without Elspeth or Brenna or somebody, and you should wear a shawl because it's colder than down in the bailey. Don't you want to know what I said?"

Maeve was cold, inside and out, and she ached the way crying always made her ache. If she were with Bridget and Kevin, Bridget would have asked her to turn pages at the pianoforte while they sang silly songs, or Kevin might have taken her for a ramble to visit the latest batch of puppies.

"All I want is to go home to Ireland. If you knew I didn't take the carrots, why did you let Cook yell at me, and then let Michael send me to my room?"

Almost as bad as the false accusations was that Lachlan had heard the whole business. To know he'd been able to speak up for her, and had waited until later to do so, made everything worse.

Even worse, when things couldn't really get any worse.

"Nobody listens when they're mad," Lachlan said, standing on the bench to drop his bit of moss into the bailey below. "Besides, I didn't want anybody to hear what I said to the laird."

A ray of cheer shone through Maeve's black mood. "You broke something, in the butler's pantry. Was it something valuable?"

"I made any noise I could so they'd stop pestering you. I didn't mean to break the platter."

Maeve's upset eased a trifle. "Will you have to pay for the platter? Kevin gave me some money for my own before I left Ireland." Kevin, who often smelled of horses and might yell at her sometimes, but only when she deserved it.

Lachlan picked another bit of moss loose, a larger patch, and peered over the stone crenellations. Maeve stood too, because the view from up here was very grand.

"I'll pay for what I broke. Da would want me to, but the laird said it was an accident, and we all make mistakes. I think he'll apologize to you." The larger chunk of moss went sailing down, down, down to land in a pot of pansies.

"Apologizing is nice. You shouldn't throw things into the bailey like that."

Because somebody could come out of the castle or the stables and get pelted with the moss, and Maeve would probably be blamed for that too.

Lachlan shot her a grin. "It's fun, but I'm cold. They'll change the flag when the party starts tomorrow. It takes two men, one to climb up, and one to keep a rope on the climber. For safety."

The party. All over again, Maeve felt the lump in her throat, the ache that was for Ireland, but not only for Ireland. The ache was because everybody was excited about that party, and nobody had time for her, not even when she asked if she could help. She turned her back to the cold stones, watching the pennant above them whip and flap in the stout breeze.

"Climbing up there wouldn't be so hard. The stones stick out like a ladder. Do you think I could see Ireland from up there?"

"I think you could fall off the roof and split your head open on the cobbles," Lachlan said. "I wouldn't like that."

Tumbling from the roof would be awful, but for a few seconds, it might also feel like flying free.

"I don't want to go back down to the kitchen."

Because an apology was a fine thing, for making the wrongdoer feel better, but a few humble words wouldn't undo the sense of betrayal Maeve felt from Cook, her brother, and even Lachlan.

"I thought I'd find you two up here." Brenna stood in the doorway to the winding steps, a shawl about her shoulders. "This was my favorite place when I was your age, but that breeze is chilly."

"I have boots to polish," Lachlan said, rising and brushing past Brenna. "Good day, my lady."

Brenna unwrapped her shawl and tucked it around Maeve's shoulders, bringing Maeve warmth and the scent of flowers. Then she sat beside Maeve and laid her arm across Maeve's shoulders.

"Did you come up here to cry, wee Maeve?"

Of course, she had, but now that somebody who was blameless and even understanding was at hand, Maeve couldn't say that.

"Lachlan broke a platter. He might have to pay for it."

Brenna patted Maeve's arm while the wind snapped the pennant's rope against the flap pole in a rhythmic flap-flap-flap.

"What was the boot boy doing, carting a break-able platter about, I wonder? Platters are heavy, and Lachlan has a fair bit of growing to do."

Platters were heavy, and homesickness was heavier still. Maeve turned her nose to Brenna's shoulder.

"I want to go home."

"I know, lass. It's good that you have some place you love so much you miss it, but missing home and family hurts too. I'm glad you're here, though."

Those words helped—some. "Can you invite Bridget and Kevin for a visit?"

Brenna withdrew her arm, and when she straightened, even being wrapped in her shawl didn't compensate Maeve for the resulting lack of warmth.

"I cannot, because your sister ought not to travel when she's close to having the baby, and I cannot tarry up here but a minute, there's so much to be done."

"I hate Scotland."

"Come here," Brenna said, moving to the side of the parapets that looked out over the loch.

Maeve hopped off the stone bench, keeping Brenna's shawl wrapped tightly about her, because the wind was worse on this side of the parapets.

"Ireland is that way," Brenna said, stretching out a hand in the direction of the loch. The water was dark today and frosted with whitecaps, and not a soul stirred on the shore. "There's water between Scotland and Ireland, but also lots of beautiful countryside. You might write to your sister, you know. Tell her everything you don't like about this place, tell her you miss her."

"That would be a long letter."

Brenna's smile wasn't that of a grown-up indulging a silly little girl. Her smile said she understood that even a silly little girl's life could be hard and lonely sometimes. "You may use my desk, and I'll have Cook send up a pot of chocolate. I can't have you taking a chill."

That felt good, to be ever so gently scolded for lingering up on the windy heights. Maeve followed Brenna down the winding steps and started on a mental list of all the things about Scotland worth hating.

The upper reaches of Angus's house were not well lit, the housekeeper, as was prudent, having closed every drape and door to keep out the chill breeze and protect paintings, rugs, and furniture from the damaging effects of the sun.

Michael found his uncle's bedroom on the third try, the ubiquitous pipe scent even stronger than usual.

The space was not unusual for a comfortably well-off gentleman's private chamber, though Angus's personal finances were becoming a mental sore tooth. A large bed dominated the room, raised two steps for warmth, swagged with burgundy velvet and adorned with matching pillows tasseled in gold.

The bed was more imposing than the one Michael shared with Brenna.

The shelves were full of books, some in French, titled in gilt lettering. A sturdy rocker sat near a large hearth, and a wardrobe occupied an interior wall. Above the hearth, where Michael might have expected a landscape of the Scottish countryside, a hunting scene, or some grand depiction of a stirring moment of Scottish history, hung another rendering of the children with the kitten.

Unusual, perhaps, but not if Michael's own mother had furnished the place.

And yet… Why would Angus, who'd adorned his bed with tasseled pillows, keep that portrait as the last thing he saw each night?

The sense of evidence eluding notice resurged, and along with it, a repugnance for the task Michael had set himself.

The search here must be thorough, so Michael

started with the wardrobe, intent on working his way
around the room. Angus was well dressed, his shirts
beautifully made, his boots a testament to the quality
of goods available when a man had coin. Formal clan
attire hung on the inside of the wardrobe door, proof
Angus meant to attend the next day's gathering.

And yet, something was off.

The wardrobe was a massive piece, as wardrobes
tended to be. Nearly as high as the ceiling, several feet
wide and several feet deep. The floor of the wardrobe
was a good foot higher than the rug upon which it sat,
however, suggesting...

The false bottom came up easily, revealing a space
packed the way a sailor might stow his goods in a
trunk. Every inch of the compartment was used, and
every article positioned for ease of access. To one side,
Michael found yet more books, including what looked
like sketchbooks.

A cold foreboding slithered through Michael's guts,
a certainty that this was a central piece of the puzzle
that must be put together if Michael was to make his
castle a home for those he loved.

Somebody moved about below stairs, a door
closed—Hugh, nosing around among the pipe smoke
and ledgers. Michael was abruptly glad that whatever
lay in the bottom of Angus's wardrobe would not be
revealed to any save Michael.

On closer inspection, the wardrobe held journals,
the entries in the same tidy hand as all the ledgers in
the office. Michael took a sketchbook off the bottom
of the stack and crossed the room to a cushioned
window seat, the better to see what he'd found.

He pushed the drapes wide and flipped open the book to a page at random. The images on the page, the precision and skill in them, gave Michael a momentary reprieve from absorbing what he was seeing. When his mind caught up with the evidence of his eyes, he endured the sensation of a great mean fist squeezing his lungs, until his very vision dimmed, and his ears roared.

Hugh found him in the window seat, an indefinite while later. "Laird?"

At some point, Michael had thrown the sketchbook halfway across the room, and he saw now that it lay open on the rug before the empty hearth, a stash of letters having come free of it as well.

What was needful was that Michael get up, gather those letters, and close that damned sketchbook, so nobody would ever see its contents.

He could not move.

"Something amiss?" Hugh asked, hovering in the doorway. "I found nothing in the family parlor but more sketches of you, your sisters, and Brenna as a child, more cutwork and some framed embroidery. Not a very manly decorating scheme, but then I suppose a dower property—"

Hugh's words landed in Michael's awareness like so many crows chattering from the parapets high above the bailey, while Michael's every certainty about life and about himself lay shattered like Lachlan's pretty platter in the dark confines of the butler's pantry.

"Laird?"

"Don't call me that, and don't you dare look at the damned book."

So, of course, Hugh glanced down at the open sketchbook. "Jesus, Mary, and Joseph."

The holy family, the very last invocation Michael might have chosen, given what was revealed in Angus's drawing.

"I said not to look."

"I'm not looking," Hugh said, toeing the book closed as if it were a source of contagion, which it most assuredly was. "You did, though. You looked at every page?"

Michael managed a single nod, and the remains of his breakfast threatened a reprise. Fortunately, Hugh was a father, a privilege Michael would never know, which was likely why Hugh could speak calmly even in the grip of fierce emotion.

"Where did this piece of excrement come from?" Hugh asked, gathering up the letters scattered on the rug.

"Bottom of the wardrobe. I want to wash my hands, Hugh."

And he wanted to kill his uncle. A small desperate hope remained that Angus had drawn those pictures from imagination, that Brenna hadn't been made to pose without her clothing for an adult male's perverted pleasure, that were Michael to read Angus's journals, he'd find a recounting of crops harvested and calves born.

Hugh shoved the sketchbook back where it had come from, replaced the floor of the wardrobe, and latched its doors. "Take this."

A handkerchief, the plain farmer's variety, sporting a half-inch tear and a small clumsy embroidered bouquet likely done by wee Annie.

Annie, whom nobody had allowed near Angus.

The small desperate hope guttered and died amid a blackness without end. Michael could not touch the flowers a little girl had sewn to brighten her papa's day.

"I want to kill him."

And Michael wanted to die. Wanted to cast himself into an endless desolation as great as the sorrow welling in his chest.

Hugh eyed the wardrobe as if writhing, slimy things lived inside and were struggling to get free.

"You saw some sketches. You can't kill a man for sketches."

They were sketches of Brenna, but perhaps Hugh hadn't realized that. Michael pressed his own handkerchief against his eyes, a bit of silk Michael stored among Brenna's dresses because he wanted the scent of her near throughout the day.

"Somebody should go through what's in that wardrobe," Hugh said.

"Nobody should have to do that," Michael retorted, letting his head fall back to rest against the wall of the window seat. "I saw enough."

Brenna in poses far too seductive for tender years, Brenna as the first harbingers of womanhood unfurled in a child's form, Brenna with trust and hope shining from her eyes, though she wore not a stitch over her small body.

And for nine long years, Michael had left Brenna to contend with the monster who'd abused her, all because Michael had never imagined a monster might enjoy devouring more than one variety of prey.

꧁

"You're quiet," Brenna observed as Michael dragged a brush through his hair. "Are you planning your apology to Maeve?"

He studied the brush, Brenna's brush, actually, as if he weren't sure how it had arrived in his hand.

"I forgot to apologize to Maeve." Then he stood before his shaving mirror, brush in hand, as if he'd also forgotten the next step in his end-of-day routine.

Rather than puzzle over her husband's peculiar mood, Brenna turned down the covers on the bed.

"Maeve probably expected you to apologize at dinner, and that's why she was so quiet. Then too, we're all tired, getting ready for tomorrow. Are you looking forward to the festivities?"

"Yes."

That small word conveyed anything but gleeful anticipation. Brenna scooped coals into the warming pan, but wasn't careful enough with the hearth tools, so a few red embers went spilling onto the bricks.

"Careful," Michael said, a bit sharply.

Brenna dealt with the small mess, closed the lid of the warmer, and aimed a smile over her shoulder at her husband.

"Tend to your washing off, Michael. Your hair is quite brushed, considering I might well put it all awry before morning."

He set the brush down and retreated behind the privacy screen, not a hint of an answering smile to be seen.

Since coming north from England, Michael had been the soul of patience, good cheer, and consideration. Something had put him off stride today, maybe something to do with working among the men earlier.

"Are you concerned that we're spending too much on tomorrow's gathering?" Because Brenna was concerned. Ever since losing a year's worth of wool money, she was concerned over every groat and farthing.

"I am not." He emerged from behind the privacy screen in nothing but his kilt, his expression unreadable.

"I've shown you my finances," Brenna said, slipping off her robe. "When will you show me yours?"

She tossed the question out in hopes it might catch Michael's interest, because whatever was amiss with him, he was behaving like a stranger—a worrisome stranger.

The look he gave her, his hands on the fastening of his kilt, his eyes...*bleak*. That look chilled as surely as the draft sneaking in under the door kept the floor toe-freezing cold.

"Every penny I have is yours, Brenna. Every pound, every...thing I lay claim to on this earth is yours for the asking." He sat heavily on the bed, his kilt still on. "We're man and wife."

Brenna sat beside him and laid the back of her hand to his brow. "You've no fever. Are you sickening for something?"

"Possibly."

A memory came to her, of their wedding night. She'd begged and begged for him to take her away with him when he joined his regiment, and he'd grown quieter and quieter, until she'd fallen asleep in his arms.

He was growing that quiet now.

"Do you need a posset?" Brenna asked, though instinct told her a posset wouldn't put her husband to rights.

"I need to sleep." He rose to push the peat and coals to the back of the fireplace, snugged the screen to the bricks, and blew out the bedside candles. "If you'd oblige me?"

Brenna rose from his side of the bed, her puzzlement edging closer to panic. "Is something wrong, Michael?"

He got into bed without taking his kilt off, and that frightened her.

"Get into bed, Brenna. Tomorrow will be a long day."

Every day was long, but the days since Michael's return had also been good days, mostly. She climbed in on her side of the big bed and did not presume to snuggle up to her husband.

"You're still wearing your kilt, Michael."

He rustled around beneath the covers until his left fist emerged holding a length of plaid, which he tossed to the foot of the bed. "Good night, Brenna."

He hadn't kissed her. Hadn't even found her hand beneath the covers and given her fingers a squeeze.

He hadn't dusted his big feet together before stretching out on the mattress.

He'd spoken a truth—they were man and wife, and soldiers home from war could be given to odd moods. Brenna ought to have taken this into account sooner. She punched her pillow, hard, then flopped down beside her spouse.

"If you continue to behave like this, Michael Brodie, I will soon miss you every bit as much as I did the first year of your absence."

"I did not deserve to be missed, but believe this, if you believe nothing else about me, Brenna. I regret leaving you behind. I regret that bitterly."

"I got over it," she said, which was in the nature of a truth belatedly admitted rather than a lie. "I did get your letter about Corunna."

He shifted to his side, so he faced her, and yet Brenna remained on her back. Whatever was wrong with him tonight, even the weight of her stare might send him out of their bed, into some dark place she could not follow.

"Mention the name Corunna to any soldier who served in that campaign, and you will fill him with a sorrow and dread that…" Michael's voice trailed off.

Brenna waited, because his letter had been short and factual. A headlong retreat across more than two hundred miles of northern Spain, the French in pursuit, pounding at the stragglers, at times near blizzard conditions ensuring the camp followers were the most vulnerable, and army discipline disintegrating into looting and mayhem.

When the remains of the British Army had straggled, sick and exhausted, onto the coast, the evacuation ships had taken two more days to reach them.

"You spared me that, Michael. You spared me all that brutality and violence, all that sickness, injury, and disease. You talked about the horses that had to be shot, hundreds of them, foundered and starving, the wounded left under horrific conditions. I might easily have been with child, or even had a child…"

He was over her without warning, an avalanche of heat and husband.

"Hush. For the love of God, please hush. I do not deserve your forgiveness." His arms held her in a desperate embrace, and yet he made no move to kiss her. No arousal nudged at Brenna's sex; no tender caress swept across her brow.

"There is nothing to forgive, Michael. You fought your battles. I fought mine, such as they were." She tightened her arms around him. "We have the rest of our lives together, and I, for one, am grateful for that. Very grateful."

He shuddered, as if a sexual paroxysm claimed him, or a great grief. When he rolled back to his side of the bed, Brenna at first let him go.

"What is wrong, Michael? I am your wife, and I will endure much if you ask it of me. Your silence cuts at me."

"Some silences are meant to be kind. You understand that. You probably understand that far better than most." A spate of sentences. Brenna drew encouragement from his loquaciousness and possessed herself of her husband's hand.

"Most silences need to be broken. I've been looking for a way to bring up some difficult matters, Husband. Old business, as it were. I haven't known how, but after we've seen to this nonsense tomorrow, I will want some of your time."

She hadn't meant to say any of that, though darkness was certainly appropriate to her declaration.

"You have already endured much as my wife, Brenna. I am more sorry for that than I can say."

"You're daft." Brenna cuddled up to his side and slid an arm under his neck. "You haven't been home long enough to properly try my patience." She kissed his cheek. "Go to sleep, and when we've rendered every man, woman, and child in the shire feeble with drink, and the old ladies have danced the lads under the table, we'll clear up a few matters."

She kept her arms around him, though he was inert in her embrace. He'd survived the retreat to Corunna and worse, and yet, Brenna felt as if she held not a veteran, but a casualty.

For the cheek she'd kissed had been wet with tears.

"What has you planted here, quiet as a tomb?" Hugh put the question to his laird, because Elspeth had bid him to keep close watch on the man. Without any intention on Hugh's part, the entirety of the previous day's awful developments had come spilling forth in Elspeth's hearing, and when she'd finished swearing and stomping about the clearing—Hugh had become very fond of this little clearing—she'd charged Hugh with keeping watch over the laird.

While Elspeth tried to split her vigilance between the child Maeve, and a very busy Brenna.

Michael tossed a sprig of mutilated heather off into the undergrowth. "You were right."

Neil often spoke in the same fashion—a handful of words wrenched from him, leaving the listener to puzzle meaning as much from the silence as the syllables.

"I am frequently right, though my brothers are loath to admit it." Hugh took the place beside Michael on the bench. "I am guessing, though, in this case, I will rather I was not such an infallible fellow."

He would rather his laird had started in drinking, as the men in the village had earlier in the day. A Highland celebration that did not start until sundown would start far too late in the day, and waste hours that might be spent dancing and eating.

"You are a good fellow," Michael said, rising. "What you were right about is I should have searched all of Angus's effects when I had the chance. Something sticks in my mind about the contents of that wardrobe."

The contents of that wardrobe would stick in Hugh's mind when he was an old blind man.

"These are yours," he said, fishing some letters out of his sporran. "I didn't read them."

He hadn't had to, because they were letters a young soldier sent home to his even younger wife. They would have been full of love and longing, like every letter Hugh had ever written his Anne.

"These were…"

"With that other," Hugh said, the word "sketch-book" having acquired connotations worse than any curse word. "I don't think your lady wife ever received this correspondence."

The clearing was a peaceful place, particularly in late afternoon when the golden summer sun slanted down through the trees, birds flittered about, and a lone squirrel chattered high above. Hugh had made some wonderful memories with Elspeth here, and it was good to have those memories now, when Michael rose off the bench and kicked a sizable rock many yards away.

"I am full of murder," Michael said softly. "As full

of murder as if my regiment had just broken another endless siege, and every soldier fallen outside the city walls is screaming from his unshriven grave for vengeance against the enemy. I am not full of justice, Hugh, I am full of murder. Sick with it, and I fear I'll find no cure."

Crazy talk, but the man had cause. "You cannot do murder. You have a party to host."

Michael sent another rock hurtling down the slope. A deer went crashing up the path a moment later, and the squirrel ceased making a sound.

"Brenna wants to talk to me. The only reason I am standing here in my lordly finery, the only reason I am not sharpening my dirk and hunting my uncle down like the traitor to decency he is, is because my wife has old business to discuss with me."

"Then you'll put aside your murder long enough to listen to her."

The fight—the murder, disgust, rage, whatever—ebbed enough that Michael's shoulders dropped.

"It's myself I want to kill most, you know. I've puzzled out that much."

Hugh was far out of his depth, and yet, Elspeth had raised a few questions, about that sketchbook and Neil, and the names—four younger fellows, two lasses—penciled on those six leases set aside from the others.

"How will taking your own life help Brenna now?"

"It won't. I am sick and reeling, Hugh, but you needn't worry that I'll end my life and leave Angus Brodie laird of anything or anyone I care about. I'm the worst husband that ever took a wife, a poor friend, and a miserable excuse for a man, but I'm not that craven."

For all he was tall and handsome in his fancy dress, for all that his wife probably shared none of those conclusions, the laird was imperiled by what he'd learned yesterday.

"Angus is down at the pub," Hugh said, rising from the hard little bench. "Every spare servant is getting the castle ready for the gathering this evening, and that means Angus's house is again deserted. I've wondered where the money came from that supports Angus's fancy mistress in Aberdeen."

"I know where the money came from," Michael said, turning his face up to a shaft of sunlight and closing his eyes. "I know exactly where it came from, though now more than ever, proof is necessary."

He might have been a saint transfigured by remorse, so sorrowful did the sunlight render his features, and in that sylvan, peaceful, fraught moment, Hugh understood something more painful, even, than what he'd seen in those awful drawings.

"A part of you still loves your uncle."

Michael opened his eyes. "He taught me the dances, Hugh. He taught me to sketch and to fish. So often, when my father could see nothing except that I would be laird someday and must be tough and strong, Angus was the one who made sense of my childhood injuries to pride and distracted me from my sulks. I cannot…"

This was what imperiled an otherwise strong man, a contradiction of the heart so powerful, Hugh could find no words to comfort the one suffering it.

"What will you do, Laird?"

Michael spoke gently. "If it had been Annie in those drawings, Hugh, what would you do? Or Lachlan?"

Hugh said nothing, for the question was rhetorical and the answer was...murder.

"Exactly," Michael said, heading for the path. "Keep an eye on Brenna for me, please. The guests will soon assemble, and my wife will expect me to open the dancing with her."

He strode off through the undergrowth, not along the path, but in a direct line up through the bracken and heather toward the empty dower house.

Seventeen

THE DAY HAD BEEN BUSY, LOVELY AS ONLY A SCOTTISH summer day could be, and nerve wracking as hell, for Brenna had hardly seen her husband.

"Where's Michael?" Brenna asked Milly St. Clair. "I thought he was with your baron."

Milly and her baron were both in borrowed Highland finery, sporting Stuart plaid, as loyal subjects of the Crown were entitled to wear. Through the passage into the great hall, St. Clair and the musicians were adding a table to the buffet already groaning with food.

"He might be among the crowd outside," Milly said, peering through a window. "Every man, woman, and child has gathered in the bailey, and it's quite colorful."

"Michael and I will open the dancing." Brenna stole her hundredth glance at the clock and wondered why she and Michael hadn't practiced dancing together. "If he hasn't left the shire."

Would her request for some time to clear up old business have sent him away? Could he have known she'd meant for him to learn of her past with Angus?

"You must not look so worried," Milly chided softly. "This is a party. It's Michael's welcome home, and his first celebration as laird. Everybody is intent on enjoying themselves."

Elspeth was intent on ordering the menfolk around as she had them pick up the empty table and carry it to the other end of the buffet.

"Have you seen Maeve?" For Brenna had delegated keeping track of the girl to Elspeth and hadn't spotted Maeve since midday.

"She's probably out among the neighbors, making all manner of new friends with their children," Milly replied. "We should be out there too."

Making small talk, while Brenna wanted nothing more than to find her husband and ask him why, after barely speaking to her before bed, he'd slept with his arms wrapped around her through the entire night.

If he'd even been sleeping.

"Elspeth, you'll cease giving orders now," Brenna called. "Let the musicians tune up, tell MacDowell to tap the first keg, and get you out into the bailey to snabble Hugh for the first dance."

Somebody set his corner of the table down on somebody else's toe, or near enough to occasion foul language, and Brenna's impatience coiled more tightly. Violence was an aspect of many celebrations, at least once the whisky had been flowing for a few hours and the children all put to bed.

"Come, you two," St. Clair said, winging an arm at each lady. "The Baron Strathdee will be along any minute, and if we're not out visiting in the bailey when he arrives to collect his baroness, my life will be forfeit."

"Or your toes," Brenna muttered. "Where *is* the Baron Strathdee?"

St. Clair suffered a minute hesitation in his progress toward the French doors opening onto the bailey. "He's on his way, I assure you."

"Are we in a hurry, Baron?" Brenna asked, for St. Clair had resumed his escort at a brisk pace indeed.

"We are not, but the evening is pleasant, and I'm sure you'll want to show off your finery as much as I want to show off my wife."

What Brenna wanted was to be done with the entire gathering, to find Michael and dragoon him off to share a blanket under the stars. A woman could explain some things better that way, with a wee dram at hand and no castle walls to hear her tales.

"There's your baron," Milly said as they emerged from the ballroom onto the terrace. "He looks splendid in his formal attire."

Michael looked...splendidly furious. Coldly, beautifully furious as he strode up the path from the dower house.

"Stay near me," St. Clair muttered, sliding an arm around his wife. "Both of you women, stay near me."

Michael was carrying something. Brenna couldn't see what, though the crowd parted near the back to make way for him.

"Angus Brodie!" Michael bellowed. "Show yourself now!"

Foreboding rose up inside Brenna, a foreboding that had slept beneath her heart for years.

"Michael," she called, "now is not the time."

He gave no sign he'd heard her, no sign he could hear any words of reason.

"Angus Brodie, show yourself to your laird!"

Michael's words rang out over the crowd, who came to an uneasy, milling quiet.

"I'm here," Angus said, sidling through the throng to mount the steps not six feet away from Brenna. "Are we to have a disagreement before the drinking has even started?"

His attempt at brusque jocularity fell as flat as if it had been dumped over the parapets above.

"We are to have an explanation," Michael said with soft menace. "All of us here are ready to listen to your explanation." He spoke from the middle of the crowd, and even as angry as he was, Brenna wanted him closer— wanted him where she could look into his eyes, where she could clap a hand over his fool mouth lest years of silence come to an end in the wrong place at the wrong time.

Something went sailing over the heads of the crowd to land at Angus's feet.

"Explain that, Angus Brodie," Michael spat.

"It's a leather satchel," Angus said without glancing down. "I suspect half the folk gathered here have owned something similar, and they would not trespass on my privacy to locate this one."

And abruptly, Brenna was glad for St. Clair's steadying hand on her arm. Neil MacLogan was at her back, and Hugh on her other side. Wherever Maeve was, Brenna prayed she'd stay there, because the mood of the crowd was anything but festive.

"That," Michael said, marching up the steps, "is a leather satchel I made for my dear intended years ago with my own hands. It's a clumsy effort, a boy's effort, but I labored over it long, wanting the young lady to have the finest gift I was capable of giving her. The leather on the shoulder strap doesn't match the hides I used to make the bag, because I could not afford to make the entire satchel of the better leather, and I put extra knots in the lacings, so the bag would be sturdy."

Hugh swore viciously under his breath, while Brenna sustained a discordant sense of relief: Michael was confronting Angus about a stolen birthday gift, not bringing up years of intimate perversion.

Then a sensation like vertigo seized her, for that very bag—

"You stole from your own people," Michael said, his voice a low, vicious lash. "You took a year's worth of wool money, saw Brenna and her cousins blamed for your larceny, cast tenants off their holdings when your thievery meant they couldn't pay their rents, and presented yourself to me as the relation who'd held my estate together when I was soldiering far from home."

"I recall that bag," Hugh MacLogan said, staring at Angus's feet. "I recall how Brenna treasured it, for all it was a homely thing for a lady to carry her belongings about in. And you spent the money you stole from us on your expensive whore down in Aberdeen, didn't you, Angus Brodie? We went cold and hungry so you could cavort in style, while all held Brenna in contempt for being your victim."

An ugly murmur went through the crowd, silenced by Neil MacLogan's voice.

"Not an expensive whore," Neil said. "An expensive brothel, catering to men who prey on the very young. The only problem with that brothel is that the woman who owns it then preys on her own clients, charging them exorbitantly for her silence."

The ugly murmur swelled and blended with a sense of past and present crashing together over Brenna's head and drowning her in memories and emotions held in check for years.

"Michael." The roaring in her ears and dimming of her vision said she'd soon lose consciousness. St. Clair's grip on her arm became necessary if she was to stay upright. "Michael, *please*."

He could not hear her over the jeering and accusations of the crowd, and yet, Brenna needed desperately to reach him. "Michael, you must not—"

Words were useless against the rising tide of outrage coming from the clansmen and women in the bailey. As both nausea and darkness tried to obliterate her will, Brenna used the last of her determination to reach for the one source of strength remaining to her.

She grabbed Michael's hand and held on tight.

❧

Violence rose up in Michael's mind and body, a gleeful, primitive impulse that would glory in ending Angus Brodie's life. He knew bloodlust—any soldier who'd breached the walls of a besieged city knew bloodlust—but this was a far richer inspiration, its current higher, faster, and deeper for being driven by outrage and vengeance.

"Michael."

Somebody tried to get his attention, a pesky little midge of a distraction as the crowd seized on the horrified, delighted sense of having found an outlet for years of misery and victimization. Their hatred of Angus Brodie was converted in a few moments from a shortcoming any Christian would wrestle into ashamed submission, to a source of righteous pride.

"I'm sorry, laddie," Angus muttered. "I am so verra sorry. If you must kill me—"

Laddie.

"Michael, *please*."

Laddie.

"This is getting ugly," St. Clair said. "I'm taking the women—"

Fingernails bit into Michael's hand as a whiff of lavender assailed him.

"Michael, stop them. You must stop them." Brenna slammed into his side, the very person to whom Angus had done the greatest injury.

"St. Clair, take my wife—"

"*No!* I will not be sent away while you do murder because an old man turned thief! Not murder, Michael, never that. *This is our home.*"

Somebody yelled for a rope; somebody answered that a knife would do, and many knives would do even better.

"Michael, *there are children here*. You cannot do this." Brenna's hold on him became desperate. "You shall not allow this to happen."

She was asking—begging—that he shut the beast back in its cave, that he find self-restraint when every instinct screamed at him to do murder, and on her behalf.

"Michael, please don't. I could not live with myself if I condoned such rapacious behavior."

She'd chosen a word even Michael could not ignore: *rapacious*, from old Latin roots, meaning to seize and carry off. In his years of soldiering, Michael had seen a bloody lot of seizing and carrying off, but rapacious behavior required first that a man's honor be carried off. His reason, his pretensions to civility.

His ability to govern his own evil impulses.

Neil MacLogan took Angus by the shoulder in a punishing grip, but when he would have shoved Angus down the steps, Michael found his voice.

"Hold!" Michael used the bellow that could be heard over battle, over riot, looting, and the screams of women subjected to the aftermath of battle. "I am your laird, and I said *hold*!"

The crowd settled into an uneasy, seething quiet.

"He deserves to die," a woman shouted. "My boys are gone, and I'll die alone because Angus Brodie had to have his rents."

"So he could go down to Aberdeen and be wicked!" another called out.

On Michael's left, Angus's expression was a mask of regret that would make not a one of his many victims whole, and yet, he said nothing in his own defense.

On Michael's right, Brenna was tucked against him, her cheeks wet with tears.

He wanted to avenge the wrong done her in the most immediate, violent manner possible, but as Brenna wrapped her arms around him, Michael recognized that impulse as self-serving. If he'd stayed home to be a proper husband to her, Angus's thievery, at least, could have been averted.

"Brenna has been wronged not only by Angus," Michael said, loudly enough that his words could reach every corner of the bailey, "but also by each of us. When Angus stole that money, he took coin from you. He took bread from the mouths of your children and elderly, he took your rents, but from Brenna, he took all of that, and *he took her good name.*"

Michael waited for the crowd to again quiet, while Brenna sagged against him, perhaps in relief rather than devastation.

"Brenna was the victim of a crime, a young woman alone, who'd bargained well for her people, who'd never given any of you cause to doubt her. When you might have taken up for her, you instead listened to Angus—a man you didn't even *like*—and you blamed her, cast aspersion on her, and turned your backs on her, though you knew she was without a husband or father's protection."

The ugly mood turned quieter, shame diluting righteous bloodlust.

"Brenna says that Angus should be brought up before the justice of the peace." The relief Michael felt in Brenna was unmistakable now. "She says we are not to do murder while our children stand watch. If we bring harm to Angus Brodie tonight, without giving him a chance to present evidence or speak in his own behalf, then we place ourselves beyond the realm of decency, as he has."

Milly St. Clair had taken up a position on Brenna's other side; Sebastian crowded close to his wife. Hugh had his arm around Elspeth, while Neil and Dantry MacLogan flanked Angus.

"Go home," Michael said, fatigue pitching his voice lower. "There will be no gathering in the great hall.

As your laird, as the man who for years did not protect Brenna Brodie or safeguard her happiness, I am telling you all to go home. Unless she wills it otherwise, you will have to go through me if you seek to take justice into your own hands with respect to Angus."

The quiet from the crowd shifted, perhaps in relief that murder was to be denied a village entitled to it, perhaps in shame.

Vera MacDonald stumped across the cobbles toward the gate. "I have letters to write."

Mairead Dolan was next, dragging a random child with her. "As do I."

The menfolk were apparently not as willing to heed Michael's guidance, except for Davey MacCray. "I've drinking to do, particularly if you'll send some of that food down to the village."

Martin Dingle fell in step beside Davey as they trailed after Vera and Mairead. "Then I've an inn to open and a barrel to tap."

The moment eased enough that Michael could wrap his arms around his wife and wonder how in the hell matters between them could ever come right, when Lachlan's voice pierced the shuffle of feet and the mutters of the dissipating crowd.

"Laird, you mun come now! Maeve's on the parapets, and she canna get doon!"

❧

Brenna's head lifted from Michael's chest. "Michael, we have to help her. The dew falls on those stones, and they're slick, and she's—"

When Brenna might have pelted back into the

castle, Michael stayed her by virtue of their joined hands. "Wait, Wife. A crowd up there will only complicate things. I need one man, the same as if we're changing the flag. You fetch a blanket, for the child will be chilled."

"I'll come," Neil said. "I climbed to the flagpole as a boy many times." A look passed between Neil and, of all people, Angus.

Angus, who was uncomfortable with heights.

"Don't stand here arguing," Brenna pleaded, wrenching free of Michael's grasp. "I'll scramble to the roof myself, but we can't leave her there, frightened, chilled, unable to come down—"

"I'll go." At those words, the remaining crowd, as one body, paused to regard Angus. "I'll get her down. Neil is a stranger to the child, she's out of charity with her brother, and I am...I am on good terms with the girl."

"Let him come," Brenna said, and for Michael, that decided the matter. "And on Monday, he goes before the justice of the peace."

"Aye," Angus said, as if Brenna's pronouncement determined not only their present course of action, but every outstanding issue on all sides.

They traveled up the shadowed steps in a quiet, tense parade. Michael, Brenna, and Angus, the crowd having again formed below.

"Wait here," Michael said to his wife as they reached the top of the steps. "We'll get her down to you safely, I promise you." Though slick old stones, an unpredictable wind, and the encroaching night made his promise more of a prayer.

Brenna wanted to argue, wanted to charge onto the parapets and snatch the child from the roof herself. Michael saw that in her eyes, and saw as well that she trusted him to keep his word.

"Be damned careful, Michael Brodie. I love you far too much and have waited far too long for you to come home. Step carefully along the side of this mountain."

He well could take a bad step and fall to his death, and yet, her words were worth risking his life for.

"I love you too, Brenna Brodie."

They kissed each other on the mouth, a spontaneous mutual impulse that further fortified Michael as he faced the gusting wind coming off the parapets. He took down the rope looped on a hook at the top of the staircase, intent on securing it around his waist, when movement caught his eye.

Angus had already climbed onto the crenellations.

Without a rope, while Maeve huddled above them at the base of the flagpole, a silent heap of shivering terror.

"Angus, for God's sake get the rope around you."

The older man paused, standing on the very parapet, as if he'd soar out over the bailey and take an aerial tour of the loch.

"I'll be safe enough, and I'll make sure wee Maeve is safe too. What could you be thinking, child, to climb up to that flagpole with nobody to mind you?"

His voice was conversational as he began the ascent that required use of strategically placed rocks up the vertical wall that joined the parapet and the roof over the stairway.

"I w-wanted to see Ireland."

"You might have asked Brenna to show you some

picture books and guide books," Angus said, gaining the lip of the roof. "Or I might have sketched you some landscapes. The wind's a bit brisk up here, isn't it?"

His tone was so matter-of-fact, at complete variance with the terror roiling in Michael's guts, the wind slapping the pennant and its rope against the pole, and Maeve's shivering.

"I wanted to see h-home," Maeve said, "over the water. Far, far away. I want to *go* home."

With a grunt and a heave, Angus made the perilous transition around the gutters circling the roof, only to slip and scramble for purchase on the climbing stones.

"Be careful!" Maeve cried.

"You needn't worry about me, child," Angus said, his tone gently chiding. "The matter wants another try is all. Lachlan is fretting about you. He's a good lad, is Lachlan MacLogan. You should not have given him cause for anxiety."

"Lachlan said Ireland isn't home for me anymore."

Angus had again shifted his weight up around the gutters, though the effort had cost him. He remained on the edge of the roof, breathing heavily.

"You knew the lad was right," Angus said. "You belong to us now, and you knew you might visit in Ireland, but your family is here now. You must be chilled to the bone, wee Maeve."

The last part was the most difficult, because the roof over the steps was of standing seam tin construction and conical. A steep slope, dewfall, age, and in places, moss, made the going treacherous. Had Angus been wearing a rope...

"Maeve Brodie, you will turn loose of that flagpole,"

Angus said, as if teasing her. "This is no place to spend the night when there are entire tables of desserts awaiting below." He teetered, slipped, and ultimately fell up the roof incline to land beside Maeve at the pinnacle. "It's a grand view, child. I'll give you that."

"Is that Ireland?" Maeve asked, pointing out over the loch. "That high, high peak behind the hills. Is that Ireland?"

Brenna came out onto the parapets far enough to pass Michael a soft Brodie tartan, then retreated to the top of the steps, out of the wind.

"I cannot say if that's Ireland or Scotland," Angus replied. "It might well be a bit of Ireland, and there's none up here to say otherwise, is there? Now give me your hand, child, or Lachlan will get first pick of those desserts. I think you might fancy the lemon tarts."

"I don't like lemons," Maeve said, unwrapping one hand from the flagpole and putting her palm in Angus's grasp. "Lemons are sour. I'm scared."

"No need to be frightened. Your brother and Brenna are waiting just below, and they won't scold you, wee Maeve. They'll scold themselves for not keeping better watch over you."

This was the Uncle Angus whom Michael had grown up with, the nice fellow who could put a small boy's fears and puzzlements into perspective. This Uncle Angus was a source of sense and safety when a lad thought he had few allies and many challenges.

A man of sense and safety should have worn a rope.

"Uncle Angus is right," Michael said. "I've owed you an apology since yesterday, Maeve, over that business with the carrots. I was wrong not to say I was sorry sooner. Do you forgive me?"

He raised the question because he needed the child's forgiveness, and because he needed to distract her from the peril she faced on her descent.

"I was mad at you," Maeve said, the wind snatching at her words. "You didn't even listen. You never take me up on your horse."

"I'm listening now, and I hope you're listening to me. Keep hold of Angus's hand, and don't try to stand up. I want you to scoot down the roof, slowly, slowly. By inches. Angus will hold your hand as long as he can, and if you slip, I'll catch you."

Though on that small, slick conical roof, she might well fall in the wrong direction.

"I'll be c-careful."

"You'll be warm and stuffing yourself with cream cakes in no time," Angus said. "Down you go, slowly, slowly, like your brother said."

Maeve heeded Angus when she might not have paid any attention to Michael's cautions. She clutched at Angus's hand, crouched, and inched down the roof, one foot, then another, then the first foot again. Michael positioned himself below her, his heart hammering, his arms upstretched.

"Well done, wee Maeve," Angus said as she hit the limit of his reach. "Only a few more feet, and Michael will catch you. That's my brave girl."

Her fingers slid free of Angus's grasp, and she paused, halfway down the roof. "I'm scared."

They were all bloody terrified.

"You're nearly down, Maeve," Michael said as a

stiff gust set the rope to whipping against the pole. "Another three feet, and you can dangle your feet over the edge. I'll have you then."

"Will you scold me?"

Please God, allow the child to live so she might endure many scoldings.

"I will not scold you for wanting to see home, but we will talk. You and I and Brenna will talk about how we can make the castle more of a home to you." Just as soon as Michael put a stout, locked gate across the door to the roof terrace, and hid the damned key from all save Brenna. His arms began to burn, even in the frigid wind. "Now get you down, please, so we can all get out of this breeze."

The rest was easy. Maeve scooted to the edge of the roof, dangled one little boot, then the other over the edge, and tipped herself the last few feet into Michael's embrace.

"You're safe," he said, clutching the girl to his chest as a cheer went up from below. "Thank the Almighty, you're safe."

She was also chilled to the bone. Michael let Brenna wrap the blanket around the girl but did not put her down. "Have some hot chocolate, at least, Maeve, and then Brenna will tuck you in lest you develop a lung fever. A tot of whisky might be in order. Lachlan will want to see you too."

"I can tell him I saw Ireland."

While in Michael's worst nightmares, he'd see his wee sister, crumpled and unmoving on the cobbles below.

"You tell him you did indeed see home, and I'll be by to say good night too."

He kissed the top of her head and set her on her feet, his own balance as unreliable as if he were standing on a slick roof in a high wind.

"Get Angus down," Brenna said, taking Maeve's hand. "And thank him."

She kissed Michael on the cheek and disappeared down the steps, Maeve's hand in hers, the tartan eclipsing all but the top of the child's head.

Leaving Michael to again face the bitter wind.

"Brenna said to thank you," he called up to his uncle.

Angus remained kneeling at the foot of the flagpole, his gaze fixed on the far peak Maeve had dubbed a bit of home.

"You cannot fathom that, can you, laddie? That Brenna could thank me for anything." He rose, a bit stiffly, his age showing. "Neither can I. It's beautiful up here. Captivatingly so."

Captivating was the word of an artist, not the vocabulary of a scheming, perverted old man, not even the word of an uncle.

"Angus, get the hell down. Now." The way his uncle gazed out over the hills and peaks as the sun dipped closer to the horizon made Michael uneasy.

"So you can haul me off to the gaol?" Angus asked, taking a cautious step away from the flagpole. "Do you suppose I'll fare well at the hands of justice, such a one as I?"

"Better than you would at the hands of a half-drunken, righteous mob."

Another cautious step. "D'ye think so? Felonies are serious business. I've had occasion to look up the penalties for several of them. The law does not deal in pleasant fates." Angus slipped, caught his balance, and resumed gazing out over the loch.

While Michael wrestled back the urge to point out that Brenna's fate, thanks to Angus, had not been pleasant, and she'd done nothing to deserve the misery he'd visited on her.

Neither had Neil MacLogan. Neither had Jack Deardorff and God knew how many others, at brothels in Aberdeen, or on the Brodie holdings.

"I'm weary, Michael," Angus said, sliding his foot another six inches down the incline. "I'm tired of my own wickedness, and yet, I can find no reprieve from it. Before I found that damned establishment in Aberdeen, before I stole that money to keep the diabolical Fournier creature silent, I had hoped some-day..." He managed another two steps, bringing him halfway to the lip of the roof. "I had hoped someday to be free of what I am, but there is no freedom to be had. None."

"We can stay up all night arguing over your worst transgression," Michael said, "but get the hell off this roof. Maeve will worry about you." As Michael was, despite all odds to the contrary, worried about him.

As even Brenna might be.

Michael's words gave Angus pause. "Maeve might fret for me at that. She doesn't like lemon drops. Did you hear her say that?"

"I did." Whatever the hell lemon drops had to do with anything.

"You will tell the child I slipped."

Angus had worked his way down the roof to where the parapets met the wall. At his left lay the roof terrace. To the right… Michael hiked himself onto the parapets and did not look down.

"Angus, you're not going to slip. Stop jabbering and get moving."

"You may tell Brenna I slipped as well. I was never fond of heights. She'll believe you."

"Another three feet, and you'll be able to climb down along the wall. Stop being dramatic." Though Angus sounded contemplative rather than dramatic.

"Brenna saved more than my life tonight," Angus said. "She saved this castle and all who call it home—I understand that—but there's no saving me."

The expression on Angus's face was hopeless, also… peaceful, and yet, Michael pleaded with his uncle anyway. "Let me get the damned rope. Please, Uncle."

Angus shook his head and edged closer to the lip. "Laddie, it's not your fault. None of it is your fault. Maybe it's not even entirely mine."

On that soft observation, Angus spread his arms and tipped forward. Michael dived forward fast enough to snatch hold of his uncle by the forearm as Angus hung suspended over the bailey.

"Take my other hand," Michael bit out. "For God's sake let me pull you up."

Angus tipped his head back, the sheer weight of him straining every muscle and sinew Michael possessed.

"I cannot, Michael. I am sorry—so sorry—but I simply cannot."

He let go of Michael and fell, while in the bailey, all was silence.

"I heard every word." Brenna whipped off her shawl—the beautiful Brodie tartan shawl she wore only on special occasions—and wrapped it around her husband's shoulders.

Michael slid down the stone wall to sit at its base, out of the worst of the wind, his back supported by the parapets. "Maeve?" he whispered. In all his clan finery, he was as white as a winding sheet.

"I gave her to Elspeth and Hugh, and they'll make sure she's kept out of the bailey. Come away from this cold place, Michael."

He focused on her, blinking as if trying to put a name with her face. "You love it up here."

"We'll talk about that." Brenna took his hand and tugged, which was rather like tugging on Wee Bannock when the beast was in the mood to tarry at his grass. "Michael, I don't want to stay up here another minute."

"We'll put up an iron gate," he said, making no move to rise. "You heard every word?"

She'd said as much. "Angus wasn't right, in his head and in other ways. That wasn't news."

Michael rested his forehead against Brenna's thigh, his posture bewildered and defeated. "He was my uncle."

She ran a hand over Michael's hair, which had grown damp in the evening air. "And he risked his life to save Maeve."

Please let that be an end to it, for nothing Angus had said quite revealed the nature of his worst transgression where Brenna was concerned. Given everything else to fall on Michael's shoulders, Brenna would spare her husband that, at least for now.

Michael lifted his head to gaze up at Brenna. "Angus abused you terribly."

Night was stealing across the sky, clouds making the sunset early and beautiful. "Michael, he stole from us all and abused our trust, but we'll lay him to rest in the family plot."

Michael shook his head in weary denial, and all the upset Brenna had endured in the past twenty-four hours rose up in one sudden, enormous urge to run.

To run not from Michael, but from the knowledge in his eyes.

"I'll bury him wherever you please, Brenna, but that's more than he deserved. I saw the sketches, and I know what he did."

"No."

Michael held her hand in an implacable grip while Brenna's heartbeat skittered with the need to flee this confrontation. She wasn't ready, and Michael was in no condition himself to hear what she might disclose.

"I know of Angus's transgressions, Brenna," he said, his head tipping back to rest against the wall. "What I do *not* know is how I can ever be a husband to you, when I had a clear indication of Angus's problems before I even left here."

Michael's hand was warm. All of Brenna was cold—she could not feel the cold, but she knew it to be enveloping her—while Michael's grip on her was secure and warm.

"I do not understand what you're saying, Michael Brodie, and I am not sure I want to."

Eighteen

A BOOT SCRAPED ON THE STEP BEHIND BRENNA, THE sound making Michael's lawfully wedded—and bedded—wife jump as a pistol shot would have.

Sebastian St. Clair emerged from the stairway, the wind snatching at his hair and at his Stuart plaid kilt.

"Hugh is dealing with the details, below. The musicians had first go at the food, and Elspeth is sending the rest home with various families or to the kirk. The barrel and the desserts went to the inn."

He went on, barking out information in his precise, aristocratic English, and at some point, Michael rose from the stones, his hand still grasping Brenna's. He'd never seen his former commanding officer rattled—not ever—and yet, shutting St. Clair up was imperative.

Angus was dead, and the musicians had first go at the buffet?

"Maeve and Lachlan?" Michael asked.

"Saw nothing," St. Clair replied, the first useful piece of information he'd shared. "Thank God for that mercy. When word spread Maeve was trapped up here, the children were all hustled away. Maeve and Lachlan are drinking chocolate in the solar, and they'll not be allowed to stir from there until they're put to bed."

"My thanks for the report." Michael could somehow form words—a relic from soldiering days—while Brenna remained a silent wraith whose hand he would never let go. She should leave him, of course, and not for a paltry nine years. "St. Clair, if you would continue to manage things, my wife and I…"

He trailed off and took the shawl from around his shoulders, using it to envelope Brenna and bring her against his body.

"This view, these damned stones, they remind me of France," St. Clair muttered. "Of that bloody Château. Come down, you two, before you catch your—before you catch a lung fever. I'll send Milly up here next if you don't come with me now."

"We're coming," Michael said. "Give us a moment."

St. Clair disappeared down the steps, his muttering, if Michael weren't mistaken, including a deal of French cursing. St. Clair had faced more hardened officers on the field of honor than any other five men of Michael's acquaintance, and yet, the baron had been near tears.

Why had Michael disclosed his knowledge of that damned sketchbook to Brenna, and why now?

Because his common sense was another of the bloody heaps on the cobbles below. God help him, his marriage was probably down there, bleeding its last as well.

"You're shivering," Michael said. "I should be shivering. Come along."

She resisted as he moved toward the steps. "Michael Brodie, where are you taking me?"

❦

Michael had been like this on their wedding night. Soft-spoken, considerate, distracted, and utterly fixed on some purpose Brenna could not divine—until she'd woken to his note, explaining that he'd gone to join his regiment early.

He'd been planning his escape from their marriage then, and perhaps he was planning it anew.

"I'm taking you out of this wind, Brenna Maureen. You'll want Elspeth, and a wee dram, and—" He stopped in the doorway to the stairs, shadows and granite behind him, night coming on over the castle roof. "You can't possibly want me for a husband. I don't see how you could want any husband."

They held hands, and yet Michael leaned not against his wife, but against the cold, hard stones of the castle.

"How could you *have* me, Brenna? How could you bear to be intimate with me, after what you'd suffered as a child? I can understand why Angus chose death, I can understand—" Michael's breath gave an odd hitch, and he shook loose of Brenna's grasp. "You'll want to check on Maeve."

A shudder went through him, and Brenna knew, by the sick sinking in her bones, she *knew*, Michael was just then piecing together the threat Angus had posed to Maeve.

"I'll not lose you too, Michael Brodie." She marched past him, snatched his wrist into her grasp, and dragged him into the stairwell. "Much was taken from me by that awful man, but I will not lose you too. If I must explain the whole of it to you, I shall, but there will be no more running off, keeping our well-meant silences, and allowing pains that should bring us together to separate us."

For she wanted to run off, wanted to tear off across the hills and never look back. Angus had doomed her to looking back, but she could at least look back with Michael's company to fortify her.

"You don't have to tell me, Brenna," he said, following her down the winding steps. "I can move my things. You'll have peace, at least. You won't have to see me strutting about, so proud of my—"

He stopped, back to the wall, eyes closed, and Brenna had the sense her husband was in the grip of an illness, one that might overtake him if she allowed it.

"Stop this," she said, slipping her arms around him. "You are entitled to your self-loathing, if that's what this is. You are entitled to loathe *me*, but you are not entitled to leave me again, Michael Brodie. That didn't work very well, if you'll recall, and we're stronger people now. I forbid you to abandon me again."

She prayed they were stronger people, though the notion she could forbid her husband anything was a desperate fiction.

"Brenna, he saw you naked. As a child. Many... many times. He *touched* you, I'm sure of it, and if he—" Michael fell silent. By the flickering light of the sconce below them, tears glistened on his cheeks.

And that...that was the worst of the legacy Angus had left behind. Not that he'd betrayed Brenna's innocence, preyed upon her loneliness and ignorance, and exploited a child's trust, but that he'd continued to take from her the normal, prosaic gifts of a happily married woman.

Brenna kissed her husband.

"Angus didn't—he never...I was a virgin when I first made love with my husband. I have my husband to thank for that. I'd love him to my dying day for that alone, but in fact, I love him for many reasons."

She'd avoided the word "love" for years. Tender sentiment was a source of weakness and bewilderment, and it flooded her now, rendering her strong in a way that astonished her.

"Brenna, hush." Michael stayed propped against the wall, head back, eyes closed as if she'd just admitted to hanging felonies. "I don't deserve your sentimental declarations."

"I'd slap you with my sentimental declarations if I could. I hoarded them up, storing them where even I couldn't see the truth of them. We're leaving this castle, and we shall talk."

She would talk, and he would listen.

He opened his eyes. His left hand came up, and with one finger he traced her hair back from her brow.

"I owe you that. I didn't listen to you on our wedding night. I'll listen now."

A small portion of Brenna's anxiety slinked back under her heart, where she'd learned to manage it. The rest flapped about inside her, like the castle pennant in a punishing wind.

"Come with me, then, and we'll find some quiet, where you can listen to me properly." Where she could listen to him too.

Cook abetted them, shoving a hamper at Michael and a bundle of blankets at Brenna. Her face was lined with fatigue and grief, but she managed a wan smile when Brenna explained that she and Michael might be gone some time.

They left through the deserted ballroom, walked past all the magnificent flowers, the empty tables and chairs, the crossed swords given pride of place on walls now sporting slashes of moonlight. Without dozens of overheated human bodies and groaning tables of food, the entire space bore the fragrance of heather and roses.

"We were to have had a celebration tonight," Michael said, as if he'd not been in charge of repairing the banister railing just two days past. "A welcome home to the long-lost laird who'd come safely through the wars."

Whoever that fellow was.

"We'll have a celebration," Brenna said, pushing through the doors to the back gardens. "Though first, we'll have a wee natter."

❧

In the moonshadows of the empty ballroom, Michael was incongruously reminded of Brenna as he'd first seen her. He'd been thirteen, she'd been eight, and he'd been fascinated with her.

"She'll be yours someday," his father had said. "If all goes well, and ye don't muck it up. She'll be your lady wife, and she'll be yours."

Michael had been too young to understand that marriage alone did not confer dominion or possession of a woman's heart on her spouse. The privilege of keeping a lady's heart safe was earned, and he'd failed his wife miserably.

And yet, that small Brenna had been much like the lady leading Michael into the summer night.

"You're still a determined soul," he said as they passed a patch of daisies looking pale in the moonlight. "You still go after problems instinctively. You attack them without any thought they might have no solutions."

She shot him a look suggesting the moon was affecting his wits.

"They mostly do have solutions, it's we who lack the vision to see them, and I'm certainly guilty of that."

She should leave him. That would solve too many problems, and yet he could not bear it if she did.

"Angus stole our letters, Brenna. Yours and mine, both. I don't know as he even read them. He simply took them from the post. And from us."

Brenna paused at the postern gate, while Michael shifted the hamper so he could get at the latch.

"He took more than a few letters, Michael. I'm glad he's dead, though I understand your feelings are more complicated."

She reported her position with breathtakingly unapologetic assurance, and of the two—her relief at Angus's death, and her acceptance that Michael's emotions might not match her own—the second caught Michael's interest.

"I don't want to feel anything." Though Michael loved his wife, and that was...that was still good.

"You will feel me leaving you here by the gate if you don't get moving, Michael Brodie. Down to the river with you, before the grass gets any more damp."

"Brenna, you need not be anxious. My wishes prevailed for nine years, and even had they not..." He could give her this. He could give her absolute control over their fate, and she deserved that, at least. "Even had they not, based on what has transpired, our marriage will be as you wish it to be."

"You're daft," she said, marching off down the hill. "Marriage isn't a matter of taking turns being the baby or the queen or the laird. We don't take turns running the castle or scurrying off to France. We're *married*."

He had scurried off to France. Tail between his legs. "You have some definite notions about this marriage business."

She was quiet for the time it took them to wind down the path to the river, and Michael had to approve of her choice of location. The sound of the Dee at summer ebb was soothing, the moonlight on the water lovely. Maybe what they had to say to each other would profane such beauty, or maybe the water could carry all the hurt and misery away, down to the sea, and out of their lives.

Out of their hearts.

Brenna snapped out the blankets and more or less flung them on the grass. Michael tossed his sporran down as well.

"I don't want to tell you a thing, Michael Brodie. Angus is dead, and I want all his wrongdoing to die with him. Keep marching, you know, like a good Scots regiment, even after the colors have fallen and the pipers are silent."

Michael could not stand that she was so afraid. Despite whatever he might be feeling himself—nothing at all, too much, and everything in between—he stepped up to his wife and put his arms around her.

"What Angus did will live in your heart and mine unless we deal with it." Even then, even if Brenna shared with him every jot and tittle of her recollections, she'd still not empty her mental coffers of Angus's pernicious legacy. The same way a soldier could be felled by memories of battles past, a shaft of sunlight, a snippet of laughter, any small sensory impression might dredge up more experiences she'd shuffled away from her mind's notice.

"I am too tired of dealing with Angus to hate him," Brenna said. "Though I expect to get a second wind on my hatred. I pray for it."

"Because," Michael said, looping his arms around her shoulders, "beneath the hatred lies the hurt and the fear. Tell me about the hurt, Brenna Maureen. Tell me all about it."

❧

Michael Brodie was a brave man, though he'd be years understanding that about himself. For now, he'd see only that he'd abandoned his sixteen-year-old wife, and while there was a story there—one Brenna sensed lay at Angus's far-from-sainted feet—she'd lead the way and tell her miseries first.

"I was lonely," she said against her husband's shoulder. For years and years, she'd been lonely, but she was fiercely pleased that when she stood in Michael's embrace she was no longer lonely.

"Let's sit," Michael said, and perhaps that was wise, because Brenna's knees had gone weak at the effort to push out three honest words. "I'm sorry you were lonely. If it's any consolation, I have some acquaintance with loneliness myself."

When Brenna might have taken up a position beside her husband, the better to keep her thoughts straight and her emotions far from her own notice, he instead sat behind her, hiked his knees up, and drew her down against his chest. She was surrounded by Michael as surely as the keep was surrounded by the bailey walls. Though Michael was a good deal warmer than granite, he was no less solid.

"I don't mean I was lonely when you left for the military, though I was. I mean, I was lonely from the day I arrived to Castle Brodie. My ma had died the year before, my father and brothers were reeling with it, and there I was. Eight years old, and I knew not one soul, but that tall, green-eyed boy named Michael, who would someday be my husband."

Michael's lips grazed her temple. "He is your husband. He wants always to be your husband."

She nuzzled his throat, which bore the scent of vetiver.

"I've had some time to think on it, Michael, and while I liked you—you were *my* Michael—I also did not want you to leave me as my family had."

"Bloody hell."

"Leave me when I was small, I mean. I'd watch you, and sometimes, you'd watch me, but if my own father and brothers could pass me into the keeping of strangers, then I was easy to leave, you see. I didn't want to do anything to make you leave me before you were truly mine."

"So you were shy and coy, and I was fascinated with you."

"Angus was fascinated with me too." While Brenna wanted to focus on Michael's admission—wasn't he fascinated with her any longer?—the part about Angus was what needed telling now. "Angus was diabolically sly, Michael. He did not approach me indecently—he was kind and understanding. He answered the questions I could not ask anybody else. He offered the occasional pat on the shoulder or passing hug. He made me feel..."

Oh, this hurt. This hurt awfully, to think of how vulnerable she'd been, what easy prey.

"He made you feel special," Michael said, his voice carefully flat. "He made you feel safe, and as if you had at least one friend in the world, a friend you would protect and trust. He was the serpent in the garden of your childhood, promising much, though the cost of what he offered you was beyond your ken."

Brenna's fingers ached—she'd curled them that tightly in the wool of Michael's sash.

"Exactly. So when he'd sit me in his lap, even though I wasn't exactly comfortable, I wasn't entirely uncomfortable either. I felt privileged to be Angus's 'special little girl.'"

For a long moment, the river murmuring to the moonlight was the only sound other than Brenna's breathing. It was too soon to give way to tears, for they had much more ground to cover.

"He graduated to kissing me, on the cheek at first, and then he offered to show me how a grown-up girl kisses."

"I'm glad he's dead too," Michael muttered against her hair. "Very glad. And then what?"

Somebody started up playing the pipes in the vicinity of the castle above them. Not Davey MacCray, somebody of a more lyrical, lamenting bent. Neil MacLogan, probably.

"Then he wanted to draw me, because I was so pretty. Nobody had hair the same shade as mine. Nobody had such lovely eyes, or such a charming smile. He'd steal into my room at night and draw me in my shift. It was our secret, of course. What child doesn't think a grown-up's confidence some sort of treasure?"

"Then he took your nightgown off."

Michael said the words like a catechism, as if to give Brenna an example for how to simply express such base wickedness.

"Then he took my nightgown off." And she'd hated it, hated how his gaze changed, so he saw not her, a person, but as nakedness that should be forbidden to him. Worse, she'd hated how shame and a sense of excitement had blended in a child's heart, to leave bewilderment and powerlessness in place of self-respect.

Along with enormous fears, of abandonment, and of discovery, both.

"What else, Brenna? I know he didn't stop there."

Michael held her, as if his arms around her could contain all of her childhood confusion, all the sick dread that bordered on anticipation, all the fear of what might happen next.

"This despoiling took time," Brenna said. "Months

and even years of cozening and moving by degrees. Angus would take a chair by my bed, ask my opinion on this or that, and draw me sitting on my bedcovers. Then he'd take a place at the foot of the bed, until that's where I expected him to sit when he wasn't stealing kisses. He moved up the bed by slow degrees, like a wasting disease progresses in increments too small to measure. And one night—"

Abruptly, she could not breathe.

"Easy," Michael whispered, smoothing a hand down her hair. "It will keep for another time."

Brenna did not want to endure *another time*. Though her wish was doomed, she wanted this one night under a full moon to be her unburdening, and when the sun came up, she would bury her past along with the man who'd ruined so much of it.

"This was the night I woke up, in one sense. I was about eleven, maybe twelve. Angus had been making odd comments for weeks, about the march of time, about all beauty fading. The closer he crept to me, the more I tried to resist. I told him I already knew how to kiss well enough. Told him he had enough drawings of me. Told him I was not well. He'd grow sad when I made these comments—if I didn't hate him for what he did to me, I'd hate him for the way he manipulated with his silences and quiet looks."

"*I* hate him. I hate him more with every word you speak. I hate that I'm related to him." And yet, Michael's hands on Brenna's hair were so gentle.

"He got under the covers with me, took his dressing gown and nightshirt off, and laid on top of me. I never *saw* him, but I'll never forget the feel of him, either. He stank of his damned pipes, and he had soft, clammy hands, and he—"

"He took his pleasure on your body, though he left your maidenhead intact."

Those were not words Brenna could repeat. She managed a nod, and wanted so badly to go back in time and pluck the girl she'd been from the clutches of the monster who'd climbed into her bed.

"The w-worst part..." She took a slow breath, because the words must be set free. "The worst part was that he kissed my hands and told me next time it would be even better. I was crying—silently, but the tears were there—and he told me it would be even better. What sort of man, what sort of *creature* treats a child thus, so she's crying and naked and horrified, and then offers *that*?"

Michael said nothing—the question had no adequate answer—though to speak it aloud, to cry it out to her husband, unloosed the weeping Brenna had been wrestling back for years.

She cried for herself, for the child who'd trusted none to protect her, who hadn't entirely understood the wrong being perpetrated on her. She cried for the woman she was, who could see with adult eyes the magnitude of the damage inflicted on a lonely girl behind a closed door, in a walled garden, and in small, quiet moments that arose without warning whenever Angus saw opportunity.

"You made it stop," Michael said, long moments later. "Somehow, you made it stop."

The pipes went on, still sad, but softer, as if the wind had shifted.

Michael would desperately need to hear this part, to be reassured that his wife had not drifted from victimized child to victimized adult, and Brenna could give him those assurances.

"*You* made it stop, at least in part," she said. "More and more, you took to following me about, and I realized—I finally realized—that as long as I stayed around people—as long as I stayed near you, in particular—Angus did not dare approach me. I learned to stick close to the keep, and I made friends with your sisters. I did my lessons in the kitchens, because somebody's always coming and going in the kitchens, and I became your mother's right hand."

"I felt like an idiot," Michael said. "I was, at sixteen and seventeen, a young man. You were a child, and yet, I liked you. I liked to tease you. I liked to watch you embroider. It wasn't the same liking I had for my sisters, though I was protective of you all, and yet..."

Brenna struggled to raise herself from his chest.

"What you felt for me was the opposite of what Angus felt. In some way, I sensed that. To you I was a person to be cherished until I could take my place as your wife. To him I was a pleasure to be hoarded up and exploited as long as womanhood eluded me. I asked your mother if I could share a room with Bridget, and then I asked her if Erin might join us."

Michael gently gathered her back onto his chest.

"Because Angus was looking at Erin the way he'd looked at you. She was shy and sickly, and easily overlooked. Do you think my mother guessed?"

He didn't ask her if she'd ever gone to Lady Catherine—a kindness to all concerned.

"I don't know what your mother knew, what she guessed, what she knew without admitting even to herself, or what she confronted your father with in private. She took your sisters to Ireland, though, and Erin rallied. She also made sure we girls had a lock on our bedroom door, and said young ladies must never quibble at demanding privacy when they needed it."

Brenna's hip ached, and she had that wrung-out, floaty feeling that came with spent tears. She pushed Michael to his back and cuddled down into his embrace.

"Angus was furious with me. He found me collecting eggs one morning and told me he knew what I'd done, asking to share a room with your sisters and trailing after you like a trained hound. He ranted and railed, and told me I was growing ugly anyway, losing any appeal I'd ever had. I was no end of pleased to hear that part."

"But he threatened you."

"Oh, of course. If I ever accused him of untoward behavior, he'd see me sent from the castle. I'd never be allowed to marry the laird's heir if I told such tales. The laird's heir, especially, deserved a wife who hadn't allowed a man into her bed without a peep of protest."

Michael flipped the blankets up around them.

"War is a *delight* compared to such diabolical manipulation of a young girl's fears. Perhaps I shall lead a life of wickedness, so I might meet my uncle in hell, there to inflict upon him every misery I can devise and a few hundred I haven't thought of yet."

Hell would be a wondrous lively place, if Michael's tone of voice were any indication.

"Thoughts of revenge can comfort for a time,"

Brenna said. "Knowing it would never happen again was of greater comfort yet. Angus did not feel for grown women what he did for children."

"And then Maeve showed up. Merciful, everlasting God in heaven. She was lonely, out of place, shy, and ill at ease." Michael was so quick to grasp a pattern that in Brenna's case had gone unnoticed for years.

The wool Michael had wrapped around them, and Michael beneath her, made a cozy haven for Brenna, and increasing lassitude meant she must complete her confession before sleep and the blessed pleasure of Michael's embrace overtook her.

"I was not Angus's first victim, but I think his attentions to me were the most sustained."

His chest heaved up and down with a sigh, like the waves on the loch yielding to a passing wind.

"My dearest wife, I know. And Angus didn't limit his perversions to little girls. I had thought that young men were his preferred victims—his only victims, in fact."

Young men. Michael had been a young man. He'd been a braw, bonny fellow, who'd left for his regiment at the first opportunity. All the wool in Scotland could not have kept Brenna warm as that realization washed over her. She sat up, the blankets falling away as she searched her husband's face.

"Michael, how could you know that Angus did not limit his wickedness to little girls?"

Nineteen

SEBASTIAN HAD LAST SHOWN THIS CAREFUL, CONTROLLED quality—and sworn at length in French—before Milly had married him. Since Michael Brodie had come striding through the middle of the crowd in the bailey, the entire night had been a series of *sacre bleu*'s and worse.

"Why aren't you in bed?" he growled, prowling across the great hall. "I recall sending you up to bed more than an hour ago."

At his tone, the last of the maids and footmen melted away, leaving a half-dozen trestle tables stacked against the wall in anticipation of a return to storage.

"You did send me up to bed." After a distracted kiss good night. "You forget, however, that I am not one of your corporals, to scamper off upon your orders. Why aren't *you* in bed?" She slipped her arms around him, knowing exactly what had kept him awake.

The Castle Brodie garrison was in an uproar. As a former commander, Sebastian was constitutionally incapable of resting when anyone he cared for was threatened, and he cared for Michael Brodie a very, very great deal.

As did Milly.

As did, happily, Michael Brodie's wife.

"If you dragged me to bed, I could not sleep," he said, wrapping Milly in a snug embrace. "Michael has gone missing, and I haven't seen Brenna for some time either. It's too much to hope you've shooed her to sleep with the proverbial wee dram?"

"She has found a far more bracing tonic in her husband's company. Come with me, Sebastian."

He peered down at her, looking exhausted, handsome, and worried. "Brenna's with Michael?"

"Cook equipped them with a hamper and blankets. Michael could not have a more ferocious guard than his Brenna. She'll see him through this night." They'd see each other through all the nights, just as Milly and Sebastian had learned to do.

Sebastian led her to the enormous hearth at one end of the hall. The remains of a fire burned, the peaty scent oddly appealing, the warmth welcome. "You heard what Michael accused his uncle of?" Sebastian asked.

Milly pushed him into a well-padded reading chair and climbed into his lap. "He accused Angus of many things, but mostly of betraying Michael's trust."

"And Brenna's trust, and the trust of every person on the estate. Michael takes his loyalties seriously."

Thus, Sebastian could not sleep. "You did not keep him captive in London for two years, my love. You did not tie him to that infernal rock pile in France."

Sebastian was not like some, who needed to chatter their way through conflicting arguments and confusing facts. He was a master at keeping his own counsel and arranging details like so many chess pieces until a matter was thoroughly weighed in his mental scales. Milly made herself comfortable upon her husband's person, prepared to deal with his guilt when he was comfortable admitting it.

"Michael has suffered enough," Sebastian said softly. "Do you know, in all the years of my acquaintance with him, I've never known him to look at another woman? The ladies were forever sending him inviting glances."

Milly had seen how Michael looked at his wife, which was explanation enough for a soldier's constancy to his lady. She might have remarked as much, but at the great door across the room, a troop of kilted Scotsmen spilled into the hall, their ladies still in evening finery.

"St. Clair."

Hugh MacLogan approached the hearth, while his confreres lingered by the door. Sebastian rose, Milly in his arms, then gently deposited his wife on her feet.

"MacLogan. I'd thought the evening's gathering displaced to the tavern. We've sent the servants to bed."

The servants, as Milly well knew, had gone straight down the hill, to gossip and drink away the upset and excitement of the evening's developments.

Hugh inclined his head in Milly's direction, a Scotsman's version of the perfunctory bow. Considering that Milly had never aspired to be anybody's baroness, she made do with his civility and offered him a smile in return.

"We've been discussing matters down at the inn," Hugh said. "We believe we might perform a service for our laird and his lady, but we'll need a key. Elspeth says it's usually kept in the laird's study."

Milly had seen the heavy, ornate key ring hanging in the study, and could well imagine Brenna wearing the keys at her waist, like a chatelaine of old. Sebastian reached for her hand without looking at her, a commanding officer canvassing the opinion of his trusted lieutenant.

"Listen to him, Sebastian," she said too softly for any but MacLogan to overhear. "We're all too overset to sleep, and Michael had the right of it: Angus wasn't the only one to betray Brenna, and people need to make amends."

"Come along then, MacLogan," Sebastian said. "We'll find your damned key, and then, by God, I'll get my lady off her feet."

More muttering in French accompanied his departure, but when he came back to the great hall and had sent MacLogan and his fellows on their way, he also brought Milly a warm cloak.

"Where are we going, Sebastian?"

"Down to the dower house and then to the loch. It's not a celebration, by any means, but they'll drink, and MacLogan thought—" He settled Milly's cloak around her shoulders and fastened the frogs. "I can see you up to bed if you'd rather. We can't have you becoming fatigued."

He kept his hands on the lapels of her cloak, so Milly wrapped her fingers around his knuckles.

"What are we about, Sebastian? You need your rest too." And Milly slept ever so much better in her husband's arms.

"You were right: I did not hold Michael prisoner in London, and I did not chain him to that infernal pile of rocks in the French Pyrenees, but something or someone did."

"It's not your fault if a grown man, married to a woman he apparently adores, spent years wandering—"

He kissed her, which in addition to distracting Milly could also be counted on to make her hush.

"Something or someone banished Michael or held him captive, and I want to do what I might to end his sentence."

This undertaking meant going to the dower house, where Angus had dwelled. Milly kissed her husband, because he hated being helpless, and he looked so worried for the man who might be his only true friend.

"I want to help too. Let's be about it, shall we?"

❦

The moment had all the elements of sweetness—Michael's wife was snuggled to his chest, the summer night air was fragrant with the scent of crushed clover, a lament drifted down from the pipes played up on the parapets, and the moon hung rosy and smiling in the sky.

Michael held on to his wife lest sorrow sunder him from his soul.

Brenna had led the way, finding words for the unspeakable, offering Michael two comforts: First, the comfort, dubious though it was, of the truth. He need not torment himself with thoughts of Angus inflicting the ultimate defilement on a child, for he had accurate information about what had happened and for how long.

A *very* dubious comfort.

The second comfort was as substantial as the walls around the keep, as substantial as the hard Scottish earth beneath his back and the hills ringing the shire: Brenna had trusted *him* with her truths. Trusted him to listen, which he'd found harder by far than waging war for years on end.

Now he must afford her the same awful comforts.

"On our wedding night, I saw Angus."

"Everybody was there," Brenna said. "Had he not attended, it would have caused talk." Talk was not something Brenna ever wanted to be the object of.

"He was in his Highland finery, drinking, dancing, and comporting himself as a benevolent uncle—for all he'd tried to speak against you to me privately."

"You didn't listen to him."

"I wanted to call him out." For the first time in Michael's life, he'd seen his uncle as an opinionated, self-interested, interfering old besom who'd needed a good hiding. "But neither did I put him in his place."

Brenna levered up to undo Michael's clan sash, then went after the buttons of his shirt.

"You'd expose me to the night air?"

"I'd expose you to your wife." She subsided onto his chest, her cheek against his throat, and Michael rearranged the blankets over her. Next she wedged an arm under his neck. "You were saying?"

"It was late, I was hoping I might slip upstairs with you, and I went in search of my father, who would offer the parting toast."

"I saw you disappear and thought you were stepping out to the jakes. When the whisky flows…"

"I'd hardly had anything to drink, because drink can dull a man's—" The memory made him ill now. "I wanted to give a good account of myself when we consummated our vows, wanted a clear head. I expect you simply wanted the wedding night over with."

She smoothed his hair back and spoke right in his ear. "You expect wrong. I loved you then, and I desired you. I was nervous, aye—we were both nervous—but I had few qualms about joining you in that bed."

"Few qualms" was a far cry from no qualms, god-damn it. "I took that from you. Took away your display of courage and trust, and tossed it aside."

He waited for his wife to admit that yes, he'd wrecked their wedding night even more thoroughly than he knew, waited for her to express some honest disappointment in him. A lot of honest disappointment.

"You must be patient, Michael, and determined. This situation of ours can be described in a few minutes of blunt speech, but it has been years in the making. We'll not find our way through it overnight. I've learned that."

The piper shifted to another tune, the rhythm different, though still in minor key. A ballad, not a tune for dancing.

"What have you learned, Brenna? For I feel without any wisdom whatsoever. I am all sorrow and confusion and anger."

And hurt, of course. Mostly for her. But some for *them* as well.

"Ach, Michael. I wanted on our wedding night to prove to myself that I was *fine*, just like any other young bride. I was nervous about the kissing, but the rest of it…You would have been all unsuspecting, Michael, a new husband having his first romp with his wife. I would have been fighting with my past, and that would not have been fair to you."

Some time, when his brain could work, Michael would ask his wife to explain those notions again, for they had the ring of import about them. For now, he had a truth to add to their pile of sorry memories.

"I saw Angus engaged in perversions with Neil MacLogan."

Several heartbeats went by while the piper drew out a cadence.

"Buggering him, you mean. Neil would have been little more than a boy." Brenna's body plastered against Michael told him she was not surprised. "My cousin has never said a word about it, though it makes sense."

"In hindsight, I doubt Neil's participation was in any way…" The pipes fell silent, and Michael's arms fell away from his wife. What a boy had decided to tolerate in the interests of keeping a roof over his family's head was irrelevant.

"I told myself Neil wouldn't allow such attentions if he weren't also inclined in that direction," Michael went on softly. "The longer I considered it, the less certain I was of what I'd seen. Perhaps they'd been half-seas over, perhaps I was overreacting, though I'd entirely lost the ability to consummate our vows."

Brenna kissed his forehead, encouragement perhaps, or forgiveness. In any case, the gesture fortified him to tell the rest of it.

"Like Neil, I said nothing. When I reached the coast, I sent a letter to my father, telling him I'd seen bitter words between Angus and Neil, and asking him to keep Angus away from the MacLogans. In short, I lied. To my father, to myself."

Michael wanted to weep with the shame of his silence, with the horror and bewilderment. He wanted Neil MacLogan to confront him and pound him flat, and he wanted Neil to leave the shire forever.

"Did Neil see you?" Brenna's question was soft and inevitable.

"Nobody was tending the sconces by that time, so no, Neil did not see me, and neither did Angus. I want my flask, though, for I will never stop seeing the look on that boy's face." Despair, rage, and resignation beyond what any adolescent ought to lay claim to. Neil hadn't been as small as Brenna, but he'd been several years away from shaving.

Brenna kissed him on the mouth this time.

"Your sporran is by our feet, if that's where your flask has got off to. Neil has managed, and when he might have seen Angus murdered tonight, he did not. We must take comfort from that."

What or whom did Neil take comfort from?

"He seems devoted to his family." Was Neil ever to have a family of his own? "I could not bed you after having seen that. I didn't bed a woman until I came home to you, Brenna, and Angus is largely the reason why. To think that my uncle..."

Brenna climbed off him, the loss of her weight and warmth engendering panic in Michael's chest.

"Where are you going?"

"I could use a tot." She produced his flask, took a sip, and passed it to him, then got settled on the blankets beside him. "That's fine drink, Mr. Brodie. So Angus queered your efforts at a wedding night, but that's not entirely why you took off, is it?"

She shook her head when Michael offered her the flask back, so he fortified himself with half the contents.

"He was my uncle. He taught me which birds sing what songs. He tried to help me learn to sketch, and he always had a kind word for me when my father had been too demanding. How could Angus be...?"

"Good and evil?" Brenna eased to her back. "I don't know, Michael, but he surely was. Shall we make a night of it out here? The stars are beautiful."

"I'm his nephew, his blood." There was the problem, the unsolvable conundrum that had hounded Michael across battles, sieges, and even into peacetime.

"I saw him commit what I knew was a grievous wrong, but because I'm his nephew, I told myself Neil could have stopped it, there was drink involved, men get odd notions as do teenage boys, everything gets out of hand when the hour grows late and the whisky's flowing. I made all manner of excuses for my silence, because I was his braw, bonny nephew."

Brenna was quiet for a long time, and though Michael knew she could offer him no absolution, he waited on her next words.

"A long time ago, I *was* his special little girl. I *was* a lot of things Angus Brodie tried to tell me were the sum of me, and I know better, now. You'll talk to Neil."

Ah—an unlikely shaft of wisdom amid the night's sorry recitations. "I can talk to Neil, but still...I was Angus's nephew."

She rose over him, bringing the blankets with her.

"Go to sleep. You *are* my husband, I *am* your wife, and that's what matters now."

In a manner that was entirely wifely without being in the least erotic, Brenna kissed him. She pursued the task with enough inventiveness and determination that Michael absolved himself of thinking up a rejoinder to her very accurate observation.

He was her husband; she was his wife.

And that was a start.

❧

"Something bothers me," Brenna said, shifting a few inches so an unobliging bump of Scottish ground no longer dug into her hip.

"You're awake." Michael shifted too, dragging his kilt out from under his backside. "We seem to have bivouacked on our own private alarm grounds."

The sun wasn't quite up, but the singing of the birds said it soon would be.

"Are you angry with me, Husband?"

He stopped wrestling the covers. "Nobody can force a man to make love with his wife, Brenna Maureen."

And yet, he was unhappy. Unhappy was a vast improvement over the previous night's hard slog through awful memories.

"I wanted to make love with my husband." She had needed the reassurance that they *could* still make love, needed emphatically to be Michael's wife, not Angus's victim.

Michael's sporran went sailing several feet off into the grass, followed by a large dancing shoe, laces flapping against the fading stars.

"And I wanted to make love with my wife. I wasn't sure, after all that had been said"—another shoe went sailing—"that you could stand for me to touch you like that."

He turned his face up to the fading stars, his mouth bracketed by fatigue for all they'd shared a few hours' sleep on their blankets.

"I wasn't sure you could stand for me to *ever* touch you like that. We should probably get dressed," he said more softly.

Enough talking, in other words.

"You might touch me like that again first," Brenna suggested. "You were half-asleep, after all, and not entirely on your mettle."

He'd been more than half-asleep, and she'd been more than half-desperate. Their coupling had been brief, silent, and entirely graceless.

Also miraculous.

Michael knelt up enough to get his kilt around his hips.

"One swiving proves little, Brenna. We'll have awkwardness. *Intimate* awkwardness. When I think…" He sat back on his heels amid the blankets, his kilt half-fastened. His hair stuck up in odd directions, and a beard made his jaw bristly by the dawn's early light. "Brenna, marriage to me will be so difficult. We've made a start, but around any corner, behind any innocent line of poetry will be setbacks and bad memories. I need to know now if you have any doubts at all about us."

He needed to know if she had doubts about *him*, for nobody fought a battle like they'd waged the previous night alone. And he was right—there would be more skirmishes, none quite so bitter, though.

"I love you," Brenna said. "We'll have awkwardness and sorrow, but we'll have rejoicing and peace too. I daresay we'll also have children. Where is my shift?"

Michael tossed her a wad of linen.

"Children." He'd apparently forgotten what the word signified. "*Children?* You think—" Down he went, into their tangle of tartans, felled by a single word. "Children. God in heaven, children."

"You do know where babies come from?" Brenna asked, pulling her shift over her head. She went fishing for her stays next. "Wee bairns, who cry and drool, and have their papa's smile. They do other things too, not nearly so endearing, like grow up and leave home. You'll have to do my laces."

He rallied, sitting behind her and pulling her laces not nearly snug enough. "Maybe we should wait before we think about starting a family." His suggestion was cautious, and offered while he tied off her laces. "You were wearing a skirt and blouse."

"I'm wearing a smile," she said, drawing Michael's arms around her waist. "The time for waiting might already be past, Michael Brodie. Are there any names you favor for our firstborn?"

He knelt up behind her, enveloping her in a snug embrace.

"I love you too, Brenna Maureen MacLogan Brodie. I love you more than I can say, but please let's not be picking out names just yet."

He was genuinely daunted, and it had nothing at all to do with...the past. Brenna started to laugh at her brave soldier, Michael wrestled her to her back, and they were still laughing and tussling among the blankets when Sebastian and Milly St. Clair found them twenty minutes later.

☙

"The scouts have found us," Michael whispered in Brenna's ear. "Poor St. Clair looks like he's been up the entire night."

"Clan attire becomes them both," Brenna said, batting Michael's hands away from the buttons of her blouse. "Best put your shirt on, Husband."

She was so brisk, so fragile, and so wise. They had needed to talk, they had needed to make love, and they had needed—desperately—to laugh so hard their bellies ached. Now, they apparently needed to face the coming day.

And to find some proper clothing. The thought made Michael smile as he pulled his shirt over his head and got it right way around, for life did go on, and that was good.

"St. Clair, good morning. My lady." Michael stayed sitting on the blankets while Brenna passed him his shoes.

"Strath—Michael. Baroness. I trust we're not intruding."

"Another five minutes, and you would have been," Michael said, lacing up his shoes. "Pardon my blunt speech, Baroness."

"I like your blunt speech," Brenna said. "St. Clair, I know you're a guest, and English, and allowances must be made, but why are you hauling her ladyship about in the morning dew, when the woman needs her rest?"

"I slept," Milly St. Clair said. "We camped, more or less, by the loch. The entire village was there too. Seems it was a night for admiring the stars. Also drinking whisky and telling stories. Neil MacLogan can make even bagpipes sound sweet."

What were they trying to say? Brenna had her shoes on, a shirt and skirt, also a few underthings. Her hair was in complete disarray, and the whole of her smelled of lavender and clover.

"I will fall in love with you every day for the next hundred years," Michael muttered to his wife. Such extravagant sentiments were their due, after the night they'd put in. Also the God's honest truth.

She winked at him. "I'll fall in love with you every night, then. We'll share the work. Yonder baron has something on his mind."

St. Clair usually did, but for the first time in Michael's memory, his former commanding officer looked *worried*. Michael rose, his shirt half-buttoned, his kilt hanging low on his hips, and helped Brenna to her feet.

"Spit it out, St. Clair. Is the clan emigrating en masse? Are we being sued for restitution of the funds that were stolen?" He would not say his uncle's name, might never say it again.

"It isn't like that," St. Clair said. "Your people undertook to do a bit of housecleaning, and they hoped you and your lady would come admire their efforts."

Whatever this housecleaning was, St. Clair was nervous about it—though his baroness was not.

"The sun will soon be up," Brenna said, taking Michael by the hand and leading him toward the path along the base of the hill. "I, for one, need a decent breakfast and some strong, hot tea. I want to explain to Maeve that there's been an accident involving... there's been a sad accident, but we're inviting her sister for a visit at the earliest opportunity."

Of course they were.

Michael let Brenna chatter as they made their way to the shore of the loch, while ahead of them, St. Clair held hands with his wife. As they emerged from the trees, the sun crested the horizon, turning the surface of the loch into a bright blue mirror of the morning sky.

"This looks like the aftermath of a battle," St. Clair observed, for everywhere, bodies sprawled, some on blankets, some around the remains of campfires. The MacLogans were heaped together near a wagon, no horses or bullocks in evidence.

"I'd say the whisky won," Michael observed. "What's piled in the wagon?"

"Have a look," St. Clair suggested, turning a half barrel bottom up so his lady might take a seat.

The first impression to hit Michael was a whiff of pipe smoke. Then the sunlight landed on the gilt edge of a framed painting that stuck out from a pile of clothing—kilts and cloaks in the Brodie plaid, boots and shoes, a great lot of maroon velvet.

"It's all from the dower house," Brenna said. "Everything he owned." Around them, people stirred, stretched, and yawned. "I can smell that god-awful tobacco. What is it all doing here?"

"MacLogan called it cleaning house," St. Clair said.

"Your people thought the time to remove the last tenant's effects was now, not when some future Lady Strathdee might have need of the place."

For even St. Clair apparently understood the present Lady Strathdee would never dwell in that house.

"Thoughtful of them," Brenna said. "I suppose we're to burn it?"

"I like the idea of burning it," Michael said before Brenna's thrifty nature could ruin a wonderful gesture from their people. "I like it a lot."

Brenna drew closer to the wagon, though she touched nothing. "I don't want to see even the ashes on the shores of our loch. I don't want any reminders at all."

Footsteps crunched on the stones behind them.

"You'll want this, if you're going to light a bonfire." Hugh MacLogan had a box in his hands, and a crease across his cheek from having slept on something. Neil and Dantry stood a few paces back, looking every bit as disheveled, and slightly worse for drink.

"Tap another keg," Michael said, "and send word to the castle we need some food down here. Bread, cheese, ham, simple fare, for we've a bit more work to do."

"What's in the box?" Brenna asked, regarding Hugh as if his offering smelled much worse than pipe smoke.

Michael spared MacLogan the admission. "Journals are in there, Brenna, along with sketchbooks and other garbage that should never again see the light of day."

MacLogan set the box down. "We opened none of it, and we made sure nobody else did either. We packed up the bedroom and allowed no one through its door while we did."

Brenna pulled her shawl tighter in a gesture that had nothing to do with the breeze coming off the loch.

"Our thanks," Michael said, hoping he still had a handkerchief in his sporran. "If you could spare us a bit more effort, that wagon needs to be emptied."

"Emptied?" Hugh asked. "It took half the night to fill it."

They'd be a lifetime emptying that bloody wagon, nonetheless. "What I have in mind won't take long at all."

❧

The flames were beautiful.

As the sun spilled down the hillsides and the scent of heather blended with a whiff of lamp oil, the row-boat bobbed gently a few feet from the loch's stony shore. Books caught first—art books, mostly, but not all. The velvet bed swagging caught, and the scent of the smoke became more acrid.

The little vessel rode low in the water, its makeshift sail luffing gently in the breeze. When Michael set the last box aboard at the stern, Neil cast the rope securing the boat to shore into the fire.

The silence on shore was broken by the sound of Michael splashing up onto the beach in his bare feet. He put his arm around Brenna's shoulders, and that was…that was wonderful.

As wonderful as wrestling the truth with him through the night, as wonderful as making love with him, as wonderful as waking up to teasing and more honesty.

And to friends and family, and *this*.

"How deep is that water?" Brenna asked, letting her head rest on Michael's shoulder.

He was quiet for a moment, while the flames rose higher and the boat made a stately progress toward the middle of the loch.

"My father told me it was at least two hundred feet deep at the center. Deep enough." The boat slowed as the flames enveloped the cargo from bow to stern. "I love you, Brenna Maureen Brodie."

Their marriage had acquired the loveliest punctuation. Any sentence, any sentiment, might be anchored with those three words, and they'd always be appropriate.

"I love you too, Michael Brodie."

The crowd on shore watched in silence as flames consumed the sail. The boat floundered and then slipped into the depths of the loch—stern, amidships, then bow.

Until all that was left were placid, concentric surface ripples that faded before they reached the shore.

"Well done," Neil MacLogan said softly. "Well damned done." He swung his niece up onto his back and headed off toward the trees, his brothers and his nephew following. The rest of the crowd dissipated with no more ceremony than that, until Brenna was alone with her husband on the quiet beach.

"I favor the names of the angels," Brenna said, turning to tuck her arms around Michael's waist. He was lean and strong, full of courage and the occasional flaw, and he was hers. He'd been hers even when he'd been off soldiering too.

"I'm named for—" Brenna *felt* the understanding blossom in Michael as he went silent. "What if we have a girl, Brenna? Or all girls? You'd name a girl Gabriel or Raphael?"

"Michaela," Brenna said. "Let's go home, Husband. I'm in need of a bath, and our bed."

"I'm in need of my wife."

Whatever that had to do with anything.

Arm in arm, they wandered up the path, past the clearing, through the postern gate, and into the gardens. All the while, they argued over what to name their firstborn, until Brenna diplomatically changed the subject to how they should go about tearing down the enclosure of the walled garden.

Their first of seven daughters arrived a mere eight and a half months later, and they named her Gabriella Michelle Maureen Brodie. She was red-haired, freckled, full of energy, and the terror of all save the St. Clair's oldest boy, who alone among all the children, could safely refer to the young lady as Gabby.

Acknowledgments

Have you ever been working on a jigsaw puzzle, and had the sense that the pieces you needed most must be the ones the cat has batted under the rug? Then somebody who has more worthy things to do than work on a jigsaw puzzle comes strolling by and randomly plucks five pieces from the pile and puts them exactly, precisely where you just spent half an hour square-pegging the wrong pieces.

And then the nice person wanders off, and you finally, finally have all four corners and most of the border.

Joanna Bourne (*The Rogue Spy*) did that for me with this book. I was utterly bumfuzzled with regard to some plot points—all right, the plot in general—and she asked me a few surgically precise brainstorming questions, and lo, my book came together in my mind.

Thank you, Jo, for all the wonderful books you write, and for the wonderful questions you ask at the most wonderful time.

In case you missed the rest of
the Captive Hearts series, read on
for excerpts from

The Captive

and

The Traitor

Now available from
Sourcebooks Casablanca!

From
The Captive

IN HIS PERSONAL HELL, CHRISTIAN DONATUS SEVERN, eighth Duke of Mercia, considered the pedagogic days the worst of a horrific lot—also the most precious. The days when his captors used his suffering to teach the arcane art of interrogation might cost him his sanity, even his honor, but they also ensured he would some day, some night, some eternity if necessary, have that sweetest of satisfactions—*revenge*.

"You see before you the mortal form of a once great and powerful man, Corporal," Girard said, pacing slowly between the table his prisoner had been lashed to and the damp stone wall where the corporal stood at attention.

Girard was a stranger to hurry, a necessary trait in a torturer. A big, dark, lean acolyte of the Corsican, Girard lived in Christian's awareness the way consumption dwelled in the minds of those it afflicted.

"Our duke is still great, to my mind," Girard went on, "because His Grace has not, as the English say, broken."

Girard blathered on in his subtly accented French, and Christian translated easily. As Girard's ironic praise

and patriotic devotion blended in a curiously mesmer-
izing patter, Girard's superior, Henri Anduvoir, lurked
in the shadows.

Girard made a science of extracting truth from
those reluctant to part with it, and pain was only one
tool at his disposal.

Anduvoir, on the other hand, was a simpler and
in some ways more-evil soul, plainly addicted to
hurting others for his own entertainment.

Christian filled his mind with the lovely truth that
someday Anduvoir, too, would be made to suffer.

"*Yet.* Our duke has not broken yet," Girard went
on. "I challenge you, Corporal, to devise the torment
that will break him, but be mindful that our challenge
grows the longer His Grace is silent. When God put
Mercia into our hands months ago, we sought to know
through which pass Wellington would move his troops.
We know now, so what is the point of the exercise?
Why not simply toss this living carcass to the wolves?"

Yes, please God, why not?

And then another thought intruded on Christian's
efforts to distance himself from the goings-on in that
cell: Was Girard letting slip that Wellington had, in
fact, moved troops into France itself? Girard played a
diabolical game of cat and mouse, hope and despair, in
a role that blended tormenter and protector.

"We yet enjoy His Grace's charming company
because the duke serves another purpose," Girard
prosed on. "He did not break, so we must conclude he
is sent here to teach us the breaking of a strong man.
One might say, an inhumanly strong man. Now…"

A boot scraped, and Christian divined that

Anduvoir had come out of his shadows, a reptile in search of his favorite variety of heat.

"Enough lecturing, Colonel Girard. Your pet has not told us of troop movements. In fact, the man no longer talks at all, do you, *mon duc*?" Anduvoir sucked a slow drag of his cigar, then gently placed the moist end against Christian's lips. "I long for the sound of a hearty English scream. Long for it desperately."

Christian turned his head away in response.

"A quiet man, our duke." Anduvoir expelled smoke through his nose. "Or perhaps, not so quiet."

He laid the burning tip of the cigar against the soft skin inside Christian's elbow with the same care he'd put it to his prisoner's mouth, letting a small silence mark the moment when the scent of scorched flesh rose.

The blinding, searing pain howled from Christian's arm to his mind, where it joined the memory of a thousand similar pains and coalesced into one roaring chant:

Revenge!

❦

"Lord Greendale was a man of great influence," Dr. Martin said, clearing his throat in a manner Gilly was coming to loathe.

"His lordship enjoyed very great influence," Gilly concurred, eyes down, as befit a widow.

The bad news came exactly as expected: "You should prepare for an inquest, my lady."

"An inquest?" Gilly gestured for her guest to take a seat, eight years of marriage to Greendale having taught her to produce an appearance of calm at will. "Theophilus, the man of great influence was universally disliked, approaching his threescore and ten, and the victim of an apoplexy in the midst of a formal dinner for twenty-eight of his most trusted toadies. What will an inquest serve?"

"Countess, you must not speak so freely, even to me. I will certainly be put under oath and questioned at length. I cannot imagine what the wrong words in the hands of the lawyers will do to your reputation."

His wrong words, over which he'd have no control, of course. A just God would afflict such a physician with a slow, painful death.

"Reputation matters little if one is to swing for murder."

"It won't come to that," Martin said, but he remained poised by the door, bag in hand, as if lingering in Gilly's presence might taint him not with her guilt—for she was innocent of wrongdoing toward her late spouse—but with her vulnerability to accusations.

"What am I to be charged with?" Stupidity, certainly, for having married Greendale, but Gilly's family had been adamant—"You'll be a countess!"—and she'd been so young...

Dr. Martin smoothed a soft hand over snow-white hair. "You are not accused of anything."

His lengthy, silent examination of the framed verses of Psalm 23 hanging over the sideboard confirmed that Gilly would, indeed, face suspicion. Her life had become a series of accusations grounded in nothing more than an old man's febrile imagination.

Because the physician was eyeing the door, Gilly fired off the most important question, and to Hades with dignity.

"Who's behind this, Theophilus? My husband is not yet put in the ground, and already you're telling me of an inquest."

"Lord Greendale himself apparently told his heir to see to the formalities."

And to think Gilly had prayed for her husband's recovery. "Easterbrook ordered this? He's still in France or Spain or somewhere serving the Crown."

"Easterbrook would have left instructions with his solicitors, and they would in turn have been in communication with King's Counsel and the local magistrate."

Men. Always so organized when bent on aggravation and aspersion.

"Shall you have some tea, Theophilus? It's good and hot."

"Thank you, my lady, but no." Martin turned toward the door, then hesitated, hand on the latch.

"You needn't tarry, Theophilus. You've served the family loyally, and that has been far from easy." He'd served the family discreetly, too. Very discreetly. "I suppose I'll see you at the inquest."

He nodded once and slipped away.

As Gilly's tea grew tepid in the pot, she sat down with pen and ink, and begged an interview with Gervaise Stoneleigh, the coldest, most astute, most *expensive* barrister ever to turn down Greendale's coin.

And that decision very likely saved her life.

From
The Traitor

THE BULLET WHISTLED PAST SEBASTIAN'S EAR, COMING within an inch of solving all of his problems, and half an inch of making a significant mess instead.

"Die, goddamn you!" Lieutenant Lord Hector Pierpont fired his second shot, but rage apparently made the man careless. A venerable oak lost a few bare twigs to the field of honor.

"I shall die, *bien sûr*," Sebastian said, a prayer as much as a promise. "But not today."

He took aim on Pierpont's lapel. An English officer to his very bones, Pierpont stood still, eyes closed, waiting for death to claim him. In the frosty air, his breath clouded before him in the same shallow pants that might have characterized postcoital exertion.

Such drama. Sebastian cocked his elbow and dealt another wound to the innocent oak branches. "And neither shall you die today. It was war, Pierpont. For the sake of your womenfolk, let it be over."

Sebastian fired the second bullet overhead to punctuate that sentiment, also to ensure no loaded weapons remained within Pierpont's ambit. When Pierpont opened his eyes, Sebastian gazed into loathing so intense as to confirm his lordship would rather be dead than suffer any more of Sebastian's clemency.

Sebastian walked up to him and spoke quietly enough that the seconds could not hear.

"You gave away nothing. What little scraps you threw me had long since reached the ears of French intelligence. Go home, kiss your wife, and give her more babies, but leave me and mine in peace. Next time, I will not delope, *mon ami*."

He slapped Pierpont lightly on the cheek, a small, friendly reminder of other blows, and walked away.

Michael Brodie snatched the pistol from Sebastian's grasp, took Sebastian by the arm, and led him toward their horses. "You've had your fun, now come along like a good baron."

"Insubordinate, you are. I thought the English were bad, but you Irish give the term realms of meaning Dr. Johnson never dreamed."

"You are *English*, lest we forget the reason yon righteous arse wants to perforate your heart at thirty paces. Get on the horse, Baron, and I'm only half-Irish."

"You fret, *Michel*, and one wants to strike you for it. The English are violent with their servants, *non*? Perhaps today I will be English after all."

Michael climbed aboard his bay, and Sebastian swung up on Fable.

Burnished red eyebrows lowered into a scowl. "You would ride a white horse," Michael groused. "Might as well paint a target on your back and send a boy ahead to warn all and sundry the Traitor Baron approaches."

Sebastian nudged his horse forward.

"Fable was black as the infernal pit when he was born. I cannot help what my horse decides to do with his hair. That is between him and his God. Stop looking over your shoulder, *Michel*. Pierpont was an officer. He will not shoot me in the back, and he will not blame you for sparing all others the burden of seconding me."

"How many duels does that make, your lordship? Four? Five? One of these honorable former officers will put paid to your existence, and where will Lady Freddy be, then?"

He took out a flask and imbibed a hefty swallow, suggesting his nerves were truly in bad repair.

"You should not worry. These men do not want to kill me any more than I wanted to kill them."

❧

In Millicent Danforth's experience, the elderly came in two varieties: fearful and brave. Her grandmother had been fearful, asking for tisanes or tea, for cosseting and humoring. Like a small child, Grandmother had wanted distracting from the inevitability of her own demise.

By contrast, Lady Frederica, Baroness St. Clair, viewed her eventual death as a diversion. She would threaten the help with it, lament it gently with her friends, and use it as an excuse for blunt speech.

"You are to be a companion, not a nursemaid. You will not vex me with your presence when I attend my correspondence after breakfast. You will appear at my side when I take the landau out for a turn in the park. Shall you write this down?"

Milly returned her prospective employer's beady-eyed glower calmly.

"I will not bother you after breakfast unless you ask it of me. I will join you when you take the air in the park. I believe I can recall that much, my lady. What will my other duties involve?"

"You will dine with me in the evening and endure the company of my rascal of a nephew if he deigns to join us. What, I ask you, is so enticing about a rare beefsteak and an undercooked potato with a side of gossip? I can provide that here, as well as a superior cellar, but no, the boy must away to his flower-lovers' club. Though he's well-mannered enough that he won't terrorize you—or no more than I will. Are you sure you don't need to write any of this down?"

Yes, Milly was quite sure. "I gather you are a list maker, my lady?"

Blue eyes lit up as her ladyship reached for the teapot.

"Yes! I am never so happy as when I'm organizing. I should have been a general, the late baron used to say. Do you enjoy the opera? One hopes you do, because nothing is more unendurable than the opera if one hasn't a taste for it."

Her ladyship chattered on about London openings she'd attended, the crowd in attendance, and the various solos, duets, and ensemble numbers. Her diatribe was like a conversational stiff wind, banging the windows open all at once, setting curtains flapping, papers flying, and lapdogs barking.

"You're not drinking your tea, Miss Danforth."

"I am attending your ladyship's recitation of my duties."

The baroness clinked her teacup down on its saucer. "You were estimating the value of this tea service. Jasperware is more practical, but it's so heavy. I prefer the Sèvres, and Sebastian likes it too."

"The service is pretty," Milly observed. They were using the older style of Sèvres, more easily broken, but also impressively hued. "Meissen or Dresden aren't as decorative, though they are sturdier."

The baroness used silver tongs to put a flaky golden croissant on a plate. "So you are a lady fallen on hard times?"

She was a lady who'd blundered. Paid companions did not need to know that fifteen years ago, Sèvres was made without kaolin, fired at a lower temperature, and capable of taking a wider and more bold palette of hues as a result.

"My mother was a lady fallen on hard times. I am a poor relation who would make her own way rather than burden my cousins any further."

"Kicked you out, did they?" Her ladyship's tone suggested she did not approve of such cousins. "Or perhaps they realized that underneath all that red hair, you're quite pretty. One hopes you aren't delicate?"

"I enjoy excellent health, thank you, your ladyship." Excellent physical health, anyway. "And I prefer to call my hair auburn."

The baroness snorted at that gambit, then poured herself more tea.

"Eat up. When Sebastian gets back from his morning ride, he'll go through that sideboard like a plague of locusts. If you prefer coffee, you'd best get your servings before he comes down in the morning. The man cannot abide tea in any form."

"The plague of locusts has arrived."

Milly's head snapped around at the mocking baritone. She beheld...her opposite. Whereas she was female, short—*petite*, when the occasion was polite—red-haired, and brown-eyed, the plague before her was male, tall, green-eyed, and sable-haired. The divergence didn't stop there.

This fellow displayed a casual elegance about his riding attire that suggested time on the Continent. His tailoring was exquisite, but his movement was also relaxed. The lace at his throat came within a whisker of being excessive, and the emerald winking from its snowy depths stayed barely on the acceptable side of ostentatious, for men seldom wore jewels during daylight hours, and certainly not for so mundane an undertaking as a hack in the park.

This biblical plague had...sartorial éclat.

Again, the opposite of Milly, who generally wore the plainest gowns she could get away with, and had never set foot outside London and the Home Counties.

"Miss Millicent Danforth, may I make known to you my scamp of a nephew, Sebastian, Baron St. Clair. St. Clair, Miss Danforth—my new companion. You are not to terrorize her before she and I have negotiated terms."

"Of course not. I terrorize your staff only *after* you've obligated them to a contract."

Milly did not regard this as humorous. Her ladyship, however, graced her nephew with a smile.

About the Author

New York Times and *USA Today* bestselling author Grace Burrowes hit the bestseller lists with her debut, *The Heir*, followed by *The Soldier*, *Lady Maggie's Secret Scandal*, and *Lady Eve's Indiscretion*. All her Regency and Victorian romances have received extensive praise, including starred reviews from *Publishers Weekly* and *Booklist*. *The Heir* was a *Publishers Weekly* Best Book of 2010, *Lady Sophie's Christmas Wish* won Best Historical Romance of the Year in 2011 from RT Reviewers' Choice Awards. *Lady Louisa's Christmas Knight* was a *Library Journal* Best Book of 2012, and *The Bridegroom Wore Plaid*, the first in her trilogy of Scotland-set Victorian romances, was a *Publishers Weekly* Best Book of 2012. *Darius*, the first in her groundbreaking Regency series The Lonely Lords, was named one of iBooks Store's Best Romances of 2013, and *Once Upon a Tartan* won Best Scotland-Set Historical Romance for 2013 from RT Reviewers' Choice Awards.

Grace is a practicing family law attorney and lives in rural Maryland. She loves to hear from her readers and can be reached through her website at graceburrowes.com.